"YA GOT TO BE CAREFUL ABOUT BLAMING," IKE SAID.

''Ya get caught up in it, ya may miss the blessing.''

Blessing? Where was the blessing in being betrayed by friends? Voice brittle, Libby said, ''It's kind of hard to see it that way.'' Fighting tears, she turned toward the fire.

Ike gazed into the coals Libby was stirring, his thoughts reeling back over the years. ''Ever tell ya about the time we were headed for the poor farm? Mom and my sister Cicely and me got lost. The shadows were starting to fall, and my mother was out of ideas. She asked God which way was the way to go; said she wasn't taking another step until she got an answer. She'd hardly got up off her knees when along come this red-haired fella.''

''Uncle Willie,'' said Libby.

''Willie was sorry-looking and none too sober. I was ready to bolt and run. If I had, I'd of missed out on the best blessing of my life. Until you came along.''

Libby spoke Ike's name, and turned to meet his waiting embrace.

He stroked her damp cheek, catching a tear on his thumb. ''It's all right, Lib. God's not going to hang us out to dry.''

Other Avon Books by
Susan Kirby

AS THE LILY GROWS
PRAIRIE ROSE

When the Lilacs Bloom

SUSAN KIRBY

AVON BOOKS  NEW YORK

This is a work of fiction. Names, characters, places, and incidents either are the product of the author's imagination or are used fictitiously. Any resemblance to actual events, locales, organizations, or persons, living or dead, is entirely coincidental and beyond the intent of either the author or the publisher.

AVON BOOKS
A division of
The Hearst Corporation
1350 Avenue of the Americas
New York, New York 10019

Copyright © 1997 By Susan Kirby
Published by arrangement with the author
Visit our website at http://www.AvonBooks.com
Library of Congress Catalog Card Number: 97-93171
ISBN: 0-380-78505-6

First Avon Books Printing: November 1997

AVON TRADEMARK REG. U.S. PAT. OFF. AND IN OTHER COUNTRIES, MARCA REGISTRADA, HECHO EN U.S.A.

Printed in the U. S. A.

WCD 10 9 8 7 6 5 4 3 2 1

For Reggie.
Once, when you were a boy,
you gave me a rose.
This is my rose to you.
You make your dad and me proud.

Acknowledgments

I am indebted to several individuals who shared their knowledge and, when lacking the answer, directed me to others who were equally helpful: Robert Coombs, for trusting me with your vintage maple materials; Gary Gaudette, President of Leader Evaporator Company; Betty Ann Lockhart, maple author and expert; Warren Lyndaker, President of American Maple Museum; Steve and Glaida Funk, whose expertise far exceeds maple syrup making.

In addition, I wish to thank Lettie Busey, Marilyn Kirby, Donna Twist, and Fayetta Mitchell. Your mothering hearts provide inspiration in story and in life!

Prologue

Illinois
October 1904

A pumpkin moon lighted the road from the town of Edgewood to the grove of trees known as Old Kentucky. The air was crisp and pungently autumn. Libby had chattered much of the three-mile journey. Now as the team rattled over the railway crossing, jostling her against Ike, she ran out of words.

They continued a few dozen yards and stopped at a wide spot in the road. For a brief time the railroad had spawned a settlement here. All that remained now was the crossing with its depot, its grain dump and elevator, and the cabin shrouded in trees. Two giant oaks on the west side of the cabin stood out from the others. Their trunks were grown together at the base, their moon-washed limbs entwined in a lovers' embrace.

"Wait here, while I make a light," said Ike as he stopped the wagon.

Libby watched him wade through the drifts of leaves to the porch and disappear inside. Motherless since the age of ten, she came to this moment long on love and short on information. Her corset was too tight, her breath

1

too shallow. Her pulse leapt as a light went on inside.

Its soft yellow glow poured out the yawning entrance, lighting Ike's way back to the wagon. At twenty-five, there was in his broad shoulders and easy gait the quiet pride and the sinewy strength of the Illinois farm country that was his home. He tipped his head back and reached up to help her over the wagon wheel. His hair curled over his battle-scarred ear and touched his collar. Libby's gaze met his as he lifted her to the ground.

His gray eyes crinkled at the corners. Smiling eyes. "You're lookin' tuckered out. Why don't ya jest stand here and keep the horses company while I unload the wagon?"

The butterflies were in her chest now. Their powdery wings rose to tickle her throat as she held her ivory skirts off the ground and stood by as he carried the paper-wrapped quilt and her valise inside. The assemblage of dishes and linens and tableware and leftovers from the wedding dinner followed. And finally, her trunk. Libby retrieved the last two gifts from the wagon. One was a bare-rooted offshoot from the lilac bush that grew by the back gate of her childhood home. Her brother Jacob had dug it up and carried it on the train with him as he came north for her wedding.

The other was a cookie jar, shaped like a rose. The gift had been left in the porch swing at the house she shared with her father and brother. There was a tiny chip in the petaled lid, unnoticeable until the lid was lifted. Pink with green petals painted at the base, it was pretty and durable-looking, though obviously not new. It had been nicely wrapped. But there was no card attached.

Ike entered the cabin from the backyard. His footsteps rang as he came across the plank floor. The mystery of the cookie jar was driven from Libby's mind as he met her in the open door. The light was behind him. Libby sensed more than saw that he was nervous, too.

"Reckon I should carry you over the threshold?"

"Not if you have to ask."

Ike's soft laughter broke the spell. Libby left the lilac slip on the porch, but cradled the cookie jar in the crook of one arm as he lifted her off her feet and carried her inside. He set her on her feet and called her Elizabeth Watson Galloway.

Her married name had a melody all its own. She accepted his waiting kiss. It was a gentle kiss, followed by another and another, each kiss making a shadow of the modest tokens they'd exchanged over their brief courtship. He spoke plainly without words. She belonged to him now and he to her. It would be all right. They'd find their way. Tonight, and forever. Ike built a fire in the stove, then left her to return the team and wagon to the barn.

Night treated the cabin more kindly than the burning summer sun by which Libby had viewed it months earlier. Soft hissing lamplight spilled over the table. It enfolded the cast-iron cookstove in its circle of light and shone dimly on the dry sink and baker's cabinet, handcrafted and given by a friend. The bed was a dark shape in the distant corner.

Libby placed the cookie jar on the table. She took off her gloves and hat and made her way to the bed. The cornhusks rustled in the mattress as she spread the gift quilt over the sheet and blanket. It made a splash of color in the barren room. She ran her fingers over the quilt with its stitched pictures of tufted fields golden with harvest, fence lines, and a road curving toward the distant woods that was now her home. The figure in the buggy, with its tiny flame of red hair, was her.

But there was nothing of Ike in the quilt. Nor had the other gifts been given with a man's interests in mind. Why hadn't she bought him a present? Better yet, fashioned one with her own hands? Or her pen, since words were her gift? Libby opened her trunk in search of her tablet of paper. But she stopped, suddenly certain of what she wanted to give him. It was a gift that would take time.

Family. It settled over her so surely, so right, she felt born to it. Ike, with his mother and sister so far away, had been too long without that blessing. She breathed a prayer to God, who had brought them to this moment. Thanked Him. Petitioned Him. And thought with quiet wonder of herself, not so much as the giver but as the vessel waiting to be used in the giving of what only God could create.

1

The sun rose on a perfect Indian summer day. The fall colors were sharp and clear. Here and there, cobwebs drifted in the air as Ike led Libby on a rambling walk through the trees of Old Kentucky.

A coal miner's daughter from the southern part of the state, Libby had grown up near wooded hillsides, much of which had been harvested for supporting timbers in the mines. But this was prairie timber, virgin growth. The soil was rich, and the trees were giants, their autumn leaves carpeting the ground and crowding out the sky.

Southbound geese winged overhead as Ike pointed out Hascal Caton and his grandson Frankie McClure fishing on the bank of Timber Creek. The elder was speckled with salt-and-pepper whiskers, the younger with freckles. Libby was fond of children, and ten-year-old Frankie, with his red hair and agile mind, was a favorite of hers. Hascal, on the other hand, was prone to spreading rumors and other general mischief-making. Short, squat, and spry, he embodied her childhood fancy of leprechauns. As a writer, she was intrigued by him. But as the new bride in the neighborhood, she felt vulnerable to his mischievous gaze as he peered at them from beneath the shade of his leathery hand.

"If it ain't the honeymooners," Hascal drawled.

"Howdy, Hack." Ike grinned at the old man, thrust his shoulders back, and called to Frankie, "Fish bitin'?"

"Not so's ya'd notice." Frankie beckoned toward the rusty tin can at his side. "Got some line and plenty of bait, if ya want to join us."

"Can't today, I'm showin' Lib around. But thanks for askin'."

Hascal poked his grandson with an elbow. "Hitched a day, and already he's draggin' her along with him. It's that or hug her good-bye. Ain't much of a choice, is it?"

"Wasn't for Ike." Frankie's cheeky grin included them both. "I was tuckin' a letter into the mailbox when I saw you two step out on the porch earlier."

"You did?" said Libby, surprised. "I didn't see you."

"That's cause Ike was huggin' on ya, blockin' yer view."

Hascal cackled. "See thar! You two been settin' a bad example for the boy."

Abashed, Libby ducked her head and whispered as they walked on, "We couldn't set a worse one than Hascal himself. I'm not letting our children anywhere near the old scamp."

Ike squeezed her hand and chuckled. "I wouldn't worry about that just yet."

They angled west, came out on the road that meandered through Old Kentucky, and took it back to the house. After lunch, Ike found a shovel at Libby's request. She was planting her lilac bush when Billy Young came along in his mail cart.

A robust, good-natured fellow, Billy had served with Ike in the elite First U.S. Volunteer Cavalry during the Spanish American War. He was Ike's best friend and a good friend of Libby's as well.

"Did you bring me any good mail?" Libby called to him.

"I don't remember seeing your name on anything. Though I do have something here for a Mr. and Mrs. Isaac Galloway. Fit anyone you know?" Billy held a white envelope just out of Libby's reach.

"Hand it over, or I'll tell Chloe Berry what a big tease you are," warned Libby.

"That could help. She's got a nice laugh, but she doesn't seem to know when to use it," said Billy.

"Could be yer tryin' too hard to make her laugh and not hard enough to romance her," said Ike, coming off the porch to join them.

"Listen to him, married one day and he's the expert." Billy grinned and handed Libby the letter.

It was a card of wedding congratulations from her friend Catherine in St. Louis. She sent regrets that an unavoidable conflict had kept her from the ceremony. Libby wondered if Catherine's stepfather, Chester Gentry, was the "conflict." He was Ike's father's half brother, but there was a rift between them over some long-ago wrong done to Ike's family when Ike was a boy. Libby knew of it in a general way, though as yet Ike had avoided painting in the details.

Billy visited a minute, then went on his way. Libby and Ike trekked over the Chicago and Alton Railroad tracks and across the bridge to Ike's sap house, where he would cook maple sap into sirup next spring. The timber that Libby's uncle, Willie Blue, had entrusted to Ike enfolded the sap house on all sides. The road leading into Edgewood passed the front of the sap house. Beyond the trees to the east of the building was the gound Ike farmed for Miss Maudie.

"Goin' to be a struggle, Lib. But I'm hopin' to save enough to buy this farm, should Miss Maudie ever agree to sell," Ike confided as they stood looking over a field of golden corn waiting to be harvested.

"Is that what you want? Your own farm?" At his nod, Libby slipped her hand into his. "Then that's what I want, too."

"It'll take hard work, a lot of patience, and some pinchin' times," he cautioned.

"I don't know much about farming, but I do know how to make do in pinching times," she said as they continued on to the barn. Libby found a rake there among the tools and carried it home.

Prone to letting leaves take care of themselves, Ike pulled up a chair on the porch and looked on as she tackled the leaves piled up around the cabin. He smiled to see her go at it so industriously, for the ground would be covered again by morning.

"Where are ya goin' with them?" he called from the porch as she filled a bushel basket with leaves.

"I thought I'd give my lilac bush some protection for winter," she said.

He looked askance at the slip they had planted. "Ya reckon that's really a lilac?"

"Of course it's a lilac."

"How can ya tell?"

"Jacob told me it was."

"And you believed him? Shoot, Lib, he was havin' a little fun with you. Broke it off a tree jest to see if you'd stick it in the ground."

"Ike Galloway, bite your tongue! He did no such thing."

"Sure he did," said Ike, just to see her eyes sparkle. "But you go ahead and coddle it if ya want to."

"I thought I would," she said with a sniff.

Ike rocked up on the back legs of the chair, locked his hands behind his head, and was stretching his feet toward the hitching post when she swerved onto the porch and dumped the bushel of leaves on his head. He bolted upright, toppling the chair, and, with a shout of laughter, shook off the leaves and chased her across the yard.

Libby squealed as he tackled her in the mountain of leaves. As they flung leaves, rolled in them, and laughed like children, she wished that this day they had set apart for themselves could last forever. But it was slipping away all too quickly.

For supper, Libby reheated leftovers from yesterday's wedding dinner. She sliced large wedges of cake for dessert. They ate side by side on the porch and watched twilight shadows spill over the surrounding trees. The pink hues against the treetops made Libby think of the rose cookie jar waiting to be filled with tasty morsels to satisfy Ike's sweet tooth.

It was almost dark by the time Ike went to the barn to care for the horses. Libby stayed behind and wrote in her journal, describing their wedding, their new home, and their first day together. When she had finished, she put her journal away and went out on the porch to watch for Ike's return. The air had turned chilly. But she was beguiled by the drowsy peace of birds settling into the trees, locusts singing, and purple shadows turning to night's hues as the moon rose over the woods.

"Could get some frost tonight," said Ike, stepping out of the darkness and onto the porch. "Cold and clear."

"And lots of stars," said Libby.

Seeing her shiver, he opened his jacket. "Come here and I'll warm ya up."

Libby tunneled her arms beneath his warm jacket. Relishing their shared body heat, she thanked God for this man who had so tenderly unlocked the mystery of marital union. The oneness she'd felt with him had swept away her timidity of the previous night. Snuggling close, she said, "I wonder how many years it takes a lilac bush to bloom?"

He lapped his coat around her and chuckled. "You and yer lilacs. Three years, I reckon. Maybe four."

"I was wondering . . ." Hesitant to reveal how little she knew, she tried a roundabout approach. "I was thinking about lilacs and babies and wondering which will come first."

He went so still, her face grew hot. Had she assumed too much? Been too forward?

"Family's important to you," he said finally.

She felt his chin brush her hair as she nodded.

"And two ain't a family?"

"Two babies?" she said.

"I meant you and me. One, two. That isn't enough family for now?"

Concerned she'd injured him, Libby tightened her arms around his lean torso. Last summer, when he had been so deathly sick with malaria, she had first realized she loved him, even though she was being courted by Angus Cearlock at the time. But that had worked itself out, and Ike was healthy now. Stalwart and strong and something more, something that tugged, like strings attached to her soul. Struggling to answer his question, she said, "I didn't mean it wasn't enough. I was just wondering how long it will be before someone calls me mama."

He tunneled his hand beneath her hair, stroking her nape. "What's yer hurry?"

Libby could hear his heart thumping through his shirt as she rested her face against him. It was the joy that came of giving she was anticipating. Feeling shy, she said, "Last night, I realized that not one of our wedding gifts was tailored to your interests. I felt bad because I hadn't thought to get you something special. Then I realized I did have a special gift to give you, and that gift is sons and daughters."

He gave no response. She drew her head back and looked into his face. Something hovered unspoken in his eyes. She caught her breath. "You *want* children, don't you?"

"Sure, I do. But I'd like to have ya to myself for a while." He kissed her and added, "Besides, I want to be settled so we can do justice to children, should God choose to bless us with them."

The reminder that children were God's workmanship seemed at odds with his assumption they could pick the time. Was such a thing possible? Libby lifted her gaze to his. "Are you saying we have control over the timing?"

"I hope so. If we're careful."

She needn't have worried she'd been too forward with him, for he told her then in plain words about keeping track of her monthlies and judging by them when it was best to abstain from lovemaking.

"I don't want 'em to be deprived, Lib," he added. "If we have any, I want them to have better than I did."

Libby had known lean living, too. She had grown up in a hard-bitten mining town. She had given up school at age ten to run her father's household and take care of her baby brother, David, after her mother died in childbirth. And yet not once had she felt deprived. It was a hard thing for her to understand.

He didn't want her gift. Not now, anyway.

Libby felt a shadow pass over her soul. She glanced at the lilac bush, the twig he had teased her about, and felt an odd affinity with it, for bushes and wombs were made to blossom. Weren't they? *If,* he'd said. Not *when.*

Ike lay awake long after Libby fell asleep in his arms. He couldn't crowd out the disappointment he'd seen on her face when he'd spoken of taking precautions against having children right away. *God, what a bitter irony if it should turn out that the precautions weren't necessary.*

There was a theory among some of the men who had served with him in Cuba that the fever associated with malaria could leave a man sterile. *Was I wrong not to tell her?* But to tell her something like that, he would have had to come a lot closer to the subject of sex than was considered decent for unwed couples. If he told her now, would she think he had deliberately waited until her choices were gone? Ike dodged the thought and reminded himself that it was only a theory.

A theory held not by men of science, but by a few battle-scarred men of war.

Still, uncertainty nagged at Ike enough that the next time he was in Edgewood, he stopped by Dr. Harding's office and confided in him.

"I've seen cases when a high fever crippled the brain," said Doc. "But I can't say I've seen any conclusive evidence of fevers burning up the fruit of a man's loins." He looked past Ike to someone in the doorway. "What is it, Sarah Jane?"

Ike turned to find Sarah Jane Brignadello standing in the open door. Mrs. Bee, as she was known to folks in Edgewood, was Doc's sister and a self-trained nurse. She was good with a needle, be it a wound or imported silk she was stitching. Libby adored the woman, though she conceded that the one thing Mrs. Bee couldn't seam up was a confidence. Ike wondered how long she'd been standing there.

"Chester wants you to come out to Erstwood right away," Mrs. Bee said to her brother. "Ida's fainted and hit her head on a corner of her dressing table."

"Fainted?" echoed the doctor in alarm. "What made her faint?"

"I have no idea; Chester didn't say. Smelling salts brought her around, but apparently, she needs stitches. I'll ride along with you, Melville."

Ida Gentry was Dr. Harding's other sister. Ike got to his feet. "I'll get out of yer way, Doc, so you can git goin'. Thanks for your time."

"Glad to be of help." Dr. Harding clapped him on the shoulder and as he reached into his pocket, said, "No, no. There's no charge for separating science from old wives' tales."

"Did Libby come to town with you today?" asked Mrs. Bee, as she shook the wrinkles from her brother's suit jacket.

"Yep. She's over at the newspaper office, leavin' her articles for next week's *Gazette* with Mr. Gruben. We're going to meet her father at Baker's for lunch."

"Merciful patience, I just remembered! I can't go

with you, Melville. Mrs. Baker's coming over this afternoon for a fitting. I'm making her wedding dress.'' Mrs. Bee held Doc's jacket while he slipped in his arms. She glanced at Ike and added warmly, ''Mrs. Baker is such a delightful person. Libby must be pleased she'll soon have a new stepmother.''

''Libby's brothers were plannin' on comin' for Christmas anyway, so having a Christmas wedding makes good sense,'' Ike said, for Libby's widowed father was to marry Mrs. Baker on Christmas Eve.

''We really miss Libby here in town,'' said Mrs. Bee as she bustled about, collecting Doc's eyeglasses and black medical bag. She wagged a finger at Ike as he edged toward the door. ''You take good care of her, now, you hear?''

As he went to meet Libby, Ike wondered whether telling her about his conversation with Doc constituted ''good care.'' Or would it just worry her? He had a high opinion both of Doc's skills and his knowledge. If he said it was an old wives' tale, then it must be. Now was no time to be starting a family anyway. When the moment was right, if Libby failed to bear a child, he'd tell her.

2

January 1905

🌹 January's bite numbed Ike's fingers and toes. His scarred ear ached from the cold as he tramped from tree to tree with his auger and bit, drilling small holes for maple taps.

Libby followed after him with spiles and buckets. The snow-purled woods made a foil for her bright hair, wind-burned cheeks, and blue eyes. Seeing her pause to take in the view, Ike followed her westward gaze to see the sun riding the treetops, spilling red-gold rays through the network of limbs. Shadows covered the snowy ground like giant-sized chicken scratches.

"He's scolding you, Ike." Libby tipped her head back and pointed out a squirrel, chattering from a high branch. "Asking how would you like it if he came and drilled holes in *your* house."

Ike straightened. His speculative gaze skipped from the squirrel to the horse-drawn sled with its dwindling pile of wooden buckets. He'd gone hungry enough times in the past to appreciate such a clear shot. But there was Libby to consider. She would cook game if he brought it in gutted and skinned, but he had a feeling it would hurt her to see him shoot it. Deliberating, he tugged his woolen cap down low on his brow. "Ya think he'd like to come to supper?"

"He says thank you very much, but he's made other plans," said Libby, recoiling at the thought of her keen eye being the means of the squirrel's demise. "So have I. I left stew simmering on the stove."

"Softie."

"Stringy," she called back. "Squirrel, I mean. You skin it and pick out the buckshot and all you have left is string. You know how I like it best?"

"In the treetops?"

"That's right."

"About what I'd expect from a city girl."

"I'm not a city girl."

"You aren't what I'd call a country girl," he said. "So what are ya?"

"Don't rush me, I'm thinking," she countered. She circled a tree, then wheeled around and retraced her steps, circling it again, looking for the tap hole. "This *is* a maple, isn't it?"

The wind snatched the wood curlings from the tip of his auger as he pointed. "South side of the tree. Little lower. There ya go," he said, as she found the hole.

Married less than four months, they had emerged from their drafty cabin to tap Ike's stand of sugar maples in Old Kentucky, also known simply as "the grove." Ike looked Libby's way again and found her standing still. An aspiring writer, she was prone to bouts of gazing and wool-gathering. He called to her, asking, "Ya writin' a piece in yer head, are ya?"

Libby wiggled her numb toes and returned his smile. "As a matter of fact, I wasn't."

"Ya haven't froze in place, have ya?"

"No."

"Then what're ya standin' there lookin' at?"

"You." She cocked her head to one side, studying him as if he were a painting on the wall. In bright sunlight, his eyes were the gray of prairie fences, with undertones of deep blue. He hadn't taken time to shave that morning. There was an auburn haze on his cheeks and jaw. Long exposure to sun had weathered his face and gilded the tips of his eyelashes. "I was looking at you and thinking how to answer your question *What are you?* I'm your girl, that's what I am. And I'm congratulating myself on making such a fine catch."

"Yer not so bad yerself."

There was music to her laughter. Truth was, in his mind she was the catch, adventuresome and optimistic, uncomplaining over the lack of comforts in their primitive cabin. The sight of her upturned mouth and slim curves, well padded by winter wraps, distracted him from his race with the waning afternoon sun. Her step had lost some of its bounce. He called to her, saying, "Stay where ya are. I'll get the buckets while ya rest a minute."

He intercepted her uphill trek to the horse-drawn sled, grabbed some buckets by the rope handles, and placed them on the ground at her feet.

Libby plunged her mittened hands into her coat pockets. "Is it just me, or is the temperature dropping?"

"Could be," he said. "If yer rested, grab yer hammer. We're running out of daylight."

"You're awful pushy for a fellow who pays in kisses. Which reminds me, I haven't been paid," she added.

He grinned and landed a careless kiss that missed her mouth and hit her eye.

"Some kiss," she said, drying her eye with her mitten. "Were you expecting change for that?"

He chuckled and let himself be distracted. Truth was, with her windblown curls framing rosy cheeks and her bright eyes glistening at her own joke, she was hard to resist. As the kisses turned from playful to passionate, Ike put a little more distance between himself and her pliant mouth, and said against her ear, "Will that keep ya on the payroll for a spell?"

Libby linked her hands behind his head and pursed her lips, pretending to give his question due consideration.

"Yer not thinkin' again, are ya?" he asked.

"Here I was about to make you an offer you couldn't resist."

"That's what I'm afraid of," he said, for he was vulnerable to all of her advances, whether playful or sincere. A regular temptress, she was, lighting sparks at will. And him, just captivated enough to be honored she took the trouble.

But the richness she brought to his life didn't ease his certainty that he had married her too soon. That old saying about two living as cheaply as one might be true if you didn't mind living precariously. He minded—not for his sake, but for hers.

The cabin was rough in the winter. They'd awakened after the first winter storm to find snow drifting through the cracks in the walls and ice glazing the top of the water bucket. It had put a knot in his gut, for it was his responsibility to keep her in good health. Keep her well fed and clothed and cared for, and he didn't want to get reckless and complicate their struggles by bringing a child into their lives.

Libby looked over her shoulder at the discordant sound of Ike's tuneless whistle. Christ had won the battle for his heart nearly seven years ago as he lay near death on foreign soil. But there were difficulties in his past he hadn't shared with her. Those hardships had given him an intimacy with his Maker that often dwarfed her own faith. Yet he wasn't without fears. He watched for her monthlies closer than she did, and while desire quickened easily between them, he was more disciplined at checking it than she was.

Libby knew now that it was the gift, not the giver he was setting aside. It helped to remind herself that there were gifts God wanted to give her, but found her unprepared to receive. Patience was one such gift. With that in mind, she cooperated with Ike in putting off a family, even though it went against her own wishes. That being the case, it helped as she worked toward their common goals, to hold a mental picture of each accomplished task that brought her closer to the day when Ike would be ready to receive the blessing of a family.

Libby broke off a twig and used it to clean sawdust from the next tap hole. Holding the twig between her teeth, she pulled one fur-lined mitten off with her knees and retrieved a spile from her coat pocket. It was about the diameter of her finger, half a foot long and made of elderberry. The softness of the wood made it easy to trench with a pocketknife, which was why Ike favored elderberry and sumac for spile-making. But because the wood was soft, she had learned to be careful with the hammer, and not split the spile as she tapped it into the tree.

The holes for the spiles, slanting upward into the tree to catch the sap, were about a foot and a half off the ground. That left enough clearance to slip a wooden bucket on the ground under the spile.

Their friends, the McClures, were going to help them with their sirup venture. But Libby was glad that today, the first day of her first sirup season, she didn't have to share Ike with anyone. She told him as much a while later as she strode after him, helping care for the horses in the chilly barn with its blended scents of animals and dust and hay.

"Between the timber work and the sap-cookin', you'll soon be glad for more hands," Ike said as he pitched hay down from the loft. "Frankie's big enough to be a real help."

Frankie McClure had just turned eleven. He had a sister Opal the same age as Libby's youngest brother, David. But it would be a couple of years before those two would be strong enough to be much help with the sap-gathering.

Libby twined her arm through Ike's as they started

home on foot. "How many Frankies would it take to run a sirup camp?"

"I don't know, Lib. How many Frankies do ya think ya could tolerate?"

She gave his question due consideration. "Maybe I'll wait for Ikes instead."

Ike shoved his hands in his pockets, the direction of the conversation provoking a familiar discomfort. He denied the source of it, reasoning instead that she was young and didn't understand that too soon and too many children was a ticket to disaster. He reasoned that he was protecting her against that danger. Vivid was the boyhood memory of standing beside his widowed mother, his belly empty and his heart hot with shame as she pleaded for help from his dead father's half brother. Ike shook the memory loose and glanced at Libby to find a pensive expression shadowing her eyes.

Trying to recapture the closeness of a moment ago, he tugged on an overhead branch and showered her in a miniavalanche. She scooped up a handful of snow and chased after him. The clear cold air rang with their laughter as they crossed the bridge throwing snow at one another, raced over the Chicago and Alton Railroad tracks and on toward the cabin, located at the edge of timbered pasture on the south side of a frozen dirt track.

Out of breath and perspiring beneath her layers of clothing, Libby left Ike on the sleepy eyelid of a porch that shaded the front windows of their cabin while she dashed across the road to the row of mailboxes. The *Gazette* came on Saturdays, and she was eager to see how many changes the editor, Lucius Gruben, had made to the pieces she had written. She brightened to see that one of her Old Kentucky news articles had made the front page.

Aware of Ike tramping inside with an armload of firewood, Libby scanned the article hurriedly, then slowed her pace and was reading it word for word, hungry to learn from the revisions her editor had made, when the smell of woodsmoke distracted her. Sparks and billowing plumes shot from the chimney into the purple sky. Libby let herself into their drafty cabin and rescued the stew from the stove.

Ike met her chiding glance from his hunkered-down position beside the stove. She was fussy about her stove. Made him feel like a schoolboy caught with a spit-wad. "Jest knocking it into coals is all."

"Yes, well the sky is on fire with your pyrotechnics!"

"I heard redheads was partial to fireworks," countered Ike. "Or is that only when they're makin' 'em?"

"Out of the way before you get on the bad side of the cook," said Libby, with a nudge.

He made another foray with the poker while she shrugged off her coat and scarf, then let her take his place at the stove. Libby settled several chunks of seasoned maple onto the glowing coals, then washed her hands before covering the table with a hand-stitched cloth. She added a splash of color with a shallow wooden trough. It was filled with pine cuttings and cones she had gathered from the woods.

Ike liked the care she took to make things attractive. Wanting her to know he noticed, he said, "If I'd of known it was pine-cone stew, I'd of shot that squirrel."

Libby saw the compliment paraded as teasing. Words were her gift, not his. She smiled and passed him two plates. "Just for that, you can dish up the stew while I open a jar of peaches and slice some bread."

They held hands and said grace and talked of the coming sirup season as they ate their meal. Ike was eager to try out the sirup evaporator he had had shipped from Vermont last autumn. It was the most modern on the market and capable of producing the best quality sirup. That and the sap house he had built had taken all of his savings.

"How many years will you get out of it?" asked Libby, stunned when he revealed for the first time how much he had paid for the evaporator.

"Fifteen, maybe twenty, if we're careful."

Feeling better, she said, "We're set for a long time, then?"

"So long as we don't burn the pans," said Ike. "We'll have to watch that real close. You can ruin 'em, and they're pricey to replace."

Libby's heart quaked at the thought.

"There's other equipment to make things easier. But we'll have to acquire it bit by bit, if we're going to save some profits for a down payment on a farm."

Libby tore a piece of bread in half and shared it with him. "Do you really think Miss Maudie will sell?"

"I don't know. If she won't, we'll look elsewhere."

Libby knew he was partial to the acres he'd been farming since he'd mustered out of the cavalry. She pushed the apple butter his way. "You wouldn't be too disappointed?"

"You can't buy what isn't for sale. Anyway, if she won't sell, I reckon God's got somethin' else in mind."

"Something better, maybe."

"Maybe," said Ike. "If it comes to lookin' elsewhere, it'd be nice to find a piece with a house on it. That's the one drawback to Miss Maudie's piece."

"It wouldn't have to be anything fancy."

"Weathertight, though," said Ike. "Somethin' this cabin ain't."

"We're saving money," she pointed out. "It's nice of Decatur and Naomi to let us use it."

He appreciated her underplaying the misery of nights when the temperature dipped and the wind kicked up. But it didn't relieve him of the responsibility of making things better when and where he could. "When sirup work lets up, I'll see what I can do to shut out the breeze. Shouldn't set us back much. I'll get by using what I have at hand."

And some ingenuity, thought Libby. He might not be much good at expressing his emotions, but his mind was keen, and his hands were skilled. They were rough hands, and chapped from the cold, yet handsome to her in their ability to mend, build, adapt, and create.

After supper, Ike settled near the stove and leafed through the Leader Evaporator Company catalog while Libby cleared the table and washed the dishes. His goals required patience, hard work, and God's blessing of good weather upon which both farming and siruping depended. He wanted to replace his hand-whittled spouts with manufactured ones next year. He pored over the bucket page, too, and jotted down some figures in a ledger he kept.

Libby poured water from the drinking bucket into the stove reservoir to replenish what she had used washing dishes. It would take a bit before it was warm enough for bathing. Ike had put his ledger away and was reading from the Bible as she sat down to write in her journal of their day in the woods. She kept her entry brief, for she was looking forward to giving the weekly newspaper a thorough read. "Have you seen the paper?" she asked.

"Haven't had it," said Ike. He shifted his feet to the nearby crate of kindling and went on reading to himself.

Libby looked a moment longer, then stopped short and protested, "Ike! You're sitting on it."

Belatedly, he saw that he was. He held back a smile. "I suppose ya want me to get up."

"Well, I wouldn't want to put you out."

"Then sit down." He tipped over the crate of kindling, planting his feet on the floor as he pulled her onto his lap.

"Now see what you've done," said Libby, trying not to be the first to laugh.

"It's yer fault for distracting me. Sashaying by with the lamplight in yer hair and sighin' like you was feelin' left out."

"I was not! I was going to read the paper before I bathed."

"Well, ya found it."

''For all the good it's doing me. My water's hot by now.''

''Then what's keeping you?''

Libby warmed at his grin. She settled more comfortably into his lap and laid her head against his shoulder, all the while making a token offer at odds with her true intentions. ''If you'd rather I left you alone, I'll go in the other room. Or upstairs. Or dancing,'' she said.

He chuckled. ''Dancing'' was her silly answer to the silly question he had asked one night when he'd awakened to find her slipping out of bed. But if she was wanting to bathe, he'd get out of her way for a spell. He gestured toward the empty rack over the front door. ''Looks like I've got careless with my gun.''

''Leave it in the barn?''

''Must have,'' he said. ''Suppose I'd better fetch it home.''

''We wouldn't want the horses having a shoot-out,'' she said, for he didn't *have* to go. But he would. She knew why, too, and it didn't have anything to do with the gun. Libby sighed and slid off his lap and braced herself for the draft of air and the emptiness of the cabin in the wake of his going.

The cold night air stung Ike's lungs as he headed for the barn. There wasn't much privacy to that bathing screen of hers. Just unbleached muslin stretched over a wooden frame. With the lamp behind it, she made a handsome silhouette, splashing water in the basin and humming to herself through chattering teeth. He felt no shame in admiring those curves, was proud to think they belonged to him. But it was taxing to his restraint, and now was no time to get careless.

3

November 1905

The cabin at Old Kentucky was more primitive than Libby's childhood home in Thistle Down had been, but Ike's handiwork and her care gradually produced, if not comfort, then at least a rustic charm.

In addition to the usual tasks of keeping a home, Libby had planted a garden and spent the past summer storing away the fruit of her labors. But with the approach of her second winter in Old Kentucky, she was missing what she hadn't missed in a while, and that was company.

Reared in town with three brothers and easy access to neighbors and friends, she had felt a similar lonesomeness during her first weeks in her new home. But the novelty of being married, of sharing, of learning and growing closer with Ike had carried her over the rough spots. Now it was her writing that drove back bouts of loneliness while Ike was busy with the corn harvest. She kept track of the farmers out their way and how the harvest was proceeding. Marriages and sicknesses and courtships, church news and school news and a grain spill over by the depot all made it into the *Gazette* with her byline. The pay was modest, but she was learning a lot from her editor, Mr. Gruben, and it made her proud to contribute to the household income in her own small way.

Waiting for Ike to come home, Libby opened her journal and penned a confession:

Ike is in the barn putting the finishing touches on what is supposed to be a surprise. But I got so curious over what he was doing out there every night that I peeked. He's made a bathtub! It's round like a barrel, only shorter, and lined in copper. He's even put a hinged lid on it to pull down when not in use.

The teakettle was humming. Libby closed her journal and strode through the open door separating the summer porch from their one-room cabin. Supper was in the warmer, the table set, with some pretty autumn seedpods and grasses arranged in a vase in the center. She took the kettle and a clean towel back out to the porch and set them beside the gray granite basin on the water bench, where Ike would splash the day's toil from his hands and face.

The porch was a result of his ingenuity. He had closed off the front six feet of the cabin. The wall he put up reduced their living quarters to size that could be adequately heated with the cookstove, and created the enclosed porch in the process. The sunlit space was utilitarian as well as serene, and a cozy nook for reading and writing.

The north-facing windows were wide with divided panes, providing a panoramic view of the woods as well as the railroad and the small station to the east of the tracks. A passing train blocked the dirt road that would bring Ike over the bridge, the crossing, and home.

Libby flung her shawl over her shoulders, crossed the road to the mailbox, and returned with the *Gazette*. She was skimming her own contributions to the paper when she came across an article concerning the Friends of the Library. They were planning to meet in Henry Ketchum's cornfield on Monday morning for a corn-picking fund-raiser.

It was a worthy cause, and the chance to get together with ladies she hadn't seen in a while. Best of all, Mr. Ketchum's field was less than a mile as the crow flies. The train rattled on down the tracks with a thin wail. Seeing Ike coming over the crossing, she walked out to meet him.

"Late for supper, am I?" he asked, heart lifting at the sight of her.

"A little." Hoping to tease him into revealing his not-so-secret secret, she saved the news of the library fund-raiser and asked instead, "Lose track of time in the field?"

"I wasn't in the field, I've been in the barn."

"Husking corn?"

Ike had meant the tub as an anniversary present. But with the press of harvest, he'd missed their wedding date. He draped an arm over her shoulders, and short-ened his long stride to match hers. "What is it you been wantin' ever since we moved in?"

Libby leaned into him as they walked along. She sucked at the corner of her bottom lip, pretending to be stumped. "I give up. I thought I had everything I needed."

"I didn't say *need*, I said want."

"Oh! In that case, the answer is books. I want to write lots and lots of books and sell every one. We'll build a house with indoor plumbing." She caught the corners of her shawl in her hands and swung ahead of him, stretching her arms wide. Turning, walking backwards, she saw suspicion dawn on his face and arched him a coy smile. "I told you about Catherine's house, didn't I?"

The little snoop! She knew! Biding his time, figuring out how to turn the tables on her, he said, "Seems like ya did, but tell me again. What part did ya say ya liked best?"

"Singing in the bathtub. Why do you ask?"

He grinned and shrugged and whistled off-key.

Seeing that he knew that she knew, and was having some fun of his own, Libby let it drop for the moment, and mentioned the corn for books project.

"Corn for what?" he asked as she rattled off the heading of Mr. Gruben's newspaper article regarding the library fund-raiser.

"Books. The ladies are going to pick corn, then sell the corn to buy books."

"Wantin' to pick corn, are ya?" he said, and wagged his head with feigned regret. "Ya should of told me b'fore. I'd of been takin' ya to the field with me these past weeks."

Indignant, she reminded him, "I offered! You turned me down."

"Ya got enough to do here at the house."

"In other words, you figured I'd just get in your way."

Catching her hands, he pulled her back to his side. "Ya ain't in my way now."

Libby lifted her face for his kiss as they walked along, then picked up where she'd left off. "They're meeting at Henry Ketchum's at ten o'clock on Monday."

"Yer talkin' about the field south of us?" Ike slowed his pace. That was Gentry ground, and he didn't want her stepping foot on anything Gentry owned. He couched the truth in guarded tones, saying, "Lib, the storm that skipped over our fields last August hit Henry hard. His corn's lying on the ground."

Libby heard the shift in his voice and saw that his mouth had lost its upward lift. Her gay spirits of only a moment ago escaped like wisps of smoke. *I should have guessed!* Chester Gentry owned land all over the country, including nearby fields and some timber adjacent to Ike's. Their trees touched, but their lives did not.

"Henry's rheumatism's actin' up. He hasn't made much headway at gettin' the corn gathered," Ike was saying. "With the harvest in full swing, I doubt Gentry's anxious to take hired hands out of more productive fields to go help Henry. Don't suppose he thinks he should have to."

Libby said, "I'm not sure what you mean."

"Him and Ketchum share-farm," Ike explained. "Gentry furnishes the money for seed and stock to keep things runnin'. Ketchum does the farmin' jest like I do for Miss Maudie."

Uncertain what that had to do with the library, Libby said, "I'm sorry for Mr. Ketchum's bad health. But at least the library stands to profit from Mr. Gentry's generosity."

"Generous would be givin' ya a straight-standing field."

Libby drew her shawl closer as Ike sat down on the porch step to take off his boots. "Mr. Gentry isn't giving Mr. Ketchum's half away, is he?"

" 'Course not, he can't do that."

"Then what's the problem? It appears to me that the library owes Mr. Gentry a debt of gratitude for allowing them to profit off his misfortune."

"Jest don't knock him over, pattin' him on the back, that's all I'm saying."

As if Mr. Gentry didn't deserve a word of thanks! All Libby knew for sure was that Ike's estrangement with Gentry dated back to an incident in childhood when Ike's mother, newly widowed, had traveled with her children from Missouri to seek Mr. Gentry's help. From what she'd heard of it from other sources, Mr. Gentry's treatment had been lacking in benevolence. But Ike's mother had found help elsewhere and it wasn't too long before Mrs. Galloway remarried. So why did Ike hold this lingering grudge?

Meekly, she said, "I know you don't like Mr. Gentry. But he does have some good qualities."

Ike kept his head down, unlacing his boots, thinking maybe he should be more direct and just say he didn't want her on Chester Gentry's land. He didn't examine too closely his reluctance to do so.

"You always see the good in people," she persisted.

Boots in one hand, forearms resting on his knees, he said, "Leave it alone, Lib."

"I don't think I can," she replied, for she had been instrumental in getting the library started in Edgewood. "What am I supposed to do—sit on my hands and refuse to help because it's Mr. Gentry's field?"

Warily he countered, "I never once said you couldn't go."

"No," she said, the leaf crumbling in her hand. "But I can see the hair rise on the back of your neck, just talking about him."

"Go on, then, if that's what yer wantin'."

Her temper sparked at his tone. She lifted her chin. "I thought I would."

But Libby was wanting more than that. They'd both shared from their past. But there were two things Ike wouldn't talk about. One was war and the other was his grudge against Chester Gentry. The anguish in his voice as he bolted awake in the throes of battlefield dreams hinted at scars beyond those of his tattered ear, and she would sooner die than pick at them. But this business with his uncle was different.

Yes, he and his mother and sister had received shabby treatment, and not the sort she would expect from a man like Mr. Gentry, who was known for doing his civic duty. But it had been years ago. Was it really so unforgivable?

Ike ate supper, then returned to the barn to wax the lid he'd made for the bathtub. He'd been planning to give it to her tonight. He wouldn't now. She had a right to go to Gentry's field if she wanted to, but he didn't have to like it. Nor did he want her thinking he was trying to sway her into doing otherwise. As if he had to buy her loyalty with a bathtub.

A quiet presence inside him told him to dig deeper, but he wasn't wanting to hear. All he could see was the contempt on Gentry's face as he left a worn-out woman and two hot, hungry kids standing in the blazing sun while he passed judgment from the shade of his porch. He'd had his cook fix them a packet of food, but the words he had spoken had negated even that small kindness.

"I warned Morgan when he left for Missouri not to expect any more help from me. That goes for his whelps and his common-law wife."

It was the first time Ike had heard the word. But he had understood the tone. His mother may have made some mistakes, yet in his mind, she'd lived closer to the faith she had come to profess than did Chester Gentry that day. Or any day since.

It was a hard thing to forgive, and even when he thought he had, it would creep back over him if he looked too long or too hard at Gentry. Best thing he knew to do was stay away from him. He didn't know how to explain that to Libby without telling her that his parents hadn't been married. Nor did he think he should have to.

Timber Creek Church, the little country church at the west edge of Old Kentucky, shared Pastor Shaw with the newly established New Hope Church in Edgewood. The minister took the rails to and from town, traveling by his own handcar. During the summer months, Timber Creek Church had early-morning service, but during the fall, winter, and spring, their worship services were held in the afternoon.

Pastor Shaw arrived at the crossing in the early afternoon. The McClures, who lived deep in the woods down a lane opposite Libby and Ike's cabin, took Pastor Shaw the remaining distance to the little white church along the banks of the creek that wound through Old Kentucky. After worship services, Ike offered the middle-aged pastor a ride back to the depot where he had left his handcar and was relieved when he accepted.

Libby hadn't been too talkative since the previous evening, and Ike wasn't looking forward to an afternoon of being careful of one another. He said to the pastor as they neared the cabin, "If yer not too pressed for time, why don't ya come in and visit a spell b'fore ya head back to town?"

Pastor Shaw accepted and offered to accompany Ike to the barn first, to unhitch the team. But Ike hitched them to the rail out front instead. Ordinarily, Libby jested with Ike over the measures she would take, should his horses nip at the lilac bush they had planted the day after their marriage. Today, she set her jaw and clamored down from the wagon seat before he could help her.

Libby stoked up the stove and made coffee while the men visited on the sun-warmed summer porch. She cut generous wedges of peach cake and, when the coffee was made, added it to the tray.

"Decatur and I were talking on the way to church about Mr. Ketchum's troubles," Pastor Shaw was saying as she reached the doorway.

She stopped. Ike's chair was blocking the door. His hands were laced behind his head. The only way past was to ask him to move or brush against him, and she couldn't bring herself to do either.

"Mr. Ketchum's son is trying to get an early discharge from the navy so he can come home and help him get his part of the crop out," Ike was saying. "If he doesn't swing it, Decatur and I can lend Henry a hand, once Gentry gets his half out."

"It won't take Chester long," said Pastor Shaw. "He's made the New Hope Ladies Aid the same offer he made Friends of the Library. Only he didn't put a time limit on it. He said the ladies could pick until they got tired of it. The ladies are wanting funds to finish out the kitchen in the basement of the new building." He chuckled. "If I know them, they'll leave nothing but fodder. As for Ketchum's half, keep me posted, Ike. If you men go to shuck it out, I'd like to help."

Pastor Shaw came to his feet in deference to Libby. "Let me help you with that, Libby."

Belatedly, Ike turned in his chair to see her standing behind him, about to pass the tray over his head. She retreated a step to guard the tray from a collision as he came to his feet and reached for it. "Here, Lib. I'll take it."

Ike saw her eyes flash as she pulled her hands away, relinquishing the tray. He couldn't see what she was so mad about. She was going to Gentry's field. *Wasn't that what she wanted?* He gave the tray to the pastor, and pushed his chair Libby's way. "Sit down. I'll fetch another one."

"Ike and I were talking about Mr. Gentry's benevolence," said Pastor Shaw, as the gruffness in Ike's voice resonated through Libby.

"Yes," she said, scarcely noticing the pastor's measuring glance. "We talked about it ourselves just yesterday."

Pastor Shaw set the tray on the water bench and waited until Ike had returned to distribute the plates of cake. He admired the blue fruit jars of jams and jellies and canned garden produce crowding the scarred top of a workbench; he praised her enterprise regarding the tied bundles of dried, sun-washed herbs that hung from exposed rafters above the bench.

Libby flushed at his kind words, but the potpourri of color and scent held no appeal for her today. Even the view from their summer porch and the sun coming through the windows failed to divert her attention from the misery of yesterday's quarrel.

They were finishing their coffee and cake when pale-haired Opal McClure emerged from the woods. She skipped up to the door, calling Libby's name. "Frankie's gone fishin' and I ain't got nothin' ta do. Would ya come out and play, Miss Lib?"

"An irresistible invitation, if ever I heard one. Go on, don't keep the child waiting," urged the pastor.

Appreciating his understanding, Libby cut a piece of cake for Opal, slung a shawl over her shoulders, and went out in the yard to join the girl. Her thin face lit up at the sight of the cake.

"So what do you want to play?" asked Libby, dropping down on the step beside her.

"House," said Opal, around a mouthful of cake. "If ya got a rake, we'll make us a house of leaves. Iffin it suits," she added, so as not to appear bossy.

Libby said that it did, and in short order, they had arranged piles of leaves to form a "pretend" house. Opal assigned herself the role of Mama and cast Libby as all the other parts, including the doctor who came to visit the ailing man of the house.

"Let's say ya take yer pay in eggs, Dr. Lib."

"All right. A dozen will be sufficient."

"Make it two on account yer such a good doctor. Can ya fix the mister up the way ya did Ike?"

"Well, maybe. Put the hot water on to boil and I'll get some more bandages from the buggy," said Libby in her best pretend voice.

"Not *them* hurts. I mean the ones Mama was talkin' about, the ones ya cain't see makes a feller melancholic."

Libby flushed at Opal so innocently parroting words not meant to be repeated and struggled with the unpleasant sensation of wanting to defend herself for not living up to them. But why should she be a party to a grudge, and in effect, justify Ike for holding on to it? Getting to her feet, she said, "I'll get a match, and we'll burn these leaves."

Opal picked at a knee scab showing through the hole in her brother's hand-me-down coveralls, and pleaded, "Cain't we play in 'em a bit more first?"

"All right. But just a few more minutes."

Opal brightened and said in her best Mama voice,

"Ya have ta take yer tonic if ya want ta git better. Hold yer nose now and swaller it down."

Submission, the word dropped to mind. Libby had re- sisted, thinking she shouldn't have to give in when he was wrong and she was right. But there was no healing in a standoff.

Libby took Opal's imaginary tonic from her imagi- nary spoon. She scrunched up her face and clutched her throat, making Opal giggle. Smiling herself, she surren- dered to the prod of her heavenly Shepherd's staff urg- ing her to higher pastures. If Ike really didn't want her picking corn in Mr. Gentry's field, even for a good cause, she wouldn't.

Frankie came along shortly thereafter to fetch Opal home. Libby bid the children good-bye, then went back inside to join the men. By and by, Pastor Shaw thanked her for the coffee and cake and prepared to go. In so doing, he mentioned that his wife planned to help husk corn at Mr. Ketchum's.

"Reckon Lib'll be seein' her tomorrow, then," Ike spoke up. "She's planning on helpin' too."

Libby lifted her face and saw as their eyes met that his words were not grudgingly given. *He was miserable, too*. The realization brought tears to her eyes. She ducked her head and cleared away the dishes, while Ike walked the pastor to the crossing to help him get his handcar back on the rails. When he returned, he called to her from the door.

"I'm taking the team over to the barn. You want to ride along?"

Heart lifting, she nodded and reached for her shawl.

They rattled side by side over the railway tracks, east a few dozen yards, over the bridge, past the sap house, and out of the woods. The barn was surrounded by pas- ture and a field of partially picked corn, the stalks stand- ing in shocks. Libby helped care for the horses while Ike tried to find the words to say the trouble was be- tween him and Gentry and if he had made her feel it was a breach of loyalty to pick corn in the man's field, then he was wrong.

Why was it so hard to say he was sorry? He finally gave up trying. It wasn't the way he'd meant to give her this present when he'd first started building it. He'd meant to get her away from the house under some pretense. Install the thing. Have it full of water and ready for her use on the night of their anniversary. Now, feeling foolish over the sentiment, he lifted the horse blanket that was covering it. "Take a look here, see what you think."

Trying to erase the awkwardness left by their quarrel, Libby played the clown, widening her eyes and saying with feigned astonishment. "A bathtub? For me?"

A slow grin tipped his mouth up at the corners. "Who'd ya think?"

Wondering why a kiss on the jaw seemed such a risk, Libby landed it and kept moving, circling the tub, lifting the lid, running her hand along the shiny copper lining. "Thank you! What a beauty!" She stroked the lid, fingers following the grain of the wood. "You'd never guess it was a bathtub, with the top down. It looks like a table."

"It'll do the job, I guess."

"You're being modest, Ike. It's handsome and ingenious and I'm fair overcome with surprise."

Ike chuckled at her acting. "How long have ya known, Lib?"

"Not long." She laughed, telltale color sweeping up her neck.

Watching her hands move over the wooden cover, aching for the touch of those cool white fingers, he shook his head. "I don't know what I was thinkin', marryin' a town girl, doesn't know a thing about keepin' her nose out of the barn."

"What's there to know?"

"Why, jest what I said. That it's a place ta be respected as a man's hideaway."

"Hideaway?" She arched him a glance. "What would you be hiding away? Besides my bathtub?"

"Nothin'," he said with studied nonchalance.

"Then you won't mind if I take a look around?"

"Suit yerself. Jest so ya stay out of the loft." He stood there long enough to let her get up the ladder, then climbed up after her.

"There's nothing here but straw and hay and an owl," she called loud enough to startle the owl.

"Ya didn't look good enough," said Ike as the bird took wing.

Libby swung around to find him with his feet spread and his hands locked loosely beneath his arms. She knew as their eyes met what he had in mind. Heat swept up her neck. Feeling foolish for having fallen for such a prank, she asked, "How do I know that tub's going to hold water?"

"You bargainin' with me, Lib?"

"Should I be?"

His gaze was soft with desire as it moved over to her in the dim, dusky loft. "Come here and I'll tell ya."

She went to him. His mouth against hers nursed the hurts of their recent quarrel. At length, she said, "It's cold up here. Let's take our bathtub and go home."

His arms tightened in a silent promise to keep her warm.

Distracted by a fleeting motion caught out of the corner of her eye, she asked, "Was that a mouse?"

"Let's call it a shadow."

"Ike, it was a . . ."

"Shadow," he insisted, his mouth warm against hers in the dusky sweet-smelling loft.

"A bath first, all right?" she said, but he smothered her words with a long, deep kiss and whispered her name.

She searched his face, those strong lean familiar lines, and searched for the words to say she was sorry they had quarreled, but she didn't want to tarnish the moment. "I love you, Ike."

"I know."

What a joy! Neck deep in soap suds, singing and soaking by candlelight while Ike sat by the stove on the other side of the screen, whittling sap spiles and waiting his turn. Libby thought fleetingly of cracking that closed door regarding his hard feelings against Mr. Gentry. Restored harmony kept her from trying. The truth was, the man could love her into anything. Even silence.

4

❧ "Stop by the barn on yer way by if ya want a huskin' hook," Ike said as he was preparing to leave for his own fields the next morning.

"How does that work?" Libby asked.

"It's a hook ya strap to yer hand. Helps ya open the sheath. Reckon I'll be in the field by the time ya come. I'll jest set it there by the door, where ya can find it easy." He kissed her good-bye. "Have fun and leave some corn for the Ladies Aid."

Libby smiled and waved him out the door, then set about condensing her morning chores into a couple of hours work. According to the paper, the ladies were taking along box lunches for a picnic when the work was done. She packed herself a lunch, a second one for Ike and left it on the table with a note, that, on a whim, she signed with a heart.

The pungent smell of late autumn wafted on the air as Libby stopped by the barn. Ike was nowhere to be found, but he'd left the husking hook as promised. Taking it with her, she cut across the pasture and back into the woods, then angled south toward Henry Ketchum's field. The trees were stark giants with their branches ex-

38

posed, their castaway leaves rustling underfoot.

She crossed the fence where Ike's timber ran out and looked back across his cornfield, which skirted the trees. It was more than half-harvested. The standing shocks waiting to be used as fodder for the livestock resembled an Indian village. As Libby turned south to walk along Henry Ketchum's cornfield, she was struck by the contrast. Ike hadn't exaggerated. Henry's field was a tangled mess strewn across the ground.

The sight of Sarah Jane Brignadello coming from the other direction in her husband's tinker wagon drew Libby's eye away from the flattened corn. She lifted her hand and quickened her stride, reaching the wagon just as Mrs. Brignadello halted the team.

The handsome little lady, known to her friends as Mrs. Bee, was old enough to be Libby's mother. In her youth she had been a circus performer. The gold braid on her cape matched the gold trim on her hat and a flourish of elaborate gold stitching on her layered skirt. Her smile, as she climbed down from the wagon, nursed a lonesomeness Libby hadn't realized she was feeling.

"I told Paulette you'd be here," she said, and gave Libby a quick hug.

"Paulette's with you? Where?"

"Right here." Mrs. Bee knocked on the wall of her husband's brightly painted huckster wagon. She winked at Libby, put her hands to her mouth, and called, "How are you ladies doing in there?"

"Let us out of this cracker box!" One voice rose above the cacophony of female voices.

Surprised, Libby exclaimed, "Maddie Cearlock! Is that you?"

"Of course it's me. Ouch, Catherine! That's my foot you're trampling."

"Catherine, too?" Libby laughed in glad anticipation. "What are you two doing here?"

"Other than being rattled and banged to death? Let us out, would you?"

A pounding fist and Maddie's insistent bellowing for release crowded over Catherine's laughter and the beehive hum of the other ladies stirring to disembark out the back door of the wagon. Libby rose on tiptoe, trying to reach the wooden latch that held the door closed.

Mrs. Bee ground-tied her team. "I'm coming, I'm coming! Merciful patience, ladies!" she exclaimed, and circled to the rear of her husband's enclosed wagon. She brushed Libby to one side, unfolded a hinged step from the tailboard, and climbed up it to turn the wooden latch.

Women poured out the door and onto the ground—Mrs. Shaw, Paulette Harding, the Berry girls, Maddie and Catherine among them. Catherine was fair and petite and sunny of disposition. Maddie was statuesque and dark and strong in her opinions. The two were lifelong friends. They had become sisters-in-law as well fifteen months earlier, when Catherine's brother Angus married Maddie.

The women crowded around Libby, warming her with hugs and friendly inquiries and swiftly traded news. Chloe Berry and her sister Dorene, who had married Earl Morefield a month earlier, were the nearest in age to Libby. Chloe was still single, despite Billy Young's faithful courting. But Dorene, all smiles, looked as if marriage suited her. Maddie and Catherine were several years older. Maddie had become a mother since Libby had last seen her. Catherine, whom Libby hadn't seen in over a year, had two children—Tess, who was two, and Thomas, who was born the month after Maddie's twins.

"What are their names again?" Libby asked as they talked over one another, trying to catch up on all the news.

"Louisiana Lace and Purchase."

Catherine dimpled. "They're adorable and their auntie doesn't mind saying so. Named for the St. Louis World's Fair honoring the Louisiana Purchase, you know."

"I know! Maddie wrote and told me the name she'd chosen months before her time." Libby laughed, and added, "Of course, you didn't know you were going to have to divide the name between two, did you, Maddie?"

"Had I known, I would have run for cover! We call them Lace and Chase," added Maddie with a maternal smile and a tilt of her proud head.

Henry Ketchum came limping across the field from the direction of his chicken coop of a house at the south end of the field. His forehead was lined from a habitual squint. He nodded to the group in general, then shifted his cane to the other hand. The ladies fell silent as he opened his pocket watch. He pressed his nose almost to the face of it, then straightened again. "Ya have two hours, ladies."

Maddie tugged at her smooth-fitting kid gloves. "Could I trouble you for a husking pin before we get started, Mr. Ketchum?"

"I ain't shore but what Mr. Gentry'd want me passin' out huskin' hooks," hedged Henry. "Ya get to grabbin' fast, and it's easy to slice yer other hand with 'em. Or yer neighbor, if yer crowdin' too close."

Libby waited for Maddie to tell poor nearsighted Henry who she was. But Maddie challenged him instead: "Tell me, Mr. Ketchum. Who peels the potatoes at your house?"

"Why, the missus, of course."

"So she can wield a paring knife, but not a husking hook?"

Henry's leathery face darkened at the stir of stifled laughter from the ladies. He hitched his britches and shifted his arthritic bones and muttered to the sky.

Catherine Morefield, stepdaughter to Henry's employer, said, "Never mind, Mr. Ketchum. Some of the ladies brought their own, but the rest of us will get along just fine without them."

"Miss Catherine?" Henry fumbled for his glasses.

One stem was broken and he had a hard time balancing them on his nose. "Well, I swan, it *is* you, Miss Catherine. I wasn't expectin' you here this mornin'. What're you doin' up here from St. Louie?"

"Visiting with Chester and Mama. They miss me a little and their grandchildren a lot." Catherine smiled, and added, "You know Angus's wife, don't you? She came down on the train from Bloomington yesterday and graciously agreed to help us."

"Beggin' yer pardon, Miz Cearlock. I didn't recognize you," Henry said to Maddie, his manner suddenly solicitous. "You tell Angus hello for me."

"I will, Mr. Ketchum," said Maddie. "Now about that husking hook . . ."

"That's our Maddie. She'll make an issue over anything!" muttered Catherine for Libby's ears alone.

Grinning at the mix of affection and exasperation in Catherine's voice, Libby played the peacemaker and gave Maddie the palm hook Ike had left for her.

The weather had been dry, sparing the corn from rotting on the ground. The women organized themselves in such a fashion so as not to hit one another with flying ears. Libby, Maddie, Catherine, Dorene, and Chloe picked into one wagon; Sarah Jane, Paulette, and Mrs. Shaw picked into the other. Most of them were farmborn and -reared, and familiar with the process. But the job would have been easier had the cornstalks been standing. Libby soon wished she'd kept her husking hook. Maddie was making better headway than she in parting the husk from the corn.

As were the Berry girls. Libby watched in admiration as Dorene grabbed an ear in her right hand, ripped back the shucks with the hook in her left palm, twisted the ear free and flung it toward the wagon with her right.

"You do that like a pro, Dorie," said Libby. "You, too, Chloe."

"We should," said Dorene with a smile. "We've had some practice. Haven't we, Chloe?"

"Lots of practice," chimed in Chloe.

Plain-featured, wholesome green-eyed girls, they took turns regaling their friends with stories of past cornpickings. Their father farmed for Miss Maudie Morefield, and had often put them to work in the fields alongside their brothers.

Dorene had moved to town after marrying. Her husband, a farm boy himself, was now working for Mr. Gruben, setting type for the newspaper. Thinking of the adjustments she had made in moving from town to the country, Libby wondered if Dorene was undergoing a similar adjustment at having made an opposite move. She asked, "Do you miss the country, Dorie?"

"Sometimes." Dorene flung an ear of corn toward the wagon, and added, "Then I remember all the work and try to figure out exactly what I miss. I remind Earl of it, too, when he starts feeling a little homesick for milking and plowing."

"It's hard to get the farm boy out of a Morefield," said Catherine, who was married to Earl's cousin. "But it can be done. Look at me. I'm living proof that a man can make a living with his head just as well as his back, if he's got an encouraging wife behind him."

Maddie baited her with a smile. "So you're saying it takes more brains to sell insurance than plow a field and congratulating yourself on providing Charlie with inspiration?"

"Now there you go, putting words in my mouth and trying to get me in trouble!" said Catherine with feigned indignation. "I thought we were here to pick corn, not pick on me."

"But you make such an easy target," said Maddie. "Doesn't she, Dorie?" Dorene chuckled, and said, "Leave me out of it."

"What're *you* standing there looking at, Libby?" Maddie asked.

Before Maddie, who was something of an instigator, could drag her into her good-natured wrangling, Libby said, "All this corn. How many ears do you think it takes to buy a book?"

"Now there's a good question," said Chloe.

Maddie sent an ear of corn flying toward the wagon. "Think of each ear as a page."

"A dog-eared page," said Libby, as she held the stalk down with her foot and battled tenacious cornhusks.

Dorene and Chloe sent their corn ears ringing against the bang-board of the wagon with unerring accuracy. A tall board at the far side of the wagon, it was so named for the noise the ears made as they banked off the board and into the wagon. It would take a good arm to overthrow the bang-board.

Catherine, Libby observed, needn't worry about that. Her pitches fell short of the wagon with enough regularity to garner some teasing from the others.

"Oops," Catherine said, as yet another ear missed the wagon. "How do I keep doing that?"

"I don't know, but I hope Charlie and the children never have to depend on you throwing them a rescue line," said Maddie.

Face flushed with laughter, Catherine ducked low so as not to be hit by air-bound ears as she went to retrieve her last three misses. She leaned under the wagon to reach the last one, flung it straight up in the air, then yelped and winced when it missed the wagon and glanced off her shoulder. Flinging her arms up to shield herself, she laughed helplessly, and pleaded, "Hold your fire while I run for cover!"

Maddie wagged her head. "Catherine, you monkey, that wasn't us! You hit yourself."

"That was *my* ear?"

Catherine's chagrin sent Libby and the Berry sisters into giggling fits. Catherine returned to them, brushing dirt and dried cornsilks from her skirt with one hand and holding the retrieved ear of corn in the other.

"Speaking of monkeys," said Maddie, "Angus left a

cartoon on my dressing-table mirror, the political over-
tones of which I found of interest.''

Catherine rolled her eyes. "Here we go."

"Picture a big young daddy monkey leaning against
a tree with his ankles crossed, his arms folded over his
chest, and his hat dipped low over his eyes," said Maddie, ignoring her. "In the tree overhead is mama monkey. She's got her nose in the air and five little monkeys
strung along the branch beside her. The caption beneath
it reads: "Thought you said we were just monkeyin'
around.""

Catherine smothered a giggle. "That's not political,
that's just plain naughty."

"Speaking in zoological context, I also believe it's
misleading," said Libby. "Monkeys don't have litters,
do they?"

Maddie grinned. "Only the passionate ones."

"Careful," murmured Catherine, in deference to
Chloe, who had no tolerance for such talk.

"Chloe's a grown woman with six sisters and three
brothers. If she doesn't know about passion by now, then
she isn't paying attention," said Maddie mildly.

"She's a nice girl," said Catherine in the same
hushed voice.

"A nice goose," countered Maddie. "She'll marry a
gander. They'll have a flock of little goslings and she'll
never quite figure out how it happened because it isn't
nice to talk about sex." Maddie said the forbidden word
with pleasure, swung around, and called to Dorene,
"Dorene! You know how men keep women from aspiring to anything higher than motherhood, don't you?"

"What could be higher?" said Libby.

"Exactly!" echoed Catherine.

"Catherine, either throw that ear of corn in the wagon
or give it to me!" ordered Maddie. She sighed, and
added, "I don't mind saying I'm disappointed in both
of you. Be still now, while I enlighten Dorene."

Catherine, stifling laughter, gave her the ear of corn.

She patted Dorene, who'd come over at Maddie's bidding, and warned, "Don't listen to her, Dorie. She's all talk, anyway. She'll outmother us all, just wait and see."

"Outmother?" echoed Maddie. "What's that supposed to mean?"

"It means you're going to have lots more babies and Libby and Dorene and I are going to make you eat every word you ever uttered to blacken the eye of motherhood. Right, ladies?"

"I have never blackened the eye of motherhood. Though in the interest of accomplishing something worthwhile with my life, I don't mind telling you that I don't intend to have any more children," said Maddie, with a toss of her head.

"Oh, pooh! There is no more valuable contribution you can make to the world than your children. Besides, Tess and Thomas want some more cousins. In fact, I think we should make a note of this discussion. Chloe!" Catherine beckoned to her. "Come over here. You may as well get in on this, too. You want a family someday, don't you? Of course you do. Here's what we're going to do. We're going to predict who will have the most children."

"Oh, for pity sake. This is childish!" declared Maddie.

"Don't be a such wet blanket, Maddie. Here's what I'm proposing. I'm proposing that twenty years from now, we all meet right here, bring our families, and count heads."

"Twenty years?" said Dorene with a doubtful blink.

"Yes, and we'll have a picnic under the trees there. How does that sound?"

"It sounds longer than my memory," said Libby. "How about ten instead?"

"All right, then, ten," said Catherine.

"It isn't exactly fair," said Chloe.

"What isn't fair about it?"

"You and Maddie have a head start."

"Chloe, you goose, the winner is the one with the fewest children, not the most!" said Maddie in exasperation.

Chloe scratched her head. "You mean if one of us doesn't have any children, we win? That isn't winning, that's losing."

"I agree," said Libby. "The winner should be the one with the most, not the least."

"Leave me out of it, then," said Maddie.

"Oh, Maddie! It's just for fun," said Catherine.

"Yoo-hoo!" yodeled Mrs. Bee from thirty yards away. "Are you girls picking corn or having a tea party? Time is running out."

Libby and her friends went back to work, picking corn and ringing it against the bang-board with renewed fervor. To Libby's fanciful ear, it sounded like a drumroll, building as they raced Henry Ketchum's pocket watch.

Jerk-peel-twist-toss. Jerk-peel-twist-toss. Libby said it to herself in four-four time, though in reality, her uneven effort more closely resembled a novice pianist murdering a musical score.

By and by, Mr. Ketchum hobbled across the field. Time was up. Pleased with what Mr. Ketchum estimated to be fifty bushels of corn, Libby and her friends spread blankets in the sunshine and sat down to eat the lunches they had brought along.

They were just finishing up when a light buggy bumped across the field. Libby recognized Chester Gentry at the reins. A rotund man with a heavily waxed moustache and an air of industry about him, he climbed out of the buggy and came their way. He tipped his hat and traded greetings with some of the ladies. Libby felt his gaze skip over her. Intuitively, she saw that he no longer viewed her as a friend of his daughter's or the young woman who had once been courted by his son. He saw her as Ike Galloway's wife, and was surprised that she had come.

Surprised? Or displeased? What was between him

and Ike to make him look at her that way? Feeling out of place, Libby sat quietly while Mr. Gentry verified Mr. Ketchum's estimate of fifty bushels, and told Mrs. Bee, who was their official Friends of the Library spokeswoman, that he would pay two cents over the current market price. As he prepared to leave, he offered Catherine and Maddie a ride home.

Catherine bade her friends good-bye, and went with her stepfather, but Maddie declined. Libby wasn't sure what to make of it. Maddie, who had complained the loudest about the ride out in Mr. Brignadello's tinker wagon, offered no explanation for refusing a reprieve.

"I'd love to see the twins," Libby said to Maddie as Maddie sat down beside her to eat. "Did they come with you?"

"I had no choice. Angus adores them, but he would sooner walk through fire than take those two on alone."

Libby laughed. "You must bring them to see me, Maddie. Really! Could you make it for lunch tomorrow?"

"I wish I could, but we're taking the early train back to Bloomington in the morning. Anything beyond twenty-four hours, and Mother and I are at one another's throats."

"You're staying at your mother's home?" said Libby. "From the way Catherine talked, I thought you were staying with Angus's parents."

"Ida invited us, and I disliked disappointing her. She's a dear, really she is. But Chester and I don't get along that well."

"I'm sorry," murmured Libby. She had no point of reference where in-laws were concerned, for she had yet to meet Ike's family. Ike's mother, Nona Kay, remarried for many years now, lived in California near Ike's sister, Cicely. The distance and train fare were unsurmountable obstacles. She shared her chocolate velvet cake with Maddie. "Perhaps you and Mr. Gentry will become better friends in time."

"Libby, our pop-eyed optimist." Maddie grinned with that indomitable spirit of hers. "Don't bother feeling sorry for me. Angus accepts me the way I am, and that's all that really matters."

And Mr. Gentry *didn't?* Sorry for Maddie and yearning suddenly for the harmony of her own little woodland haven, Libby finished eating, then retrieved her husking hook, bade Maddie and the rest of her friends good-bye, and hurried home to Ike.

5

March 1906

Ike heard the jingle of harnessing and the sucking sounds of the horses dragging the sap wagon through the slushing snow. He crossed to a west-facing window to see twelve-year-old Frankie McClure jumping free of the gathering rig, a pair of deer antlers in hand.

There wasn't enough snow to gather by sled, so they were using an iron-wheeled wagon that had been modified for gathering. It was built low so sap could be easily dumped into the wooden-staved, tub-shaped tank. There was enough room on the platform to the rear of the tank for Decatur McClure to stand, lines in hand. Ike watched him begin the loop that would bring the horse-drawn sap wagon over the earth ramp at the north end of the building.

As they disappeared beyond the north wall of the sap house, Ike turned back to the evaporator. Dominating the heart of the building, the divided pans were four feet wide and fourteen feet long. Long enough that between waning daylight and wafting steam, he couldn't see one end of the evaporator from the other. But with his good ear, he could hear the trickle of sap spilling from the feed pipe that led from the outdoor storage tank through the wall and into the evaporator. The adjustable float arm regulated the incoming flow, thereby keeping a constant level of sap in the pans. He set the float a notch deeper to allow a little extra sap into the pans so there'd be no danger of scorching, then paused beside Libby on his way to the door.

The humidity had turned her hair to tight curls. They spilled over her shoulder like flying sparks and curtained her face as she stooped to sweep a pile of dried mud into a broken-handled shovel. Her curves made a tempting target. "Yer blockin' traffic," he said, and patted her on the bottom.

"Watch it, buster," she warned, and swung around to face him.

A smile worked at the corners of his mouth. "Gettin' tired?"

"No. But I'm about to go dancing."

The only dancing he'd ever seen her do was down the long ash-strewn path to the privy behind their cabin. Grinning at her code word for nature's call, he asked, "Can ya wait just a minute?"

"Guess so." She dumped the mud she'd swept up into a bucket, put the shovel and broom to one side, and withdrew a twig from her apron pocket. "See what I pinched off my lilac bush? It looks as if it's going to bloom this year."

"Those are leaf buds," said Ike.

"Leaf buds? Not flower buds?" Disappointed, Libby held the twig with its purple rice-sized buds to the light of the nearby window, then pivoted to grab Ike's hand as he turned away. "Hey! Where are you going?"

"Thought I'd see how much sap Decatur and Frankie gathered along the C & A," said Ike, speaking of the timber closest to the railroad tracks, a tract of woods that belonged to Decatur. "You can take over fer a minute, cain't ya?"

The price of the evaporator, her inexperience, and the

ever-present risk of burning the pans made her reluctant.
"Why don't I go and bring you back a report?"

"All I need is a pair of eyes, Lib."

"What am I supposed to do if the sap starts to boil
over?"

"It won't," he said, for it was nearly time to add
wood and it wouldn't boil high until he did. Not unless
she overstirred it.

"But if it does," she pressed.

"Drop in a little cream."

"How much should I stir it?"

"Stirrin' it is what brings on a high boil, makes it
want to boil out of the pans."

Doubtfully, she said, "You're sure you want to leave
me in here alone?"

Ike nudged his cap back and scratched his head.
"Where'd I get such a sap-shy babe in the woods?"

"All right, all right. But don't get into any long-
drawn-out conversations," she warned.

Ike indicated a nearby chair. "Sit down while yer
waitin', and quit worryin'."

"Okay. But don't be gone long."

"Dancin', I remember."

"I want to check the fire, too. It probably needs wood
by now," she said

"Won't be gone but a few minutes, then you can go."

Ike's thoughts shifted to the McClures and how much
sap they'd gathered and how much remained in the
woods. February had been cold and mean right up to the
last of the month. But March was showing some promise. He was going to call on Miss Maudie again, just as
soon as he got time. If she had no interest in selling the
land in the near future, he hoped at least to get a three-
year farming commitment from her. Something in writing this time. He owed Libby more security, and while
that wasn't a guarantee of good farming years, it was
the best he could do for now.

Ike strode to the north end of the sap house just as

Decatur stopped Ike's team of work horses on the earth bank above the round wooden storage tank. The tank, elevated about eight feet along the wall of the sap house, was stationed beneath a roofed lean-to, thereby offering some protection from the elements. Its high position made use of gravity, piping the sap from the storage tank, through the wall of the sap house, and into the evaporator.

"Ya get it all?" he asked.

"Fer today, anyway," said Decatur. "We was makin' good time till a feller from the railroad come along, jaw-in' about that water tank. Looks like they'll be puttin' it up in a few weeks. Hope it ain't too much of an eye-sore, 'cause you'll be lookin' at it, right out your east window."

It'd been almost two years since Ike had first learned of the railroad's plans to sink a well and put in a water tank at Old Kentucky. It was part of a project to improve the Chicago and Alton that involved leveling and dou-ble-tracking all the way from Bloomington to Spring-field.

Ike asked, "Trees still drippin'?"

"Yep, but they're slowin'." Decatur was a long-limbed rawboned bearded man with piercing blue eyes and coarse hair that escaped his weather-stained hat and touched his shoulders. He stepped off the low-slung sap wagon, retrieved a plug of chewing tobacco from his coat pocket, and motioned for his son Frankie to drop the pipe at the base of the wooden gathering tank.

The pipe wasn't long enough to reach the storage tank. Ike put a bucket in place and balanced a narrow wooden trench between the bucket and the rim of the sap-storage tank. The trench acted as a channel for the sap as Frankie lowered the pipe. Gravity carried the flow down the pipe, along the trench, through a flannel-lined screen filter and into the wooden storage tank, which was wedged between the bank and the north end of the sap house.

"Reckon the sap'll run all night, Ike?" asked Frankie.

"Doesn't look like it. Feel the temperatures droppin'?"

"But they'll run again tomorrow?"

"Should, if the sun warms things up like it did today," said Ike.

"Need me tomorrow, then?"

"Countin' on it." Ike clapped the boy on the shoulder. From the vantage point of the steep man-made earth bank, he looked back toward the bridge, the direction from which they'd hauled in the sap. "Where's Opal?"

"She jumped off at yer cabin and said she was goin' ta see Lib and warm up," said Frankie. His trousers and coat front were damp from gathering. The breeze feathered the red hair fringing his cap as he hunched his thin shoulders, shivering in the early-evening shadows.

"Go on inside, Frankie, and stand by the firebox. Better kick yer boots off first. Lib's been makin' war on mud this afternoon."

"What's the use in havin' a dirt floor if ya have ta keep it clean?" asked Frankie.

"Ya got a lot to learn about wimmin," Decatur spoke up. He ran a hand along the nearest horse's flank and knocked a clump of mud off the hip strap that straddled the animal's powerful hindquarters. "She inside, or over at the cabin?"

"Who, Lib? Inside," said Ike.

Decatur paused in unhitching the team of horses from the sled located beneath the gathering tank. "Don't take them boots off yet," he called after Frankie. "Go git yer sister, first. Ain't nobody at the cabin, and ya know Opal cain't leave nothin' alone."

Ike watched Frankie slide down the slushy bank, lope across the melting snow and over the rutted, muddy road toward the bridge to do Decatur's bidding. He'd been doing a good job considering how young he was. A man could be proud of a son like that.

"Done with the horses for the day, ain't ya?" Decatur

interrupted his thoughts. At Ike's nod, he got a good tight grip on the lines. The horses were tired from a day of heavy hauling and eager for the barn.

Once the tank had emptied, Ike went inside to find Libby lighting the kerosene lantern. He threw fresh wood in the firebox and used the manual valve to let fresh sap into the evaporator.

"Is Decatur gone?" asked Libby.

"Not yet. He's goin' ta take care of the horses b'fore hitching up his own team and heading home." The lantern was sputtering, battling for oxygen. Ike moved it to the corner, where there wasn't so much steam.

"Where are the children?"

"Opal thought you were home and stopped off to warm up. Frankie went to get her."

"Maybe she'll put some wood in the stove while she's there."

He nudged her with his shoulder and challenged, "Ya won't let me near that stove of yers, but you'll let a child tend it?"

"You worry about your fires, and I'll worry about mine."

Ike grinned and reached for the skimmer. He moved around her as he waited for the fresh sap in the pans to come to a boil. "I thought you were goin' home."

"I am," she said, and stirred herself to go.

But the McClure children came along before she made it out the door. Their mother, Naomi, worked at Willie Blue's, Edgewood's general store, four days a week. The store actually belonged to Frankie, but Naomi served as proprietor, according to the arrangements made following the death of Willie Blue. With Decatur helping Ike, the children came to the sirup camp as soon as they got home from school.

Pale-haired, blue-eyed Opal flung herself into Libby's arms. She chattered a mile a minute about school and the rush home to help in the woods and the deer antlers Frankie had found while they were gathering sap.

"Two-point buck," said Frankie, finding Ike in the mist. "Did ya see 'em, Ike? I hung 'em on the roof of the storage tank lean-to."

"Yes, and when I come over the bridge, that tank with them antlers on it looked like a big old snail crawling up the sap-house wall," declared Opal.

Ike grinned at Libby in the maple fog. "Ya got some competition here, Lib. Opal's making word-pictures."

"She's good at it, too." Libby laughed as she caught Opal's rosy cheeks between her hands. "You get it from your mama, don't you, Opal?"

"Reckon so?" Looking pleased, Opal shared the limelight with her brother, saying, "Frankie gits her memorizin'. He won the spellin' bee at school, Lib. Spell somethin' for 'em, Frankie."

"I ain't goin' ta do it," said Frankie, sounding pained.

Ike traded smiles with Libby and motioned to Opal. "Step up here, Opal. Looks to me like yer about tall enough to skim the pans."

Opal beamed and threw her shoulders back. "Hand me the ladle."

"It ain't a ladle, it's a skimmer. Ladle's what ya use on the finish pan, and the only reason he'll let ya skim is ya cain't hurt much there," added Frankie, as if he was afraid Opal would let the job go to her head.

"Hush up, Frankie. Ike's showin' me," said Opal.

"See where the sap is feedin' into the evaporator? If ya catch the impurities there just as the sap starts to boil, I won't have to chase them all over the pans."

Opal, clad in a pair of her brother's hand-me-down overalls, cocked her pale head to one side. Using the skimmer to point, she said, "That whipped-egg-whites-lookin' stuff there?"

"That's right, the foam. That's what you want to skim out. See the bucket there on the ground? Pitch it in that. There ya go, yer doin' fine. See here, Lib, if we aren't turning Opal into a sirup-maker? Frankie, soon as we're done here, we'll test for sirup."

"We're close, goin' by what the thermometer says."
Frankie squinted to read the thermometer in the dim
glow cast by the lantern.

"The temperature can fluctuate when the air pressure
shifts. That's where the saccharometer comes in," said
Ike. He paused to insert, "Good job, Opal. That's
enough, though. You don't want to stir it any more than
you have to."

"Stirrin' makes it boil higher," said Frankie.

"That's right." Ike shot Libby a glance to see her
standing well behind Frankie. "Step up here closer, Lib,
if yer wantin' to see."

"I can see," she countered.

Ike turned back to the bubbling sap. It had taken him
all of last season to gain some confidence with the evaporator. He had it down now, and was wanting to teach
Libby. So far, he'd found a better student in Frankie.

Trying once more to spark some interest in his wife,
Ike undertook a detailed explanation as to why the front
and back foot-deep pans were partitioned into four parts
and how the fresh sap feeding into the pans entered the
flues and passed around into the front, joining the circuit
that pushed the sap that had boiled the longest into the
back pan he called the sirup pan. When it reached sirup
density, it was drawn off, filtered, and put into tin containers.

"If ya got all that, we'll move on to how you can tell
when it's getting close to sirup," he concluded.

Frankie nodded. Ike looked around to see Libby with
a rag in her hand, wiping off the handle of the empty
bucket beneath the sirup draw-off spigot.

"Ya watchin', Lib?" He waited until she came back
to his side, then took the flat-bottomed ladle in hand and
swept it through the sirup pan with a smooth sweep of
his arm. "Dip ya up a ladle full, then notice how it falls
back into the pan. When it drops dead like that, ya know
it ain't quite sirup."

"It isn't, then, is it?" asked Libby.

"No, it isn't," said Ike. "Sap drops. Sirup sheets. It'll collect along the ladle like teardrops and sheet back into the pan. Here, try it." He offered Libby the ladle.

"You do it," she said, and passed it to Frankie.

Ike let it go and continued his explanation. "There's shifts in the way it boils as it gets closer to sirup. See it goin' to finer bubbles? Won't be long now and those bubbles'll boil up big and golden. Let's test it with the saccharometer."

He took the long narrow dipper from the shelf on the wall behind him. "Lib, want to try this?"

"No thanks," said Libby. Reluctant to admit she was intimidated by the thing, she added, "You're getting too scientific for me."

He turned to see her disappearing in the mist. "Ya goin' home?"

"Yes. Opal? Are you coming with me?" Libby invited.

Enjoying her new status as skimmer, Opal said, "Be all right if I stayed here a while?"

"It's up to Ike."

Ike agreed. He said it as if he were doing Libby a favor, freeing her of the responsibility. Libby smiled and let him think so, but in reality, she was disappointed. She enjoyed Opal's company. She asked Ike, "How long are you going to be?"

"Up to bedtime, anyway. Got to empty out the storage tank b'fore I quit for the night."

"I'll bring you back some supper after a while, then."

"That'd be good."

"Like this, Ike?"

Ike turned back to Frankie. "Good! Now put the saccharometer in the cup of sirup. Some fellas make sirup with jest a thermometer. But this here instrument gives ya a good cross-check. Make a better grade of sirup that way."

"On account density don't vary accordin' to air pressure?"

"That's right," said Ike, Frankie's eager grasp a pleasing contrast to Libby's general disinterest.

Ike knew she had plenty of chores. In addition to her work at home and cleaning up after him here in the sap house, she had begun on busy days to gather the buckets close to the sap house while he and Decatur and Frankie were gathering deeper in the woods. No, he wasn't wanting to shuffle more work her way. He just wanted to share what he knew, the same way she passed along her better knowledge of grammar.

Maybe if he were to tell her that when she came back with his supper, she'd be more prone to listen. *Or was her refusal to learn her subtle way of telling him that if he was wanting help running the evaporator, he'd have to wait for sons and daughters of his own?*

6

Libby used the blunt edge of a triangular wrought-iron trivet to scrape the mud off her shoes. She had found the old fireplace trivet while rummaging through a junk pile last November and put it to use as a boot scraper. Ike had been digging a cistern at the back corner of the house at the time and collecting a good crop of mud on his shoes. As he affixed the trivet to the porch floor, he had cautioned, "Mind where yer goin' now, or ya'll trip over it."

Libby minimized the hazard by keeping a short pine bench over the trivet. She swept up the mud she'd scraped from her shoes and moved the bench back into place, then let herself inside.

The fire in the cast iron cookstove was burning low, the polished steel trim gleaming in the flickering light of hot embers. Libby scooped ashes from beneath the grate and stepped outside to dump them along the muddy path leading to the backyard privy. Hearing an engine pop off steam, she lifted her gaze to the railroad tracks skirting the back pasture as a train slowed for the depot several hundred yards ahead.

Libby filled the ash bucket with corncobs from the woodshed on her way back to the house. Corncobs made a fast, hot fire, and she was counting on a bath after supper. She added water to the soup beans to keep them from boiling dry, then began pumping water into the copper boiler.

Both the sink and the pump were new improvements. Ike had installed them after completing the cistern. The cistern water wasn't pure enough to drink, but it was softer than the mineral-rich backyard well water, and ideal for bathing and washing clothes.

Hearing Naomi McClure call to her from the summer porch, Libby hurried to let her in. Tall, auburn-haired, cheeks burnished from the cold, Naomi flashed a tired smile as they traded greetings, then peered into the lamp-lit room. "Are the younguns here?"

"They're keeping Ike company in the sap house. De-catur's putting the horses to bed."

"Brought ya some cream," said Naomi.

Gifts of cream and butter and other staples from the store was Naomi's way of repaying Libby for helping with Opal while she was working in town. Often, Fran-kie stopped by as well. But he rarely stayed, for Decatur always had chores for him to do. Grateful for the cream, Libby thanked Naomi and waved her toward a chair by the stove.

Naomi blew on her hands as she made her way toward it. "Airish out."

"Can I make you some tea?"

"No thanks, Libby. I ain't keepin' ya from supper, am I?"

"Not at all. Ike's got a lot of sap to cook down. He'll be at it for hours."

Reassured there was time for a visit while she waited for her family, Naomi said, "Couple of gals by the name of Stapleton moved into the house north of Miss Mau-die's ground. Had ya heard?"

"No! When?" asked Libby.

"Sometime last week. One of them's got a little girl, name of Joy. Ain't that a sweet name? Close to school age, I'm guessin'."

"Then the women are young," said Libby.

"The smoky-eyed one is near about my age, I'm guessin'. Thar's somethin' about that gal rings a bell with me. Cain't quite put my finger on it." Naomi smoothed her hair back from her face and unfastened the buttons on her coat. "The other'n is her mother. They was married to brothers. Second marriage for the older one."

"And their husbands?" asked Libby.

"The younger Mrs. Stapleton is a widow. Kind of confusin', her mother goin' by Mrs. Stapleton, too."

"Is she widowed as well?" Libby asked.

"The older one? No, she's married to a lawyer, but he's still back East. Mr. Gentry come into the store just as the Stapletons was leavin'. Queersome thing." Naomi's brow furrowed. "He didn't even look them gals' way and they didn't look his. Once the ladies was gone, one of the fellers sittin' thar by the stove said something about them folks he was rentin' to, and Gentry acted like he wasn't even talkin' to him."

"The house *does* belong to Mr. Gentry, doesn't it?" asked Libby.

"Far as I know, it does. Mr. Gentry grazes cattle on the ground around it."

"Then he has to have met them."

"I ain't so sure it was that kind of not speakin'. It was more like Mr. Gentry was looking right past 'em so he wouldn't *hafta* speak.

" 'Course maybe Mr. Gentry was thinkin' if he kept quiet, he'd discourage them men gathered around the stove from askin' questions," reasoned Naomi.

Libby chuckled. "That never works."

Naomi grinned. "Nope. Best they could come up with was that maybe Mr. Gentry had sold them gals the place."

Libby thought it over as she pulled ingredients out of the cupboard to make dumplings. "That doesn't seem likely. Why would he sell land he uses for grazing?"

"I don't know," said Naomi. Interest in Mr. Gentry waning, she peeled off her coat and joined Libby at the table. "Did Mr. Gruben tell ya he's goin' ta be losin' his printer's devil?"

"Earl? No! When did this happen?"

"It ain't yet. But Earl don't think he can make enough at the paper to support a wife and a youngun', too."

"Dorene's in the family way? Well now, that is news! She must be excited," said Libby, measuring flour into a bowl.

"I reckon," said Naomi. "Earl, too. He went to his aunt. Wants Miss Maudie to scare up a few acres for him to farm. 'Course it's a little late, what with spring jest around the corner."

Naomi was out of village news by the time her family came to collect her. Libby followed her as far as the summer porch, and called to the children as they dived from the wagon seat into the straw in the back to make room for their mother beside Decatur. "Are you going to stay with me tomorrow, Opal, while Frankie's gathering sap?" Libby asked.

"Can I, Mama?"

"Not tomorrow, darlin'. I'm takin' ya in town with me. I need yer help dustin' shelves," said Naomi. "Thanks anyway, Lib."

Libby took a jar of canned tomatoes back to the stove, and made breaded tomatoes while the dumplings were cooking. The wind rattled the tin on the roof as she added more cobs and some wood to the fire, then raised the wooden lid on the bathtub.

Constructed of staves like those used in kegs and barrels, it was like climbing into a barrel to bathe, except that it was only two and a half feet tall and wide enough in circumference that Libby could sit cross-legged in it. One boilerful and enough cold water to moderate the temperature would bring the water level to her waist. A second would bring it almost to her shoulders.

She dumped the first boilerful in the tub, dropped the

lid to hold the warmth, and put a second boilerful on the stove to heat before finding containers for her basket supper. There was a flat stone she kept on the stove to warm the bed sheets on cold winter nights. Libby put it in the basket to keep their food warm, then bundled up in her coat and scarf and boots for the short walk to the sap house.

Starlight shone on clumps of snow, relieving the blackness of the night as she made her way down the road over the railroad tracks. Libby could see the steam rising from the cupola and smell the woodsmoke as she crossed the bridge and the clearing and let herself into the sap house.

The blazing fire, hidden beneath the arch of the evaporator, warmed the simple frame building with its earthen floor. Libby closed the door quickly to hold the heat in. The steam deepened the darkness. "Ike?"

"Over here." His voice wafted on the sweet air.

"I've got supper." Libby moved toward the distant glimmer of a lantern in the blanket of maple clouds, listening for his voice. "Say something."

He materialized out of the steam and rumbled, "Boo!"

"Are you all alone?" Libby asked, for several of the old-timers in the neighborhood had fallen into the habit of stopping by to watch Ike make sirup. At his nod, she said, "I hope you're hungry then, because I packed enough for idlers, too."

"Enough what?" He tugged at the cloth covering her basket.

"Enough supper."

"Ya wantin' me to guess?" he asked, and made a pass over the basket with his nose.

"Ham and beans with dumplings, breaded tomatoes, and cookies."

"What kind?" he asked.

"Maple sugar cookies," she said, ever willing to accommodate his sweet tooth. "Where do you want it?"

"Right here's fine." He upended a crate close enough to the evaporator to keep an eye on the boiling sap.

Libby spread a cloth over the upended crate while Ike planted a chair on each side of it. She lit the candle she had brought along to eat by and placed it in the middle of their makeshift table. Its light illuminated the fatigue in Ike's face. Libby wondered aloud over tomorrow's weather.

"If it warms up like it did today, the trees'll run. Unless we come under low pressure."

"What is it again about low pressure?" asked Libby.

"It's a sign of bad weather comin'. If a freeze comes along, and catches the sap up in the tree, it can break the tree wide open. So the sap heads for the roots."

Ike ate quickly and went back to work. Libby finished her supper, then lingered a while, helping where needed and relaying the news of Edgewood that Naomi had passed along, beginning with their new neighbors.

"I was thinking I would bake a cake and take it to them when we're not quite so busy," Libby said.

"Be a nice way of makin' 'em feel welcome," said Ike.

"If I wait until the work slows down a little, will you go with me?"

"Depends. If it's jest womenfolk, they might feel more comfortable if you was to take Naomi and Opal with ya. How about holding the lantern while I check the thermometer?" he added.

The flame gasped for breath as Libby held the lantern over the sirup box while he tried to get a reading. "I almost forgot! Dorene is expecting."

Ike darted her a glance. "Ya want to hold that light steady? Can't hardly read the thermometer as it is, without ya wigglin' it."

"Sorry," said Libby, taking more care.

"Gettin' close." Ike motioned her to back up with the lantern.

"Now that Earl's going to be a family man, he's decided he wants to farm."

Ike swung around and peered at her in the whorls of maple fog. "Farm for who?"

"Miss Morefield." Gratified at having caught his attention, Libby added, "I'm surprised, too. I thought Earl was happy with his job at the paper."

"Must be thinkin' he can provide better as a farmer than a newspaper man," said Ike, a sinking feeling in his gut. Libby, he could see, hadn't stopped to wonder just whose ground Miss Maudie might offer Earl.

"Or it could be Dorene's idea. Her daddy's raised a big family farming for Miss Morefield. It would only be natural for her to think she and Earl can do it, too."

"She best be figurin' in how much help her daddy's had from her and her brothers and sisters," said Ike, as he tried to reel in his alarm. "Mr. Berry's notorious for yankin' his kids outa school to work."

"My father took me out of school, too," Libby reminded him.

"What else was he goin' to do? He couldn't work and look after a baby both at the same time."

"Perhaps Mr. Berry doesn't feel he has a choice either."

"Yer right. Not with all them mouths to feed."

She wouldn't want to take her children out of school to contribute to the family income, if that was his point. But she wished he hadn't turned Dorene's glad news into an object lesson. Feeling discouraged, Libby gathered up their supper dishes and piled them back into the basket.

Ike had grown quiet, too. His brow was furrowed, his jaw tense as he squinted, trying to see the numbers as he tested for sirup. Turning away, she shrugged into her coat and started for the door.

"What's yer rush?" he asked.

"You're busy, and I've got dishes waiting at home."

Putting off telling her the fear her news had prompted,

Ike said, "Come over here first. See if I can't show ya a little 'bout runnin' this outfit." Seeing her hands go still, he added, "Frankie's catching on to it easy enough. Can't see why yer draggin' yer feet so."

Stung, she said, "I'm not dragging my feet. I just don't want to risk making a costly mistake. As much money as you've invested in that evaporator, it'd be silly of me not to be cautious."

"That's what's holdin' ya back? Yer scared of it?"

"What did you think? That I was too trifling to learn?"

Seeing the hurt behind her failed smile, he said carefully, "Not triflin'. Though ya are a little dreamy sometimes."

"And you're a little pushy, since we're naming names," she countered.

He shifted his weight, seeing he'd been too hasty in his conclusions. "I reckon I misread ya."

"I don't know why. It was you who warned me how easy it is to burn the pans."

"Lib," he tried to cut in.

"If I was to be the cause of that, I'd just have to pack up my bags and move on."

He held back a grin. "Not till ya'd scoured the pans, ya wouldn't."

"About what I'd expect." Libby jerked a thumb toward the evaporator. "I'm going home and leave you with your friend, here."

"Lib, don't go. Sit and keep me company a while."

"I don't know that I want to. I'm feeling misunderstood."

"I'm feeling sorry," he said, with enough humility that Libby softened.

She stayed and filled tins with sirup and wiped up spills and fed the fires for him. Unfortunately, she forgot all about the bathwater on the stove back at the cabin while she was helping. Later, when they returned home and opened the door, steam came billowing out.

"We're lucky you didn't burn the place down," said Ike, calming down once he realized it wasn't a fire, only water left on the stove. "You gotta start payin' more attention, Lib."

Now wasn't that just like him? Cajoling her into staying and helping him, and now he was out of sorts because she'd forgotten her bathwater! But knowing he was tired, Libby took her bath, and kept her self-defense to herself.

7

The earth shook with the violence of shells that burst in eerie silence. Fighting the explosion of pain, Ike drifted out of his body, saw himself stagger and go down in the oozing mortar of mud and blood. A shell burst against his right ear, strewing tissue and cartilage and twisted fragments of steel. He watched his ear open like a gruesome weed pod and disintegrate, staining his blue polka-dot bandanna, turning his shirt red.

Ike jolted awake in the cold dark cabin. The phantom pain in his ear and the pulsing rush in his head receded at the comforting brush of Libby turning over next to him.

It had been almost eight years since he had charged up San Juan Heights with the Spanish shell fire raining down from the stone-walled citadel above. To dream of it was to slog through the jungle all over again. One of Teddy Roosevelt's Rough Riders. Young and cocky and glory-seeking, he had sacrificed his right ear and nearly died of malaria. The gory dreams, evoked by something as innocent as last evening's breaded tomatoes, were a recurring memento of his experience in Cuba.

No, it had been sparked by more than a dish of tomatoes. Libby's news about Earl Morefield wanting to farm had set off an alarm that made him susceptible to the dreams. Miss Maudie's land was farmed mostly by nephews and great-nephews. She had entrusted forty acres to Ike because the piece was isolated enough from the rest of the Morefield land that no one else in the family was interested. Until now.

The chilly stomach spasms faded, their retreat hastened by Libby's warmth. The room was dark, her breathing deep and even. She still had no inkling of trouble ahead. He'd put off telling her his fears when they were both so tired they were already tangling over little irritations.

Careful of her hair where it spilled over the pillow, he lay close to her, reasoning that Miss Maudie should have given him written notice by now if she planned to terminate their arrangement. She should know that her failure to do so gave him legal grounds to stay another season. But there were rumors of mental slips and failing health; she was vulnerable to pressure within the family in a way she hadn't been when she could still catch a horse, hitch it to her buggy, and ride over the countryside visiting her farms without any outside help.

It's been in the back of my mind for weeks I should go talk to her again, Lord. Was that You nudgin' me, tryin' to safeguard us? And me, not payin' enough attention to that quiet voice in my head?

Legally, he wouldn't have to go, not this season. But he would, if asked. Pride wouldn't let him stay when he wasn't wanted.

Ike murmured Libby's name. Lying on her side with her back to him, she stirred, but didn't answer. Ike checked the numbers in his head twice before curving his arm around her. But Libby edged away. It reminded him of her silence as she bathed last night. No singing, in and out of that tub and into bed, all business. He'd hurt her feelings. But it'd scared him, opening the door and having all that steam rush out at them. He'd thought the place was on fire.

Sap-house fires needing stoking, horses waiting to be fed, sediment to be drawn out of the flues, ashes to be emptied. But Ike lay there a moment longer, wanting to get off on a better foot with her than he had ended up on yesterday and knowing at the same time that he couldn't put off any longer telling her of the danger facing them.

He leaned over her ear and whispered, "You jest lie there and sleep, and I'll stoke up the stove this mornin'."

Libby pulled the covers up over her ears and didn't answer. Ike slipped out of bed and buttoned his pants on over his long union suit, stuffing his sockless feet into boots. It was cold in the cabin and even colder on the summer porch. He lit the lamp and stepped out the front door. The stars had given way to the deep gray of approaching dawn. The cold air stung his lungs as he fetched an armload of firewood off the open porch.

Libby sat up and combed her fingers through her hair as Ike shook the grate free of ashes. Smoke was escaping into the room instead of up the chimney. She swung her feet over the side of the bed. "Let it go. I'm getting up."

Ike whistled softly as he fanned the coals and added corncobs in place of kindling.

"Ike, it isn't drawing. You're smoking up the place."

"Come over here and do it yourself then, sleepy-head."

"Isn't that what I just said?"

"Did ya? Guess I had my bad ear to ya."

Libby crossed the room and caught her hair back out of her face as she tried to nudge him to one side. "Move."

There was a crease in her face from sleeping on her hand and a spark in her eye that looked like it could turn into a twinkle easily enough. He said to the air, "Reckon if I can cut the wood, I can burn it."

"Just keep talking, and I wouldn't be surprised to hear you in an argument with yourself."

Hunched down, forearms resting on his knees, he looked up and caught her eye. "Been that hard to get along with, have I?"

"It was uphill work last night, to borrow a phrase from your book."

"You can borrow anything ya want, jest so long as ya don't let a little steam stand between us."

"I thought about it," she said, her mouth softening, "but it seems to have evaporated."

"That's my girl." He patted her foot, planted there on the floor beside him, then rose beside her. "Suppose yer wantin' to take over, now that I got the fire goin' good?"

"Good and smoky, don't you mean?"

"Mmm-mmm," he said, drawing air into his lungs with feigned satisfaction. "Don't ya love the smell of maple logs burning?"

"Smells like smoldering corncobs to me."

"Don't be that way, Lib." He leaned down, hooked his hands under her arms and hauled her to her feet. "Come on now," he cajoled, seeing her trying to smother her laughter. "Kiss me, and let's make up."

She gave him a peck on the cheek and was turning away when he snaked an arm around her waist and pulled her against him. "That's a start. Might hold a fella to oh, say, breakfast."

Her eyes met his, reassessing the situation. After a moment, she rocked forward on her toes, and took his waiting kiss. Ike built on the spark he had kindled. He trailed kisses from her mouth to her throat, heard her breath quicken, and set about achieving all he'd hoped for in starting the day out right.

By the time he'd shaved and Libby had fixed breakfast, the sun was shining through Jack Frost's window etchings. He was running really late and refiguring the numbers in his head, reassuring himself they were safe.

They'd been swallowing meals in such a hurry, there hadn't been much grace to saying grace. Libby looked up from the table as he caught her hand. She bowed her head, her fingers curling around his. But he could feel her poised to jump up for whatever it was she'd forgotten to bring to the table—she always forgot something.

Or was she rushing on his account? Ike slowed his own impulse to hurry and brought to mind what had been in his heart while lying next to her. How she was waiting to give him the gift of family, waiting willingly without a clue to the conflicting emotions that wait produced in him. He thought, too, of her cheery industry. Tramping through the woods, helping him tap trees, cleaning up after him in the sap house, hauling sap, making time for the McClure children, carrying meals to him, and keeping the house up, too.

He squeezed her hand and began a prayer, though he could find words for only part of what was in his heart. But God knew the thoughts behind them: "Lord, thanks for Lib." *She's quick to lend me a hand where it's needed and managing all the while to keep us clean and clothed and well fed.* "For her hard work." *She's made straight and true. Sweet and light, quick to laugh and quick to love.* "For her willingness to help every way she can. Thanks for bringin' us together and teachin' us to get along."

Libby got up, opened the window, and took his cream from the cold-air window box. She reached around from behind him to set the cream on the table, then lingered behind his chair where her damp eyes wouldn't betray her. "I'm sorry, too," she whispered, then draped an arm over his shoulder and spoke of the twin oaks beyond the window. "I heard the wind blowing through them last night and thought that we've been like that ourselves here lately. Creaking and wearing at each other every time the air stirs."

He reached up and patted her cheek where it rested

against his ear. "It isn't deliberate. We're working hard
and gettin' cranky."

"Or maybe it's low pressure," she jested, and kissed
him.

It was the opening Ike had been waiting for. "Could
be you just hit the nail on the head. About low pressure,
I mean. I'm afraid there's some rough weather comin'.
Somethin' we haven't figured on."

Turning, trying to see her face as she stood behind
him, he said, "You know, don't ya, that my agreement
to farm this year for Miss Morefield is verbal? Just her
word and mine and a handshake?"

"I guess so." Warily, she added, "Why? What's the
matter?"

"Miss Maudie's land is all worked by family, except
for me and Mr. Berry. It isn't likely Dorene'll stand by
and watch Earl nudge her folks off their piece. That only
leaves us."

Libby drew her arms away and sat down. "You think
Miss Maudie is about to go back on her word to you?"

"Used to be I wouldn't have thought it of her," he
said, omitting mention of legal rights that were, to him,
a moot point. "But she's slippin' some, and not so in-
dependent as she once was."

"But Dorene and I are friends. Earl and I have
worked together at the newspaper. Surely they wouldn't
do that to us!"

As he did almost daily, Ike thought how young she
was. And trusting. He said, "I hope you're right. God
knows we need this farm. We can't get by on sirup
alone."

Libby searched his face as he resumed eating. Appetite gone, she asked, "What should we do?"

"Nothin' *to* do except wait and see."

Her mind leapt ahead, assuming the worst and working through it as she might a piece of writing that was
flawed. At length, she asked, "What about that piece of
ground just south of the timber?"

"Where you and your friends picked corn for the library?" Ike felt that familiar tightening in his chest. "Lib, ya know better'n that."

She flushed, but kept her gaze steady. "You said yourself that Mr. Ketchum probably wouldn't be up to farming it next year."

"I wouldn't farm for Gentry."

"Not even if he asked you to?"

"He ain't goin' to, Lib."

Libby knew that decision would severely limit Ike if he wanted to live near his sirup camp, for most of the surrounding farm ground belonged to Chester Gentry. His vast holdings spilled into three townships. Gingerly feeling her way, she said, "I don't understand about him. You're related. That should mean something."

"Never did before, and it's too late, now."

Ike could see she would like to question him further, but was hesitant to do so. He didn't encourage her. Staying friends with Chester's family—Ida, Angus, Maddie, and Catherine—was her choice. But he didn't want her getting any ideas about trying to build bridges between him and Gentry. Having learned she often heard only what she wanted to hear, he was careful so there'd be no misunderstanding. "I don't like Chester, but I don't hate him either, and that seems like a good way to leave it."

"Like him well enough to get to heaven, do you?"

Her soft-edged point hit its mark. He held back a sheepish grin and retorted, "Quit yer sermonizing, and pass yer cereal over here if ya've lost yer appetite."

"There's more on the stove," she said, and picked up her spoon.

Ike poured himself another cup of coffee while he was up and found himself thinking of his own parents. He remembered his sister Cicely getting sassy once and asking his mother why she and his father had never married. His mother didn't defend herself, simply used her past as an object lesson, saying there were some mistakes you couldn't untangle and to keep that in mind if ever they were tempted to get careless with love.

He loved Libby with great care. If they *did* get the rug jerked from beneath them, he would do what he had to do to get by. He sipped his coffee and glanced out the window where the twin oaks dominated the west yard. It looked as if they'd stood there for a hundred years and could stand for another hundred. The root system that kept them safe and strong wasn't visible. But it was there. *Same with God.*

As if sensing the path his thoughts had taken, Libby reached across the table and covered his hand. "It's all right, Ike. We're under God's shadow."

Under God's shadow. It was a comforting thought. The peace that had evaded Ike last night was coming over him now. It wasn't a peace of circumstances, for their position was shaky. What had changed was that his soul was braced by his soul mate and by the One who had entrusted her to him. Fear was the adversary, and it was gone, cast out by love. *Thanks, Lord, for reminding me.*

Ike was starting off for the barn when Libby stepped out on the porch after him with just a shawl thrown over her blue dress. It kindled the blue of her eyes as she looked from him to the lilac bush and back again. Her mouth curved into a smile.

"Here's something to take to the sap house with you," she said, and pressed a tin of cookies into his hand.

"Thanks, Lib."

She leaned closer and kissed his jaw. "When I get my chores done I'll be over and take a lesson on the evaporator."

"There's no hurry. I've got chores to do, then I'm going to the woods with Decatur for a while."

Libby donned an old coat belonging to Ike before she carried out the ashes. She filled the white enamel drinking bucket at the well out back. The firewood on the front porch had dwindled to only a few pieces. She was replenishing it from the wood stacked inside the back shed when the door blew closed. Arms full of wood, she gave it a nudge and met resistance, as if something was lodged against it. She was about to give it a kick when she heard a muffled sneeze.

"Opal? Is that you?"

Suddenly the resistance was gone and the door opened. Libby let herself out to find instead a dark-haired teary-eyed little girl with a quivering mouth and frightened look on her small, heart-shaped face. She had never seen the child before.

"Forevermore!" exclaimed Libby. "Where did you come from?"

The little girl's mouth puckered. She tucked her chin and dug her toe into a clump of dirty snow without answering. Libby looked toward the road. There was no one else in sight. Mystified, Libby knelt beside her and asked, "Are you lost?"

The little girl's coat gapped open as she lifted one mittened hand to wipe away a silent tear. Libby leaned down and buttoned her coat for her and tried again.

"I'm Libby Galloway. What's your name?"

"Joy," she said in a voice as timid as her gray gaze.

"That's a pretty name." Libby retrieved a handkerchief from her coat pocket. She was drying the little girl's tears when she remembered that Naomi had said their new neighbors had a child by that name. "Is your last name Stapleton?"

The girl nodded, and asked shyly, "Do you know my mama?"

"No, we haven't met. But I think I know where you live." Beckoning in the direction of the railroad tracks, she said, "If we go over the tracks and up the road through the trees about a quarter of a mile, we'll come to a big pasture where some cattle are grazing and right in the middle of that pasture is your house. Am I right?"

"The cows are gone," said the little girl. She tucked her chin, and added, "I wanted to pet the doggie."

"You have a dog?" asked Libby.

"No."

Libby let it go and asked, "Do you want to come inside and warm up a minute? Or shall I walk you home?"

"Home," said Joy, and entrusted her hand to Libby's.

They hadn't quite reached the bridge when a young woman came hurrying down the road from the north. Libby saw her stop and look toward the sirup camp.

"Mama! Here I am!" Joy let go of Libby's hand and dashed toward the bridge.

The woman's relief was apparent as she rushed to meet Joy. She scooped the child into her arms, kissing and scolding her. Libby quickened her step. But before she reached them, the mother waved and called a thank-you and, with the child's hand in hers, turned back the way she'd come.

"One of them Stapletons, I'll wager."

Libby swung around to see Hascal Caton coming up the bank sloping down to the creek.

"Mr. Caton! What're you doing down there?"

"Been checkin' my trap lines." He indicated the swiftly retreating neighbor as he came lumbering toward her. "Seems like she's in an all-fired hurry."

"Under the circumstances, I think she was more interested in getting her little girl home where it's warm than in meeting the neighbors," said Libby.

"What was the young'un doin' with you, anyways?"

"She was lost."

Hascal's eyes narrowed. "Seen a couple of Gentry's hired men and that cow dog of his headin' up through the trees a while ago. Must be bent on movin' some cattle."

"Cow dog? Joy said something about wanting to pet a dog. Maybe that's what she meant."

Hascal looped his thumbs behind his coat lapels. "I hear tell the older gal is hitched to an attorney, but I ain't never seen no man comin' nor goin'." He reached into his pocket for a plug of tobacco and changed the subject.

"Lester Morefield's uppity wife was in the store, buyin' some of Ike's sirup yesterday. Miss Maudie was with her. But she said she'd as soon git her sirup fresh off the pans." Gaze sharpening, he added, "Said somethin' about wantin' to talk to Ike anyways."

Libby's heart bolted. "What about?"

"Don't rightly know. Truth is, folks in town is sayin' the old gal's gettin' addlepated. Accusin' the hired girls of stealin' food from the cupboards and takin' her hats and sech as that." He scratched his grizzled jaw. "Shucks, them little Berry gals may not be much ta look at, but they got their pa's decency about 'em and anyway, who'd want them old raggedy hats of Miss Maudie's? Ain't no wonder she never landed her a husband. Not a bit of style to 'er."

"Could it be that she never wanted one?" countered Libby.

Hascal tugged at his whiskers and shot her a cockeyed grin. "There now, ya almost had me goin'. Jokin', wasn't ya? Well, I'll allow some men like that in women."

Libby left the old character cackling to himself and walked home. Her conversations with him usually prompted prayers of gratitude for her own dear father, but this time, her petitions were pleas to God to keep Miss Maudie from turning their lives upside down.

Libby resumed carrying firewood to the front porch, and jumped at the sound of an icicle falling and breaking over the slanting board she had nailed from the porch railing to protect her lilac bush.

Shield of faith. It was a quiet thought. They could let whispers and rumors strike fear in their hearts. Let it freeze out their friendships with mistrust and suspicion, like icicles poised to shatter and break.

Or they could trust God to look out for them. The choice seemed simple enough. Faith wasn't faith if the answer was staring you in the face.

8

Ike helped Decatur and Frankie gather sap most of the morning, then fired up the evaporator. He had a batch nearing the temperature of sirup when Hascal Caton wandered in.

"Come lookin' for ya earlier, but ya wasn't here."

"Probably in the woods."

"Speakin' of woods, I was sayin' to yer wife, it's queersome about them Stapleton gals livin' up thar through the trees without their menfolk."

His mind on his work, Ike didn't encourage Hascal in his speculation, rather, indicated a nearby bucket. "Would ya set that up here on the crate, Hack?"

Hascal passed him the bucket. "Gentry's men was moving cattle off that piece this mornin'. What do ya make of that?"

"Can ya stand back? Got sirup to draw off here in a minute, and yer blockin' my spigot."

"Ain't ya the least bit curious why he'd up and move them cattle?"

"If I was to guess, I'd say he's wantin' them closer to home while they're calvin'."

"Confound it, Galloway! Yer missin' the point," grumbled Hascal as he shuffled out of the way.

Privately, Ike agreed it was odd. But he busied himself checking the temperature of the sirup in the finishing pan.

Disappointed in his lack of response, Hascal started hauling in wood from the lean-to Ike had built onto the sap house to keep his mountain of firewood dry.

"Don't do any good to dry the wood over the summer if yer goin' to haul it in here and let it soak up steam b'fore tossin' it in the fire," Ike pointed out.

"Who says I'm lettin' it git damp?"

The arch upon which the evaporator sat housed the firebox and the ash pit. It carried the heat and the flames the entire length of the heating surface of the evaporator. Hearing the doors on the firebox creak open and the fire roar, Ike complained, "Yer interferin' with my system, Hack. I draw off a batch of sirup, and *then* I feed the fire."

"Didn't know you was so hard ta suit," groused Hascal.

Patience strained, Ike said, "Why don't ya run over to the house and see if Libby'll make us some coffee b'fore she comes over?"

"I ain't much on coffee this close to lunchtime."

"I meant coffee *with* lunch. She'd pack enough for you, too, if she knew you were here."

"Cain't say I'm hungry. I had a big breakfast. Ya got tins to fill?"

Ike nodded. "But it takes a good steady hand to fill 'em without runnin' 'em over."

Hascal shuffled to the back corner to the manufactured tank containing the sirup to be put into tin containers. Ike drew a bucket of sirup off the finishing pan and joined him there. He had received the barrel-like tank from New England just a few months ago. The spigot at the bottom worked efficiently, and proved a real time-saving device over the funnel approach he'd used last year to get the hot sirup into the tin containers.

Ike heard fresh sap running into the pans. He needed

to check his fire, but he hated to walk off and leave the fruit of his labors in Hack's hit-or-miss hands.

"How'm I doin'?" asked Hascal, as he ran sirup over the sides of the quart tin he was filling.

"A might messy, since ya asked."

"That so?" Hascal wiped a sticky hand down his trouser legs and came to his feet with an injured sniff. "Reckon ya can jest do it yerself, then."

"Didn't mean to make ya sore. Where ya goin'?" Ike called after him.

"Up through the tree ta see if them Stapleton wimmin is lonesome. Why, was ya wantin' to come?"

Ike shook his head. "Old feller like you, talkin' that-away. What makes ya so ornery, anyway?"

"What makes *you* jump down a feller's throat when he's jest bein' neighborly?" countered Hascal. "I declare! How's that little redhead put up with you, anyways? I'd say she was love-struck, if ya wasn't sech a homely cuss."

Ike grinned as he moved toward the firebox. "Reckon I'll overlook that, since ya been so helpful and all."

"Good riddance ta you, too." Hascal punched the dents out of his hat and humped toward the door, adding, "Wouldn't wanna keep the wimmin waitin'."

Ike shook his head. The old coot had more fiction in him than a picture book. He wasn't goin' anywhere but home for lunch and maybe a nap.

It had grown warm in the sap house. The draft of cool air the old man let in felt good. After feeding his fire, Ike left the door leading into the lean-to open a crack. He crossed to the west-facing window and was opening it when he saw Libby coming across the bridge with a basket over her arm.

Ike watched from the window as she stopped and looked back over her shoulder. All at once, she was moving again. Coming fast, alarm in her posture. She had reached the edge of the sirup camp when Ike saw Miss Maudie's black buggy come over the bridge. Raymond Morefield, Earl's daddy, was driving Miss Maudie.

Ike's gut clenched. He stepped back from the window and uttered a swift petition. It seemed to catch in the steam and drift back down over him as if covering him in the reminder of similar prayers he'd been making ever since last night. He drew a deep breath and tried to calm the nerves rippling over his stomach.

"Ike?" Libby called from the front door.

"Over here."

She materialized out of the maple mists. Her knuckles gleamed white on the handle of her wicker basket as she searched his face with swift, anxious eyes. "Miss Maudie's here."

"I know. Can you watch the pans while I go out and talk to her?"

Libby nodded. Clinging to the thin hope that this had nothing to do with Earl and Dorene, she said, "Maybe she's come for sirup."

Knowing better, Ike reached for his coat where it hung from a bent nail on the sap-house wall. He took a moment to run some fresh sap into the pans to make certain nothing scorched.

"Tell me what to do."

"Skim the pans if they should start ta' boil. Otherwise, things should be all right."

Libby nodded and looked for a spot to put her basket down.

By the time Ike made it out the door, Miss Maudie was picking her way over the planks he'd thrown down when the ground thawed and the path had turned to mud. Advanced in years, she made him think of a knotty fence post with her wiry gray hair and drab coat and network of wrinkles. Her cuffs were frayed, and her hat was limp and lopsided from frequent wear. She had become frail-looking since Ike had seen her last. But her manner was as direct as ever.

"Could we sit down?" she asked in her thin, reedy voice.

"Sure. It's warm inside," Ike invited.

"This will be fine. All that steam can't be good for the lungs." Miss Maudie lowered herself to the weathered bench just below the sap-house window. "I'd like to buy a gallon of sirup while I'm here. Why don't you get it for me before we talk?"

Ike opened the door and asked Libby to bring him a gallon.

Miss Maudie paid him while Libby went to get it. She passed the time of day for a moment or two before launching into a speech that sounded rehearsed: "I've always felt that there is no better life preparation for a child than to be raised on the farm. As you know, I've tried to keep family on my land so that my nephews and their children can benefit from the same rural training I enjoyed. You are the exception to that, Mr. Galloway. You and Mr. Berry, and Mr. Berry has many mouths to feed."

Miss Maudie turned her head as Libby came with the sirup. She greeted Libby, thanked her, then waited until she had gone back inside to square her stooped shoulders and return to the matter at hand. "To state the case plainly, Mr. Galloway, Earl wants land to farm. His wife is in the family way."

Ike wanted to remind Miss Morefield that he had a family, too, and that she was most likely standing on the other side of that door, holding her breath. He tried to find the words, but it was too much like hanging his head before Chester Gentry as a boy, his chest hurting from holding in the shame of seeing his mother plead for her children's next meal. Feeling hollow inside, he said, "You do what you think is right, Miss Maudie."

"No, Mr. Galloway, I am not doing what I think is right, I'm doing what's easy. I'm old and tired and not very proud of myself. But my nephews and their wives are waiting on me hand and foot these days, and it can't be all take and no give on my part. I guess when you sum it up, land has more value than an old woman's word," she said with a touch of asperity. In the same breath, she concluded, "But a body will do for her family what she wouldn't do for herself sometimes, if you know what I mean."

Ike looked toward the road where Raymond Morefield was avoiding his eye. He'd worked as an oiler on Raymond's threshing runs a couple of summers ago and until now, had found him to be a fair-minded man. "I reckon I do."

"So," said Miss Maudie briskly. "Where do we go from here? Friends? Or are you going to pretend not to see me when we pass on the street?"

Ike thought again of Gentry. But it wasn't the same. Miss Maudie troubled herself to make an explanation and to admit she didn't feel right about it. She'd been as straightforward as she knew how to be. "Gets tiresome, wearin' blinders."

"Very well, Mr. Galloway." She stood and offered her hand.

Ike shook it, then took her arm, picked up her gallon of sirup, and walked her to the road. As he put the sirup in her buggy, he heeded a heart nudge, and said, "I want to thank you, Miss Maudie."

"Thank me?" she paused in accepting his helping hand into the buggy.

"You gave me a start on yer land. You've been good to work for. I've learned a lot, and I'm grateful."

Her jaw slackened. Averting her gaze, she murmured, "You're quite welcome, young man."

He nodded to Raymond. "Take good care of her, Mr. Morefield."

Mutely, Raymond Morefield returned his nod, but offered no comment.

Miss Maudie smoothed her skirts and flicked her hand to say she was ready. "I only wish . . ." she began, as if snatching at a stray thought.

Ike had his bad ear to her and didn't hear her wish. But he saw her eyes turn glassy. Her tears surprised him, for she had always been such a tough old gal. He took no pleasure in her distress. Instead, he was freed by it. Freed from the temptation to harbor hard feelings.

Libby was watching from the sap-house window. She saw Miss Maudie's chin quiver and her hand come up to wipe her eyes as the buggy pulled away. It might have softened her, had the tears been for Ike. They weren't. They were for Miss Maudie herself. *Humiliated at reneging on her promise.*

Libby moved away from the window as Ike came back up the plank walk to the sap house. Her hands were steady, but she was shaking on the inside.

"How are ya doin'?" Ike asked, as he came in. His gaze skipped from Libby to the evaporator and back again.

Libby coughed to keep from choking on her resistance to what had just happened. "She should have kept her word to you, Ike."

"It's her land. She can do what she wants with it," he said with little emotion.

"Next year, maybe." Libby followed him through the steam. "But you had an agreement."

"Earl's her nephew."

Miss Maudie's rationalizing that Earl's need was greater than Ike's because Dorene was in the family way only sharpened the sting. *We've lost twice. Lost the farm. Lost the security even to look forward to starting a family.* Mechanically, she said, "Your lunch is there on the crate."

"Thanks, Lib. You can go on back to the house, if ya got work to do."

"I thought you were going to show me how to make sirup."

"This isn't a good time. Sap's running like crazy, and I'm runnin' behind."

The laundry was piling up at home. But Libby wanted to help him in some more immediate way than scrubbing the mud from his jeans. Taking two five-gallon gathering buckets, she started collecting sap from the trees nearest the sap house.

It was heavy work. Her feet were soon cold, her skirts damp and dirty from slogging through the mud, then emptying her gathering buckets into the holding tank that Opal had said looked like a snail clinging to the north side of the sap house.

Her fingers were numb and her limbs aching from the heavy sap buckets when Billy Young called to her from the road. He waved and turned his horse and mail cart into the clearing in front of the sap house.

"What're you trying to do, Libby? Beat Decatur out of a job?"

"I don't think there's any danger of that." Libby's hair, hastily pinned earlier that morning, was coming loose beneath her scarf. She pushed a windswept strand out of her eyes and retied her scarf. "I wasn't sure you'd be along today, the condition the roads are in."

"Pretty soupy, what with the weather warming. But it beats hammering my way into iced-over mailboxes." Billy tied his horse and vaulted to the ground. He took the buckets and swung along toward the sap house. "Say, that reminds me! Would you write a piece for the paper telling folks to quit licking their copper cents and sticking them to the bottom of the box? I'm tired of jerking off my gloves every whip-stitch to pry those confounded frozen pennies loose."

"They think they're doing you a favor, keeping them from rolling to the back of the box."

Billy snorted. "Let them tuck them into an envelope. Or better yet, mail their letters already stamped."

"Consider it done," said Libby.

"Be sure to tell them that stamping their letters isn't my job. Name names. Shame them, Lib." Taking fiendish delight in his rantings, he grinned broadly and added,

''Nice big headlines, now. Something like 'Weasels, Skunks, Penny-Lickers and Other Varmints, Beware!' Or maybe I'll write it myself. I can editorialize nicely when I put my mind to it. I used to think I might like running a newspaper.'' At her failure to respond, Billy sent her a sidelong glance. ''Somehow, I thought that would get a reaction.''

Libby blurted, ''Miss Maudie stopped by. It looks as if Earl will be farming for her this year instead of Ike.''

''So she really did it, then.''

Libby tipped her head, and said woodenly, ''You knew it was coming?''

''There were rumors circulating. I was hoping that's all they were. I'm really sorry, Libby.''

''Me too.''

Billy fell silent. He swung along at her side, carrying the buckets up the dirt ramp adjacent to the north wall of the sap house. Libby stepped back to keep from being splashed by sap as he dumped the buckets into the storage tank.

''How's Ike taking it?''

''From what he said this morning, I think he was braced for it,'' said Libby. She picked up a stick to scrape mud from her shoes.

''I'll stick around a while, see if I can't help him out.''

''Thanks, Billy.'' Appreciating his kindness, she added, ''You're a good fellow.''

''That's what I keep telling Chloe,'' said Billy with a shadow of his former humor. His mouth tipped as he lifted his hand and ambled toward the sap-house door.

Not wanting Billy's kindheartedness in staying to cause him trouble in regard to his job, Libby took his mailbag containing a handful of outgoing letters, and dropped it by the depot with instructions for it to be left in Edgewood. She attached a note of explanation to her father, Edgewood's postmaster, then walked on home.

9

🌺 Libby changed out of her muddy clothes, then strung a clothesline across the inside of the cabin and started the laundry. It occupied her hands and left her mind free to go over the events of the morning.

Because Dorene was in the family way, Miss Maudie gave her and Earl more consideration. *You and me. One, two. Ain't that a family?* Ike's words from more than a year ago came ringing back to her. Why hadn't he pointed it out to Miss Maudie?

It took Libby until evening to finish the wash. The scent of Fels Naphtha soap and steamy cotton wafted in the air as she fixed supper. She carried it to Ike and Billy, then returned to the cabin for a much-needed bath. Bedtime came and Ike still hadn't come home.

Libby's back ached from the day's work. But her thoughts were unsettled, and she couldn't go to bed until she had had a chance to talk with Ike alone. She heated milk for cocoa, dressed while the chocolate was melting, wrapped some cookies to take along, and, with lantern in hand, followed the muddy road to the sap house.

A lamp burned inside the building, turning the windows to soft yellow patches. Libby couldn't smell the hint of maple that hung in the air when Ike was cooking, or see steam rising from the cupola to meet the starry sky. But she heard Ike's low murmur as she opened the door.

The doors on the firebox were standing open. He sat in a chair, leaning toward the fire, his forearms on his knees, his hands clasped. The glow of the red-hot coals kindled a light in his eyes as he lifted his head and looked at her.

Her heart turned at the lines of fatigue on his face. "Where's Billy?"

"He left a bit ago."

"I thought I heard you talking."

"You did."

His clasped hands, his bowed head, his absorbed manner—she should have realized. Suddenly, her cookies-and-cocoa consolation seemed a shallow impulse. When she emptied her heart to God, the last thing she wanted was an audience. "I'm sorry. I'll go," she said, and backed toward the door.

Ike stretched a hand toward her. "Sit here with me a minute, then we'll go together."

"You're done for tonight?" At his nod, Libby set her basket down and hesitated a moment before asking, "Are you all right, Ike?"

"It's a setback, and I won't say I'm not disappointed. But it isn't the end of the world." His gray gaze shifted to the basket. "What'd ya bring me?"

"Cocoa and cookies."

"Sounds good."

"Shall we take it with us?"

"Let's sit here and drink it."

"Too tired to walk home?" she asked.

He denied it, but Libby suspected she'd struck the truth. She used the crate that had served as a table for a number of recent meals and poured the cocoa while he helped himself to a cookie.

"This is nice," Ike said after a minute. At her failure

to respond, he asked, "You sittin' there stewin', are ya Lib?"

Libby lifted her eyes to his. She watched the firelight play on his face and struggled between the right answer and the true one. Straining for words to express what she felt without adding to his burden, she asked, "Was there nothing you could have said to soften her?"

"I don't want to stay where I'm not wanted, Lib."

"I know. But maybe . . ."

"Maybe *what*?"

"If you'd appealed to her fairness . . ."

"And made her more ashamed?"

"She had a right to be ashamed. And Earl for putting her up to it," she added with feeling. "I can't help but think Dorene could have stopped him. Her father's in the same situation. The shoe could easily be on the other foot."

"Ya got to be careful about blamin'. Ya get caught up in it, ya may miss the blessing."

Blessing? Where was the blessing in being betrayed by friends? Voice brittle, she said, "It's kind of hard to see it that way."

"God knows what we need to get by."

Yes, He did. But the hurt was there all the same. Ashamed, Libby subsided into silence. She finished her cocoa and picked up the long-handled poker and knelt on the dirt floor to prod the glowing logs inside the firebox. The shower of flying sparks suited her mood. She gave the coals another blow with the poker. A flying cinder flew back and singed the bodice of her dress. Hastily she brushed it away, but the damage was done. She could smell the singed cotton.

"Now see what I've done. My favorite dress, too," she muttered, and turned to see Ike put his cup back in the basket with hers.

"Mine too. Matches yer eyes," he said, and moved the crate to one side.

He rested his forearms on his knees just behind her.

Fighting tears, she turned toward the fire again. The rise and fall of his breathing stirred her hair.

Gently, he asked, "Did I fail ya, Lib?"

Remorse and a fresh perspective came with her tears. All day, she had been measuring the blow in terms of how it affected their future. But his past was here, too. He had farmed this land since his return from the war. It was his sweat and toil that had gone into it, his footprints left upon the soil. His long-held dream to own it. It had come to her only lately in the rites of shared lives. Singed dress forgotten, she said, "Maybe you've got it backwards. Maybe I failed *you*."

"How could you?" he asked.

"By wanting you to reason with her."

"Wantin' me to tell her I had a family, too?"

She turned and looked into his eyes. "How did you know?"

"I could feel you on the other side of the door thinkin' it."

Libby swallowed hard. She turned away, and made another foray with the poker, carefully now. "Your way was better."

Ike took his time answering, for it wasn't *his* way so much as God's prompting. God would do that if a body'd listen. His mother had taught him as much, not by word, but by example, for she had never once spoken against Chester Gentry for turning them away. Nor had she answered those who ostracized her for accepting help from Willie Blue, a man who, in the opinion of most in those days, was a nice enough fellow, but a drunkard all the same.

Ike gazed into the coals Libby was stirring, his thoughts reeling back over the years. "Ever tell ya about the first time I set foot in these trees?" he asked. "We were headed for the poor farm, Mom and my sister Cicely and me. Chester said they'd take us in there. But we got lost. The shadows were starting to fall, and my mother was out of ideas. She asked God which way was the way to go. Said she wasn't taking another step until she got an answer. She'd hardly got up off her knees when along come this red-haired fella.''

"Uncle Willie," said Libby. It was his funeral that had first brought her to Edgewood several years ago. She stilled her hands, straining to catch every word, for it was rare for Ike to speak of those days.

"Willie was sorry-looking and none too sober. I was ready to bolt and run. If I had, I'd of missed out on the best blessing of my life." His chin chafed her cheek as he reached beyond her to close the firebox door. He took the poker from her, cast it aside. "Until you come along, that is."

Libby spoke his name. She turned on her knees and met his waiting embrace.

The fire made a ticking sound behind her as he stroked her damp cheek, catching a tear on his thumb. He brushed a strand of hair back from her face. "It's all right, Lib. God's not going to hang us out to dry."

"I know. I *do* know," she said, affirming it in her own mind.

" 'Course you do. It was you who reminded me jest yesterday of bein' in His shadow. All we got to do is trust Him to work things out. That's what I'm goin' to do, too. I'm not takin' another step till God shows me what He's got in mind."

She pressed closer and cried, partly for their losses, partly that he would look for blessings instead of placing blame. Brokenly, she said, "I thought we were making some progress. That we could begin to think about a family."

"Time'll come for that, and when it does, our pleasure in that'll crowd out all this fuss," he said. "As for Miss Maudie, what's done is done. Earl, too."

"They knew that what they were doing wasn't right. That it would hurt you. And it did hurt you, don't say that it didn't."

"I know. But I'm layin' what's left of it down right

here. I ain't pickin' it up again, and I hope you won't either.''

Fresh tears pooled in Libby's eyes, for with his words came the unspoken reminder of the author of forgiveness praying for His persecutors. The loss she and Ike had suffered diminished by comparison. Still it was a loss, not just of land, but of trust that the code of friendship was a universal one.

Much later, as Ike was bathing, Libby stepped out on the porch for firewood and looked into the starry sky, seeking understanding as she offered the confessions of a wounded spirit: *I can't hide it from you, Lord. I'm hurt, I'm angry, I'm discouraged. I can't change what I feel, yet I fear that my feelings put me at odds with You and I don't want that. So here they are, Lord, this tangled heap of raw feelings. Do what You will with them and help me, like Ike, to look for the blessing instead of nursing the hurt.*

She stood a moment longer, thinking of how Ike had supplemented his farming income with part-time jobs over the years. In so doing, he had acquired a good range of skills. He could find a job without much trouble. But could he find one that paid well enough that he wouldn't have to abandon his dream of expanding his sirup camp and, someday, buying a farm of his own?

10

It was the cornhusk mattress whispering beneath Ike's weight as he sat down on the bed that awakened Libby the next morning. The cabin was warm, but Ike's face was burnished from being outdoors. The bracing scent of winter clung to him.

Sleepily, she asked, "You've been to the barn already?"

"Done my chores and some of yers, too." He leaned closer and offered his coffee cup.

Libby sat up and took a cautious sip. Looking toward the heart of her home, she wondered how she'd slept through him shaking the grate and clanging the doors and thunking the wood as he piled it twice as high as it needed to be.

"I see you've got the stovepipe glowing that fiery shade of red," she said, and passed the cup back to him.

He grinned and offered it a second time. "Git another swallow of this, and maybe you'll be tolerable company."

A smile twitched at her mouth as she waved his offer aside. "Is the sap running?"

"Nope. We didn't get a freeze. Cooked up everything last night, so it looks like we've earned ourselves a day off. I was thinkin' we'd head into Edgewood.''

''It's Sunday. The stores are closed.''

''I know. I thought we could go to church at New Hope. Give you a chance to see yer father and Davie.''

Touched by his effort to bring some sunshine after yesterday's storms, Libby said, ''It *would* be good to see everyone.''

''If that's a yes, you better get movin'.'' He smiled as she swung her feet to the floor, then squeezed her knee, saying, ''Roads are sloppy. We'll make better time walking along the railroad tracks than fightin' the mud with the wagon.''

There was a stiff breeze as they began the three-mile walk over a rough railroad bed. But thoughts of family and friends and a good lively step kept Libby warm. The purple tips of the winter-bare tree branches glimmered in the sunlight as she and Ike followed the tree-lined train tracks south. The church bells were ringing in the crisp morning air, lifting Libby's spirits as they made their way to New Hope Church at the north edge of town.

The brick church with its bell tower and high white steeple had been built the previous year. Sugar, the old beagle, was sprawled in front of the door. She wagged a greeting and reluctantly shifted out of their way.

Libby's family was sitting near the back. Years of coal mining had left its punishing mark on Thomas Watson. He was thin and pale, with a sunken chest and shoulders stooped from heavy labor. But as he looked to see who had joined his family in the pew, his expression was pure sunshine. He gave Libby his open hymnal, then reached past her and shook Ike's hand as the service opened with a hymn of praise.

Libby had been active in the fund-raisers that had brought the New Hope building to fruition. But the building hadn't been finished until after she had married and begun attending the Timber Creek Church in the

grove. She had forged friendships with most of the New
Hope congregation, Chloe and Dorene Berry included.
Chloe was sitting with her family on the other side of
the church, Billy Young at her side. But Dorene wasn't
among the worshipers. She'd changed churches after her
marriage to Earl Morefield. *Just as well.*

Ike leaned into Libby with his right shoulder. She
rested her hand, palm down in the pew between them,
her little finger against his right thigh as he thumbed
through his Bible, looking for the Scripture that Pastor
Shaw was reciting. Libby reread the closing portion of
the passage:

*Now unto Him that is able to do exceeding abundantly
above all that we ask or think, according to the power
that worketh in us, Unto Him be glory in the church by
Christ Jesus throughout all ages, world without end.*

They were encouraging words on the heels of yesterday's news. Libby listened closely, heartened by the lim-
itless boundaries of such a promise.

The service closed with "Just As I Am," a favorite
hymn of Libby's. The third line seemed particularly
meaningful. *Just as I am, though tossed about, With
many a conflict, many a doubt, Fightings and fears
within, without, O Lamb of God, I come, I come.*

Libby's family closed around her at the end of the
service.

"Ye'll be comin' for lunch, lass?" Father invited.

"You will, won't you, Lib?" echoed David.

As he tipped up his face Libby saw that the gap of a
missing tooth had filled in since she'd seen him last. She
smoothed his dark hair. "Wouldn't miss ¨it for the
world."

David beamed. "I'll go home and put two more plates
on the table."

"Make it three, Davie, and we'll coax Mr. Elliot into
eating with us, too," Verna Baker Watson called after
him.

"All right, Mother," said David, and sped away.

Mother. Libby was thankful that Father had found such a suitable soul mate, not only for his sake, but for David's. He had lost his mother coming into the world, and Verna, who had been widowed for many years prior to her marriage to Libby's father, was filling that special need in David's life.

"We'll wait for you outside," said Verna, as other friends crowded in around Libby. Ike spotted Billy in the vestibule, and went to join him.

Dr. Harding and his wife, Paulette, and Mrs. Bee all traded warm words of welcome with Libby. As did Dorene's sister, Chloe. Grateful Chloe's loyalty to her sister hadn't come between them, Libby said, "Why don't you ride out with Billy one of these days so we can have a nice visit?"

"What? Go gallivanting across the countryside, unescorted?" Chloe peered over the top of her spectacles, poking fun at herself as the stodgy straitlaced spinster, and doing it with such good humor, Libby found herself laughing even though her sympathies were solidly in Billy Young's corner.

"Billy's a nice fellow, Chloe."

"Yes, he is, and I'm doing what I can to protect his reputation."

Libby shook her head at Chloe's affable grin. Poor Billy had been courting Chloe a long while to no apparent avail. Libby curbed the urge to prod a little further. She waved to Ida Gentry, who was waggling fingers at her from across the church, then murmured to Chloe, "Ida's lost weight since I saw her last. Is she not well?"

Chloe's smile faded abruptly. She shrugged, and said with an injured sniff, "How would I know? I'm just the hired girl. Nobody tells me anything."

"Chloe, you're much more than that to Ida, and you know it. Come on, now. What aren't you telling me?" Libby pressed.

Chloe glanced over her shoulder. She lowered her

voice to confide, "Ida saw a fancy city doctor last time she was in St. Louis, visiting Catherine. But you didn't hear it from me."

"What else didn't I hear?"

"That's all I know. Now if you were to ask me about *Mr.* Gentry, it's those Stapleton women ailing him," she added.

Mystified, Libby asked, "How do you mean?"

"I don't know how or why, but I think those gals are tryin' to pinch him in the wallet."

"Careful," Libby murmured, and Chloe fell silent as Ida Gentry drew near.

Ida looked like a bright little goldfinch in her frothy gown and tiny yellow slippers. But she also looked weary, and her hands were bony as she squeezed Libby's in greeting.

"Hello, Libby. Maddie was down with the twins yesterday. She asked me about you."

"The twins! How old are they, now?"

"They'll be a year in June. Oh my, what little characters!" Ida's violet eyes brightened. "Tell her, Chloe. Tell her how precious they are and what a joy to our lives."

"Sweet as sugar." Chloe slipped an arm around Ida and dropped a kiss on her employer's cheek before striding away.

Ida smiled after Chloe, then related an anecdote concerning her grandchildren. She was just warming up to her subject when Mr. Gentry came along.

"I rode past your place the other day, and saw the steam rising from your sugaring," Mr. Gentry said in a manner so warm, Libby wondered if she had imagined his snub last fall at the corn-picking. "In my boyhood days, neighbors got together and cooked the sap down in big iron kettles right out in the woods."

Mr. Gentry took off his glasses and folded them into his pocket. Smiling at his wife, he said, "Remember, Ida?"

"I hadn't thought about that in years. How we looked forward to sugaring season! Living in the country, we were thrilled to see people we hadn't seen all winter. Oh, my! I'd love to smell that smell again and dribble hot sirup over the snow," exclaimed Ida wistfully.

"You aren't alone," Libby replied. "We get quite a few visitors these days. Some come to get sirup, others simply to reminisce. And then, there's the old-timers, dropping in to tell Ike how it's done," she added, then flushed at the abrupt lull in the conversation at her mention of Ike. Lamely, she added, "You'll have to stop by." *But of course they wouldn't. Not with matters as they were between Ike and Chester.*

"Hello, Libby. What brings you to town?"

Grateful for the interruption, Libby swung around to return Lucius Gruben's greeting. He was the editor of the *Gazette*. While living in Edgewood, Libby had been privileged to know him through her work for the paper. She had also forged a friendship with his wife Florence. A semi-invalid, Florence wasn't with him today.

"Florence has a touch of cabin fever," said Mr. Gruben in reply to Libby's inquiry after her health. He ran a hand through his white hair, and invited, "A visit from you would be good medicine for her."

Libby promised to fit one in before the day was over. Both the Gentrys and Mr. Gruben bid her good day, then went their way, making room for other friends to pause in greeting.

At length, Libby caught up with Ike. They traded a few words with Pastor Shaw, then walked out into the sunshine to join Thomas and Verna. Verna's son, Teddy, was waiting with them. Though in his mid-twenties, Teddy made his home with his mother. A high fever in childhood had left him mentally disabled. He and Ike were friends of long standing.

"We-l-l-l, somebody's waitin' for you," Teddy said to Ike.

Though Teddy knew everyone in Edgewood and most

of the farm families, too, he never called anyone by name. "Where, Teddy?" Ike asked.

Teddy beckoned toward the street where Kersey Brignadello was motioning to Ike from the seat of his tinker's wagon. "Be right back," Ike said, and strode over to shake hands with Kersey.

Libby urged Verna and her father and Teddy to go on home, saying, "We'll be along shortly."

"Kersey wants to add our sirup to his line of products," Ike told her a moment later, as they hurried to catch up with her family.

"That was kind of him," said Libby. Kersey traveled the surrounding countryside, carrying a wide range of general merchandise. He was a popular fellow, appreciated for his wares as well as his news of those beyond the borders of the family farms.

"Saw the Gentrys talkin' to you," said Ike.

There was something in his tone that reminded her of that long-ago quarrel. Supposing the less said, the better, Libby replied, "Ida paused to say hello and took long enough saying it that Chester came after her." She slipped her arm through his and changed the subject, asking, "Do you suppose we could squeeze in a visit to the Grubens this afternoon?"

Baker's, Verna's restaurant and boardinghouse, was located on the square in downtown Edgewood. The back door of the deep, two-story building opened onto the alley and railroad tracks beyond. The front faced the town park with its bandstand and enclosed wrought-iron fence, where so many of the social events took place in fair weather. But today, as they assembled for lunch at a long table in front of the wide glass window looking out on the square, a few birds and a pair of squirrels had the park to themselves.

One of Verna's boardinghouse guests joined them for lunch. Mr. Elliot was a civil engineer hired by the C & A Railroad to take charge of some ambitious improvements under way a few miles south of Edgewood.

"I canna help thinkin' 'tis a monstrous-big undertakin' the C & A has commenced," said Libby's father.

"Indeed it is!" agreed Mr. Elliot. All through dinner, he spoke of "cuts" and "fills," of curves to be straightened and concrete subways to be built, serving drivers as well as farmers with livestock and equipment to move.

"With the weather clearing up, the project will be full speed ahead within the next couple of weeks. One of our biggest headaches will be to keep our equipment in good repair," Mr. Elliot said, then went on to lament some of the tensions that had arisen last fall due to time-consuming breakdowns. "But when the work is done, it will be a first-class railroad, straight as an arrow and double-tracked all the way from Bloomington to Springfield, as fine a railroad as this country can boast."

By the time dinner was over, Mr. Elliot had offered to use his railroad pass to take the men down to the job site for a firsthand look.

"What about me?" David asked.

Mr. Elliot beckoned cheerfully. "Come along. Teddy, you're coming, aren't you?"

"We-l-l-l, I guess I can," said Teddy, already three steps toward the door.

After they had cleared the meal away and washed the dishes, Libby visited with Verna a while, then excused herself to call on the Grubens.

11

🙚 "Libby. I'm glad you could come," said Mr. Gruben as he swung the door wide and ushered Libby inside. "Florence? Elizabeth is here."

Libby curbed a smile as she relinquished her coat, for while Florence consistently refused to use her nickname, there was no coinciding formality in regards to her home. Florence had lost a leg in a farming accident in childhood. But it was more her nature than her handicap that accounted for the unconstrained spirit throughout the cluttered white clapboard bungalow. The carpet bore a well-worn path to the back parlor, a room lined in bookshelves. The furniture was comfortably worn, and, in the center of it all, Florence sat reading a picture book to one of her cats, her crutches at her feet.

"How are you, Florence?"

"Not bad," Florence countered, as Mr. Gruben excused himself to make tea. "Push those papers to the end of the sofa and sit down. I take it your husband had more interesting things to do than visit an old woman and her cats?"

"He and Father and the boys are off on a lark," said Libby. She stretched a hand out to pet the orange cat. "Marmalade, isn't it?"

Florence nodded and stroked its lush fur. "Marmalade is a bookish cat. Watch this."

Libby looked on as Florence settled the cat in her lap, then licked her finger and lowered it to the page. The cat pricked his ears, twitched his tail, and lifted a paw as if to aid in the page-turning.

Libby chuckled and praised the cat's cleverness. "Are you still reading for Children's Hour at the library?"

"I gave that up once they moved into the new building. They have plenty of volunteers to read to the children now. All of them are younger than I, and the steps no obstacle for them." Florence subsided a moment, then with averted gaze, added, "Anyway, what do I know about children? That's what people say, you know. Because I don't have any of my own."

"You've *been* a child," reasoned Libby. "That qualifies you, doesn't it?"

"A good point, Elizabeth, but unnecessary," said Florence, as she stroked the orange cat. "I wasn't ousted, I stepped down. So you see, you needn't feel prickly on my account. I'm enjoying the library. Lucius stops by several afternoons a week and picks up something for me to read."

Mr. Gruben soon joined them with the tea tray. He had arranged Boston brown bread and wedges of cheese amidst the pot and cups. Cats rose from lounging spots in wide sunny windowsills and came with twitching noses and tails. Florence called them each by name. She distributed tidbits of cheese and chattered softly to them while Mr. Gruben and Libby went over some ideas regarding articles for the newspaper. At length, Mr. Gruben asked Libby how her freelance ambitions were coming along. She was forced to admit she'd done very little writing beyond her work for the *Gazette*.

"You've been given a gift, Elizabeth. Don't bury it," Florence chided.

"She's right, you know," said Mr. Gruben. "You should be setting goals for yourself. One of these days, you may have a family to care for. If you can't find time to write now, how will you then?''

Libby admired Mr. Gruben for a newspaper career that spanned decades. She endured his reprimand with good grace, and was relieved when the conversation shifted to a discussion of books. But when her visit drew to a close, and he walked her to the door, Mr. Gruben brought up the subject of writing again.

''Remember now, I'm expecting you to get to work on something creative. And I don't mean for the newspaper.''

''I'll do better, once sirup season is over.''

''Real writers write, regardless how busy their days.''

It was doubtful any of them helped run a sirup camp.

''They arrange their lives around it,'' he stressed.

Libby squirmed beneath Mr. Gruben's penetrating gaze, for how was she to arrange her life around writing when it had so naturally arranged itself around Ike?

It was late afternoon when Ike returned with Father and Mr. Elliot and the boys. The long walk home awaited them, yet Ike tarried in private conversation with Mr. Elliot, while Libby bid her family a leisurely goodbye.

The sun was waning as they started home. Libby tugged her hat down, turned up her collar, shoved her hands into her pockets, and tried to keep up with Ike's long stride. Along the way, he spoke of the Chicago and Alton's improvement project, describing the construction scene south of Edgewood.

''They'll be working at the grove, too,'' he added in summation. ''Decatur was tellin' me not long ago about them plannin' to put in a water system in advance of the work to be done.''

''To water the steam engines, you mean?''

Ike smiled at her terminology and explained that the improvement project created its own demand for large quantities of water. ''It's an uphill grade headin' north,

Lib, with dips here and there. They're wasting a lot of equipment, manpower, and time on pusher engines givin' trains a helpin' hand up the hills. They plan to level out the roadbed. That means steam shovels moving a lot of dirt.''

"They'll be working right by our house, then.''

Ike nodded. "Accordin' to Decatur, the water tank's going to be just east of the cabin.''

"In our yard?''

"Lappin' over the edge of it, by the sound of it.'' Ike lent his shoulder to her for balance as she stepped up on a rail to avoid getting her shoes dirty on a muddy stretch where the roadbed dipped.

"Mr. Elliot says there's a shortage of good mechanics,'' he continued. "They'll be hirin' some more, jest as soon as the weather warms up. Your father mentioned I'd worked as an oiler on threshin' runs and knew a little somethin' about gasoline engines, too.''

The purpose of his private conversation with Mr. Elliot suddenly dawned on Libby. She stopped so suddenly, she would have fallen off the rail, had he not steadied her. "Mr. Elliot offered you a job, didn't he?''

"Yep. But it'd be six days a week, as long as the weather was good. I couldn't get home except on Sundays.''

Libby's heart dropped. "Couldn't you take the train back and forth?''

"Be costly. Anyway, if somethin' breaks down, they expect their mechanics to be close at hand. They've got a camp train on site to house the skilled labor.''

"But if they're going to be doing work here at the grove . . .''

"They will, but not until next summer,'' said Ike.

"So you're not interested?''

"The wage Mr. Elliot's offerin' is a generous one. I can't make that kind of money farmin'. But I don't want to be gone from home all week.''

Still, Libby could see that the job interested him.

"They must need cooks on this camp train. I could go with you and cook for the men," she said a while later, as they left the tracks at the Old Kentucky crossing.

"That's no life for a woman." Ike slanted her a glance and added, "We'll keep prayin' about it, but somehow I can't hardly think it's what God's got in mind."

Libby didn't think so, either. Not if it meant being apart. She ambled along with him to the barn and helped care for the horses. The sky had turned to pewter by the time the chores were done. As they started home, Ike asked if she'd called on the Grubens. Libby nodded and told him about her visit.

"Florence gave up reading to the children at the library. Now she reads to her cats," she said in closing.

Ike grinned at her doleful tone. "What do you care if she reads to a cat?"

"Her life seems so narrow sometimes."

"Because she's missin' a leg?"

Libby pondered her reasons as they crossed the railroad tracks. Was Florence's disability the problem? Her spirit bore the scars of slights and oversights of others, whether real or imagined. Nonetheless, Florence had a choice. She didn't have to curl inward, hiding the best of herself. At length, she said, "It isn't her leg."

"What, then?"

"She has no one but Mr. Gruben."

Ike picked up an armload of wood off the porch and followed her inside. The fire was dead, but the chill that stirred over him as he crouched before the stove had nothing to do with their cold cabin. It was Libby's view of Florence. Narrow, she said. Because Florence had no one but a husband. Did Libby find her own life narrow at times, living out here in the trees, cut off from her family, wanting to start one of her own?

Ike had built a wood-framed screen of punched tin. It partially shielded their sleeping space from the rest of the open room. He looked up as Libby retreated behind it to change out of her good dress, and found himself wanting to follow her there. Wanting to know she was content with him and had no regrets. He couldn't ask a question like that. Not with words, anyway. He was half-way to his feet when he heard a crash on the other side of the screen.

"Lib? What'd ya do?"

"I'm all right," she was swift to reassure him. "I tripped over something. Quick, bring a light."

Ike grabbed matches from the tin matchbox nailed to a central beam and struck one with his thumbnail. He cupped in it his hands as he circled the screen to find Libby on her knees, hands resting on a crate.

"Chickens!" she cried. As she lifted her face, her eyes reflected the match flame.

Ike hunkered down beside her and lit another match. One of the hens poked its beak between the slats and pecked her finger. Libby let out a yelp and leapt back.

"She bit my finger!"

"Don't look at me," said Ike, tickled by her wording. "I know better'n to ruffle yer feathers, lettin' chickens inside."

Disgruntled at his laughter, she said, "Are you going to make a light or not?"

He struck a second match and touched it to the lamp on the stand by the bed. Its circle of light fell on a wrinkled note. "Here ya go. Maybe this'll solve yer riddle," he said.

The note was from Opal. Libby read it aloud:

> *Dear Libby,*
> *Here's a present for watchin' me after school and helping me learn to sew.*
> *It was mean of Miss Maudie to do what she did. But she's old and don't know no better. Your friend, Opal.*

The transformation from indignation to surprised gratitude was so swift, Ike was almost sorry he hadn't thought of the chickens himself.

"What a sweet gesture! Though I don't know what to do with them." Twisting around to see him better, Libby asked, "What *do* I do with them?"

"You'll have ta keep a close watch until I can get something built for them. Hawks, foxes, all sort of varmints prey on chickens. Guess we could put 'em in the woodshed for tonight."

"Help me with these and I'll change and come with you." Libby turned and presented her back to him.

Ike's hands were rough, his fingers more suited to handling horses and swinging a sap pail than unfastening tiny pearl buttons. But he worked at it patiently, and when the dress gaped open, dropped a kiss in the faint hollow between her shoulders.

Turning, smiling up at him, she asked, "What was that all about?"

"What do ya think?"

She slipped her arms around him. Her fingertips stroked the small of his back, but the circular caresses stopped as he curved his hand to her nape. She tipped her face and kissed him, then smothered a laugh against his mouth as one of the hens squawked at their feet.

"Quit now. You're stirring up the chickens."

"Opal wants to bring chickens, tell her ta put 'em in soup." Ike covered her smile with another kiss, but it was a lost cause and he knew it.

She stepped out of his arms and changed her dress to go with him, but he talked her into starting supper instead.

Ike found some grain for the hens and a shallow container to hold water. He wasn't too crazy about letting the hens wander free in the woodshed. But he figured if he didn't let them out of the crate, they'd either hang themselves sticking their necks through the slats or peck each other bald.

After supper, when the last dish was washed and put away, Libby joined Ike by the fire. She parked her feet on his lap, and coaxed him into rubbing them as she questioned him about how to care for chickens.

"I'd wait until mornin' before I put too much study into the chicken business," Ike said. "No tighter'n that shed is, varmints may get 'em, and you'd have wasted yer time."

"I wish you'd quit bringing up varmints."

"Just don't want ya fillin' yer head with useless information."

"It isn't useless at all," Libby objected. "I like learning new things. That's what makes life out here so interesting. Trees and flowers and garden and sirup. Even varmints," she said, and nudged him with her toe. "Broadens the writing canvas, so to speak. That should please Mr. Gruben. He scolded me today for being a slackard about my writing."

"For the *Gazette*?"

"No, he meant my ambition for story writing. And he's right, I have grown lazy about it." She closed her eyes and curled her toes and all but purred. "You've almost brought that one back to life. How about the other one?"

"All right. But it's goin' ta cost ya."

"Can I pay you in chickens?" She laughed at his grimace and skipped back to her writing. "Florence scolded me, too, and said I should be using my gift. Personally, I was flattered she thought I had one. Though she's a fine one to fuss at me, sitting there reading to a cat," she added, then opened her eyes and asked, "Why did you stop?"

"Three chickens won't get you much of a foot rub."

"What if I were to throw in a cup of cocoa?"

"Keep goin'," he said, and resumed kneading her foot.

"That feels so good, I'll make it six chickens." Libby

sighed, and added, "I had a nice day, but it sure is good to be home."

Her eyes drifted shut again, her lashes making a red-gold smudge against her cheek. Awash with a tenderness he couldn't express in words, Ike tickled her foot.

"Careful," she warned, cracking one eye. "You'll forfeit your feathered friends."

"Varmints can have 'em. I'm holdin' out for the bare-foot redhead. But she's too busy countin' her chickens ta notice."

"That's not entirely true."

"Isn't it?"

Libby shook her head. Mouth tilting, she dropped her feet from his lap, banked the fire, and, with attention only for him, held out welcoming hands.

12

🌸 By the light of day, the chickens were black-and-white-speckled. They had vivid red combs atop their heads and beady eyes that Libby found intimidating.

"Plymouth Rocks," Ike told her before leaving for the sap house the next morning. "If yer serious about egg money, yer goin' to need more'n three young hens. Take a rooster and a couple dozen chicks to get a good start."

He promised to pick her up some chicks at the hatchery. But not yet. It would be after sirup season before he could build a chicken coop and make a wire fence in which to confine the chickens during the day.

On Monday, Libby helped gather sap in the morning, then spent the afternoon baking. She filled the rose cookie jar with gingersnaps and had loaves of bread rising when Opal stopped by after school.

"Did ya find my note?" Opal asked.

The anticipatory pleasure shining from Opal's eyes made Libby smile. "Yes, and the chickens, too. Cute as can be, all dressed up in black-and-white gingham feathers."

Opal giggled at her description. "Then ya like 'em?"

"I certainly do." Libby framed Opal's thin face be-

113

tween her flour-dusty hands and kissed her forehead.
"Wash your hands and have a gingersnap. Where's
Frankie?"

"He went to the woods to help Daddy gather sap."
Opal crossed to the sink and pumped the black handle.
She came back to the table, helped herself to a cookie,
and watched Libby shape the remaining yeast dough into
supper biscuits. "Want I should stir yer 'spook' for ya?"

Spook was the mixture of flour, yeast, and water
Libby used as starter for her bread dough. She had re-
served a small amount upon beginning her baking. Now,
she added more water, flour, and a smidgin of sugar and
pushed the bowl in Opal's direction.

"Don't seem too punchy," observed Opal.

"It will be, by the time I bake again. So long as it
doesn't get too warm."

"Ya goin' ta teach me how to make bread? Mama
keeps sayin' she will, but it don't look like she's ever
goin' ta have time what with workin' at the store."

"I'll teach you about bread and you can can teach me
about chickens."

Pleased, Opal said, "What're ya wantin' ta know?"

"First of all, I'd like to know how to avoid getting
pecked."

"Ya ain't scairt of 'em, surely?"

"Just timid. And whatever you do, don't say anything
to Ike. I'd never hear the end of it!"

Opal's lips spread in a knowing grin. "Shucks, Lib,
a feller only teases a gal if he's sweet on her."

"Has someone been teasing you?" Libby rubbed her
hands together, peeling away the yeasty dough.

"Purdy. He's new at school. He sneaked into the
cloak room and ate the sandwich from my dinner bucket.
Left a note says I'm good with colors, almost as good
as his daddy is with a paintbrush." Opal plopped a pinch
of raw dough into her mouth. "Frankie says Purdy was
jest sweet-talkin' me so's I wouldn't tell Teacher what
he done. But I know better."

Libby shared the tale with Ike later. He didn't know of anyone named Purdy, nor was he aware of any house painters in the area.

"They're new. They was passin' through, when their team broke down," said Frankie, when Libby questioned him.

"Where are they living?" asked Libby.

"In their wagon. Purdy says it's enclosed and got a stove and everythin'."

Frankie went on to say that Purdy had a brother the kids called Dumplin and two sisters. One, he referred to as "purty good" and the other as "very fine." His showing an interest in girls startled Libby so, she let him get past her in his muddy boots. He tracked dirt all the way through the sap house by the time she caught up with him.

"A gentleman leaves his muddy boots at the door, Frankie," she said pointedly.

"Aw, Lib. I'm jest buildin' up yer dirt floor," he countered with a pained look.

It seemed to Ike as if God had reached out and touched the trees, making them flow like an unending stream. They had made more sirup in the past thirteen days than all last season. The pace had been such that he hadn't had a chance to look for work yet.

Ike stepped off the porch and looked back to the homey glow of yellow light in the cabin windows. The sun wasn't up yet, but he could smell the smoke lifting from the chimney. The air was balmy, and the ground was sloppy underfoot. He heard the plip-plip of the dripping sap as he crossed to the maple tree east of the cabin.

Libby had quibbled with him over tapping the tree. She said it earned its keep, spreading its arms over their cabin in the heat of the summer and leaving a variegated carpet on the grass in the fall. He told her to mind her bush and leave the trees to him. She quit protesting, but winced with comic drama as he tapped it.

Striking a match, Ike saw that the bucket on the yard tree was running over. Good thing it was Saturday. Frankie would be home from school to help. Narrowing his concerns to the day that was breaking, Ike lengthened his stride. By the time he finished his chores and headed home for breakfast, Libby had potatoes browning on the stove.

"Trees ran all night," Ike told her as he washed up.

She broke eggs into the skillet, then slipped up beside him to dash her hands under the stream of water he was making with the pump. "You're getting skinny."

"Hadn't noticed."

"I have."

He reached for a towel. "I'm feeling pert."

"You better tighten your belt a notch, or you're going to lose your trousers."

Hoping she wasn't going to fuss, Ike made a joke of it, saying, "You flirtin' with me, Lib?"

"No, I'm telling you you'd better slow down to a trot," she said, and turned away to dish up breakfast.

Ike picked up the salt shaker and the coffeepot on the way to the table. He held her chair, waiting for her to join him. She took cream from the window box first and set it on the table.

Ike looked up from asking the blessing to find her gazing out the window into the gray dawn. He couldn't resist a gentle needling. "Ya writin' in yer head again, are ya?"

"No. I was thinking about Naomi. She says there are a lot of people sick with influenza in town."

Ike picked up his fork. "She's Hascal's own daughter, worryin' over disease."

"Ike, you *are* thin."

"Then tie up some of those cookies for me and I'll fatten myself up on the way to the sap house."

As he handled the fork and knife, Ike's hands were dry and red from the weather. His lips were chapped, his face wind-burned. But it was his eyes that gave away his fatigue. Libby sighed, and said, "I love you."

It wasn't what he'd expected. He looked up from his plate, his expression shifting from surprise to a grin. "Now that's tricky, Lib. If yer goin' to fuss at me, do it fair and square."

Libby eyed him over the rim of her coffee cup. "You're cheeky for such a short-handed fellow. Think you can get along without me, do you?"

"Decatur's strong as an ox and Frankie's eager. But you're better-lookin'."

"Now who's tricky?" she replied, hiding her pleasure. "I'll be over as soon as I wash the dishes."

"No hurry. Decatur's goin' to need some help gatherin' b'fore I fire up."

"You're going to the timber? I'll come too, then."

"Why don't you go call on our new neighbors to the north, instead?"

"The Stapletons? I'm about out of the notion."

Ike frowned, for it was out of keeping with her open-hearted ways. "You aren't taking that yarn-spinnin' of Hascal's seriously, surely."

"Of course not," said Libby. "But I saw the younger Mrs. Stapleton at the crossing last evening when I was on my way over to the sap house with your supper. She ducked her head and doubled her pace as if she couldn't get away from me fast enough."

"Maybe she was in a hurry."

"We were headed in the same direction, Ike. We could have walked together. As far as the bridge, anyway."

Hearing a knock at the door, Ike scraped his chair back. "Probably Decatur. I'll get it." But it wasn't Decatur beyond the door, rather a man and a woman with a baby in her arms. It took Ike a second in the deep gray dawn to recognize Libby's oldest brother.

"Well, I'll be! Watch yer step. The icicles drip there and make it slick." Ike gripped Adam's hand, then held the door wide. "Better put some more eggs in the pan, Lib, we got company."

"Break the yolks and fry them hard," said Adam. He steadied his wife as she climbed the damp steps with their infant daughter.

Libby shot to her feet at the sound of her brother's voice. "Adam Watson! Abigail! And our sweet Annie!" cried Libby. "Why didn't you tell us you were coming?"

"We thought we'd surprise you," said Abigail.

"And you have!" Libby hugged Abigail, baby and all, then kissed her brother's cheek. "And just in time, too. Ike's buckets are running over."

"Lib!"

"Aren't they?" she defended in a tone that made Adam grin and turned Ike's ears red.

"I'm not aimin' to put company to work."

"You better take help where you can get it."

"I was hoping for a firsthand look at your operation, Ike. Unless I'd be in the way," Adam amended. He had an earnest demeanor, his father's square chin, and a loyalty to those he loved, evidenced in selfless ways.

"Since ya put it that way . . ."

"He accepts," Libby cut in.

Ike shuffled his feet and gave up trying to quell the opportunist in her.

Libby turned back to the baby. "Why, she's doubled in size since I last saw her!"

"Mostly blankets," claimed Abigail. She was a pretty, dark-eyed brown-haired girl not much bigger than Libby. The baby's eyes were a lovely dark blue.

Ike deposited their guests' coats on the bed behind the wood-framed screen while Libby fussed over the baby.

"My goodness, look at those sweet dimpled hands. She has her mama's round face, and her daddy's nose. And what's this? Her aunt Libby's red hair?"

"Hair?" said Adam. "She's bald as a doorknob."

"She has a fine dusting of hair, and if that isn't a hint of red, I'll eat my hat."

"So long as you break the yolks and fry them hard."

Libby laughed and resisted her brother's attempts to nudge her toward the stove. "As soon as I make a bed for Annie."

Ike brought the bedside chair to the table, then broke some eggs into the skillet and visited with Adam while Libby emptied a dresser drawer to make a makeshift bed that Annie couldn't roll out of. Abigail had no more than settled at the table when the baby awoke. Libby rocked her while Abigail sat down with the men, and ate breakfast.

Ike reheated the coffee and answered Adam's questions regarding the maple camp and asked some of his own about Adam's job at the C & A shops in Bloomington. The conversation soon turned to the ambitious C & A project and Ike's firsthand view of it. Adam was surprised to hear that Ike had met Mr. Elliot.

"I haven't met him, myself, but I rode the train to the job site last week and did some repairs on their accommodations down by Atlanta. The men down that way spoke well of him. The ones who could speak English, anyway. They've brought in a lot of foreign laborers."

"Accommodations?" echoed Libby.

Adam nodded. "Camp train. A couple of sleeping cars, a kitchen car, a dining car, and so on."

Daylight was soon shining through the windows. Ike pulled on his outdoor clothes. "I'd best get at those buckets. Decatur'll be wonderin' what happened to me."

"I'll get my coat," said Adam.

When they had gone, Libby took another peek at the baby. She touched the sleeping infant's petal-soft cheek. "Sleeping like a lamb. Is she always this good?"

"No, but I have to say she's not as fussy as Rose."

Abigail's mention of Rose caught Libby off guard. Two summers ago, an ill-conceived love affair had left Abigail in the family way. The miner she had been involved with had refused to accept responsibility, but Adam, who had courted her intermittently for years, married her. They were living in Thistle Down at the time, but Adam tried to shelter Abigail from the village gossips by sending her to live with Libby and Father and David in Edgewood. It was there that Rose had been born.

Feeling that it would be best for Rose as well as for herself and Adam, Abigail had made the difficult decision to give the baby up for adoption. The choice had caused Abigail a good deal of anguish. Thinking of the gentle circus owner and his wife who had received Rose into their hearts and their traveling home, Libby ventured, "Do you ever hear from the Bigelows?"

"I got a short letter at Christmas. Mrs. Bigelow says Rose is doing well." The words came with a sheen of tears. "Forgive me, Libby. It's just that having Annie and watching her grow makes me realize what I've missed with Rose."

Gently, Libby asked, "You regret not keeping her?"

"I can't help but wish it could have been different."

"Does Adam ever talk about it?"

"He might, if I encouraged him to," said Abigail, a tremor in her voice. "But my instinct is to leave well enough alone."

Abigail soon regained her composure and the day passed in a rush. Libby carried little Annie as she accompanied Adam and Abigail to the depot at dusk. She pulled the blanket away from the baby's face and kissed her pink cheek before passing her into Abigail's waiting arms and thanking Adam for helping Ike all day.

Adam assured her he'd enjoyed himself and offered a word of sympathy over the loss of the farm as the north-bound Prairie Express pulled into the station.

Naomi and Opal climbed off as Libby was hugging her family good-bye. Opal greeted Libby with a wide grin, then shot off for the sap house to see if Decatur and Frankie were done gathering for the day.

Naomi accompanied Libby back to the cabin. Saturday was the busiest day of the week at the store, and it showed in Naomi's demeanor. She sagged in her chair and stretched her feet toward the fire as she relayed a bit of news.

"Seems the Gentrys have canceled their trip to Eureka Springs. They go down there every year 'bout this time. Got the bench brigade at the store full of speculation as to why this year's any different."

"Maybe Ida's not up to it. I noticed when we went to church at New Hope that she was looking washed out." A puff of smoke escaped through a seam in the stovepipe. Libby adjusted the damper and added, "So are you, by the way."

"I am feelin' a little tired," Naomi admitted. "No mystery to that, though. We're goin' ta have a family addition one of these days."

Pregnant! Libby resisted a stab of envy. "That's wonderful, Naomi! How far along are you?"

"Three months, close as I can figur'."

"Decatur must be pleased."

"Ain't told him yet. He's been tryin' all winter to git me to hire somebody to run the store, at least until the weather warms. My bein' in the family way'll jest give him more ammunition."

"Still, you're excited about the baby, aren't you?"

"I'm gettin' used to the idea. But it ain't goin' to be all that convenient." Naomi paused in sipping her tea. "What're you lookin' at me like that for?"

"I'm trying to keep from shaking you." Libby gave a short laugh, and added, "I'm sorry, but I can't help it! You're like the diner complaining to the hungry waiter that the salt pork is a little too salty."

Abashed, Naomi said, "Yer the waiter?"

"Yes, and my stomach is growling!"

"I'm sorry, Lib. I didn't know. Ya've never said nothin' about wantin' a baby."

"It's a mixed kind of wanting, made worse by a day

spent with little Annie,'' Libby confessed. ''Ike is being
practical, hoping to wait until we're better situated. And
I suppose he's right. A baby would be a hardship, particularly now that he's out of work.''

''Hardships ain't pleasant at the time, I'll allow,
though I cain't say but what I've found 'em to be good
tools in the Maker's hand. Speakin' of myself, mind
you.'' Naomi stopped short, and grinned. ''Would ya
listen at me, talkin' out of both sides of my mouth!''

Libby smiled. ''So was I. Wanting to please myself
and Ike, too.''

''Well, one of ya's bound to be pleased thataway,''
said Naomi, chuckling.

When Naomi had gone home, Libby sat a moment
longer, listening to dishes rattle in the cupboard as a train
rumbled past and thinking of babies and her wish to
experience that joy balanced against Ike's reluctance to
invite more hardship.

What was missing in that equation was God's wish.
God's will for their lives. She knew that. Yet at times
her faith didn't seem too punchy, to borrow a phrase
from Opal. As if, like bread starter, she had used it up
and neglected to go to the Source for replenishing.
Lately, there'd been much time spent in the woods, little
spent in His word, and even less listening for His still,
small voice.

Vowing to do better, Libby reached for her journal
and wrote: *Lord, help me to think less of our circumstances and more of Your sustaining arm. Less of where
Ike will work, and more of the work You are trying to
do in us. Less of our preferred time and more of Your
perfect time. Help me embrace Your plan for our lives,
whatever it may be.*

13

The weather warmed late in March. The leaves on the trees swelled. The sap developed what Ike thought of as a "buddy" smell, and overnight, they were finished for the season. With Libby's help, Ike spent the last days of the month pulling the spouts from the trees and bringing the buckets in from the woods.

On Saturday, he awoke feeling sluggish, and was thankful that Opal and Frankie were on hand to help him and Libby finish washing and storing the buckets in the lean-to where the wood had been piled so high only weeks ago. When that was done, Libby scoured the evaporating pans. Decatur came for the children late in the afternoon. He helped Ike move the pans off the arches and store them against the wall before trudging home with the children.

Libby left, too, planning to start supper. Refusing to yield to a pounding headache and a queasy feeling in the pit of his stomach, Ike stayed to clean out the firebox. He was nearly done with the job when the saphouse door swung open. Chester Gentry stepped inside and thumped his ivory-handled cane against the open door.

"Anyone here?"

Ike came to his feet while Chester squinted, trying to adjust to the shift in light. Guarding his surprise, Ike leaned the ash shovel against the metal bucket. The sound directed his uncle to him.

"So there you are," Chester said pleasantly.

"Shut the door. The wind's whippin' ashes around."

Chester pushed it closed and advanced with the confident stride of a man who had found the world to be his oyster. He punctuated the silence with a tap of his cane against the brick arch.

"Mrs. Gentry and I had the pleasure of visiting with your wife in church not long ago. Her mention of the sirup-making made us nostalgic for the old days. I was hoping to see you cooking, but by the looks of it, I've waited too long."

Unmoved by his affected friendliness, Ike said, "If yer wantin' sirup, Naomi's sellin' it at the store in town."

"So I heard." Chester took off his spectacles and rubbed the moisture from the lenses. "I'll get straight to the point. I heard in town that you were looking for a job. I've got a farm about to become vacant. Are you interested?"

"The ground Ketchum's been farmin'?" A second wave of surprise fanned chilly fingers across Ike's chest.

"You come well recommended by Miss Maudie. Of course, you've made a few mistakes. You were as late as anybody in the country, getting your wheat out a year ago. But it was clear by this year's crop that you learned from that."

It was malaria that had kept Ike from getting his crop harvested on time, though he didn't waste his breath pointing it out.

Chester shifted his weight, and said, "Maybe you could think of it as a step toward patching things up between us."

"Don't know why you'd want to," said Ike with a

bluntness that would have backed a lesser man toward the door.

But Chester, his gaze steady, replied, "My wife does. So does my daughter and my daughter-in-law. They're all quite taken with your wife."

"What's that got to do with it?"

"If you'd been married as long as I have, you wouldn't have to ask."

Something unexpected flashed in Chester's eyes. *Pain?* It was gone so swiftly, Ike wasn't sure. His gaze flicked over him as he waited.

"You've seen the house and barn," Chester resumed. "I'll furnish the equipment and buy the seed. You provide the labor. We'll split the profits fifty-fifty. You can use the timber, too, if you're looking to expand your sirup operation next year. I can have Angus draw up a legal contract once Mr. Ketchum moves out."

"Don't bother."

"And don't *you* be so hasty," countered Chester, showing an edge. "I'm prepared to make this a long-term commitment. It would give you the security you lacked with Miss Maudie. A wife likes that. It's hard for women, being shifted about."

As it had been for his mother, coming from Missouri to Illinois with two fatherless children. The old anger coursed through Ike. "One thing I could always say for you was that you were a man of your word, Chester. Don't know why you'd go back on it now."

"I'm not sure what you mean."

"You stood there on yer porch and told my mother you'd warned my father he wasn't getting any help from you, and you weren't helping his kids or his wife, either one."

"She wasn't his wife."

"No, if yer set on splittin' hairs, she wasn't," said Ike, wondering why Chester would point it out again after all these years. "But she wasn't askin' for charity, jest a chance to work for our keep."

"You were too young to appreciate the position it put me in. If it seemed harsh to you at the time, I apologize."

Harsh. Arrogant. Mean-spirited. Gentry's words reverberated in Ike's head, shaking the dirt off stony emotions, honing the sharp edges. He picked up the ash shovel and hunkered down before the fire pit. His shovel scraped against the bricks, making his aching head throb.

"Put yourself in my shoes," Chester said, breaking the taut silence. "I was just weeks from my wedding date."

"What's your point?"

"Ike, I'm no prude. But face it, after living with Morgan all those years, bearing him children out of wedlock, your mother didn't—"

Ike came to his feet again and wheeled around to face him. "Didn't *what*?"

"Simmer down. I don't mean any disrespect. I'm just trying to make you see it from my point of view. Can't we sit down and talk this over like reasonable men?"

"I've had my say."

"Then put your hostility aside and let me have mine."

"Ya got nothin' to say I want to hear. Now git on out of here and quit botherin' me."

"I don't know what my brother taught you, but it sure wasn't manners!" declared Chester, his mouth a white gash. "If I was ten years younger, I'd thrash some into you myself."

"If you was ten years younger, you'd have had yer chance by now." Ike crossed to the door and jerked it open.

A prominent vein throbbed in Chester's forehead. He balled his fists, as if he were torn yet by the temptation to give him a pummeling. Ike glowered back at him, mad enough to wish he'd try. At length, Chester unclenched his fists and strode past him. He paused just short of the door, and swiveled around to get in the last word.

"I'm warning you, Ike, don't get caught up in this business with the Stapletons. They should have settled with the deeded acres. If they think I'm an easy mark, they'll soon find out they're mistaken."

"I don't know what yer talkin' about."

"There's been no communication between yourself and Mrs. Stapleton?"

"Haven't met the woman."

Chester studied him a long moment. His gaze was the first to fall. He tugged at his collar and finally conceded, "Maybe I've misjudged you. I hope I have. You've got my mother's blood in your veins, and that ought to mean something."

It hadn't when it counted. Ike waited for him to clear the door.

Chester donned his hat, and said with stiff civility, "Ida asked that I extend her regrets to Mrs. Galloway that she was unable to come along for a look at the camp. Give her our regards."

Ike pushed the door closed and gave the ash bucket a kick. It spewed a cloud of gray dust and charred coals across the floor. Head thundering, he kicked the bucket again and waited until Chester was down the road before starting home.

Libby had a pie in the oven, canned vegetables simmering, and a rabbit frying on the stove. She took the copper teapot out to the summer porch and left it on the water bench beside a washbasin. Sunshine poured through the summer porch windows, tempting her to linger. She withdrew her journal from the basket by the chair where she had left it yesterday and was about to sit down when the younger Stapleton woman passed by on foot, heading east toward Skiff's Store.

Libby's conscience pricked her, for despite Ike's prodding, she had yet to call on her new neighbors to the north. With sirup season behind them and every bucket put away, she was out of excuses. Could her intuition be off the mark? Maybe it was shyness, not unfriendliness, that accounted for what she had interpreted as a deliberate slight.

Libby sat down with her journal. The divided panes of glass with the sun coming through cast lined shadows on the page as she made a brief entry summarizing the end of the sirup season. In closing, she wrote, *I guess I'll go visit the Stapletons and see what sort of reception I get.*

"Libby?" Ike called to her from the open porch.

Libby dropped her tablet on the water bench and walked outside to meet him. His wind-burned face was dark with anger, making the whiteness of his scarred ear all the more pronounced. She stopped short. "What's the matter?"

"Did you tell Chester Gentry to come by?"

"And Ida." Libby braced herself and hastily explained, "They were remembering childhood experiences when neighbors got together to make sirup, and I got a little carried away." She hesitated a heartbeat, trying to read his face. Her throat went dry. "Don't tell me they came?"

"I all but drew you a picture, tellin' ya ta stay out of this."

"I didn't mean it in the sense of a social invitation. I was just being polite."

"Why couldn't ya leave it alone?"

"I wasn't thinking," she admitted. "You should have come after me. I would have taken them off your hands."

"It was jest Chester, and he didn't come to see the camp."

Surprised, Libby said, "What did he want, then?"

"You don't know?"

"I just told you, they were reminiscing . . ." The impatience smoldering in his eyes stopped her. "That isn't it? Then why *did* he?"

"He offered me a job."

"You mean farming? What kind of a job?"

"Ketchum's forty acres." Ike saw the leap of hope before she could disguise it. Flatly, he said, "I told ya before when you mentioned Ketchum givin' up farming that I'd never farm for Chester."

Knowing instinctively what he was thinking, Libby said, "I never mentioned you or Mr. Ketchum's farm to Mr. Gentry."

"Ya didn't drop any kind of a hint that I was lookin'?"

"No."

"You sure?"

"Of course I'm sure."

"But it *does* bother you about Gentry and me not gettin' along."

"Yes, it bothers me! It isn't right. It's damaging to him and it's damaging to you and spills over on other people."

"On you, in other words."

Though he hadn't raised his voice, his words raised welts on tender nerves. Libby turned away. But his words followed her:

"For years, Chester ignores me. Then you talk to him in church and all at once, he's here offering me a job. Libby, don't walk away. Turn around here and talk to me."

"All right," she said, turning back. "But calm down and let me find words for what I'm thinking."

"I *am* calm, and I ain't ever seen you at a loss for words yet."

Libby walked into the house. She ran out of floor at the sink. Unable to put any more distance between him and herself without abandoning her half-cooked meal, she gripped the wooden drain board and stared out across the muddy yard. *I hate mud. I hate conflict. I hate whatever it was that Chester Gentry did to Ike to make him act like this.*

The door stood open between the summer porch and

the cabin. Libby could hear his bootlaces whispering free of their eyelets. The chair grated against the floor as he came to his feet. She jumped when he called her name and turned to find him in the doorway, her open journal in his hand.

"What's this about the Stapletons?"

"I was thinking about visiting them. You said it wasn't very neighborly of me not to," she reminded, then added pointedly, "though you didn't have to read my journal to learn that."

He crossed to her chair by the stove and dropped her journal there without apology. "Do you know something about them I don't know?"

Confused, she said, "What do you mean?"

"Chester says they've got the deed to that pasture property. He said some other things, too."

"Like what?"

"I don't remember his words. But it sounded like he thought those women were scheming against him, and that I knew about it."

"Why didn't you ask him what he meant?"

"It wasn't that friendly a conversation."

"So you can't trouble yourself to question Chester a little, but you don't mind storming in here, putting me in the middle of it?"

"You put yourself in the middle, invitin' him to stop."

Libby shut her mouth and turned away again. Half a dozen shots went unfired as she struggled to hold her emotions in check. At length, she jabbed at the pieces of sizzling rabbit, and replied, "Here we are, fighting over Chester Gentry again. What has that man done to you?" At his silence, she took a deep breath, and conceded, "I'm sorry I didn't tell you about inviting him and Ida to stop by. But I don't think that's what this is about. If you weren't angry, you'd see that yourself."

"Leave it alone, Lib."

Libby heeded an inner voice and said, "All right. For now."

Her soft-spoken *For now* was still rankling Ike a while later when they sat down to eat. She bowed her head, but he picked up his fork. He couldn't find words to ask a blessing. Not while he was at odds with her.

Libby did it for him. It was a careful prayer. Everything about her was careful and quiet. As if she were tiptoeing around him.

I'd do a lot of things for her, but working for Chester Gentry isn't one of them. Maybe You could make her understand that. She sure doesn't seem to be gettin' the picture from me.

Stomach churning, Ike gave up trying to eat, scraped his chair back, and left for the barn. He fed the horses, mucked out the barn, threw down fresh bedding, and started home again. His head was pounding and though the breeze was light, it cut through his coat and chilled him.

He paused briefly to check the swollen creek. The melting snow and a couple of spring rains had brought the water to within a couple of feet of the bridge. It was choppy and muddy-looking.

The impression of being observed was so strong, Ike turned and looked behind him to see a young woman making her way toward him from the other direction. The sight of her lifted the hair on his neck, so potent was the sense of familiarity. He knew by her averted glance that she had been watching him. Was it the younger Stapleton woman?

If so, there was no reason he should know her. As the woman came even with him, she shot him a wary, side-long glance. Ike looked into eyes the same color as his own, and instantly, the years fell away. The air left his lungs. Astonished, he reached out and caught her arm.

14

❧ "What're you doin' here, Cicely?"

The woman swept a strand of honey blond hair away from her face, and said with a censoring crispness, "I beg your pardon, sir?"

The face was his sister's, but the voice was not. There was an Eastern correctness marking her speech. Embarrassed, Ike dropped his hand and apologized. "I'm sorry, ma'am. I thought you were someone else. You look just like my sister."

The woman lifted one eyebrow. She even had Cicely's cleft chin and the same sardonic quirk at the corner of her mouth. "I see."

"Hope I didn't alarm you. I'm assumin' we're neighbors?" At her nod, he said, "I'm Ike Galloway."

"I was rapidly figuring that out."

"How?"

"The eyes, mostly. And the reference to your sister. I've caught glimpses of you from a distance, of course, but never close enough to get a good look at your face."

"You *know* Cicely?"

"Your sister? No."

It was a puzzling conversation. Or maybe his throbbing head had made him dull-witted. Ike couldn't seem

132

to quit looking. He said, "I can't get over how much you look like her."

"Yes. Well, we must both look like our father, then. I'm Laila. You don't mind if I call you Ike, do you? Mr. Galloway seems a little formal, under the circumstances."

Ike gaped at her. "Who *are* you?"

"You mean you don't know?" She searched his face. "My goodness! You *don't* know. Laila Stapleton. Laila *Galloway* Stapleton," she said, with emphasis.

Ike's chest constricted. He swallowed, trying to relieve his dry mouth. "Maybe you better explain."

"What is there to say except that we have a father in common? I'm your half sister. I supposed the whole neighborhood was abuzz with it by now."

It was like missing the last step, going down hard, and waiting for the spinning to stop before you could assess the damage.

Laila's eyes warmed a little as she watched his reaction. She gave a short laugh. "Forgive me. I'm not laughing at you, I'm laughing at myself. I assumed when we moved here and you didn't come calling, that you and your wife didn't want to have anything to do with me. My mother's been gloating over my disappointment daily."

"Ma'am, I had no idea. My wife's been goin' to call, but I've been keepin' her busy." Ike flushed at the irrelevance of his excuse measured against the enormity of her revelation. "I'm sorry. Mind's kind of a logjam. How old are you, anyway?"

"Twenty-six. How old are you?" she countered.

"Twenty-six."

"My. He was busy, wasn't he?"

Ike realized she meant his father. Heat swept up his collar. Laila tipped her head to one side, watching him. Her expression turned pensive. "Mother says he was about your height, but a little heavier and blond."

"My father?"

"*Our* father," she said, her mouth quirking again.

"You don't remember him, then?"

Laila shook her head. "He left my mother for your mother before I was born. Decisions, decisions."

She said it so flippantly, Ike couldn't say whether she was trying to shock him or convince him of how little she cared. Uncomfortable, he said, "I'm sorry."

"Don't be," she said. "I'm not. I wasn't one of those children who yearned for her father's return. I had a very nice childhood with my grandparents. It used to worry me that he *might* come back and take me away. Or that my mother would find him. She looked hard enough."

"Was she hopin' to patch it up?"

"No, that wasn't what Edina had in mind. 'Hell hath no fury like a woman scorned.' " Laila shot him a cavalier grin and asked in the manner of an afterthought, "Would you like to meet her?"

Ike did. His reasons had more to do with Gentry than with Laila. He'd taken dark pleasure in throwing Chester's offer of a farm back in his face. But Chester had tainted it by suggesting he was mixed up in something that involved the Stapletons.

"Would she mind?"

"Quite the contrary. I think she'd enjoy it. When would be convenient?" Laila asked.

Her anticipatory pleasure didn't escape Ike's notice. Had her mother really gloated, thinking they were shunning Laila? Tired and a little uneasy, he thought of putting it off, yet resisted. "Would right now suit?"

Laila assessed him a long moment, then shrugged. "All right, if that's what you want. Prepare yourself, though. Edina is one of a kind."

Libby left the dishes, pulled her boots on over her shoes, and went out to close the chickens into the woodshed for the night. The tears she'd held back through a brief silent supper where she'd eaten little and Ike even less now found release.

She crossed the sloping pasture to the creek, trying to make sense of their quarrel without placing blame. Ike had made an impression in his refusal to take up a grudge against Earl Morefield. What was it he had said? Something about the danger of blame clouding blessings.

His spiritual maturity over the loss of the farm seemed in such sharp contrast to his grudge against Mr. Gentry. Libby sat down on a log and picked at the cold bark. A loose piece came away in her hand, revealing a collection of tiny eggs against the spine of the log. The sawdust surrounding the insect eggs indicated a wood-boring beetle. The eggs were harmless now, but would hatch and soon contribute to the log's decay.

In the same way, Ike's bitterness with Mr. Gentry lay dormant most of the time, only to flare up intermittently and eat away at him. Was she, in skirting the issue, throwing bark over the problem, creating a breeding ground for future problems?

Libby heard what sounded like a bull crashing through the brush and looked up to see Hascal Caton coming across the winter-bleached weeds along the railroad tracks.

Hastily, Libby dried her eyes and with spur-of-the-moment ingenuity, grabbed a long stick that looked to be about the right size for a fishing pole. She dropped the tip of the stick in the water, hoping her tears as well as her lack of a line and hook would escape his notice in the dwindling light.

"Miz Lib? That you?"

"Yes, it is, Mr. Caton."

"Thought I saw you and Ike . . . what're ya doin' thar?" Hascal ambled closer. He squinted toward the water. "That pole standin' between you and supper?"

"We've already eaten."

"Good thing. 'Cause ya ain't goin' ta ketch nothin' there. Yer bait's so skimpy, I cain't see it. And if I cain't, neither can the fish."

"Phantom fish can. They have very keen vision."

"Phantom fish?" Hascal's bushy brows beetled, creating the illusion of wiggling his hat as he scratched the back of his head. "Didn't know they grew in these waters. Ketch me a string of 'em while yer at it. I'll take 'em to the Basket and Bean social over't the schoolhouse tomorrow night."

He looked so serious, Libby was ashamed of her childish trick aimed at distracting him from her tears. "Actually, Mr. Caton, there is no such fish."

"That's all right, Miz Lib. There ain't no social either." He met her eye, and when she answered his rascally grin, said, "There now, that's better. Where's Ike?"

"Over at the barn, doing chores."

Hascal propped a foot on the log and stretched out a leathery hand. "Go hep him. I'll hold yer stick."

Libby looked at him in surprise. "He doesn't need any help."

"I say he does. Now mind yer elders, gal."

"Mr. Caton . . ."

"Don't waste yer breath, arguin' at me. See what yer man's up to. Go on, git!"

He was a shameless old busybody. An enigma, too. Libby would have stood her ground except that she suddenly remembered where she and Ike had laid to rest their last argument over Mr. Gentry. She could sit here adding teardrops to an already-high creek, or she could take some initiative.

Libby laid the stick in Hascal's outstretched hand and ignored his chuckle as he broke it into bits. She stopped in the house long enough to splash cold water on her eyes, comb her hair, and touch a little lilac-scented cologne behind each ear before following the muddy road past the sirup camp to the barn.

The horses had been cared for, but Ike wasn't there. It grew dark while Libby waited. It wasn't long before she began to feel foolish for hoping to sweep the whole quarrel under the hay, so to speak. One thing was for sure; she wasn't accomplishing anything sitting on a bucket, letting the cold seep through her. She closed the barn up tight and started for home.

"Find him?"

Libby's heart nearly tore a hole in her chest as Hascal emerged from the shadows of the bridge. "Mr. Caton! I wish you wouldn't creep up on me like that!"

"Chorin', was he?"

Pride and uncertainty silenced her.

"Ain't back yet, eh?"

"Back from where?"

"From wherever he's at."

Libby wondered what Hascal knew that he wasn't telling. Somehow, she couldn't make herself ask.

Ike's feet were dragging by the time Laila led the way up the steps to her home. She led him to the parlor. Lamplight flung eerie shadows over furnishings crowded against one wall. "I apologize for the mess, but we've had a painter working. If you'll excuse me, I'll tell Edina you're here."

By painter, Ike thought at first that Laila meant a house painter until he saw the mural in progress on the opposite wall. It was a helter-skelter of dark ovals and shadows. Looking at it gave him a bad case of vertigo.

"Ike, this is my mother, Edina Stapleton," said Laila, when she had returned with her mother.

The older woman stood with the mural to her back. The poorly lit paths of paint made Ike think of the catacombed interior of a wasp nest. It suited Edina, with her lean frame and wings of dark hair and eyes like twin stingers. Hat in hand, Ike submitted to her scrutiny.

"So. We finally meet," she said.

"Hope I'm not intrudin', ma'am."

Edina's mouth curved, but there was no warmth to it. She asked, "What happened to your ear?"

"Flyin' scraps of metal."

"Then you've learned to duck," said Edina.

"That should serve you well," murmured Laila.

Edina gave an imperial wave of her hand. "Sit down, Mr. Galloway."

Ike separated a plain straight-backed chair from the garbled furniture, but was reluctant to sit and leave the women standing. He caught Laila watching him in the manner of a doctor taking a pulse.

Edina asked, "Are you joining us, Laila?"

"I'd like to, but Joy needs me. I bought her an orange at Skiff's Store, hoping to coax her into eating a bite." Meeting Ike's glance, Laila added, "Joy is my daughter. She's been ill."

"Nothin' serious, I hope."

"A slight respiratory complaint." Laila left the room, closing the door behind her.

Ike remained standing until Edina settled on a plush red velvet chair. Even sitting, she exuded an energy. It had no sound to it, yet in Ike's head he heard the deep drone of a circling wasp.

"You have Morgan's eyes," she observed. "He had more meat on his bones, though. And he was a womanizer. Are you a womanizer, Mr. Galloway?"

"I'm married."

"So was he. Irrelevant to him, but married nonetheless."

Ike resisted the urge to rub his throbbing temples. "I'm sorry."

Faint surprise gave way to a mirthless laugh. "What's this? You're not here to defend him?"

"No, ma'am."

"Why are you here? Curiosity?"

"Of a sort," Ike admitted. "Chester Gentry seemed to think you and I knew one another. That we had talked business of some kind. "

"Indeed." Edina crooked a single eyebrow.

Again, Ike found himself thinking of a wasp, moving

one wing as it kinked a leg. "Something about family land being deeded to you."

"Deeded to Laila, actually. Before she was born. Morgan tied it up in a trust which Laila couldn't touch until she turned twenty-five." Edina eyed him shrewdly and added, "I can assure you the terms were quite specific, if you are by chance thinking that you, as Morgan's son, are entitled to a share of it."

"I wasn't."

"Why are you here then?" she asked again.

"Just wonderin' what Chester's scared of."

His answer produced her first real smile. "I'm sure it's well-known to the locals by now. I've challenged Mr. Gentry over the legality of his having claimed for himself Rachel's full estate."

"Rachel Gentry?"

She nodded. "Morgan's widowed mother. Your grandmother. According to my information, she died just a day before Morgan." A calculating slant to her expression, she rebuked him, saying, "Come, Mr. Galloway. Surely you're at least dimly aware of your own family history."

"Can't see what that has to do with anything."

"Your grandmother died without a will. Her estate should have been divided equally between her sons. That has never piqued your interest?"

"Never gave it much thought," he said.

"Well, I have. Morgan was entitled to half, and his legal heir should have inherited his share."

If she thought she had something coming, why had she waited so long to claim it? Ike asked her as much. Edina said she hadn't realized there was a claim to be made until recently, that Morgan hadn't revealed much about his family.

"Yer sayin' you never met my father's family?"

"No, I didn't. Morgan was vacationing in the East when we met. We married in haste and repented of it almost as swiftly," said Edina, her tone caustic. "But with a child on the way, divorce was out of the question. Failing at that, Morgan made hasty and inadequate provisions for his unborn child, then left with a chambermaid.''

Ike knew that his mother, Nona Kay, had grown up on the Eastern seaboard and had worked in her youth as a maid at a coastal resort. ''Laila told me you tried to find him.''

''Yes, I did. But the wilds of Missouri is a long way to run a man down on a limited budget. I did learn that the woman he ran off with bore him two children, and that they were barely scraping by. After that, there seemed to be little point in pursuing him for financial support.''

''Chester wouldn't help you?''

''I told you, I didn't know Mr. Gentry or any of the rest of Morgan's family. Not until after Morgan's death. At that time, I was contacted by the bank regarding the trust. It was the first I knew of it, but Mr. Gentry had been paying a leasing fee to Morgan for the use of the land. After Morgan died, other arrangements were made so that the leasing fee came to us. I got in touch with Mr. Gentry, using information that the bank had held as confidential until that time. That was my first contact with Mr. Gentry.''

And now she was getting ready to sue him. Ike couldn't help thinking Chester had met his match.

Misunderstanding his silence, Edina said, ''Laila was deprived of a father. I won't see her deprived of her just inheritance as well. As I told your uncle, my present husband is a very successful Boston attorney. Mr. Gentry would do well to settle this matter between us without litigation.''

Gaze narrowing, she added, ''Should you consider taking similar action, I caution you against it, in light of the circumstances of your birth.''

It was the second time in a day Ike had been reminded

of his illegitimacy. He said evenly, "You give me too much credit, Mrs. Stapleton."

"Then we understand one another?"

"No, not really. Truth is, I don't understand you at all."

Crisply, she said, "I believe we've covered it, then. I'll see you to the door."

"No need," said Ike, stirring from his chair. "I'll find my own way."

Ike went over the conversation in his head as he started home. Edina had cleared up a couple of things: He knew now why his parents had never married. And he knew what had brought Chester to his door.

It wasn't nostalgia over sirup-making or Libby's invitation. Nor was it about healing a breech. Chester, like Edina, was nervous he was going to jump on the bandwagon and want a piece of the cake, too. That's why he'd waved Ketchum's farm before his eyes and reminded him his parents hadn't been married.

Ike could have saved Chester the trip. He'd make his own way, God willing. And he'd do it by the sweat of his brow, not in a courtroom. He'd go home, apologize to Lib for gettin' mad over nothin', and see if he couldn't sleep off whatever was making his head thunder and his stomach roll.

15

꧁ Libby had donned her night shift and was giving her hair one hundred strokes when she heard Ike step in on the summer porch. The wave of relief that went over her was almost physical. She waited a moment and when he didn't come in, laid her hairbrush aside and crossed to the door. She found him sitting in the dark, hunched forward with the washbasin between his knees. Concern pushed past the constraint of their quarrel and his long absence.

"Don't you feel good?"

"Must have a touch of something."

The edge was gone from his voice. There was wordless contrition in his eyes. Relieved, she let the damage go, as if it were a scorched pan she dared not stir. She felt his forehead, almost relieved for the valid touch, but it was a fleeting relief, for the heat of his brow dragged her back to that summer day at the creek when she'd found him delirious with fever.

"Have you been taking your quinine, Ike?" she asked, for Dr. Harding insisted regular doses would ward off more bouts of malaria.

"It's not malaria."

Libby prayed he was right. She had feared he would

die the last time he had it. He was sick twice before she could help him off with his boots. At length, he shed his clothes and crawled into bed. She bathed his face with a cool, wet rag. "I warned you to slow down and get some rest."

"Hush, Lib, and come to bed." He pushed the rag away. "If I'm worse in the mornin', you can fuss then."

There was no heat to his words, just weariness. Libby banked the fire and put out the lamp. By the time she crawled in beside him, he was chilled. Just like with malaria. Cycles of fever and chills. Firing anxious petitions to God, Libby put her arms around him, trying to warm him.

"Thought you was mad at me," he said after a moment.

"I am. I'm mad at you for not taking care of yourself."

"I meant about Chester. I was wrong, Lib. I'm sorry."

Hot tears pricked the back of her eyelids. He *must* be delirious. He often showed he was sorry, but he rarely said it. "I'm sorry, too. If I hadn't said anything in church, he wouldn't have stopped by."

The cornhusk mattress rustled as he rolled over to face her. "No, he'd of come anyway."

Puzzled, she said, "How do you know that?"

"I walked up to Stapletons' to see what I could find out about what Chester meant, tellin' me not to get caught up in this business of theirs."

That's where he'd been? Hascal must have seen him go. That would explain his curious remark about seeing what he was up to. Libby waited in silence for him to continue.

"Turns out Edina—that's the older one—was married to my father. She's reasonin' he stood to inherit half of his mother's estate. That'd be Rachel, my father's mother. I never knew her, but that's where Chester got some of the land he owns."

Morgan, Ike's father, and Chester had had the same mother, but different fathers. Ike's father, Libby knew, had been half-grown before Ike's grandmother married a wealthy bachelor and bore him a son, that son being Chester. Reading between the lines, she gathered Morgan had sown some wild seeds and left his family to harvest the consequences.

"Seems Rachel didn't leave a will," Ike went on. "My father died, so Chester got it all. That's what Edina says, anyway. She thinks she's got somethin' comin' to her. Or her daughter, at least."

"Her daughter?" echoed Libby. "You don't mean . . . ?"

"Yes, Lib. Seems that gal livin' up there with her is my half sister."

A half sister! And he hadn't even known! Libby digested the news in silence. Confused, she said, "But if this . . . this Edina was your father's first wife, how would she stand to inherit anything?"

"She was his only wife."

Ike felt Libby go still beside him. He gave her time to absorb the full meaning of his words, then told her about meeting Laila on the bridge and all that had transpired since. He came full circle, repeating Chester's remark concerning his mother. "Guess he must have been thinkin' a tenant farm was better'n I had any right to expect, considerin' my pedigree."

"Chester had no right to talk to you like that!" said Libby, her dander stirred. "No wonder you told him you didn't want the job."

"I told him before that. But he was pushin' me to change my mind."

"He was? Why?"

"Best I can figure, he was thinkin' if I was on his payroll, I'd be less likely to get ideas from Edina."

"You mean he's worried you'll sue him? Ike! You wouldn't do that."

"No, but he doesn't know that. Must be picturin'

heirs comin' out of the woodwork, eatin' away at his fortune.''

Libby was quiet. At length, she said, "It's too bad you had to find out this way. About your parents, I mean.''

"Not being married?" Finding it hard to get comfortable, Ike changed sides again. "I already knew.''

"You did?'' Libby raised up on one elbow.

"I figured it out when I was a boy. Somethin' Chester said.''

"How come you never told me?''

"It was b'fore you, and nothin' to do with you.''

Picking at the covers, she reasoned, "I told *you* about Abigail and Adam's trouble.''

"I'd pretty much figured it out anyway. A man doesn't let his wife go stay with relatives when she's in the family way. Not unless there's trouble.''

"You didn't let on to me that you knew.''

"Course I didn't. It wasn't any of my business. Same with my folks. We all make mistakes. If God can forgive and forget, why do we keep diggin' at our sins?''

His words didn't distract Libby from his admission that he had deliberately chosen not to tell her about his parents not being married. Had he worried she wouldn't understand? Unable to let it rest, she asked, "What did Chester say that gave it away? About your folks not being married, I mean?''

Ike was reluctant to speak of it. But he could see that his failure to tell her was what made it so difficult for her to make sense of his resentment toward Chester. "He said he'd warned my father when he left for Missouri not to expect any more help from him. Said that went for his whelps and his common-law wife, too.''

"Oh, Ike!'' she said, as if he had squeezed blood from an open wound. "That was heartless.'' She laid her face against his feverish back, and whispered, "How could he?''

Ike found her sympathy harder to take than anything

Chester had said. "It doesn't matter. It was a long time ago."

"Yes, it does matter, Ike. It matters to me."

Her cool hands moved over his hot skin. It wasn't the touch of a lover, rather a mothering caress, as if she'd like to reach back and comfort the boy he had been. Ike never had liked anyone feeling sorry for him. From the time his father had spoken his dying words to him, he'd known men looked after women, not the other way around. *Take care of your mother*. He'd failed more than he'd succeeded. Been a worry and a headache and a heartache to her more times than he could count. *Just as his father had been to his grandmother*. Rachel, whom Ike had never known and rarely thought about.

Ike didn't want to follow in his father's footsteps. After the war, when God had finally gotten through to him, he'd made amends to his mother. Now it was Libby that Ike feared he would fail. He couldn't tell her that. So he lay, letting her gentleness whisper through him, and after a while, he gave in to it and found that it wasn't so bad after all. Or maybe he was just too sick to care.

Libby lay awake long after Ike dropped off to sleep. *Common-law wife*. Those toneless words made all the difference in her ability to understand his long-standing grudge against Chester. Why *hadn't* he told her before? Was it his illegitimacy that had stopped him? Or had he feared the truth would prejudice her against what little family he had?

Uncertain, Libby resumed her preoccupation with Ike's fever, praying that he would awake feeling much better. Instead, when dawn came, Ike was worse. He slept fretfully throughout the day and couldn't eat. Even the liquids she coaxed him to drink came back up. He couldn't seem to get comfortable, and he'd developed a cough.

By the second day, Libby's relief that it wasn't malaria had turned to anxiety that Ike's sickness was just

as threatening. She continued bathing his aching head
with cold rags, rubbing a mixture of warm turpentine
and goose grease into his chest, spooning liquids past
his cracked lips. She left the cabin only long enough to
fetch wood, care for her three chickens, and do Ike's
barn chores.

Night came and Ike's fever escalated. Libby listened
to his labored breathing, to the twin oaks creak in the
yard and thought how, should one fall, there would be
no nightly lullaby. She pleaded with God with heart-
borne fears.

God's thought-borne reply asked her to consider her
up-and-down faith. It was so clear and startling an impression that she couldn't shake it off. Each time she
returned to Him in concern for Ike, it was there.

Yet Ike did get better. By the next morning, his fever
had broken. Libby felt a rush of relief that was in itself
a prayer of gratitude. But it didn't settle God's unsettling
question concerning her faith, a comfortable faith in
which she had felt secure.

Ike rolled out of bed. His head was dull, and his legs
were weak. He spent the morning oiling his boots and
making sirup spiles, and when he tired of that, pored
over his sirup ledgers and equipment catalog.

In the afternoon, he went outside and hauled some
firewood from the woodshed to the front porch. He was
tired by the time he came in, but the weakness was gone.
After supper, he closed Libby's chickens in for the night
and went to the barn to do his chores.

It was dark by the time he got back. The cabin was
steamy with Libby's bathwater heating. Her practiced
gaze moved over him in silence. She must have been
satisfied with what she saw. For the first time in four
days, she didn't try to feel his brow or rub grease into
his chest.

"So how are the horses?"

"Survivin' nicely," he countered.

"Told you." She poked gentle fun at him for doubting she could fill his shoes for a few days.

He hung up his hat, and said, "Come here."

She came. But she soon squirmed out of his embrace and took her bath, then warmed the leftover water for him with water from the stove. They kept up a running conversation from separate sides of the muslin screen while he bathed.

"Naomi's in the family way," Libby told him.

"That so? I'll be!"

"She hasn't told Decatur, so don't say anything."

It wouldn't have occurred to him. "I'm goin' to have to move the horses out of Miss Maudie's barn soon."

"Where will you put them?"

"Decatur's said I'm welcome to use his back pasture, if I don't mind fencin' it in. Goin' to have to get a barn up by winter, though."

"Did I tell you Abigail's expecting, too?"

"Yesterday," he said, and went back to his barn-planning. "I figur' a thousand board feet of lumber's the least I can get by on."

"She says Adam's hoping for a boy this time."

"I know. Ya read her letter to me. I talked to the fellas at the sawmill last week, and they've agreed to trade logs for cured lumber."

"Little Annie won't be much over a year when the baby comes."

"Means sawing about twice the trees I'll need to pay 'em. Goin' to be a job."

She was quiet a minute, then asked, "Ike? Do you ever wonder if we're thwarting a blessing? By being so careful, I mean. About . . . well, you know."

Abruptly, he quit thinking in board feet. All afternoon, he'd been watching her flit about her household chores, smelling like chicken soup and laundry starch and that lilac scent that clung to her. But he'd parked his yearning and let it sit, for he'd done the numbers and he knew it wasn't risk-free now. Toweling himself off, he said, "Thought we'd been over this b'fore."

"I know. I'm just saying it seems inconsistent to trust God with some things and not others."

Like babies. Ike stepped around the screen to point out that God had given man the ability to think and plan and that to do so wasn't a lack of trust at all, so long as those plans were committed to Him. What were those qualifying words in James? *If the Lord will, we shall live and do this, or that.* But the words got stuck in his throat.

Her skin glowed the way it always did when she got out of the tub and warmed herself by the fire. She sat with one leg tucked beneath her, her arm making a graceful curve as she brushed her hair. Like waves of spun copper, it whispered over the tucks and tatting and pink ribbon tie of her hand-stitched night shift, sparking to the hairbrush, shaping and reshaping itself to her contours with each pass of the brush.

"Ready?" she said, one bare foot reaching for the floor.

Even that tiny, white high-arched foot was beguiling. Ike nodded and banked the fire and thoughtlessly put out the lamp before she reached the bed. There was no moon shining through the window to light their way. He heard her feeling her way along and moved blindly toward her.

"That's my foot," she protested.

"This must be the rest of ya, then," he said, as they found each other in the darkness.

He surprised a girlish laugh out of her as his arms closed around her. He loved that laugh. Everything about her was provocative and endearing, filling him with sharp regret for all the times his desire for her and hers for him had been thwarted by his determination to be responsible, to be safe. He tucked her closer to his heart and kissed her and said against her hair, "You're wishin' it was you, instead of Naomi and Abigail, aren't ya, Lib?"

"I didn't say that.'

"You'll make a good mother someday. Makes me feel bad about makin' you wait."

She kissed him back, once, twice, and then again. "It's all right."

"No, it's not. I married you too soon. If I hadn't been in such a hurry, I'd of used my head and planned things better."

Startled, she put her fingers over his mouth. "Don't say that. I'm not sorry. Not for one minute have I ever been sorry. You aren't, are you, Ike?"

The pang in her voice made him wish he hadn't told her what he himself had thought so often. Womanlike, she misunderstood. She led with her heart, he with his head. That wasn't likely to change. But maybe it wasn't a bad thing. Maybe God planned it that way. It drew them both to the middle.

"*Are* you?" she whispered again.

His restraint, tenuous at best, melted away. For once, he didn't let the numbers rule. He romanced the hurt from her voice, knowing as he did so that he was putting to the test the theory Doc said was nothing but an old wives' tale.

16

It was the sound of Ike's feet hitting the floor that awakened Libby in the gray morning light. Fearing he was sick again, she sat up and flung the covers back. "Ike? What's the matter?"

"Somethin's after yer chickens."

He jerked on his trousers, shoved his feet into his boots, and bolted out the back door. Libby leapt up and ran out after him just as two boys shot across the pasture. The bigger of the two boys had a chicken by the legs. It hung upside down from the boy's scrawny hand, its neck limp as a noodle.

"Why, they've killed one of my hens!"

The smaller of the two humped along with an awkward gait. Looking back, seeing Ike overtaking him, the boy shouted, "Run, Purdy, run!"

The trailing boy tripped, tumbled end over end, slammed into the privy, and howled like he'd been murdered. Ike sailed by him, intent on catching the boy with the chicken. But Libby, seeing the fallen boy cradle his arm, jerked her night shift up to her knees and raced across the pasture. The arm looked as lifeless as her poor chicken.

"Ike! I think he's hurt!"

The alarm in her voice brought Ike around. He retraced his steps, leaving the second boy to escape along the wooded creek bank. The first boy screeched and scooted backward on his bottom as Ike hunkered down beside him.

"Easy, we're just trying to help," said Libby.

"Hurts. Hurts bad," cried the boy, protecting his arm.

"That's enough, now," said Ike. "Hold still and let me have a look."

The arm was limp, and seemed to dangle uselessly. Libby shuddered involuntarily and clutched Ike's shoulder. "You'd better get Dr. Harding."

"Doctor?" the boy yelped. "No doctor for me, no sir."

Ike's narrowed gaze shifted from concern to suspicion to something harder to read. "What's yer name, son?"

"Dumplin Field."

"Where's yer folks?"

"Don't have any."

Remembering where she had heard the name, Libby leaned closer to Ike and whispered, "He does *too* have parents. Or at least a father. Opal said he was a painter."

"Opal? She knows these boys?"

"One of them ate her lunch, remember?"

Ike picked up the boy's cap, brushed the mud off of it, and handed it back to him. "Where do ya live, Dumplin?"

Dumplin hugged his arm and bunched up his face, moody with silent determination. His freckles stood out like smudges of mud.

"We're only trying to help," coaxed Libby. "Where do you live?"

"No place."

"All right, then. Jest lie there," said Ike. He got to his feet. "Come on, Lib. Yer shiverin'. Let's go in."

"Ike!" Libby protested. She hurried to keep up as he strode toward the cabin. "You can't leave him lying on the wet ground with a broken arm."

"His arm ain't broke. He's playing decoy while Opal's admirer makes off with yer chicken."

Libby shot a glance back over her shoulder. She saw the boy leap to his feet and tear away, chortling as he went. There was a ring of victory in his gurgling laughter that ignited her temper. "Why, the little fiend!"

"Forget it." Ike caught her hand to keep her from going after him.

"Wringing my hen's neck before she could lay a single egg!" Libby fumed as Ike tugged her toward the house. Humiliated over being bamboozled, she jerked off her dirty slippers just inside the door and huffed, "He ought to be a stage actor. I'd have sworn his arm was broken."

"Withered, I'm guessin'. Probably been that way from birth."

"Withered?" Libby felt a heart pang crowd over her indignation. She paused, swung around, and looked out the door again. "Still, that's no excuse for stealing. I would have fed them if I'd known they were hungry."

"So do you want to whup 'em or coddle 'em?"

Peeved, she said, "Everything is always so black-and-white to you, isn't it?"

"Includin' the chicken." He grinned.

"You're so clever, I'll let you break it to Opal that Purdy, who admires her so, is nothing but a poultry thief."

Ike crossed to the stove to get out of her line of fire, but she came after him, saying, "I'll do it."

"Just tryin' to help."

"Uh-huh," she said. "Move."

Ike emptied the ash pan for her, then left to do chores. She was dressed with breakfast waiting when he returned, wanting to know, as they sat down to eat, if a chicken coop could be locked up. He interpreted the question as a nudge.

"I haven't forgot it, Lib. Though I'd just as soon

Purdy and Dumplin took the other two off yer hands and saved me the trouble.''

"Reward them for stealing?" She sniffed. "That would be just the thing for their characters.''

"So what're you going to do?''

"I don't know yet. It depends on what kind of parents they have." Seeing him swallow a grin, she defended, "All I'm saying is, I'd like to know a little something about their situation. If their father is indeed a house painter, as Opal said, it looks as if he ought to be able to feed his family. On the other hand—''

"I don't think it's houses he paints," Ike inserted. He told her about the mural in progress at the Stapletons' house.

"You mean he's an *artist*?" Libby lathered a biscuit in butter. "There can't be much call for that in these parts. Maybe the boys really are hungry.''

"If that's it, their father better find himself a more profitable trade. Though it'd be my guess those boys are a handful, even when their bellies are full.''

Libby shrugged and dropped it, but Ike saw that problem-tackling look come over her face and knew he hadn't heard the last of it. He relished the last bite of potatoes and eggs, his thoughts shifting to barn-building. "What've ya got planned this mornin', Lib?''

"I'm going to bake bread and fill the cookie jar. Why?''

"Thought I'd go to the timber, spot a few trees to fell. But I can put it off a spell if ya want to go with me later.''

"I'd like that.''

"Guess I *could* work on that chicken coop this morning.''

She ignored the reluctance in his voice, and asked, "More coffee?''

He smothered a smile behind the rim of his cup and downed a few bitter grounds with the last swig. "No, thanks. Think I'll see what they're doin' down there by creek, b'fore I git started buildin'."

"The creek?" Libby carried their plates to the sink and looked out the south window. A group of men were milling between the back pasture and the railroad tracks, not far from the creek. "Is that where they're putting in the water tank for the C & A?"

"Nope. Told ya, the tank goes just east of the house. They might be gettin' ready to dig the well, though."

Moments later, Libby kissed him out the door and reached for her wooden bread trough. She put a pie together from canned fruit while the bread dough was rising, mixed up some cookie batter, punched down the dough, shaped it into loaves and let it rise again, all the while wondering over the circumstances of the boys who had raided her makeshift chicken house.

By the time her baking was done, the morning was spent and Ike was still at the south end of the pasture. He was deep in conversation with a stout man in a dark suit and derby. Libby didn't know when he'd appeared on the scene, but she didn't recall seeing him there earlier.

Turning her attention to lunch, Libby heated soup left over from the previous day. She was slicing bread, still warm from the oven, when Ike came in the back door. The gentleman in the suit was with him. Libby recognized him now. It was the gentleman they had met at Verna's several Sundays ago.

"Lib, you remember Mr. Elliot, don't you?"

"Yes, of course." Libby shed her soiled apron and offered her hand. "How nice to see you again, Mr. Elliot."

"Delighted, Mrs. Galloway." Near in age to Libby's father, Mr. Elliot bowed over her hand, a gesture so natural to him, it didn't seem the least out of place in their rustic cabin. "Your husband didn't tell you he'd invited me to lunch. I hope you don't mind."

"No, of course not. In fact, I was about to invite you myself."

"Thank you for your kindness," he said, his smile as courtly as his bow. "The camp train was supposed to be here by now, but there's an engine stalled on the line, and it can't get through. Perhaps that was a blessing in disguise. I don't know what you're cooking, but it smells delicious."

It wasn't the lunch Libby would have fixed had she known the engineer in charge of the entire C & A project would be dining with them. But Mr. Elliot was a gracious guest and a good conversationalist, talking at length about the ongoing C & A project aimed at leveling the road for swifter, more efficient railroad travel. His words concerning the cuts and fills underway just south of them brought to mind Biblical words about making a highway for God.

" 'Every valley shall be exalted, and every mountain and hill shall be made low: and the crooked shall be made straight, and the rough places plain,' " quoted Libby.

"Why, Mrs. Galloway!" said Mr. Elliot. "You've captured it exactly. Isaiah, isn't it?"

Ike pushed his plate back, and warned, "Be careful about gettin' her started. She came near to winnin' a memory verse contest a couple of summers ago."

"Ike, that isn't so. I came nowhere close to winning," protested Libby. But as she rose to clear the table, her mouth curved at the memory of that long-ago box social. Though she had attended the event with Angus Cearlock, Ike had shared her lunch that day, and she had thereafter been aware of him in a way that surpassed mere friendship.

Libby snapped out of her reverie as Mr. Elliot used her table to spread papers detailing the plan for the water system that was under way. She listened from the sink with mounting curiosity and expectation as Ike asked questions about the well, the steam-powered pump and underground piping which would carry the water uphill to the water tank that the crew would be building.

"That sounds like my train," said Mr. Elliot, at the sound of a distant whistle. "Is there anything else before I go?"

"No, sir. I think we've covered it," said Ike.

"The men are Hungarians, recruited fresh off the docks back East. They haven't been in the country long enough to know the language, and communication is tricky. But I pride myself in being a good judge of character, and I think that overall, they are decent men. You get them to give you a good day's work for a good day's pay, do your job, and we'll get along just fine."

"I'll do my best," said Ike.

"I'm sure you will." Mr. Elliot clapped him on the shoulder and said in parting, "I'll check back with you in the morning. Mrs. Galloway, thank you again for the lovely meal."

"It was a pleasure. I hope you'll come again, Mr. Elliot."

The door had hardly closed behind him when Ike grinned broadly. "Looks like I've got a job right out the back door."

"So he *did* hire you!" Libby had been all but certain, judging by the conversation.

"Keep me busy for a while, anyway. I'll be overseeing getting the water system up and runnin'."

"You mean he put you in charge? Ike!" Her eyes widened. "What happened?"

"The foreman couldn't make the men understand him. Mr. Elliot came along, overheard him talkin' rough and makin' threats. He fired him on the spot."

"Good for him! I could tell he was a fine man." Heady with the feeling of being looked after by God Himself, Libby added, "And a good judge of character, by his own admission!"

Ike tugged at her hair as she flung her arms around him. "Didn't I tell ya to look for the blessin'?"

"From looking *for* to looking *at!* Aren't you excited? We should celebrate!"

"Good idea. Cook up those chickens."

"Ike!" she protested.

He laughed and patted her on the bottom as he broke the embrace. "I've got to get back. How about slicing up some of that bread and somethin' to go with it? Those men haven't had any lunch, and they won't be gettin' any until the camp train comes along."

Libby agreed to wave her apron from the door when it was ready, freeing him to go on his way. She sliced cheese that Naomi had brought to her a few days earlier and made sandwiches of her fresh-baked bread, then took the lid off the cookie jar in open invitation. When the coffee was ready, she gave the signal.

The men washed at the back pump, but were reluctant to enter the house. They stood at the edge of the yard, a tidy group dressed in dark trousers and white shirts. One even wore a string tie. Libby suspected it was her presence accounting for their unease. She suggested to Ike that it might be a good time for her to take some cookies and call on the Stapletons.

Ike had noticed how the men kept their heads down in Libby's presence, careful not even to look at her. If the foreman that Mr. Elliot had fired was any measure of it, these men had faced enough discrimination, suspicion, and hostility in their short stint in America to make them cautious.

He warned her, saying, "Ya may not get much of a welcome from Edina. But Laila's agreeable enough."

Libby slipped into her coat, pinned on her hat, and left by the back door so the men would understand she was leaving. The past week had been dry and the road was starting to settle some. Just as Libby turned up the north road, Dr. Harding and Mrs. Brignadello came along in the doctor's buggy.

"Libby! We were thinking of stopping by your

cabin," called Mrs. Bee, motioning her brother to halt the buggy. "Naomi said Ike was sick."

"He was, but he's fine now," Libby assured her.

Dr. Harding was a pragmatic fellow. Upon learning of Libby's errand, he urged her to postpone her visit, as Edina Stapleton was not feeling well.

"We're on our way there right now," said Mrs. Bee. She turned to her brother, and added, "Though I'd dearly love to stay and visit with Libby. Can you get along without me, Melville?"

Dr. Harding assured her he could, and at Libby's request, agreed to deliver her cookies and pass along to Edina Stapleton her wishes for a speedy recovery.

Libby explained about the railroad laborers at the house, and suggested they allow the men to finish their meal before returning to the house. Mrs. Bee nodded her understanding and remarked over the beauty of a few early wildflowers as she accompanied Libby to the bench in front of the sap house. They moved the bench into the sunshine. Mrs. Bee gave a halfhearted summary of the news from town as they settled side by side.

Wondering what had happened to subdue her usual animated, bustling, busybody friend, Libby ventured, "You look tired, Mrs. Bee. Has the doctor been keeping you on the run?"

"We've been busy, thanks to this recent wave of influenza," Mrs. Bee conceded. "Naomi wanted us to stop and see her father while we're out this way. He's been down with it since Friday."

"I didn't know," said Libby. With Ike sick, she'd seen nothing of Naomi or the children, her best source of information.

"Ida has it, too," said Mrs. Bee. "We just came from there. Of course that's the least of her troubles. Had you heard?"

"Heard what?" asked Libby.

Mrs. Bee's eyes misted as she told Libby that a surgeon in St. Louis had removed a cancerous growth from the base of her sister's neck almost two weeks ago.

"I'm so sorry," said Libby, stricken with concern for both Ida and Chester Gentry. "I had no idea."

"Chester's tried to keep it quiet. Helpless isn't something he's used to feeling. I don't think he knows how to cope."

"It must be difficult for all of you," Libby commiserated.

Her words of sympathy opened the floodgates. Libby put her arms around Mrs. Bee and listened to her tearful account of her sister's dismal prognosis. Fighting to regain her composure, Mrs. Bee dabbed at her eyes, and confessed, "I feel so inadequate, Libby. I want to do something for her, but there's nothing I can do. Nothing that really counts."

"I'm sure she draws comfort just from your presence," murmured Libby.

"I hope so," said Mrs. Bee. Her sister lived a mile out of town on a lovely country estate they called Erstwood. "I'm going to try and make it out to see her more often, now that the roads are drying. I thought I'd make her a yellow bed jacket. She's always loved yellow."

"I'm sure she'd like that," said Libby. She had never met a better seamstress than Mrs. Bee.

When the men had had adequate time to eat and return to work, Libby urged Mrs. Bee home with her. She made tea, joined her at the table, and pushed the cookie jar her way.

Mrs. Bee helped herself to a sugar cookie. Her eyes lingered on the rose cookie jar, but her thoughts were of her sister. "Ida used to have a jar like this. It was Chester's mother's," she said as she sugared her tea.

The revelation gave Libby a jolt because of the mysterious nature by which the jar had come to them. However, it seemed so unlikely that Ida would have been the gift giver, she reasoned away the evidence, saying, "It's a common design, I suppose."

Mrs. Bee nodded agreement. "Kersey stocks similar jars in his wagon. They've always been popular with farm families. And speaking of Kersey, tell Ike he needs more sirup. It's sold very well on his route."

"It has? That's wonderful," said Libby.

"Let's see. Where was I?" said Mrs. Bee, tapping a finger against her chin. "Oh, yes. The cookie jar. Ida tried to give it to Catherine, but Catherine didn't want it. She's accustomed to such lovely things. Not that this isn't lovely, too," Mrs. Bee hastily amended.

"It was a wedding present. I've always admired it."

"It is pretty. I'll have to ask Ida what she did with hers. If she remembers."

Libby's heart turned at Mrs. Bee's clouded expression. She had mentioned earlier that the growth was at the base of her neck. "Her memory has been affected by her illness?"

"Chloe thinks she gets things a little mixed up sometimes, and Chloe should know. She waits on her hand and foot. Chester scolded Chloe for suggesting it, but I suspect he's just denying what he can't yet face." Eyes glistening, she added, "The man has his faults, but he's always been devoted to Ida. Even when we were children, he was tender with her. It broke his heart when she married Mr. Cearlock. Mr. Cearlock was a bachelor, quite a bit older than Ida and well-to-do. But they had a good marriage. Ida was devastated when she lost him. There she was with a broken heart and two small children to raise alone."

A faint smile came like watery sunlight. "Chester was patient, giving Ida ample time to grieve, so patient, in fact, he nearly let some other fellows get the jump on him. But I declare, you never saw a happier man than he when Ida finally consented to marry him. Chester's been a good father to Ida's children, too."

Libby knew that was true. In her brief courtship with Angus, he had spoken well of his stepfather, as did his sister, Catherine.

"With Catherine in St. Louis, and expecting another child, and Angus so busy with his law practice, I'm afraid they won't be able to spend as much time with their mother as they might like. I hope Ida's friends don't fail her."

"Oh, Mrs. Bee! Surely they won't."

"People mean well, Libby, but they have their own lives to lead." Mrs. Bee toyed with the cookie-jar lid, as if seizing what lay at hand to distract herself from what lay ahead. Libby saw her finger pause over the small chip.

"Ida's had a nick, too. There must be a weakness in the way they're seamed together," said Mrs. Bee. She returned the lid to the jar, unaware she had solved a riddle Libby had puzzled over every time she filled the jar.

17

There was less than an hour of daylight left by the time the camp train came along and the men quit for the day. Ike took Libby to the woods with him to select the trees for his barn-building project. Libby related how her planned visit with the Stapletons had been postponed, because of Edina's bout with influenza.

"Seems to go around about this time every year," remarked Ike.

"Mrs. Bee says Hascal's caught it, too," said Libby.

"That explains why he hasn't come to see what we were doin' there by the tracks."

The leaves were starting to come out. The trees had a ferny green freshness about them that would soon deepen in tone as the leaves uncurled and spread and blocked out the sky. Wildflowers were lifting showy faces to the sun. The yellow violets brought Ida more sharply to mind. The violet hue of her eyes. Her preference for yellow. Yellow gowns, yellow slippers, yellow fans, and ear bobs. *If the cookie jar had been a yellow rose instead of a pink one, would she still have parted with it?*

Why had she made a gift of it? Did Mr. Gentry know? Libby felt certain he didn't. That Ida hadn't signed the card indicated she hadn't confided in Mr. Gentry before making the gift. A thank-you note, had it fallen into his hands, would have given her away.

"Hey, pokey. Are ya comin' or not?" Ike turned back and found Libby trailing behind him. The gaiety of her fistful of violets was at odds with her woebegone expression. He stopped short. "Lib? What's the matter?"

Tears blurred Libby's eyes as she told him of Ida's tumor and how Mrs. Bee had cried when she imparted the news. "I thought the last time I saw Ida that she looked tired. But I had no idea it was something so serious."

Ike remembered the flash of pain he had glimpsed in Chester's eyes five days earlier. Belatedly, he understood it. "Hate to see anybody have that kind of trouble."

His tone echoed, *Even Chester*. Libby should have known him better than to fear it might be otherwise. She went on to tell him about the cookie jar, and how Mrs. Bee had innocently unraveled the mystery of that anonymously given gift. "I wonder what made her do that?"

Resisting the idea, Ike said, "You sure it was Ida?"

"Who else would it be? Certainly not Chester. Catherine was in St. Louis. She sent a gift by post. Angus and Maddie gave us a linen tablecloth. Anyway, if Maddie'd had anything to do with it, she would have given it outright."

"Must have been Ida, then. But I sure can't think why she'd want to."

Neither could Libby.

"Ought to give it back," said Ike.

"You will not! It would hurt her feelings. Anyway, it's mine now, and I'm keeping it."

Sometimes Ike didn't know what to make of her. Near tears one minute, ready to fuss over a cookie jar the next. All he meant to say was that if the jar had belonged to Chester's mother, then it was Chester's, and not Ida's to give.

Still, he preferred sparks to tears. He'd seen his mother cry only twice in his life, once when his father died and again, as they left Chester's house that long-ago day. He hadn't known then and didn't know now what to do with a woman's tears. Even yet, he felt a lingering disquiet that there was something else wrong with Lib. Something she wasn't telling him. He asked, "You sure yer all right?"

Quietly, she said, "I want to go see her, Ike."

"Aw, Lib. What good'll that do?"

Seeing the inflexible shape of his mouth, Libby tucked her chin to hide another sting of tears. "This has nothing to do with you and Chester. Ida's ill, and she needs to know people care."

"Send her a card, then. If she's that sick, she probably ain't up to much company anyway."

Libby heeded an inner Voice and resisted the urge to press. The cushion of molding leaves hushed their footsteps as they walked along.

Ike felt the weight of Libby's silence. It sat there like unfinished business while he struggled with his pride. There was one thing he'd credit Chester with, and that was his devotion to Ida. Chester would either put his own feelings aside and accept Lib's gesture for what it was, or he would react like a wounded bear guarding a cub. Ike figured his inhospitable reception of Chester five days ago would tip the scales against Libby. Then there were the Stapletons' antics stirring Chester into a stew of mistrust.

God, I hate seein' her go to Gentry's door. Hate riskin' havin' her slighted by him. Though maybe that's what it would take for her to understand that all things were never equal. Not even in sickness. Not with people like Chester Gentry.

At length, he said without looking at her, "Have to wait till the roads settle a bit. No point in makin' the horses drag through the mud."

Libby knew that the road was clear enough. Dr. Harding and Mrs. Bee had had no trouble getting through. But if Ike needed time to get used to the idea, she wouldn't jostle him.

In the days that followed, April spilled a few showers, but kept an overall sunny disposition. Libby soon had a bit of garden turned and a few early root crops in the ground. By the time her onions were showing green whiskers against the rich black soil, Ike's men were making good progress in getting their well-digging, pipe-laying, water-tower building project under way.

Youth was the main common denominator among the men. They were overcoming their shyness of Libby, yet remained polite and respectful, doffing their hats as she approached every afternoon with sandwiches or baked treats. They thanked her in foreign words and universally understood smiles. But mostly, Libby's knowledge of them was based on Ike's shared impressions of the men.

Nick Seredy, a short, stocky fellow with the bushy hair and brows and whiskers that seemed from a distance to all run together, was the only married one in the bunch. His wife cooked and did laundry for the men. Saul Semmelweis, a princely curly-haired man full of laughter and music, was so fussy about his grooming, he carried a comb along with his pocket tools. Fritz Nikisch, with his broad nose and flat face, was as animated as his brother Joseph was stoic and silent. Arthur Reiner had a need to talk, and was beginning to do so in a pigeon English spattered with grammatical glitches that traced themselves back to Ike like a lead rope. Last of all was Hans Liszt, a nearsighted fellow who communicated so well with gestures that he was the official interpreter whenever there was confusion to iron out.

They were a varied group. Ike praised them when they did well and was patient with their mistakes. Soon, they were teaching him words in their native tongue. Sometimes, Ike had an idea they weren't being honest with him about the meaning of the phrases. There couldn't be anything that side-splittingly funny about "Quittin' time," "Train's coming," or "Fetch a hammer."

One afternoon, Libby stepped out the door about dusk to hear a cheer go up. She walked down to the creek to find the men having a log-rolling contest in the creek, Ike in the midst of them. Another day, they'd strung a rope from a tall branch and were timing one another to see who could climb it the fastest. Decatur was with them that day. Libby wasn't sure yet that it wasn't him who'd greased the rope before Ike took a turn. Whoever was responsible, the whole bunch of them hooted and hollered when Ike got about four feet off the ground, hit the greased spot on the rope, and slid back down to the ground, just like hitting a patching of ice on a board-walk.

There was something wholesome and heartening about seeing the boy come out in each of them. Ike's haggard look, come of sickness heaped upon the compressed labor of sirup season, soon lifted. He was Ike again, revitalized and tireless.

Grateful for the camaraderie that had sprung up among the men, making Ike's job easier, Libby gave impromptu English lessons with her afternoon snacks and expanded on them in the evening as Arthur, Fritz, and monosyllabic Joseph helped Ike fence in the back pasture for the horses and close a small area off for her chickens.

The days trickled past. Ike moved the team from the barn, as well as the wagon, his tools, and some sirup equipment he'd stored there. He put what he could in the sap house. He emptied the woodshed of everything but Lib's chickens and divided what was left between the woodshed and another small shed behind the cabin, managing at length to get everything but the wagon under cover.

*   *   *

Laila Stapleton and her daughter Joy returned Libby's cookie tin one cheerless cloudy afternoon. Libby thought her striking, with hair the color of white-clover honey, a dimpled chin, and eyes the same shape and shade as Ike's. She looked down to greet Joy, and saw those eyes repeated. It startled a laugh from her.

"My! How did I miss that before? You have Ike's eyes!"

"And here I thought they were mine," said Laila.

Admiring the New England correctness of her speech, Libby said, "I've been anxious to meet you. But first it was sirup season, and then when I finally started up that way, Dr. Harding turned me back. How is your mother feeling?"

A muscle quirked at the corner of Laila's mouth. "Well enough to be giving the painter grief. He's not the most dependable of fellows."

"Would that be Mr. Field?" asked Libby.

"You know Lafayette Field?"

"No. But I've met the boys." Libby told Laila the circumstances. The story drew Joy's attention to the two chickens pecking in the dirt just beyond the summer porch. The little girl slipped out to investigate.

"Boys that far out of hand at seven and eight ought to be a real nuisance by the time they reach adolescence," said Laila. Her mouth curved in a mirthless smile. "Edina's threatened them with dire consequences should she catch them stealing potatoes from the cellar again."

"I understand they have some sisters."

"Yes. The older two come to the house to play with Joy sometimes. They're pretty girls. They nearly do justice to their names." Laila crooked an eyebrow and said, "Pretty Good and Very Fine. Imagine, giving children such names!"

Libby blinked, then smiled at the realization she'd mistaken their names for descriptions when Frankie had first mentioned the girls. Tactfully, she said, "It's a bit unusual."

"For anyone but milksop Sadie, it would be." Laila held her arms as if cradling a baby. "Papa, what shall we name this Purdy boy, dis whittle dumplin? She's a pretty good baby. Yes, she's very fine! Two of them, Papa. Mama's puddin' and punkin'."

"There's more?"

"Oh yes! And another one on the way, judging by Sadie's girth." Eyes sparking, Laila concluded, "Lafayette fancies himself to be quite the talent. I don't pretend to be a patron of the arts, so I'll not be overly critical of the man's abilities. However, I will say this: if he and Sadie are going to procreate like field mice, he ought to sacrifice his art for his family and she ought to let someone rename those children!"

"I suppose they do get teased," said Libby, thinking of Dumplin and his withered arm.

"I'm sure they do. Which accounts for the boys' being such a handful," said Laila carelessly. "The girls are tame by comparison. I suppose they take after their mother. If Sadie were a clock, it'd take a good shake to get her ticking again."

"It can't be easy, traveling around in a home on wheels with all those children to care for."

"Depending on the kindness of strangers, that's what it amounts to," said Laila. Her mouth winked in that now familiar corner quirk. "Edina had no idea, when they parked their wagon down along our bend in the creek and let Lafayette talk her into a parlor mural, that he would make it his lifetime work. But once into a thing, Edina never backs out of it."

Libby wondered if that applied to her threatened lawsuit against Mr. Gentry as well. Thinking it a subject best left alone, she made tea and took it back out to the summer porch, where Laila could keep a watchful eye on her daughter.

Laila eventually brought the conversation around to

Ike. In a direct fashion that Libby found discomfiting, she asked, "You say Ike's working for the railroad? Who is farming his ground?"

Libby explained that the ground that Ike had previously farmed was no longer at his disposal. Laila followed up with a question about the timbered acres Ike owned, and the sirup camp, which she assumed had been left to him by Morgan Galloway. Libby corrected her assumption, explaining it was her mother's uncle, Willie Blue, not Morgan, who had left the piece of timber to Ike.

"And your home?"

"It belongs to our friends, the McClures."

At length, Laila admitted, "I guess I had the impression that Ike and his sister were the favored ones. But Father doesn't seem to have done so well by them either."

It was on the tip of Libby's tongue to point out that Morgan Galloway had tried to make a life for his family on a Missouri homestead. But she curbed the words, uncertain why she would feel the need to defend a man she knew so little about. Or that Ike would even want her to.

Opal and Frankie stopped by after school. They acknowledged Libby's introduction of Laila and went on into the house. Soon thereafter, Laila came to her feet and thanked Libby for the tea.

Libby mentioned Sunday services at Timber Creek. Laila showed some interest, but confessed she was uncertain what her reception would be. Libby remembered Naomi speculating that the Stapletons were wary of rejection by the community owing to their battle with Mr. Gentry. Admittedly, Libby felt tugged both ways, particularly with Ida so ill. Nonetheless, she invited Laila and Joy to ride along with them on Sunday.

But Sunday came and there was no sign of them at the hour Libby had told her they would be leaving.

Three of Ike's crew went along with them, long legs swinging from the back of the wagon.

Laila and Joy came in late, the mud on their shoes indicative of how they had traveled. They slipped in beside Libby, filling in the only remaining gap in the pew. Libby smiled a welcome and shared her hymn book. Laila had a clear sweet voice that captured Saul's ear. Or perhaps it was her striking appearance that drew his eye. Standing to the right of Ike, Saul leaned forward and looked past Ike and Libby once, twice, and then again, stealing peeks at Laila.

For the third week in a row, Pastor Shaw reminded his flock of Ida Gentry's continued need for prayer. He also mentioned the terrible earthquake that had taken place in San Francisco. It was the first Libby had heard of the deadly quake and the resulting fires that burned out of control, adding to the heavy loss of life.

After services, Arthur, Joseph, and Saul put their heads together for a moment. The next Libby saw of them, Arthur and Joseph had set off on foot through the woods. But Saul was waiting by the wagon. He gave Laila a hand up while, from the other side, Ike handed Libby onto the seat.

Joy rode in the back with Saul. Judging by her giggles, she was finding him entertaining. Apparently the procedure of making inroads with a woman through her child wasn't singular to American men. Though in Laila's case, she was busy questioning Libby about Ida Gentry's illness, and seemed not to notice her daughter's captivation with the curly-haired Saul.

"I had no idea," said Laila when Libby had told her the nature of Ida's illness. "How serious is it?"

"Her chances of recovery don't look good," murmured Libby.

"Lib's going to call on her soon," said Ike.

That he should bring it up surprised Libby. His glance betrayed little. Feeling off-balance, she said, "Yes, I am." She caught her breath and added, "You'd be welcome to come with me, Laila."

"Thank you, but no," said Laila quickly.

Libby shot Ike a seeking glance and was relieved to find approval. *That's what he'd wanted her to say. Why?* Baffled, she murmured, "Perhaps another time, then."

Laila looked past Libby and targeted Ike for one of her blunt questions: "Edina got the impression there was a rift between you and the Gentrys. What exactly *is* your relationship with them?"

"Chester's mother was my grandmother, same as you," said Ike.

It wasn't what Laila had meant at all. But apparently she knew a closed book when she saw one. She pursued it no further.

A short while later, Ike stopped the team in front of the cabin. Libby invited Laila and Joy to stay for lunch. Joy seemed eager, but Laila declined. Ike offered to drive her home. She seemed about to refuse when she glanced toward the back of the wagon. "Let Saul here do it. Edina should enjoy that."

"Ya won't let her abuse him, will ya?" said Ike.

Startled, Libby murmured, "Ike!"

"It's all right, Libby." Laila smiled and said, "Relax, Ike. Mother can be hospitable when she chooses to be. Anyway, she's looking for someone to do some work about the place. You wouldn't want to deny your friend a business opportunity, would you?"

Ike walked to the back of the wagon and had a gesturing conversation with Saul. A moment later, Saul was on the wagon seat with Joy wedged between him and Laila.

Ike watched them rock along the muddy, rutted road. He shook his head and muttered, "I got a feelin' that girl's trouble even when she isn't tryin' ta be."

"Is that why you were so cagey about the Gentrys?" asked Libby, watching him loosen his tie.

"She don't need to think she can move me around

the checkerboard in her and her mama's game with
Chester,'' he said, and rid himself of the starched collar,
too. "And I don't want her causin' trouble amongst my
men, either."

"Why, Ike! She never even looked at them."

"No, but they were lookin' at her."

"I think you're making too much of it. There's a language barrier that's no small problem and anyway,
they're all so shy . . . "

"Shy? Is that what you think?" Ike shook his head
as if she'd fallen to earth from another planet.

18

Ike started the men to work early on Monday and called it quits at four o'clock. Decatur and Frankie came along as he was hitching up the wagon. They loaded a crosscut saw, axes, wedges, and other tree-cutting tools into the wagon and headed over the railroad tracks and the bridge and into Ike's woods.

One of the trees Ike planned to take down was leaning to the north. Experience had taught him if you dropped a leaning tree in the direction it wanted to go, it was likely to split when it hit the ground. Arthur, Saul, Joseph, and his brother Fritz showed up as he and Decatur were studying how to bring it down.

"Ya ain't goin' to git any boards out of a split log," said Decatur. "Hafta drop her the other way."

Looking south, Ike said, "Between that ash there, and the oak. Goin' to be a tight fit."

"Git yer boys here ta slick it up with axle grease," said Decatur, rolling up his sleeves. "See if she won't slide right down betwixt 'em, jest like tongue and groove."

"Daylight's wastin'," said Ike, taking his ribbing over the rope incident in stride. "Best get to sawin'. Or did ya want to talk her down?"

174

"Naomi'd be the one for that job. She kin jaw the ears off a man. Talkin' a tree down'd be no chore atall." Decatur paused in lifting his end of the saw to dart a glance toward Frankie. He lowered his voice. "Not that she ain't quiet when she wants ta be. Got a young'un on the way and durned if she didn't even stir herself to tell me."

Ike could tell he was strutting pleased. "So when's it comin'?"

"September. I give her a week to find somebody to take over fer her at the store."

"She agree to it?"

"Not what ya'd call willin'ly. But there ain't no need in her wearin' herself out, runnin' back and forth like she does."

There was no heat to the words, but Decatur put enough energy into his work that Ike, manning the other end of the crosscut saw, had a suspicion that he and Naomi were still disputing it.

Glad it wasn't his problem, Ike concentrated on the job at hand, keeping a good steady rhythm as they cut into the north side of the tree. Arthur seemed to know something about felling trees. When they'd made some headway, he came with the glut, a long, tapered, wooden wedge, and began driving it into the cut. Thereafter, it was teamwork. Arthur continued to tap the glut and tap it as Ike and Decatur cut until slowly they'd raised the tree from the lean and it was standing straight.

Arthur backed off and studied the situation while Ike and Decatur stood looking on. Arthur clasped his forearms together and made a twisting motion, warning that the tree could easily twist and fall into the lean despite their efforts. Ike knew as much, knew, too, it'd be good for nothing but firewood if it did. He looked to see that Frankie and the rest of the men standing south and west of them were well out of the way before he and Decatur went to the other side of the tree and started the horizontal undercut. Arthur began to pace and fidget.

Decatur paused to wipe the sweat from his face and muttered, "Give him yer end, Galloway, b'fore he shakes it down on us with his trampin' feet."

Ike gave Arthur his end of the saw and fetched a wedge from the wagon. It was bigger around than the glut and made of steel instead of wood. He waited until the beginning of the undercut had eased some of the pressure off the glut, knocked the glut out and drove the wedge so that the wedge was now holding the tree upright.

Arthur took the handle off the saw on his end and worked the blade into the cut behind the wedge. He and Decatur began sawing from the lean side of the tree. As they did so, Ike tapped on the wedge. He kept tapping, directing the tree past center toward the undercut. All at once there was space on top of the wedge. The tree was going down. Ike gave the "All clear" shout, and the men on the saw sprang away.

The shout echoed through the woods, and kept ringing. But the voice was different, and the language, too. As if in slow motion, Ike saw Joseph racing the falling tree, waving his arms wildly. Saw little Joy hunkered down, gathering wildflowers. Saw her look up. Then swivel and freeze at her mother's screamed warning coming from behind her. *Dear God!*

Ike's last glimpse before massive limbs blocked his view was of Joseph closing in on the girl from one direction, Laila from the other. The top limb caught on a towering oak, snapped, and doubled back. It skinned the bark of the oak as it slithered down its length, splintering and popping like lightning even as the tree struck the ground. The earth shook beneath his feet, its tremors reverberating in Ike's bones as he ran. Pounding feet and terrified shouts filled the woods. He could see nothing but pitching leaves and twisted broken limbs. Nothing of Joseph, of Laila, or Joy.

A spasm of cold terror cut through him as he came around the brush of the tree top and saw Laila on the ground, dazed and bleeding, but swiftly coming to the realization that her daughter was under the treetop. She let out a shriek that was Joy's name, staggered to her feet, and pulled wildly at the branches.

"My baby. My baby!" Her frantic cries rent the air.

One high fork of the tree fit snug to the oak trunk it had hit on the way down. It braced the upper central portion of the splintered treetop a foot or so off the ground. But it was a precarious bracing.

"Git her to leave off yankin' at them branches!" Decatur barked at Saul.

Saul understood the tone and the gesture. He picked Laila up as if she was weightless and got her out of the way, while Ike wormed through the splintered branches, sick with dread. Fritz approached from the other side of the treetop. His shouts matched Laila's despair as he crashed through the branches, looking for his brother.

All at once his tone changed. But Ike's flawed hearing was hindered by Laila's shrill screams. He spotted Joseph's boot, wriggled closer, and heard Joy whimpering. Joseph's foot was at an odd angle, the leg pinned. Fritz, in his haste, put weight on the branch. Joseph moaned. The sound of raw pain cut through Ike, but he was alive! Thank God, they were both alive!

Ike shouted for Decatur to fetch the cutting tools and unhitch the wagon while Fritz, moving more carefully now, spewed rapid-fire words in his native tongue. Joseph gave a groggy reply.

Ike called to the little girl, "Joy? Can ya hear me, Joy?"

"Mama? Get Mama!"

Ike picked his way carefully through the branches, looking for her and catching only a glimpse of her small hand poked from beneath Joseph's lean sinewy frame. "Yer mama's right here. She's jest got a scratch or two. What about you?"

"He kn-nocked me d-down. M-make him m-move."

"There's a limb pinnin' him down. You lie real still

now, while we do some figurin' here and we'll git ya out.''

The men braced the tree with sapling poles to eliminate the danger of shifting before using the team and a rope to elevate the treetop enough to free Joseph and the girl.

Joy, protected by Joseph's body, had escaped with a few scratches. Joseph wasn't so fortunate. He was badly scraped and bruised, and his leg was broken. Laila had a gash on her forehead and another on her face. Both looked as if they could use stitches.

In short order, the men had loaded Joseph into the wagon for the ride into Dr. Harding's office. Ike helped Laila onto the seat. There was no real need to take Joy along, but Laila, badly shaken, was unwilling to leave her behind.

Ike sent Frankie up the road to tell Edina what had happened, and asked Decatur to tell Libby not to wait supper, that he would be late. Joseph moaned with each jolt of the wagon as they made their way out of the woods and onto the road. Laila climbed over the seat into the box of the wagon and tried to brace Joseph as they made their way over the rutted road. She cleaned the blood from his face with the hem of her skirt and talked to him, just as if he could understand. Joy joined her in the back of the wagon, patting Joseph's broad brown hand with her small dimpled one.

By the time they arrived in Edgewood, the business square was dark and deserted. Reluctant to put Joseph through any more jarring, Ike parked the wagon in the alley behind the doctor's office, left him in Laila's care, and went on foot to Dr. Harding's home.

Dr. Harding said he'd need his sister's help, so Ike fetched Mrs. Bee from her home. They worked on Joseph for a long while before finally turning to Laila. It was after midnight before her cuts had been cleaned and stitched.

''The leg will mend well enough. He's bruised pretty

badly. I don't want him stirring around, not before the end of the week," said Dr. Harding.

"You're keepin' him here, then?" asked Ike.

"I think that would be best."

Mrs. Bee loaned them a couple of blankets as they prepared to make their way home. Laila wrapped one around her shoulders and the other one around Joy. Ike gathered up enough loose straw to make them comfortable in the back of the wagon before starting out. But once Joy was asleep, Laila joined him on the wagon seat.

Ike had left his jacket in the woods. The air was sharp through his shirt. They hadn't gone far when Laila unwrapped the blanket from her own shoulders and spread it to cover his back, too.

"You take it, I don't need it," said Ike, for the familiarity of her gesture made him about as uncomfortable as he could remember being in a long while.

Firmly, Laila said, "It's cold! You can share or you can have the whole thing, take your choice."

"I'll take it, then, and you can crawl back there and wrap up with Joy."

Laila gave a short laugh. "When I was small, I used to imagine what you would be like. Actually, it was the idea of a brother I was enamored with. Though I featured you as slightly more gallant."

She put Ike so strongly in mind of Cicely that he said, "Take it then, and quit aggravatin' me."

"Isn't that what sisters are for?"

Ike shook the blanket off his shoulders. "Maybe, if we was ten. Truth is, yer a stranger to me."

"I'd like to see that change."

"Maybe it can't."

She was quiet a moment, then said, "I see."

"I'm not sure you do."

"Of course I do. There isn't room. That's all right. I appreciate your being honest. And believe it or not, I understand. I had a soul mate once, too. He filled my whole life and gave me Joy."

Ike was ashamed, for she was right in part. He wasn't looking for more obligations, somebody else to be responsible for. But Libby filling the better part of his life was only part of it. He shouldn't care if Laila and Edina took Chester for a cleaning, but for some reason, he did. Not for Chester's sake. *God, if only it could be that simple!* Being as honest as he could, he admitted, "I don't like what yer doin' to Chester."

"Why is that?" asked Laila, growing defensive. "Do you think we deserve to get nothing?"

"Takin' from Chester isn't goin' to fix it."

"I don't know what you mean."

"I think ya do. You just won't admit it to yerself. What ya wanted was a father."

"I told you before . . ."

"I know what ya told me, and I know what I see." The team made its way through a wet spot. The mud sucked at the horses' hooves as Ike battled the temptation to cast aside responsibility toward a sister he hadn't asked for and didn't want. But he knew that was willful and a luxury God wouldn't afford a man when somebody was sitting there needy, right under his nose.

"Today, when that tree was comin' down and you couldn't get to Joy fast enough, you wouldn't have traded a hair on that girl's head for anythin' of Chester's, would ya?"

"Of course not!"

"Then how important is it, gettin' back at Morgan the only way you know how?"

"You don't understand. How can you?"

"I wasn't a whole lot older than Joy when Dad died, that's how. I grew up fast and took some pride in bein' a self-made man. Then I realized what I'd made of myself wasn't much to boast about."

"You won't get any argument from me."

It was said with enough anger, Ike realized he'd hurt her. She'd revealed more than she'd meant to, admitting she had fantasized as a child about the siblings she had never met. Maybe she had thought a brother could fix the loneliness. A brother, a sister, a child, a mate. *He filled my whole life*, she'd said of her dead husband. But from personal experience, Ike doubted it was so. As much as he loved Lib, there were spaces she wasn't meant to fill. Doubting he had the words to explain that to Laila, he let it drop, and asked, "I've been wonderin', what was Joy doin', she didn't see that tree comin' down?"

"Picking wildflowers."

"Distracted her, I guess."

"Joy has quite an imagination. She gets caught up in her own little world." Laila shivered and hugged the blanket closer. "I could see it unfolding before my eyes, but I couldn't reach her, and I couldn't make her hear me."

Ike supposed God knew that feeling. Folks bein' distracted by what they could admire and touch and handle. Filling the spaces, thinking it a good fit, until something else caught their eye.

"It's hard, I reckon, bein' both mother and father to a child," he said.

"She had a good father. For a while."

"She still does," said Ike. "So do you, if you'd quit runnin' from Him."

"How would you know?" she said tartly.

"I did it enough times, I ought to know. He ain't ever run away from me, though."

"You're a religious man."

"Because I know who my Father is?"

Ike saw in her silence that he'd made her as uncomfortable as he had been when she'd tried to share the blanket. He remembered her remark on what was their father's shame, having two women with child at once. Odd that she could speak of it with no embarrassment, yet squirm over the truth that would heal her loneliness in a way that he, her half brother, never could.

Laila was silent the rest of the way home. Ike carried

Joy to the door for her. She thanked him in that correct Eastern way of hers. "Ike?" she called as he was turning away. "You may be right, in part. There is some vindication involved in going after what would have been Father's. But there's a need, too. It isn't easy for a woman to provide for herself and her child. If it were your wife left with a child to raise on her own, would your advice be the same?"

"Wouldn't have to advise Lib. She'd know."

She studied him for a long moment. The battle against doubts, old hurts, and frustrations showed in her eyes. "Even if I were willing to let it go, Edina would pursue it," she said finally, her voice dropping to a whisper.

Ike knew it wasn't for fear of Joy awakening. It was her mother she didn't want overhearing her. "You don't have to let her drag ya down with her."

"There isn't much bend in you, is there?"

"So I've been told."

"She's my mother, Ike."

Yes, and already Edina had fed Laila enough bitterness to kill a mule. She'd get the job done, too, if Laila let her. Ike turned and made his way back to the wagon.

The eastern sky was showing a tinge of pink as he approached the railroad tracks. He spotted Hascal sitting on a milk can near the station. Hack jumped up like he'd been watching for him and came toward the wagon on a stiff-legged hoppity gait.

"Talk about *me* bein' ornery," Hascal called to him and got his hand under a tracing strap on the near horse.

Ike said, "What's stuck in yer craw?"

"Confound it, boy! I looked the other way last time ya ambled on up to them Stapletons. But that's a brazen piece of work, ridin' down the road with her, and the roosters already crowing."

Meaning Laila. Tired, and short of patience, Ike said, "We're related. Now let go of my horse."

"Related to a skunk, that's what you are! Blast yer hide, if you ain't Morgan Galloway all over again! Ya had me thinkin' better of ya, Ike. Ya railly did.''

"You finished?"

"No, I ain't finished." Hascal scowled back at him. "I come close to tellin' Miz Lib last time jest what you was up to, and danged if I'll cover fer ya again!"

"Git on back to yer milk can, Hack, and tend yer own knittin'."

Ike slapped the reins over the backs of his team, left Hack growling in the road, and went on home. The sun was rising by the time he'd unhitched the wagon and turned the horses loose in the pasture, but Libby wasn't stirring yet. The stove was burning warm enough, he figured she'd been up waiting for him half the night.

It would be time to go to work before long. Hardly seemed worth shedding his boots and clothes to grab a few winks. Ike locked his hands behind his head, propped his feet on the kindling box, and rested his eyes, his thoughts walking backwards over the day just past, pausing over bits and pieces.

Laila's scream as the tree crashed toward Joy. Fritz, tearing at those branches, frantic for his brother. Decatur proud over Naomi carrying his child, a pride tempered with concern that came out quarrelsome. Caring wasn't risk-free, and it caused trouble if it wasn't handled right.

I had a soul mate once, too. He filled my whole life and gave me Joy.

Laila's words told him something about Libby that he wouldn't have heard if Libby had said them. Libby would have him believe that children were to be her gift to him. But he knew that was only partly true. And for him to say he was protecting her from hardship by being careful not to start a family too soon was only half the truth. He was protecting himself, and not from hardship alone, but from adding to his list of vulnerabilites. Having to admit that he didn't want to feel anything for Laila had brought that truth home.

Ike swung his feet off the kindling box and opened the stove door to check the fire. His failure to open the damper and let the fire breath first led to the usual drift of smoke. Libby stirred and mumbled, "Good faith, Ike. Do it right."

It *was* a good faith. It asked something of a man, but it yielded high returns if a fella gave heed and let God shape him instead of trying to shape everything himself. He unlaced a boot, thinking of the richness of God's treasures. Lib was one such treasure with gifts of her own. But he'd been treating the one fashioned to unify like a leaning tree that could so easily twist and fall on his best-laid plans.

He stood up and lit the lamp and looked toward the bed where she was stirring, pushing her hair out of her face and moving her hand over the bedside table, looking for her slippers. "How's Joseph?" she asked, her voice still husky with sleep. "Did you bring him back with you?"

"Doc wanted to watch him a few days. Told him we'd come get him on payday. The boys'll be wantin' to go to town, anyway." Ike unlaced the other boot as he gave her the details concerning Joseph. "He'll lose his job with the railroad. They won't pay him to sit around ten or twelve weeks and let his leg heal."

"No, I suppose not." Libby could see he was thinking if it weren't for his tree-cutting Joseph would be sleeping in the camp train right now. She threw back the covers. "You're blaming yourself."

"Guess I am," he admitted. He caught a glimpse of creamy white skin as she untwisted her night shift and came to her feet with a flash of firm, graceful limbs.

"You can't undo it, Ike. Be grateful it wasn't worse. And Joy! I shudder to think what it would do to Laila if anything happened to that little girl. I hope she fell on her knees and thanked God. I know I did."

"She gave Him a glance," said Ike.

Her face clouded. "Why are you so hard on her?"

"Somebody needs to be. Edina's planted a seed of meanness in her and watered it real good."

Libby remembered Laila's discomfiting mockery of the Field family. "You're right, I suppose. Still, I like her. I'm going to pray for her. For the Field children, too. I've been thinking about them, and wondering if God shoved them under my nose for a reason."

"To git rid of them chickens, that's why," he said.

"Seriously. I want you to be thinking about them," she said, and came to tend those home fires she was so partial to.

Not right now, he couldn't. All he could think about was her. He got between her and the stove, spreading his feet and arms and teasing her a little as she tried to reach past him to get to the stove. "Hascal saw me takin' Laila home and got the idea I'd been steppin' out on you."

"Stepping out? Why, that meddlesome old busybody. If he'd keep his mind . . ."

"B'fore you tear him up like a sack, you ought to know he took your part and gave me what for."

That *did* surprise her. Hascal usually took the view that women brought all their troubles upon themselves. "You set him straight about Laila, didn't you?"

"I tried to, but he didn't listen. You want to have a little fun with him?"

"Ike, are you out of your mind? Hascal Caton would rather tell a lie when the truth fits! You look him up and straighten him out."

Ike moved closer, drawn past her sparks and flames to her supple, silky-haired softness. "Maybe I'll let you. You seem primed for the job."

"You bet I am! That he could think for one minute that you would do such a thing!"

"I'd have to be crazy, wouldn't I? Living with a fiery, red-haired temper . . . temptation. I was goin' to say temptation."

She fought laughter, and prompted, "Red-haired temptation. Go on."

"Well. I was thinkin' . . ." He stopped, uncertain how

to tell her exactly what he had been thinking. He tucked a curl behind her ear and traced a sleep crease in her cheek. Her skin was rosy pink, still warm from the covers. "It's been a strange day and a long night, but it's made me take stock and remember where I've placed my confidence." He cupped her face between his hands and kissed her. Let his hands fall to her shoulders. His thumbs caressed the smooth white column of her throat. He could feel her pulse quicken.

"I forget, too, sometimes." She put her arms around him and tipped her face to his, inviting him to kiss her again.

"Yes, well, ya make that kind of forgetfulness a habit, and b'fore long you think the world's resting on yer shoulders," he said, and obliged her, meeting her half-parted lips. "But it isn't. God's met our needs."

"Yes, He has, hasn't He?"

Talked out, he kissed her in earnest. She felt good to him, the way a woman was supposed to feel to a man when God sanctified their togetherness, knitting into their souls a need for one another. She felt good and she smelled good and he was tired of being careful. He kissed her again, and though the numbers were about as wrong as they'd ever been, said against her mouth, "Let's go back to bed for a while. Want to?"

Libby had grown accustomed to his carefulness, but there was no semblance of restraint in this passion he was kindling. There was a lot he was leaving unsaid. Consequences he hadn't raised, not in concrete words, anyway. Half-afraid he would change his mind, she gave assent, whispering, "I love you."

"Me too." He closed the stove door with a socked foot and lifted her into his arms.

Libby laced her hands around his neck and smiled. "What's this? You haven't swept me off my feet since the day we were married."

"Been that long, has it?"

"Yes, and you had to ask then. *Reckon I should carry you over the threshold?* Remember?"

He grinned at her gentle mockery, and surprised a laugh out of her, dumping her unceremoniously on the bed, saying, "You goin' to kiss me or are ya goin' to chatter?"

19

Ike got word to Mr. Elliot concerning Joseph's injury. He came to the grove and at Ike's suggestion, agreed to let Decatur take Joseph's place until Joseph was back on his feet. Joseph, in the interim, was going to stay at Willie Blue's while his leg mended and take Naomi's place, clerking.

Libby's father, Thomas Watson, agreed to help Joseph with the language and anything that required a sound pair of legs. Thomas spent his days at Willie Blue's, anyway, serving as town postmaster, and had for some time been doubling as store clerk on the days Naomi didn't work.

Libby knew that Naomi's work at the store had relieved the isolation of a lifetime in the woods. She understood Naomi's reluctance to give up the job. But she could also understand Decatur's position. The constant travel to and from town and the long work hours were taxing Naomi's endurance as she entered her fourth month of pregnancy. So, as a compromise of sorts, Libby offered her summer porch for Naomi's use as a small branch store.

It was a good location, just a few hundred yards off a north–south road that was used both by the locals and by those who were passing through. Ike reasoned that with the steady increase in rail service, Naomi could expect some trade from those who embarked and disembarked at the station as well as local farmers using the rails to move their grain and livestock.

The idea pleased Naomi and suited Decatur so well, he quit grumbling about it, once Naomi agreed to limit her hours. Libby moved her belongings off the porch and into the cabin and in the week that followed spent her evenings helping Naomi make the space into a small store. Naomi, skilled with wood and tools, installed shelves against the wall. Libby and Opal painted the shelves, washed the windows, and helped Naomi sand and stain the top of the old workbench. It would double as shelving and a sales counter.

On Thursday, Libby was giving the workbench a final sanding between finishes. Opal stood nibbling a cookie as she looked on.

"Jest think, Mama. This time next week, you'll have customers crowdin' in here." She brushed cookie crumbs off the counter. "If Purdy and Dumplin comes shoppin' here, ya'd better turn 'em upside down and shake 'em good b'fore ya let 'em out the door. Couple of thieves, that's what they are. Somebody took a pencil right off Teacher's desk today. I'd bet my red dress it was one of them!"

"Opal, accusin' folks when ya don't know the truth is the same as robbin'," Naomi reproved her. "Yer takin' their reputation, and that's worth more than gold."

"Purdy and Dumplin' don't have no reputation," said Opal.

"They do so," said Frankie. He was on his way out with the basket of sandwiches and cookies Libby had asked him to take to the woods for the men. "Don't hafta worry 'bout it gettin' stole, though. Who'd want somethin' that shabby?"

Opal snickered. "See, Mama. Even Frankie knows they's rotten."

Opal had been breathing fire over those boys ever since she learned they'd killed Libby's hen. Libby blew away the dust from her sanding, and said, "Maybe all those Field boys need is a little refinishing."

"Don't think they's goin' to stand still for ya sandin' on 'em, Lib," said Frankie with a grin. "But I could whup 'em for ya, if ya want."

"You'll keep yer hands to yerself, that's what you'll do, Frankie McClure," said Naomi. "Anyway, yer missin' Lib's point. Looky here how we've raised the grain of the wood. A good finish brings out the beauty that's there in the wood all the time. Same with people. Everybody's got beauty in 'em, wantin' to be noticed."

Seeing the look of superior child knowledge Frankie and Opal exchanged, Libby didn't waste her breath trying to convince them that their mother's point was valid. Instead, she said, "David has a birthday coming up. I was thinking I'd have a party for him. You two are at the top of my list. I thought I'd ask Joy Stapleton as well. Maybe the Field children would like to come, too."

"A tea party?" cried Opal.

Frankie snorted. "Now if that ain't cissified and addlepated."

"Frankie, take that basket on out to the men and quit botherin' yer sister," said Naomi.

Frankie departed on a mincing step, trilling, "A tea party, a tea party, oh goody goody, a tea party."

"Bet Pretty Good'd come to a tea party," Opal called after him. "Frankie and Pretty Good sitting in a tree, goody, goody, goody, goody, k-i-s-n-g. Yer ears is red, Frankie. Ha, ha!"

"Yah? Well, you cain't spell."

"Can too."

"Can not," Frankie called back, the breeze stirring his red hair.

Naomi placed a hand on her abdomen and eased a long-suffering sigh.

"I think we'll call it a birthday party," said Libby. "I'll check with Father and Verna while we're in town on Saturday, and make sure they haven't already planned something for David."

"The girls is all right, but I don't know why ya'd ask Purdy and Dumplin, after what they done," grumbled Opal.

"Good Book says to 'do unto others as you'd have 'em do unto you,' " reminded Naomi.

"Yep, and them two's done all they're goin' to do to me," announced Opal. "Either one of 'em gits out of line and pow!" She plowed her fist into her palm. "Right in the kisser!"

"Then I guess you'll be missin' Davie's party, on account of Lib wouldn't want ya whippin' her guests," said Naomi firmly.

"Oh, all right!" said Opal. "I'll wear my red dress. Cain't be fightin' in my red dress on account I don't want ta muss it. Miss Bee made it for me, ya know."

Libby smiled. "Yes, and it looks lovely on you."

Mollified by the compliment, Opal said, "Even if ya didn't invite them two, they'd sneak along after Pretty Good and Very Fine, jest to see what they's missin.' "

"Maybe if folks did more inviting and giving, those two would do less sneaking and taking," suggested Libby.

"I jest hope they don't ruin Davie's party," said Opal.

Libby hugged her, and said, "David will think any party his best friend helped plan is a wonderful party. You *are* going to help me plan it, aren't you?"

Opal turned into sunshine and beamed her way into the cabin to find Libby's cookbook and choose a cake recipe for David's birthday party.

"Ya got a sweet way with young'uns, Lib," observed Naomi. "Ya need some of yer own."

Libby smiled, for the possibility of having one of her

own seemed more real to her than it had ever been, now that Ike's caution was broken.

Ike's days had been filled with the water-system project, his evenings with tree felling. He had made good headway, thanks to the help he received from Decatur, Saul, Arthur, and Fritz. By Thursday, they had three logs on the ground, denuded of branches and ready to go to the sawmill to be exchanged for dried lumber for his barn. The rest would be cut up into firewood for next sirup season, but there was no rush about that. He'd have to cut at least two more trees.

Mr. Elliot showed up with the men's checks on Friday. After touring the job site, he walked to the house with Ike and accepted Libby's invitation for lunch.

"I'm pleased with the progress the men are making on the project," he said, as the meal drew to a close and they lingered over coffee and peach cake. "But I feel it only fair to tell you I'm not sure I can guarantee their next paycheck."

Ike set his coffee cup down carefully. "What're ya sayin', Mr. Elliot?"

"I'm afraid the project is in jeopardy because of the earthquake."

Ike's misgivings gave way to alarm as Mr. Elliot explained that the funds for the project had been on deposit in a San Francisco bank and that the bank had been destroyed by the fires that raged through the city after the earthquake.

"Everything is in chaos. I'm afraid the funds to complete the project can't be recouped," said Mr. Elliot. "Now, I don't want to offer false hope, but because of the increasing grain and stock commerce here at the grove, the C & A may make completion of the water system a priority anyway," said Mr. Elliot. "If so, they'll find the revenues locally, regardless of the fate of the larger project."

"When will ya know?" asked Ike.

"I'm on my way to the field office now to try and get some concrete answers."

"Yer fixin' to tell the men, aren't you?" asked Ike.

"There are hundreds of emigrant laborers in the same position as these men, Ike. I can't play favorites and give some advance notice over others. Anyway, it's up to the C & A to give them official notice, not me." Reading Ike like a bold type, he added, "They won't appreciate you getting ahead of them."

Oh Lord! Libby's heart was in her throat as the conversation limped to a painful halt. Just a few short weeks ago, Mr. Elliot had bubbled with enthusiasm over the C & A project. It had sounded as if the work would go on for several years, as if Ike and his men would have a job indefinitely and make good money. Now what?

Up-and-down faith. A silent Voice retraced the words etched upon her mind weeks earlier. Libby crossed to the sink and stood with her back to Ike and Mr. Elliot, looking out over the pasture to where the men were working, no idea that their future hung in limbo.

"Thank you again, Mrs. Galloway, for your hospitality," said Mr. Elliot, as he prepared to go. "I'm sorry to be the bearer of bad tidings. But the work *will* be done, if not this year or next, then soon. And when it is, we will look back at the uncertainty of this moment and wonder how we could have ever doubted."

Mr. Elliot's assurances gave little relief for the present. Libby went through the motions of walking him to the door. Ike left with him, saying he'd see him to the station. He wasn't gone long.

"What're you going to do?" Libby asked when Ike returned to get the hat he had left behind.

"Men are waitin'. I'm going back to work," he said.

"I didn't mean this minute."

"I know what ya meant. I jest don't know the answer."

Ike caught a glimpse of her face before she turned her back. He hadn't meant to let the words go sharply. He saw her fight off hurt. Trim her shoulders. Rub at the dishes with a tattered old rag.

"I'm sorry," he said, tone softening.

"It's all right," she murmured.

No, it wasn't. Nothing about it was right. She kept her head down, her back to him. Her hair was neatly arranged at the back of her head. The light coming through the window revealed the cheapness of the comb holding it there. Her homemade cotton dress, though neatly pressed and smelling of starch, was worn thin across the shoulders. She had turned the collar to hide the frayed edges.

The plates clattering against each other filled the stillness of the cabin as Ike fought the helpless feeling that life was working in his hands like a greased rope. He hoisted himself up only to be jerked and jarred back to earth. He reached out to touch her, to offer reassurance, only to realize he couldn't even give her that.

"What if I miss my monthly?"

Ike flinched first at that all-too-real possibility, and then at the realization he had made her afraid of her own dream. Trying to restore what he'd taken, he straightened his shoulders, and said, "Then we'll have somethin' to look forward to, won't we?"

Her breath caught. "You mean that?"

He slipped his arms around her, kissed the loose tendrils curling sweetly against her nape, and lied through his teeth just to ease her worry.

" 'Course I do."

She turned and locked her slim arms around him. "You're right," she said with fierce wonder. "You're right! Forgive me! Why is it that every time we bump into a wall, my faith pools down around my ankles like a pair of saggy cotton stockings?"

Something inside him jerked at her words. He knew the wall she spoke of, every stone, every chink in the mortar. It was the one he kept trying to detour around. He didn't have to lie, offering false assurance when rock-solid promises were right there for the taking. "God's in this somewhere. Don't know how, but He is. A man can plan and plan, and it don't amount to much if He isn't in it." He squinted against the light glaring through the window, and sighed. "My men . . . they deserve to know what's happening."

Libby's eyes dampened as he emptied his disappointment and his distress over men who were not his at all. "What're you going to do?"

"I'm goin' to tell them."

"Even though Mr. Elliot said not to?"

"Lib, that was a risk he took when he told me, he knew that. Anyway, he didn't tell me not to. He said the C & A wouldn't like it."

"The implication was there," said Libby.

"Can't help it. These men stand to lose it all. Their food, their lodging, their pay. Seems to me they deserve a little warning. Maybe I'll introduce 'em to some people while we're in town tomorrow. Let it be known they're good men, hard workers, and reliable."

"And if they find other jobs and the railroad decides to finish the water system? You'll have lost your workers," said Libby.

"There's several hundred men goin' to be in the same fix . I can't look after all of them, but I'll do what I can for mine."

Libby knew by the set of his chin that he would do it, even if it meant providing food and lodging for them himself. She said, "Maybe I better put in some more garden."

"Be a good idea."

She followed him to the door, adding, "It's time you were picking up some chicks at the hatchery, too, and building that . . ."

"Chicken coop, I know."

Libby finished the dishes, then went for a walk in the flower-spangled woods. There was a high bluff that overlooked the railroad. She followed the steel rails with her eye, to the north, to the south. It was easy to see from there that it did indeed follow the lay of the land. *Like her up-and-down faith.*

Slowly, as she waited upon that still, small Voice of God, an understanding of the phrase seeped into her soul. Life's peaks and valleys might alter the course of her days, but they shouldn't set the course of her faith. Her Lord had made the climb. She had only to keep her eye fixed on Him and not be distracted by the uncertain terrain along the way.

Show me how to make it a steady climb. She sat amidst the wildflowers with her chin resting on her knees, and prayed for peace in the face of uncertainty. Prayed for Ike and his men, and for Mr. Elliot, who though discouraged, had the faith to believe the project would someday go on. If he could put that kind of faith in a man-made project, then how hard could it be to trust God in His ongoing project with man?

20

Ike had offered to help Decatur haul part of the stock from Willie Blue's out to the summer-porch store on Saturday. Hans rode into Edgewood with Decatur's family. Arthur and Fritz made the short trip with Ike and Libby. Mr. Seredy stayed behind, as did Saul.

Edina Stapleton had hired them both to do some repairs on her place, and Mrs. Seredy, to help with some spring cleaning. Currently, it was temporary work to be fit in when they had free time. But should the railroad project fall through, Edina had enough work on the place to keep one man busy full-time, and perhaps a second man on a temporary basis. Ike wouldn't have wanted to work for her, but the Seredys seemed willing, and Saul was downright eager. His admiration for Laila, Ike knew, had something to do with that.

Libby climbed down from the wagon at Baker's. She planned to visit with Verna and David before seeing to some errands. "I'll meet you at the store in a while," she told him, and waved as he drove on with Arthur and Fritz climbing from the wagon box onto the seat.

There was a crowd at Baker's. Verna was busy with a Saturday morning breakfast rush. A girl Libby hadn't met before was helping her in the kitchen.

David was standing on a crate in front of the sink, washing dishes. He turned with dripping hands, and a welcoming grin to introduce the girl as May. Libby traded a few words with the girl, then left her to her cooking. She quizzed David about his schoolwork and Father and any news of Adam and Abigail as well as her brother Jacob in Thistle Down. At length, Libby got around to the possibility of a birthday party.

Pleasure leapt in her little brother's eyes. "A party? You mean it?"

"Of course I do!" Heart-warmed at his delight, Libby brushed a fringe of dark hair off his forehead. "If it's all right with Father and Verna."

Before she could stop him, David shot out into the dining room. He returned in short order with Verna's permission, then wheedled, "How about helping me finish these dishes, Lib? Then I can run over to Willie Blue's and tell Father. I'm supposed to help Joseph this morning, anyway."

"Joseph, is it?" said Libby with a smile.

"I'm his legs. That's what Father says, anyway."

"I guess that's reason enough to hurry you along." Libby mussed his hair and tied on an apron. Once the sink was empty of dishes, David made his escape.

Libby was getting acquainted with May when she heard footsteps on the back stairs. Turning, she saw Dorene Morefield coming down the steps. It was the first time they'd seen one another since Ike had lost the farm to Dorene's husband, Earl. Dorene stopped short at the sight of Libby, then gathered the flowing skirt of her Mother Hubbard dress and, without a word, darted back up the stairs.

So be that way. Libby thrust out her chin. But nobler words whispered a quieter message. Belatedly, she called a greeting after Dorene. Too late. A door swung shut at the top of the stairs.

"Dorene's still working?" asked Libby when Verna returned to the kitchen.

"No, she's a guest," said Verna. "May, why don't you go on out to the dining room and clear some tables? I'll take over here."

"A guest?" said Libby, when May had gone. Several weeks earlier, as she was helping Ike move his things out of the barn, she had seen the Morefield men with a ten-span of mules, dragging a herder's bungalow onto Miss Maudie's property. It was to be Dorene and Earl's home. "I thought Dorie and Earl had moved out to the farm a week or two ago."

"They did," said Verna, whipping eggs in a bowl. "But the baby's coming any day and Dorene's nervous about being so far from town. She's afraid Earl will be in the field when she needs him to go for Dr. Harding."

"Can't her mother or one of her sisters stay with her until after the baby has come?" asked Libby.

"I guess not," said Verna.

All those sisters, and not one of them could spare a few days for Dorie? Noting Verna's reluctance to discuss it, and knowing full well the reason, Libby vowed to rise above her natural nature. She asked, "Why not?"

The sausage in the heavy iron skillet sizzled under the press of Verna's spatula-wielding arm. "October to April, Libby. Think about it."

All at once Libby stopped short. "You mean she was . . . Oh!"

"Exactly," said Verna. "I don't think her family realized either until a couple of months ago. It's no disgrace to them, but they seem to be taking it that way."

Immediately, Libby thought of Abigail, and how Libby had felt when she had learned that her marriage to Adam was a "hurry-up" one. Embarrassed, disappointed, humiliated, and angry. Yes, angry, for it had seemed a blight on their family honor. She understood the Berrys' reaction. And Dorene's hasty retreat up the stairs. Again, she rallied forces lest spite gain the upper hand, and said without malice, "I hadn't realized."

"There was no reason you would," said Verna, tossing eggshells into the slop bucket. "I told Dorene she was welcome to stay here until the baby comes. I really didn't expect Earl to let her. But perhaps he didn't have any choice. Dorene is devoted to him, but still, it's her first child, and she's scared."

Dorie had worked at the restaurant for several years so, of course, Verna was sensitive to her difficulties. Libby said, "Perhaps when the baby comes, things will change. Babies are awfully hard to resist."

Verna nodded agreement as she checked a sheet of baking biscuits. "Still, that isn't much comfort right now. Dorene can't seem to settle here. Not with any peace of mind. The strain isn't good for her."

Libby could see it was a sorrow to Verna. After the pain Earl and Dorene had inflicted in the loss of the farm, she doubted she could be unbiased enough to be of any real comfort to Verna in her concern, or to Dorene herself, for that matter. Yet she couldn't erase the mental picture of Dorene's happiness last fall at the cornhusking. She had seemed so well suited to marriage. And here she was, just a few months later, separated from Earl by her own fears. Libby couldn't imagine being away from Ike for days on end. *And about to bear his child?*

It was Abigail's trials that brought to mind the lesson that love, freely given, could bring healing. How could she so swiftly mislay that hard-earned knowledge that the one who held on to the hurt needed it as much as the one who had inflicted it? Hesitantly, Libby said, "You know, Verna, Dorie and Earl aren't without neighbors."

"That's true. But Dorene hasn't had time to get to know them."

"She knows me."

"Yes, but . . ."

"Because of the farm, you mean?" Libby smoothed the wide crocheted yoke collar she had pinned over her favorite blue dress. It concealed tiny stitches that closed up the burn hole made in the bodice the night she had knelt before the evaporator firebox, stirring the coals and coming to terms with the loss of the farm. "I won't pretend that isn't still a sore spot. But I'm trying . . . I'm really trying to get past it."

Verna flipped eggs onto a plate without comment.

Libby flushed and tipped her chin. "If Dorie wants to go home to Earl, you can tell her I'll check on her."

"Are you sure, Libby? Maybe you should talk with Ike first."

"Ike would want me to," said Libby, knowing it was true. "With the weather so mild, I'd enjoy the walk to her house."

Thoughtfully, Verna said, "I'm sure she'd be more comfortable at home. Thank you, Libby. I'll tell her."

Arthur and Fritz went along with Ike to the blacksmith shop, where he left tools to be sharpened. He introduced his men and explained their circumstances. The next stop was the hatchery. Ike paid for two dozen chicks and the supplies Libby would need to get started raising chickens. He didn't want to load the chickens until they were ready to start home, so he arranged to stop by later for his purchases. Again, he introduced Arthur and Fritz and let it be known it was likely they would be for hire soon, should anyone be interested in good men. He did so once more at the bank, where Arthur and Fritz cashed their paychecks. Both men bought bank drafts, for they were sending a portion of their pay back home to loved ones who were hoping to join them in the States.

By the time Ike walked into Willie Blue's on the heels of his men, the store was crowded with farmers and Saturday shoppers and folks coming in to get their mail. Ike had counted on as much. A word dropped at Willie Blue's was as good, maybe better, than running an ad in Mr. Gruben's *Gazette*.

Naomi had done some rearranging to accommodate Joseph. He was seated behind a short table just inside the door, with his leg propped up on an orange crate. The cash register was on the table, along with a roll of brown paper and a spindle of string. A somber fellow, Joseph brightened at the sight of Arthur and Fritz.

Ike grinned at the men's spate of animated conversation. He clapped Joseph on the shoulder in greeting, and started for the back of the store to say hello to Libby's father. As he drew closer, he saw that the back door was propped open. Hans and Decatur were already at work, loading some supplies into Decatur's wagon. Thinking he'd take his wagon around back, too, Ike turned to retrace his steps and nearly ran over David.

"Watch out!" David warned.

Ike steadied the crate of soda pop the boy was carrying. "Sorry, Davie. Didn't see ya standin' there. Lib's over at the restaurant, wanting to see you."

"I know. We talked," said David. "She's going to have a party for me out at the grove."

"That's what I hear. Where are ya goin' with that?"

"Decatur's wantin' some soda for the other store."

"Ice some down, and I reckon you could twist my arm."

"I'm going to do that, just as soon as I'm done here," said David. He squeezed past a young woman as she knelt in the aisle to wipe her child's nose, and rushed on toward the back of the store. Fritz, with Arthur at his heels, loped down a parallel aisle, outdistancing Ike in their haste to reach the mail counter.

The regular crowd of loafers was clustered around the stove. Ike caught the tail end of a yarn as he waited for the young mother to shift out of his way. It sounded like Major Minor, but he couldn't see him for the farmers encircling the crates and barrels and wooden chairs where the old-timers sat tossing in their two cents' worth as the conversation turned to the C & A project.

"Here comes some of them furriners now," Hascal Caton's clamoring voice reached Ike's ears. "I reckon they know iffin' the project is on the skids. Not that you kin make heads or tails of that gibberish of theirs.''

''*Ach*, Mr. Caton, I'm thinkin' these are Ike's boys. The big-shouldered lad a-coomin' favors our Joseph consideraby.'' Ike heard Thomas's lilting tongue in the mix of conversation.

''Ike's, aire they?'' Hascal replied. ''Pains me to say it, Tom Watson, but iffin' those boys could make ya understand 'em, I reckon they'd tell ya a thing or two about that son-in-law of yers ya wouldn't much like hearin'.''

Hack Caton, you old rascal! Alarm stirring, Ike squeezed past the woman and child, trying to reach Hascal before he shot off his mouth. But his path was again blocked, this time by two elderly ladies picking through the sewing notions and drowning out Thomas's soft-spoken reply with their complaints about the price of cotton thread.

''Excuse me, ma'am. Comin' through. Excuse me,'' he urged.

One white-haired lady glared. The other smiled sweetly, and shifted out of his way. But already it was too late.

''I know what I seen, Thomas,'' blared Hascal in strident tones. ''That Stapleton girl sittin' up thar on the wagon seat with a blanket wrapped around her shoulders and the devil gleamin' right out of her eyes. Knowed from day one she wasn't no account. Her and her mama, either one, livin' up thar past the trees, no man on the place.''

''The young woman in question is Mr. Galloway's sister, so let's put an end to this nonsense, shall we, Mr. Caton?''

Ike stopped short. *Chester Gentry?*

''Sister?'' snorted Hack in disbelief.

''Yes, sister,'' said Chester, a glacial edge to his voice. ''Morgan's first wife's girl.''

Surprise stirred over Ike as he stood back, an unseen witness to the terse exchange. Hack didn't take well to being corrected. He held in general contempt anyone he perceived to think himself of higher social standing, and Chester chief among them.

"Shoulda knowed Morgan couldn't content hisself with one gal," he struck back. "It'd be too blamed easy to keep track of his offspring thataway."

"Men in glass houses, Mr. Caton. Men in glass houses." Chester dropped the warning and let it sit there while Ike stood torn between retreating and wading on through.

Retreat won out. *Men in glass houses.* His hesitation had cleared his thinking. Chester was vulnerable to what he couldn't change, and what he couldn't change was blood. When he said, "Morgan's first wife," he wasn't being generous for generosity's sake. It was family pride he was protecting, not Ike's reputation, and not Ike's mother's name.

Ike shook the thought loose and scanned the store on his way back through. He was relieved to see no sign of Libby. She'd be put out if she knew that Hascal had been rattling over the very thing she'd warned him to straighten out. And she wouldn't limit her displeasure to Hack, either.

The *Gazette* office was Libby's next stop. Mr. Gruben was ensconced in a chair, his feet on the desk. Dust motes danced in the sun-washed window as he pored over a reference book, meticulous as always about researching his articles for the *Gazette*.

"Good morning, Mr. Gruben. I hope I'm not interrupting."

"Libby!" Lucius Gruben slammed the book closed, launching a new bevy of dust dancers. He came to his feet and circled the desk to wave her into a chair. "Just the person I wanted to see. What's this about the C & A project being scrapped?"

"What makes you think I know anything about that?" she replied, avoiding a direct answer.

Mr. Gruben cleared a corner of the desk and propped a hip there. "Fine, fine. Save what you know for the article. I'd like it on my desk by noon."

"I'm sorry, Mr. Gruben, I'm not free to do that."

"I'll make it my lead."

"I'd be risking Ike's job if I poked my nose in the railroad's business."

"If my sources are correct, he hasn't got one for long."

Libby steeled herself against the observation, and said, "If you have sources, you don't need my help."

"Of course I need your help. You're my best journalist."

"I'm your only journalist," said Libby, smiling. She crossed a knee and swung a foot. "How's Florence?"

"Florence always blossoms in the springtime right along with her flowers. Are you sure you don't want a shot at this? It's big news. A *true* journalist would jump on it."

"I'm sure."

Mr. Gruben finally let it drop, though not without looking disappointed. He circled back to his desk chair. "So tell me. How are you coming along on your creative writing?" At her shamefaced wince, he said, "What's your excuse this time?"

Libby sidestepped the question and tore a page out of her notebook. "I've got a nice article here about the new store that's opening on the porch of my home. The Front Porch—that's what Naomi's calling it. Just your basic dry goods. She hasn't much room. I've been helping her get ready."

"You call *that* an excuse?"

Heat crawled up Libby's neck. She offered a second article. "This piece deals with the water system Ike and his men are putting together. The rest is news bits. One about the narrow miss with the tree felling. I suppose you've heard all about that by now."

Mr. Gruben sucked on a noxious cigar, his face growing more blustery with each puff. "Very well, Elizabeth. If you're bent on wasting your talent, so be it."

"I've been a little busy."

Palms flat on the desk, he leaned in a half-standing position behind his desk and spoke with a bite. "I've gone through three printer's devils since Earl quit and I'm currently running the whole paper by myself, so don't tell me about busy. Commitment! That's what separates the serious writers from the hobbyists."

"Yes, sir," she said meekly.

"A page a day would be a start."

"I'm sure it would," agreed Libby, startled by the unprecedented sparks.

Abruptly, he dropped back into his chair, and asked gruffly, "How's Ike?"

"Fine. He's waiting for me over at Baker's."

"Then quit wasting my time and his, too." Mr. Gruben knocked cigar ash off his jacket and ground it into the floor.

Libby was halfway out the door when a thought occurred to her. If that intimidating flash of temper was any indication, overwork was taking a toll. Overcoming her intimidation, she retraced her steps. "Mr. Gruben? Would it be presumptuous of me to suggest that you have a talk with Billy Young?"

"About what?"

"He tells me he once entertained the notion of going into the newspaper business."

"Can he write?"

"He says he can."

"What sort of an education does he have?"

"He's taught in an Eastern college, I know that much."

"He has, has he?" Mr. Gruben picked up his book, leaned back in the chair, and called a grudging, "I'll look into it. Thank you, Libby."

Willie Blue's was one door down from the *Gazette* office. Libby bumped into David on the sidewalk in front of the store. There was a block of ice in a feed sack at his feet. He was breaking it up with a hammer to ice down a tub containing bottles of soda.

She leaned over, and whispered, "You might go next door and ice Mr. Gruben down."

David grinned. "He's been cranky lately."

"So I noticed. Is Ike here?"

David nodded. "He was pulling his wagon around back the last I saw of him."

"Thanks, Davie."

"Lib? How come I never knew Ike had a sister living out your way?"

"Did Ike tell you that?"

"No. But Mr. Caton was saying something about seeing her with Ike. He says she's devilish."

Alarm ruffled Libby's nerve endings. Warily, she asked, "What was said to give you that idea?"

By the time David had finished his account, Libby could have used a little cooling down herself. Certain half the town had heard only half the information, the sordid, inaccurate half, she circled around to the back of the store where Ike and his men were helping Decatur load the wagons with stock for Naomi's new store.

Ike was grinning over something Decatur was saying as they heaved a fifty-pound bag of sugar into the wagon. As unconcerned as you please! The cluster of nerves tangled in the pit of Libby's stomach caught fire.

"So Mr. Caton's played the town crier, has he?"

Ike swung around, took one look at Libby's flashing eyes, and knew his goose was cooked. "B'fore ya start, jest let me say I ain't seen Hack all week. If I had of, I'd of told him."

Her eyes shifted to Decatur before coming back to him. Abruptly, she let the matter drop. "I've finished my errands. I'm going to call on Ida now."

"How're ya gettin' there?"

"I'm walking."

"If you'll wait a minute, I'll have one of the men take ya."

"That should give Hascal something new to talk about, shouldn't it?" she said with enough frost to wipe out an orchard or two.

Gentry's place was a mile north of town on a dirt road that got pretty sticky this time of year. But then, maybe she'd walk off some of that pepper. Aware of Decatur watching them with barely disguised amusement, Ike shrugged, and said, "All right, if that's what ya want. I'll come by that way and pick you up on the way home."

"Don't forget my chickens," she said.

"Be watchin' for me, Lib. We'll be done here in an hour or so."

It was his way of saying he wasn't coming to the door after her. *As if she would expect him to.* Libby turned away without a word.

21

Erstwood, as the Gentrys called their country estate, was a brisk, half-hour walk. The sunshine and pleasant spring breeze put the Hascal Caton incident into proper perspective and restored Libby's good humor.

The recently built, three-story house with its painted gingerbread towers and deep verandas rested like an elegant jewel on a well-manicured hand. The house was skirted by young trees and lush grass and vibrant flower beds that gave off a sweet perfume as Libby's skirt brushed their borders.

Chloe expressed glad pleasure over Libby's unannounced visit. She led her into the richly carpeted and draped reception room and climbed the open staircase to tell Ida she had a caller.

From her conversation with Mrs. Bee, Libby expected to find Ida confined to bed. She waited for Chloe to return with word of whether or not Ida was feeling well enough to receive a caller. But to her pleasant surprise, Ida came downstairs to meet her. She was wearing an exquisite dress made of layered yellow organdy. But as she drew closer, the yards and yards of filmy feminine elegance couldn't disguise her frailness. Libby thought of a faded flower as Ida grasped her hands and kissed her cheek.

"I can't tell you what a pleasure this is. Sit down, Elizabeth." Ida indicated with fluttering fingers the plush claw-foot sofa.

Now that she was here, Libby struggled with what to say. "Your flowers are lovely, Ida. I planted a lilac bush a year ago last October, and was hoping it would bloom this spring. But it doesn't look like it's going to."

"It's a little early yet for lilacs. Isn't it?" Ida added, as if doubting herself.

"Yes. It will be a few more weeks."

Ida seemed relieved. She confided, "My memory fades with my strength these days. I have to reach back and work really hard, searching for something that would have come easily just a month ago."

"Mrs. Bee told me about your illness," said Libby. "I'm so sorry, Mrs. Gentry."

"Thank you, dear. But I'll not waste our time together with a catalog of complaints. There are important things to speak of when you know you're dying. Of course, we all know that. We just busy ourselves pretending we don't, don't we, dear?"

"I hadn't thought about it, but I suppose that's true."

Ida was pleased with her answer. She confided, "Catherine thinks it's gruesome to mention death. But how am I to grow accustomed to the idea if I'm not free to speak of it?"

Libby made herself say, "You can speak of it to me, if you like."

"Thank you, dear. How have you been?"

"Just fine."

"And your husband?"

Surprised she would ask, Libby said, "Ike had a bout with influenza, but he's well now."

"I believe Sarah Jane mentioned as much. She comes several times a week to see me."

Ida rang a small bell, then chirped away like a little

bird, flitting from one subject to another. Chloe soon came bringing a tea tray and date bread still warm from the oven. She stayed, at Ida's invitation, and had refreshments with them, then left with the tea tray.

"How is your husband, dear?" Ida asked again, when they were alone once more.

Jarred, Libby said, "Ike? He's fine, Mrs. Gentry."

"I'm glad to hear it. He's Chester's nephew, you know."

"Yes, I know." Doubly saddened that Ida's thin and pale appearance told only half of the story, Libby steered the subject away from Ike. "I assume Maddie's staying busy with the twins. I haven't had a letter in a long time."

"Maddie and the children were here for several days early in the week. Or was it two weeks ago?" Ida pondered for a moment, then waved her hand dismissively. "She's a good little mother, and good for Chester, too. I like a woman who speaks her mind, don't you, Elizabeth? How is your husband?" she asked, before Libby could respond.

"Very well, thank you."

"And his sister?"

"I beg your pardon?"

"The young woman living up there in the cow pasture north of the grove. I can't think of her name. She's upset Chester, I know that much. Do you suppose she's striking back at Chester for his neglect all those years ago?"

Beginning to regret the impulse that had brought her here, Libby murmured, "I know too little about it to have an opinion on the matter."

A frown drew twin puckers over Ida's eyebrows. "I don't believe I ever knew her. It was before we were married, wasn't it? I recall Chester saying he sent her away. Or was it the girl's mother he sent away?" Ida rubbed her temples. Her violet eyes clouded. "I'm unclear on the details. I do recall Chester sending her away because he feared I would be jealous. Isn't that the dearest thing? He shouldn't have done it, of course. But then we all do things we shouldn't do. I know I have." Ida smiled sweetly and asked, "How's Ike?"

"He's fine." She fidgeted, nervous for Ida, lest she stray where Chester wouldn't want her to go. Warm to the tips of her ears, Libby stretched a hand toward the nearest table and indicated a vase bedecked in frolicking monkeys. "This is lovely. Japanese, isn't it?"

"Yes. It's a Monkey Vase. I'm fond of decorative vases. Particularly pottery."

Libby seized the moment. "That reminds me. Mrs. Bee stopped by not long ago. She commented that my cookie jar looked very much like one she'd seen at your home. It's pink and shaped like a rose."

"Oh, that." Ida wrinkled her nose. "It was Chester's mother's. I never cared for it much. I was going to dispose of it, but Chloe wouldn't hear of it. I gave it to her."

"Chloe?"

"My little jewel," said Ida, nodding. "You know Chloe, don't you? I'd be lost without her."

Many women called their hired girls their little jewels, but Ida said it with such affection, Libby knew she meant it. Abruptly, she was ashamed that her curiosity over the jar had weighed heavily in her desire to call on Ida. She had been so captivated with the whimsy that Ida was the giver that she felt a little let down now. Why had it seemed so important to her?

Seeing that Ida was tiring, Libby brought her visit to a close. As she came to her feet, she said, "Is there something I can do for you, Ida? I'd like to do something."

"You have, my dear. You have brightened my day with your visit. You'll come again, won't you?"

"I'd be happy to, as long as you feel up to it."

"Oh, yes! I enjoy having visitors. My battle with influenza really knocked the stuffing out of me. But I'm growing a little stronger and thinking of all the calls I must return. Chloe said she'd be happy to drive me about, if Chester isn't free to do so.''

"A drive in the country is always good for the spirits," said Libby. She embraced her in parting. "Give my love to Catherine and Maddie.''

"I will, dear. You don't mind if I let Chloe see you out, do you? I'm feeling a little weary.''

Chloe materialized so swiftly, Libby knew that she had been lurking just out of sight. When they reached the door, Chloe looked back over her shoulder, then stepped out on the veranda and closed the door behind her.

"She's getting a little balmy," said Chloe, the fierce protectiveness of her expression dulling the bluntness of her words. "But she was pleased you came. I could tell. Thank you, Libby.''

"I was happy to do it.''

Chloe plucked a clothespin out of her apron pocket. Rolling it between her hands, she said without looking at Libby, "I should have told you about the cookie jar.''

"I love the jar, Chloe. Thank you, a year and a half late." With a touch of reproof, she added, "Of course, when a person doesn't leave a card, she really can't expect a thank-you note.''

"No card? Of course there was a card." Comprehension dawning in her eyes, Chloe said, "You mean there wasn't? Forevermore! Did it blow away, do you suppose?''

"Perhaps. Not that it matters. I'll treasure it all the more for the mystery involved, and because it was you who gave it. By the way, I saw Dorie this morning at Baker's.''

A shadow crossed Chloe's face.

"She turned when she saw me and ran back up the stairs.''

"I'd run, too, if I were in her shoes.''

Searching for words to ease what she knew Chloe was feeling, Libby said, "Chloe, she needs you.''

Chloe wheeled around and walked back inside, but not before Libby saw the glitter of tears in her eyes. For a moment, the clock turned back to those dark days when Abigail was carrying the baby that wasn't Adam's. Where was little Rose today? On a mud lot somewhere in America, watching elephants dance and ladies in spangled costumes on swinging bars and bareback horses?

The day, so bright when she arrived, now matched her cloudy spirits. Libby lifted her skirts, navigated the wide steps and walked down the lane to wait for Ike.

"Get to see Ida, did ya?"

Libby jumped as Ike rose from a grassy spot between the road and Gentry's front gate. "Where's the wagon?"

"Rain's brewing. Decatur was anxious to get back to the grove with the store stock. Arthur and the boys drove our wagon."

A shower-scented breeze lifted Libby's hair and teased her skirt. "So we're walking home?"

"No, we're walkin' back to town, havin' an early dinner with your family, and takin' the train home."

"We are?"

"Yes, we are," he said, pleased at having surprised her.

"You didn't forget my chicks, did you?" she asked as they set off toward town.

"Nope. Forgettin's got me into enough trouble for one day."

Libby saw him tip his cap back and look up at the sky. She said, "There's not much point in your trying to read the weather when you can't even read Hascal Caton."

His sheepish grin deepened his dimples. "Can ya walk a little faster while yer bawlin' me out?"

"I'm not going to bawl you out. It's too petty to bother with."

"What's the matter?" asked Ike, wary all of a sudden. "Did Chester give you trouble?"

"Chester wasn't there."

"But ya did see Ida?"

"Yes. And she was very sweet. She invited me to come back. I suppose I will." Libby waited for him to offer some weak excuse why she shouldn't, but he didn't say anything at all.

A starling beat its wings across the adjacent field and lost itself in sulky low-slung clouds. The winter wheat sighed in undulating waves of green. Libby followed the dark sky and verdant field until they blurred. "Do you ever catch a glimpse of something inexpressible?"

"Out there?" he asked, following her gaze.

"No, in here," she said, and laid her hand over her heart.

He shook his head and reached for her hand, lacing his fingers through hers. "What's wrong, Lib?"

Libby averted her gaze and eased out a sigh. "Ida's preparing to leave this world. Dorene's preparing to bring a child into it. And they're both struggling."

The words fell short of capturing that fleeting image of continual motion, like a train that never stopped. The world was full of people embarking and disembarking at different stations in life, some of them hard stops. Dismissing the image for a more concrete explanation, Libby told him about Dorene being at odds with her family and wondered aloud where little Rose was and if she was happy and whether she would ever be told who her real mother was and how she'd come into this world. "Why does everything have to be such a struggle?" she asked, as Edgewood loomed ever nearer.

"I don't know. God puts a lot of stock in perseverance, I guess." He squeezed her hand, and said, "So yer goin' ta look in on Dorene, are ya?"

"Only if she wants me to." Libby tipped her face to his, saying with a little frown, "Seems kind of extravagant, taking the train home."

"I just got paid. We're takin' the train."

He walked along, one hand in his pocket and his

shoulders thrown back, whistling snatches of some half-familiar song. Curious all at once, she asked, "So how has your morning gone?"

"Saw Mr. Elliot in town. He says they're finishing the water system. We should have it done in another month."

"And then?"

"He says I've got a job with his firm anytime I want it. They contract projects from railroads all over the country. Looks like he'll be startin' on some work for the Toledo, Peoria, and Western Railroad north and west of us about forty miles."

She caught her breath. "It's decided, then? They're scrapping the project?"

He nodded.

"Are you interested in working for Mr. Elliot?"

"He made me a good offer. I'd be workin' for him, not any one railroad, and learnin' somethin' about civil engineerin' in the process. But it'd take us all over the country, Lib. I ain't sure you'd be suited to that kind of movin' around. Especially with most of yer family here."

Her heart dropped at the very thought. "What of your dream of the farm?"

"Can't have a farm without some money, and I'd make it a lot quicker working for Mr. Elliot than with any job I'm likely to find here at home."

"And the sirup camp?"

"Sirupin' shouldn't be a problem. The sort of projects Mr. Elliot's firm takes on have to be done in milder weather."

"So you are thinking about it," said Libby, almost breathless with the speed of events.

"I don't know, Lib. Let's pray about it a while, and not get in any big hurry, makin' up our minds. I'd like to get a barn up before too long and a . . ."

"Chicken house," she said.

He grinned and pulled her to his side. "Could you

forget about chickens long enough for me to buy ya a new dress?''

"I don't need a new dress."

"I say ya do." He tugged at the wide crocheted yoke, hiding her mending. "Can't have ya wearin' patched-up clothes."

"I have better dresses," she said. "I just happen to like this one."

He smiled, not fooled in the least, then tugged at her hand as thunder snarled off in the distance. "Come on, walk a little faster or yer goin' to be jumpin' over puddles."

Thinking a good hard sprint was just the thing to blow the cobwebs free, Libby challenged him to a race. "One, two, three, go!" she cried, and broke into a run.

Ike let her get a few feet ahead, then bumped her as he breezed past. Two strides ahead, he turned and ran backwards, teasing, "Come on, slowpoke."

"I'm holding back for the final sprint," she claimed.

The New Hope Church at the edge of town was only a stone's throw away when the growling thunder made good on its threat. Libby lifted her skirts as the skies opened, and sped across the churchyard on Ike's heels. They took the steps in twos, panting for breath beneath the sheltered entrance and chortling over their narrow escape.

A bolt of lightning splintered across the sky. Ike said, "Maybe we better wait it out inside."

Libby followed him into the silent church. He stopped so abruptly, she bumped into him. "What's the . . . matter?" she whispered the last word, as he turned to silence her with a warning glance and a backward nudge.

Resisting, Libby stretched on tiptoe to look over his shoulder. They weren't alone in the church. Chester Gentry sat near the front of the sanctuary, his forearms resting on the back of the pew in front of him. His hands were clasped, his head bowed. Deep in the throes of private sorrow, he hadn't heard them come in. *Dear*

Lord! The prayer caught in Libby's throat, for his agonized weeping was like the sound of the twin oaks rubbing limbs in the wind.

The joy of sharing a race with the rain leaked out of her in a wash of empathy. Yielding to Ike's silent, insistent prodding, Libby backed out the door after him. Wordless, they hurried down the steps, preferring the chilly spring shower to standing beneath the sheltering portico and risking encountering Chester with tears on his face. Libby released a deep, shuddering sigh and pressed closer to Ike.

22

One, two, three days late. Four, then five. In the week since Libby had asked Ike about the very situation now facing her, he had divided every waking moment between his water-system project and making firewood out of the limbs left from his tree felling. Once again, he was working too hard, and Libby didn't want to stir a false alarm. Particularly not when every day of work completed on the water system brought him a day closer to unemployment. *Unless he took Mr. Elliot's job offer.* Though they had been praying about it, she felt in her heart that he wouldn't. The Illinois prairie was Ike's home, and he wasn't anxious to stray from it.

Something to look forward to. That's what he'd said the last time they'd talked of this possibility. *Did he mean it, Lord? Or was he only saying it to put my mind at ease?*

Over the past days, Libby had watched and waited and prayed. Now, on her knees cleaning the stove in preparation for Saturday's birthday party, she relinquished her doubts unto Him who was able to do above and beyond her fondest request. *It's in your hands, Lord. Babies are Your workmanship. Prepare Ike to receive this news, and please, please, may it be a joy to him and not a worry.*

When Libby had finished her work, she made a pot of tea and joined Naomi out on the summer porch. It was the store's fourth day of operation. Word of mouth was traveling, and business had been brisk that morning. But the afternoon was wearing thin, and the little store was empty.

"Yer awful quiet," said Naomi, as they took their tea onto the open porch and sat side by side on the step, enjoying the spring sunshine.

Libby hesitated a moment, then confided, "No female complaint to complain about."

Naomi's glance was bluntly assessing. She asked, "Yer late?"

"Going on five days, now."

"And ya never been five days late b'fore?"

"Yes, though rarely," said Libby.

Naomi took a cautious sip of her tea. "The C & A project foldin' is a concern then, I reckon."

"A bit," Libby admitted.

"Have ya told Ike yet?"

She tugged at a near twig on her lilac bush. "I thought I'd wait until I was sure."

Naomi nodded and patted the little mound that became more prominent when she sat down. "Ain't no point in gettin' worked up until yer sure."

Unable to keep from relishing the possibility that life was growing within her womb, Libby reached an arm around Naomi and said with soft wonder, "Just think, if I am, they could be playmates."

"Friends, like their mamas." Naomi chortled. "That'd be nice, wouldn't it?"

Talking about it made it so much more real. The sunshine coming through the windows dazzled with promise of gifts given from the hand of a generous, loving God. Motherhood. Could it really be? Mother. Mama.

Mommy. Libby closed her eyes and embraced the sweet, fragrant whisperings.

Saturday came, and still no little "visitor." Libby's expectations continued to soar. A week. Had she ever been a week late? She couldn't recall. She finished frosting David's birthday cake, licked the knife, and dropped it into the granite dish basin.

Libby hummed as she scurried about getting things ready. David had caught a ride out from town earlier in the day. He was outside, watching Ike and his men working on the C & A's water tower. That was where Frankie wanted to be, too, but Naomi had left him minding the new store while she and Opal went home to change for the party.

Libby could hear Frankie through the wall as she donned her new muslin petticoat with its pleated dust ruffle. He was twisting Earl Morefield's arm into taking some oranges home to Dorene.

Dorene hadn't had her baby yet, but she had come home. Libby had been to see her twice a day over the past week. Dorene had opened the door that first morning, smiled tentatively, and said, "I'm fine. Thanks for checking. Would you have a cup of coffee with me?" By the time their cups were drained, the awkwardness was bridged.

As Libby slipped into her new shirtwaist, she prayed for a similar reconciliation between Dorie and her family. She tugged at the banded cuffs where the full sleeves with their embroidery insertions came together, then climbed up on a low stool before Ike's shaving mirror to adorn the collar of the sheer batiste shirtwaist with her mother's ivory cameo brooch.

"Fetchin'," said Ike, stepping in the back door to catch her preening.

"Think so?" Libby braced a knee against the sink board, and took another look in the mirror.

"Got anything for a sting?"

Libby winced in sympathy and stepped off the stool. "Wasp, hornet, or bee?"

"Wasp. But it was Saul, not me. His eye's about to swell shut. Laila's liable to come along and think the boys've been fighting over her."

"Again?"

"Don't know what yer grinnin' about," he said mildly. "She's troublesome, gettin' them all riled up."

Saul and Fritz had had a bit of a pushing match on Sunday. The gist of it seemed to be that Saul thought his part-time job with the Stapletons gave him first shot at Laila. Fritz objected on his brother's behalf. Apparently, Joseph had misinterpreted Laila's tender care of him on the ride to town after he'd broken his leg.

Libby nudged Ike in the ribs and said with a tilt of her chin, "It isn't Laila's fault that your men are making boys of themselves, mooning over her."

"You women. Always sticking up for each other."

"Careful," said Libby, making a face at him. "You're starting to sound like Hascal Caton."

"Every once in a while, Hack's right on target."

"I wish you'd let me know when that happens. Sounds like front-page news for the *Gazette*."

A grin tipped his mouth. "Feelin' sassy today, are ya?"

It wasn't sass. It was pure undiluted joy, and she was going to share it with him before the day was out. Libby laughed and gave him the container of soda paste and a flying kiss to the jaw, then closed the door behind him and finished dressing.

Her new skirt, made of an ivory-colored lightweight fabric, was fitted to the hips, then fell to her shoe tops in dainty pleats. She'd no more than fastened the placket when the door leading in from the store creaked open and Purdy and Dumplin slipped in.

Overlooking their failure to knock, Libby greeted them warmly. Earlier in the week, she had sent Mrs.

Field and the younger Field children an invitation. She asked, "Is your mother coming?"

"Can't. Doctor's on his way," said Dumplin.

"Oh, dear. Is someone sick?"

"Havin' a baby is all," said Purdy. "The girls are coming and Puddin and Punkin. Mama said thanks for letting them come. They'll be along with Laila and Joy."

"A new brother or sister. You must be excited!" said Libby.

Purdy shrugged. "Be all right, I guess."

"A pony'd be nice, though," said Dumplin, so sincere, Libby struggled to hold back a smile.

"And Mrs. Stapleton? Is she coming, too?" she asked, for common courtesy had dictated including Edina on Laila and Joy's invitation.

"No. Pretty Good says Miss Edina doesn't like your husband. Ouch!" Dumplin yelped, and jumped at his brother's pinching fingers. "What's that for?"

"Shut up is what for," muttered Purdy, and swung his gunnysack to the floor.

"Oh, dear," said Libby, her eye on the sack. "I told Opal no gifts."

"It isn't for the party, it's for you," said Dumplin. "Show her, Purdy."

"In here or outside?"

Seeing the gunnysack move under its own power, Libby crossed hastily to the back door and flung it open. "Let's go on out in the yard, shall we?"

Ike paused in nailing braces between the stout beams constructed to support the water tank at full ninety-five-thousand gallon capacity. He dragged his sleeve across his damp brow and watched Billy Young pull over to the side of the road in his mail buggy.

Billy secured his horse and ambled over. "Looks like you're working yourself right out of a job."

"Yep. I'd say three more weeks will catch her," said Ike, over the drumbeat of hammers.

"Your boys get their woman trouble ironed out, did they?" asked Billy, noting Saul's puffy eye.

"Not so's you'd notice," said Ike.

Billy grinned and tipped his hat back, a sparkle in his blue eyes. "Why don't you introduce me to the gal, and I'll solve this little problem of yours?"

"Chloe Berry won't think much of that idea," said Ike with a dry glance.

"Might do her good. She's awful sure of me."

"Yes, and if yer smart, you'll keep her that way."

Billy chuckled and nodded toward the crossing. "Is that her coming now?"

Ike looked to see Laila swinging up the road, hand in hand with Joy and four more little ragtag children. "Yep. Lib's havin' a birthday party for Davie. Must be the Field young'uns with her."

Billy took another sidelong glance at Ike's half sister, slapped his hat against his thigh, and asked, "Is it just me, or did she get all the looks in the family?"

Ike saw how Billy turned away from the road so as not to give Laila the idea he was overly interested. He grinned, and said, "Ask Lib about that."

Billy chuckled and took a turn along the freshly dug ditch where the pipe lay in readiness to carry the water from the well there by the creek uphill to the water tank. "You're moving right along. Are you going with Mr. Elliot when you're finished here?"

"I don't know, Billy. I can't say I'm uninterested. At the same time, I hate the thought of uprootin' Lib. Not to mention all I got to do around here."

"Picked up your boards from the sawmill yet?"

"Not yet. Haven't had time to stake the barn out, either. One of these nice clear nights, I'm figurin' on layin' it out by the North Star. Get it sittin' nice and straight."

"Let me know when you're ready to put her up, and I'll come out and help."

"Thanks, Billy. I'll do that."

"If you're not going to accept Mr. Elliot's offer, maybe you'd like a mail route."

Ike looked at him in surprise. "How's that?"

"I gave notice today. I'm going to work for Mr. Gruben."

"At the paper? Well, I'll be!"

"I'm going to start out setting type and learn my way through the business. If things work out, maybe I'll take over for Mr. Gruben when he's ready to retire."

"Good for you, Billy," said Ike. "Lib know yet?"

"She was the one who suggested Mr. Gruben give me a try." Billy turned his hat in his hand, and asked, "What do you think?"

"About the mail route?" Ike shook his head. He'd made better pay working for the railroad the past month than he could make in the next three as a farm laborer, and the mail route paid even less.

"What're you waiting on?" asked Billy.

He wasn't sure. *A nod from God, maybe.* Something to assure him that if there was a right choice, he was making it.

David's birthday cake, covered by an inverted pan so as not to attract flies, was in the middle of the makeshift table Ike had thrown together of boards and two sawhorses. Opal had decorated the brown-paper table covering in glued twigs, tiny stones, and colorful Indian corn. Libby's laundry bench was in line with one side of the table. Purdy balanced the gunnysack there, opened the neck, and shook out a live rooster.

Libby yelped and jumped back, then lurched forward again as the chicken fluttered his wings and flew onto the table.

"Watch out, he'll spur you!" warned Purdy. "See

here?'' He hiked his pant leg and showed off some angry scratches on his bare foot and ankle.

''Shoo, rooster. Get off the table,'' scolded Libby, just as Opal came around the side of the house in her party dress. The Field sisters were with her, little Joy Stapleton, and two towheaded, thumb-sucking toddlers. Laila followed close behind them. Spotting the chicken, she stopped at the end of the table and came no closer.

''Hey! Git off my tablecloth!'' Opal came to Libby's assistance, waving her arms and clapping her hands. ''Git, shoo! Git!''

The rooster gave them the evil eye, dipped his noggin, and pecked a piece of Indian corn glued to the paper table covering.

''Ya ornery old rooster!'' cried Opal, incensed. She hopped up on the bench and waved the skirt of her red dress, shouting, ''Leave off peckin' at them decorations, ya hear. Shoo! Git!''

The rooster cocked his head to one side, pecked at the kernel again, jerked his neck, and looked so perplexed, the children got tickled. Libby grabbed the broom off the back porch and tried to prod him off the table. He squawked and hopped over the broom.

''Whack him, Lib!'' ordered Opal.

A skilled escapist, the rooster hopped on top of the inverted pan that covered the birthday cake. He spurred Libby's broom, threw back his head and crowed at her, sparking laughter from the children. All but Opal. She jerked the broom from Libby's hand and took a swing.

''Watch the cake!'' cried Libby. But too late. The broom connected with the pan and swiped it out from under the rooster. The chicken went one way, the pan another and the cake, straight into Laila's arms.

Billy Young ambled around the side of the house just in time to catch the last act. ''My! That was a nice catch!''

Naomi, coming from the other direction, stopped short. ''Ain't that Pa's rooster?''

"No, ma'am, he's a runaway," said Purdy, smoothly.

"We caught him down by the creek," chimed Dumplin, hugging his lame arm against his round tummy as Libby, flushed and perspiring, reached for the cake, so gingerly balanced in Laila's hands.

"Careful! Cain't have a party without cake!" cried Opal. She jumped to hold the door. Libby carried the cake at arm's length rather than risk her new outfit. She came back outside to find Laila peeling the frosting off her shirtwaist and wiping it on the brown paper covering the table. Libby winced at the damage.

"I'm sorry, Laila. I don't know how things got so swiftly out of hand!"

"Them two, that's how!" Opal pointed an accusing finger at the Field boys.

"Opal, go on around front and git yer brother," said Naomi. "Boys, thanks for returnin' Pa's chicken. Maybe we could use yer sack to keep him in, once Frankie ketches him for us."

"Skilled diplomacy if ever I heard it," remarked Laila as Libby urged her toward the house.

"We'd better get that waist in cold water before the chocolate sets. I'll find something for you to change into."

"Thank you, Libby, but I don't think anything of yours will fit. I'd better go home and change," said Laila. "Joy? Are you coming?"

Libby saw the little girl's pixie face fall. "Let her stay, I'll watch her."

"Excuse me, ma'am," inserted Billy Young. "If you'd like a ride home, I'm at your service."

"Who is this fellow?" asked Laila, looking almost as haughty as the rooster had from his cake-pan perch.

"Billy Young. He's perfectly harm..." Libby stopped, embarrassed at such a shoddy introduction.

"... less," said Billy, making a little circular motion with one hand as if to draw it out of her. His dark hair tumbled over his brow as he swept off his hat. "And you must be Ike's sister."

"Laila Stapleton," Libby offered belatedly.

"It's a pleasure to meet you, ma'am."

Billy's blue-eyed smile fell short of charming Laila. She ignored his proffered arm, but did accept his offer of a ride home. Libby apologized again for all the trouble, then looked to see one of the Field girls fingerpainting in the chocolate frosting Laila had left behind. On the brown table covering, she had depicted Hascal Caton's stolen rooster.

"My goodness, you're quite the artist," exclaimed Libby.

The little girl licked the icing off her fingers and blushed to the roots of her pecan brown hair. When asked her name, she gave it in a barely audible whisper. "Very Fine."

She had eyes like a frightened fawn and an angst-ridden expression that squeezed Libby's heart. Libby asked, "Does everyone in your family draw as well as you?"

"Nope," Dumplin answered for his sister. "Just her."

"And you must be Pretty Good," said Libby.

"Yes, ma'am." Hair the same rust color as the inside of Libby's teapot framed the child's freckled face. She looked to be about Opal's age. Less timid than her sister, she volunteered the names of the look-alike toddlers. "This is Puddin, he's two, and this is Punkin, he's three."

Libby knelt before them and welcomed them both, then introduced David to the Field children and to Joy Stapleton. Needing to repair the cake, she sought Opal's help, saying, "Opal has some games planned. Opal? Why don't you get things started?"

Libby left Naomi overseeing the children and went inside to cook fresh frosting and piece the crumbling cake back together. The damage was considerable. It took longer than she had expected. When she returned, the bigger boys were racing across the pasture and the girls, along with Puddin and Punkin, were in the woodshed, playing with the baby chickens.

"What happened to the games?"

"You don't want to know," said Naomi, shaking her head. "Them boys make Frankie look like an angel. No wonder their mama stayed home. Enjoyin' a little vacation from her brood."

"No, she's home adding to it," said Libby. "Dumplin said the doctor was on his way."

"Seven kids in a wagon?" Naomi shook her head.

Libby shaded her eyes and looked across the fenced pasture to the creek bank, where the boys had discovered the climbing rope that Ike and his men had left tied to an overhead branch. They were soon taking turns, swinging out over the water on the rope. Dumplin, not to be limited by his withered arm, joined in.

"Give 'em a minute, and I reckon they'll all be on the other side of the crick and the rope'll be on this side," said Naomi.

The words were no more than out of her mouth when Dumplin lost his one-handed grip on the rope and splashed into the water with a shriek. "I can't swim! Help! Help!"

Libby leapt to her feet and was over the fence and halfway across the pasture when Frankie pulled Dumplin out of the water. Having concluded he was no worse for the wear, Libby ordered the boys away from the water, then returned to put the finishing touches on the party table.

By the time Billy and Laila returned, and the children came to the table for cake, Libby was trying to remember what it was about the Field boys that tugged at her heartstrings.

It was, to say the least, a lively party.

23

When the party was over, Laila left with Joy and the Field children in tow. David caught a ride back to town with Billy Young. Opal and Frankie went home to do their chores, and Naomi returned to her store tending, freeing Libby to check on Dorene. She pulled a handful of radishes and green onions from her garden before setting off over the railroad tracks with a wave to Ike as she passed.

"I'm off to Dorie's."

"Runnin' kinda late, aren't ya?"

"I'll hurry," she said, and quickened her step. Ike and his men would quit for the day within the hour, and he'd be waiting for supper.

Libby found Dorene sitting on a bench in the yard with a cowbell in her hand. Her swollen feet were propped up on a stump and her shoes were lying in the grass beside her. She brightened at the sight of Libby. "Libby! Thank goodness. I was afraid I was going to have to shove my poor feet into those shoes, and walk across the field."

"Why? What's the matter?" asked Libby.

"Earl gave me this bell to ring if I needed him, but I guess he's too far away to hear."

Libby's pulse quickened. "Dorie! Is it time?"

"I'm beginning to think so. I took a nap after lunch and woke up with a backache. Then, about an hour ago, I started having short twinges fanning across here," she said, drawing a hand over her lower abdomen. "But the last few have been sharp, and not so short."

"I think the doctor may be at Fields' place up there by the creek."

Relief washed over Dorene's pinched features. "Then it shouldn't take him long to get here. So long as Earl catches him before he heads back to town."

"I'll hurry," said Libby. She paused to ask, "I could go to the Fields' myself, if you'd rather have Earl come and wait here with you."

"I don't think Earl would be much help coaxing a baby into the world when he can't even prod a splinter out of his own thumb," said Dorene.

There was something of the scared little girl trying to laugh at thunder that caught at Libby's heart. *Next January, it would be her, facing this moment, born of union and nine months of waiting.* She dropped to her knees, clasped Dorie's hands in hers and made swift petitions for God's protection, for strength and for courage for her friend. Seeing the tears standing in Dorie's eyes, Libby kissed her cheek and squeezed her hands once more. "I'll be right back, and I won't leave you again until Dr. Harding comes."

Dorene caught her lip between her teeth as she nodded. Pain flickered in her face. She tugged her hands free, caught a sharp breath, and gripped her abdomen. Libby flew over the barn lot and across the field to get Earl.

Ike made himself a sandwich, then ambled out to the store. He traded a few words with Naomi, then glanced out the window and down the road, but saw no sign of Libby.

"She's been gone longer than usual," observed Naomi as she prepared to close the store for the day.

"Yep." Ike drew a chair into the open doorway between the cabin and the store, thinking he'd go see what was keeping her as soon as he finished his sandwich.

Naomi was in a talkative mood. She had old Hack's knack for storytelling. Ike was chuckling over her account of the birthday party when a buggy stopped out front.

"Sounds like yer gettin' a late customer."

Naomi paused in hanging up her shopkeeper's apron. She peered out the wide window, then drew back with a start. "Doubt she's here to shop."

"Who?"

"Ida Gentry."

"Ida?" A tremor of surprise stirred through Ike as he came to his feet. "Reckon she's here to see Lib."

"Libby told me about callin' on her. Surprised she's up to returnin' the call, though," said Naomi. "From all I hear, her mind's failin' fast."

Ike stopped in the doorway leading out to the open porch, for Ida wasn't alone. Chester was on the ground, facing the buggy, about to lift his wife down. Ida peered momentarily at him over Chester's shoulder, then seemed to forget he was there. She brushed a fly off Chester's collar. "It was lovely to take a ride, but it's good to be home."

"We aren't home yet, dear. You wanted to call on Mrs. Galloway, remember?" Chester's voice was a gentle prod.

"Oh?"

The vacant light in Ida's eyes put Ike in mind of a sputtering flame dulled by a sooty chimney lamp.

Hearing Ike's approach, Chester paused in helping his wife down and swung around to face him with a cold, desperate fire in his eyes. It charged the air between them. The silence was deep and abrupt. It compressed the air in Ike's lungs until with blinding insight, he understood the cause.

The tables had turned. Ike was on the porch, holding all the cards that counted. A smirk in Ida's direction would be lost on her, but it would gash Chester to the soul. *As he had been gashed there in the hot August sun all those years ago. Helpless in his youth to shield his mother, as Chester was now helpless in shielding Ida.* Ike summoned the bitterness. The rancor. The knotting in his gut that would enable him to settle that old score.

But it wasn't there. The harbored enmity had cooled on the rain-washed steps of the church a week ago. He was stripped without it. Sweat trickled down his neck. His limbs were weak. Someone in his flesh and bones moved down the steps and toward the buggy. Someone who sounded like him stretched out a welcoming hand to Ida Gentry.

"Lib's gone to check on Dorene Morefield. But I'll run and get her if you don't mind waitin', Mrs. Gentry. Won't take me but a few minutes."

"Dorene Morefield," said Ida, looking puzzled. "Would that be one of Lester's girls?"

"No, Mother," said Chester, and though she was his wife, not his mother, he spoke with such a wealth of tenderness and devotion that no other word would have fit so well. "It's Chloe's sister. You remember, Dorene Berry? She married Earl Morefield."

Ida's confused expression cleared. "Oh, yes! Of course! But I didn't realize Dorene lived out this way."

"Why don't you come on inside and make yerselves comfortable? Lib'll be disappointed if I let ya go without her gettin' a chance to visit with you."

Chester's reluctance was palpable. Ike could feel it in every fiber of his being. Smell it so strongly that surprise slammed through him when he deferred to Ida, saying, "It is your choice, Mother. Do you want to wait?"

Ida seemed incapable of making the decision until Naomi stepped out on the porch and offered her a cup of tea. Naomi led the way into the cabin and settled Ida in a chair at the table.

Chester followed his wife inside. He wrapped her lemon-colored shawl more snugly over her shoulders. His entreating gaze sought Naomi's. "You'll keep her company, Mrs. McClure?"

At Naomi's nod, Chester relaxed his guard. "Maybe I'll go check on my new tenant, then. I'll be back shortly, Mother." He turned to Ike. "I'm headed your way, if you want a ride."

Ike debated a moment, then climbed into the buggy with Chester. Neither of them spoke until they had crossed the railway tracks.

"The younger Mrs. Stapleton paid me a visit this week to say she was dropping her suit against me," said Chester without preamble. "Perhaps you knew that?"

"No," said Ike. Into the stiff stillness, he shot Chester a sidelong look and added, "Guess she's got some Galloway grit after all."

"If she does, she must have learned it from you," Chester countered abruptly. The softness that his wife rendered in him had vanished. "She sure didn't get it from Morgan."

Ike's resistance to hearing about his father from Chester bespoke a gut instinct that the truth, when it came, wasn't going to be gilded. He held his tongue, suddenly wanting to have it over with.

"Morgan was the proverbial prodigal son. He wanted and got his inheritance years before he had any rightful claim to it," said Chester, swift, blunt, and unyielding. "He squandered it and came back for more. My father put his foot down. It was his intention to see that Morgan never got another dollar from the family coffers. His will was worded to keep my mother from overriding his wishes, should she outlive him. As it turned out, he didn't give her enough credit. Mother's lack of a will was not an oversight, as Edina and your sister seemed to assume. It was her way of honoring Father's wishes."

"What are ya tellin' me for?"

"I want it out in the open." Chester laid the buggy

reins over his knees as they plodded along the green-canopied road. There was something in the painstaking way he unhooked his wire-rimmed spectacles from each ear that made Ike think of lifting a halter off a horse's ears. "Was my father hard-nosed toward Morgan? God is the judge of that. Have I been hard-nosed toward you? Yes, I see that I have. But I haven't cheated you out of an inheritance, if that's what you're holding against me."

"It isn't," said Ike. "Told you before you've got nothin' I want."

Chester's folded glasses paused en route to his pocket. "If I was standing in your shoes, I'm not sure I could let it go so easily," he said, as if unable to put aside his common horse sense.

The words sat there between them as they traveled over the bridge and to the sap house. It struck Ike that now, as all those years ago, it wasn't poverty or plenty that sailed or sank the ship. It was Who steered the rudder. Twice in a week, he'd felt heart sorry for Chester Gentry. He felt even sorrier now. Nobody had been any more generous than Chester in contributing to the funds that had built New Hope Church. And here he sat, so close to being free from life patterns that encumbered him, and yet so far away. Like the rich younger ruler who came to Jesus and went away sorrowful, mastered not by his wealth but by his misplaced confidence in it.

But who was he to point a finger at Chester? How many times had he let the tug of a deep-seated grudge master him? Ike summoned the courage to be honest. "Last time we talked, you said you were sorry for bein' harsh toward my mother and sister and me. I should have been man enough to accept your apology. If the apology still stands, or even if it doesn't, I forgive you."

Chester's jaw slackened. Though he wasn't moving, he seemed to settle deeper into the seat. Weariness weighted the corners of his mouth. They fell in line with his drooping moustache, giving his whole face a worn, ragged look. He studied Ike for a long moment, then shifted the reins and offered his hand.

Ike took it, returning the firm grip.

"Thank you for your kindness to Ida," said Chester, his voice grown husky. "She's . . . important to me."

Mutely, Ike nodded, for it was easier to shift the conversation to Ida. Walls didn't fall without the thunder of crumbled stone and the lung-choking dust of dying enmity. "Lib's been prayin' for her. Folks at church, too."

Chester's eyes dimmed with unshed tears. He set his jaw and offered, "I'd like to think He'll make her well. If He'd just do that for me, I'd give Him anything I've got."

"I reckon He will. One way or another."

Chester flinched. Ike grew hot, thinking maybe he'd gone too far. But it was the truth he thought as he climbed down from the wagon. *Thank God it was true.* Just as it was true that Chester had all that he had because God let him have it. It was God's, including Ida. Ike wished he had the words to tell Chester that, for if he could once understand, then he'd know where his treasure lay. But words were Libby's gift, not Ike's. It was she who had told him months and months ago to let this grudge go. And she was right. He felt freer than he had in a good long while. He lifted his face as he stood beside the wagon and said, "Thanks for the ride, Chester."

Chester tipped his hat, chirruped to the team, and drove on down the road. Ike strode across the flower-beaded woods skirting the sap house, and over the fence onto the property he had so recently farmed. Doc's horse nickered softly as he passed on his way to the door of the herder's shack where Earl and Dorene made their home.

Earl came to the door. A solidly built young man with a clean-shaven jaw and sharp, dark eyes set amidst finely chiseled features, Earl generally had a confidence about him that ran toward cockiness. But not tonight. Tonight he was nervous as a trapped cat. What with moving his things out of the barn and Earl moving in, Ike had seen enough of Earl since losing the place that the awkwardness between them had dulled a bit.

Ike asked, "Congratulations in order yet?"

Earl flashed a weak grin and plowed a hand through sleek black hair. "Doc says it'll be a little while. You're here for Libby, I guess." He winced at a guttural moan from the other room. "Don't suppose you'd let her stay and take my place a while?"

A smile worked at the corners of Ike's mouth. "I'll leave that up to Lib. But one of you is goin' ta have to come sip tea with Ida Gentry."

Ida was almost asleep in her chair by the time Libby made it back to the cabin. Ike had forewarned Libby on the walk home that Ida's mind wasn't clear. Even then, she was startled that Ida had to be told who she was before she recognized her.

As they visited, Ida perked up a bit. She shared a few stories about her grandbabies and was laughing over Libby's playful account of David's birthday party when Chester returned for her.

It gave Libby a jolt to hear Ike invite Chester in and offer him a cup of coffee. Chester declined, saying they needed to start home, or darkness would catch them on the road. He was helping Ida from her chair when her eye fell on the rose cookie jar.

"Forevermore!" she exclaimed. "Chester! It's your mother's cookie jar. Now how did I misplace that? No matter, so long as it's found. Bring it along, dear."

Libby found herself in the embarrassing position of trying to explain to Chester how the cookie jar had come into her possession. Chester looked just as uncomfortable.

"It's Libby's, Mother," he said gently.

But Ida, in her sweet way, was adamant that he bring it. Chester, accustomed to doing her bidding, seemed at a loss. Ike settled the matter by carrying the jar out to the buggy himself.

Libby's regret over the lost jar was nothing in comparison to her anxiety over Ike's reaction to Ida taking it from her. She knelt before the stove and was feeding corncobs to the fire for supper preparations when he came back in. She braced herself, certain he'd have a few choice words over the incident. *Please God, not now, not when I'm all primed to tell him about the baby.*

He crossed back to the stove and sat down. "Guess it would have been brassy to empty out the cookies first," he said, tugging at his ear with boyish regret.

Relief rushed over her. Nerves dancing as the moment drew closer, she laughed and promised, "I'll make you some more. But not tonight. I've got supper to fix and then, if it's not too late, I'd like to dash over to Dorie's and see if she's had her baby yet."

"Can't that wait until mornin'?"

"It could. But I'd like to see this baby being born and figure out what I've let myself in for." Heart pounding, she dropped another handful of corncobs into the fire, and left the door gaping open as she looked up to his face gone still. Color rushed over it. *Pleasure? Surprise? Dismay?* She caught her breath in strangled prayer as he found his voice.

"You miss yer monthly?"

"Yes."

"How late are ya?"

"A week."

"Yer sure, then?"

"Pretty sure."

He caught her hand in his and brought her to her feet. Even as he pulled her into his arms and rested his chin on the crown of her head, Libby wondered if it wasn't just a ploy to hide his true thoughts from her.

Ike did some quick math in his head and asked, "January?"

"Yes."

"A new baby right b'fore sirup season. And just when you were gettin' over bein' shy of the evaporator."

Refusing to be humored by his bantering, she said, "I know it makes things harder for you. The truth now—are you upset?"

He shook his head. "The truth? I'm kinda surprised it hasn't caught up with us before now."

Ike knew that wasn't all of the truth, but he figured it was the part she needed to hear. He heard her breath go in a rush, and fit a thumb to her chin to tilt her face up where he could see it better. Her cheeks were flushed from the corncobs roaring and the firewood catching. "Lib?"

"Yes?"

"Close up the stove door. I cain't see ya for the smoke."

She laughed and flung her arms around him and buried her face in the crook of his neck. Chuckling, he kissed the tear from the corner of her eye and teased, "What's this? And here I thought this was what you'd been wantin'."

"It is. More than anything."

The rest of the truth, Ike faced later as he let himself into the sap house after walking Libby back to Dorie's. He lit a lantern and honed sharp edges on the axes he'd been using, chopping wood for next sirup season.

Knowing a baby was coming changed things considerably. Building a barn, catching up on things around here while he watched for a job that made good use of his abilities without uprooting them was now a luxury he couldn't afford. He'd have to take Mr. Elliot's offer. He didn't want to dampen Lib's pleasure tonight by telling her so. There'd be time enough for that in the weeks to come.

The quieter part of the truth Ike would never have to tell her was about the war and old wives' tales. He thanked God that his past hadn't thrown such a long shadow as to catch her in it, too. He thanked God for

Libby. For Mr. Elliot's offer. For Laila's courage in refusing to go on swallowing doses of her mother's bitterness. He prayed for Ida Gentry, too, and, finally, for
Chester.

24

Libby sat on the open porch step on a late Sunday afternoon, her open journal propped on her knees. She smiled as she scanned her most recent entry, for the exhilaration of having helped with the delivery of Dorene and Earl's raven-haired baby boy leapt off the page.

In the two weeks since then, she'd barely had time to write her *Gazette* articles, much less focus on the creative writing Mr. Gruben kept admonishing her to begin. Feeling guilty over her failure to follow through on her good intentions, Libby picked up her pencil. The sound of backyard hammering receded as she brought her journal up to date:

> *It's been a job staying caught up on my baking for Ike and his men now that Dumplin, Purdy, Pretty Good, and Very Fine are stopping by after school with Frankie and Opal. I wish the cookie tin I bought from Mr. Brignadello's huckster wagon was indeed "magic" as he professed with that salesman twinkle of his. For each cookie taken, another one appears. Very clever, Mr. Bee! Who could resist such a whimsical pitch?*
> *We went to town yesterday after the men re-*

ceived their final checks. I walked out to see Ida again and was warmly received, though to be honest, I'm not sure she knew me. Physically, she seems stronger, but mentally, she continues to decline. Pastor Shaw came while I was there. He gave me a ride back to town and brought to mind those words about life being a vapor, here for a little while, then vanishing. I thought of the maple mists and how they waft so sweetly, yet briefly before lifting through the cupola, heaven bound. I'm trying to fill my days accordingly and trust God with Ike's decision to work for Mr. Elliot, even though it means we'll be apart for a while.

Bolster me, Lord. Prepare me for tomorrow's parting. Libby looked across the rutted road into the woodlands, seeking strength in the Power that called such beauty into being. The trees, like awakening giants, had stretched their limbs and uncurled their green fists as God lavished earth and sky and everything in between in cool rich shades and varied textures.

Hascal Caton emerged from the lane that led from Naomi and Decatur's house deep in the woods. Unaware of Libby there on the porch step, he looked into all five mailboxes standing in a row. None of them were his. He picked up his mail in town these days, along with his daily dose of gossip. At Libby's greeting, Hascal gave a guilty start away from the mailboxes and came on his humping gait to meet her.

He eyed the row of milk glasses at the end of the porch and glowered. "That little Frenchie ort to be tarred and feathered and rode out of these woods."

Mystified, Libby echoed, "Frenchie?"

"Wanderin' about with a box of paints under his arm and puttin' on airs jest like his young'uns ain't been pilferin' the neighborhood!" groused Hascal, as blustery as a March day.

"Mr. Caton, who *are* you talking about?"

"Why, the Mar-key Day La-Fay-et, that's who! Ain't ya seen him, comin' and goin' from that painted-up gypsy wagon of his, and him all gussied up in a suit and shiny shoes and his cat-whisker moustache waxed and curled?"

"Oh! You mean Mr. Field!"

"Mr. La-Fay-et Field, who'd ya think?" he said, bobbing his hoary head. He rocked back on his heels and narrowed his eyes. "I'm warnin' ya, Miss Lib, no good'll come of lettin' them little pint-sized Frenchies on the place. Why, listen at 'em, poundin' away in the woodshed. Beatin' the feathers off yer little yeller chicks, more'n likely."

"I wouldn't worry about that too much, Mr. Caton." Libby flipped her journal closed, lest he peruse her private thoughts the way he did the mailboxes. "The children have a vested interest in those chickens. I gave each of them one of their own."

"Ya did what?"

Libby explained that the children were coming each day to care for the chickens. When the hens began to lay, it would be their job to collect the eggs.

"Tarnation, Miss Lib, it'd be a heap less bother jest to do them things yerself and keep them little chicken cluckers off the place!"

"Perhaps. But I'd miss their company."

Hascal rocked back on his heels, thumbs hooked in his suspenders. "Don't know what Ike's thinkin', goin' off leavin' you here alone at the mercy of them hapless young'uns. Mark my words, they'll hep themselves to whatever ain't nailed down b'fore he comes home ag'in."

"Shame on you, Mr. Caton, having so little faith in children. And after they've worked so hard moving the wood out of the woodshed, and building perches and such."

"So that's what all that bangin' is."

Libby nodded and urged, "Go around back and have

a look. You'll be amazed to see what they've accomplished.''

''Danged addlepated nonsense,'' Hascal muttered, and lumbered around back to find fault.

Not nearly so confident as she let on, Libby hoped that she hadn't waded into deeper waters than she could handle where the Field children were concerned. She had made the chicken offer because she sensed needs in the children that were going unmet. However she hadn't realized then that, in coming weeks, Ike wouldn't be around to back her up. It was only after he'd talked to Mr. Elliot and ironed out the details just a few days ago that she'd understood the dramatic change this job would make in their lives.

Libby resumed her journal account:

> *Mr. Elliot has contracted a job with the Toledo, Peoria, and Western Railroad about forty miles from home. Ike will make a good wage as an oiler, keeping the steam-driven shovels in good repair. He will be staying on a camp train, and be on call at all hours should there be trouble. While I could probably find boarding in the nearby town, it would be a pointless expense, for Mr. Elliot estimates the work will take about a month.*

Libby tugged at a branch of the lilac bush growing near the step. Its leaves were the size of mouse ears, but the only touch of purple came from the violets she had planted at its base. Two squirrels played tag in the twin oaks, and a rabbit nibbled on tulip greens just a stone's throw away. The earth, so ripe with promise, emitted a fertile fragrance.

Libby breathed deeply of spring and rested her hand over her abdomen. Her eye wandered to the trackside water tank bordering their east yard. It had no roof. That would have to be done before winter. But for the time being, Ike's work was done. Decisions were made, to-

morrow was a fresh page in their lives, and today was
hurtling along. She put her journal away and circled to
the backyard.

"That's it, yer gettin' the hang of it, Purdy," she
heard Ike say. "Dumplin, give them chicks a rest and
come hold one end of this board for me, will ya?"

His way with the boys pleased Libby. Was this baby
a boy? A son to tag at his heels? She would think about
that, not tomorrow and good-byes.

Ike had postponed his barn-building plan and made a
deal with Laila, who was hiring Saul and the Seredys
full-time. She intended to raise a few cattle on the lush
pastures surrounding her home. Horse power was needed
to raise the crops to supplement grazing. Their agreement gave her the use of Ike's horses throughout the
spring, summer, and autumn months in exchange for
boarding them.

After the boys had gone home and Ike's bags were
packed and supper was nothing but a pile of dishes in
the sink, Libby rode with him to take the team and
wagon up to Laila's place. Joy Stapleton waved to them
as they passed the Fields' gaily painted wagon home.
Pretty Good and Very Fine looked up from picking wildflowers, smiled shyly, and waved, too.

"Do you suppose Joy's wandered off again?" asked
Libby.

Ike patted her knee and called her Mother Hen.
"Mind yer own business, Mrs. Bee," he said, borrowing
a line from Kersey Brignadello, who tried without suc-
cess to discourage his wife's lively interest in other
folks' affairs.

"All I meant was, she seems a little young to be at
the neighbors' this close to dark."

"I reckon Laila knows right where she is," he reassured her.

Libby let it rest, her thoughts shifting from Joy to the
separation awaiting them at dawn. The remaining hours

must carry them over a month of days and nights. She resisted melancholy, wanting to spend the time well so that the parting picture would draw Ike's thoughts to harmony and cheery home fires waiting for him.

She tapped her feet and tried to teach him the words to a Scottish song, learned at her father's knee, a lilting, good-humored melody. "It's custom-made for gandy-dancing," she said, and nudged him with her shoulder. "You can belt it out when you're laying new steel and think of me."

"I don't plan on layin' any steel, Lib. Jest monkeyin' with the steam engines, is all."

"All right, then. How about a love song?" She twined both arms around him, and laid her cheek against his strong shoulder.

"There ya go, flirting with me again."

"Yep," she said, and he laughed.

Just beyond the trees the land opened to fading sky and an expanse of emerald pasture. A white clapboard house and a collection of outbuildings sat at the edge. Ike stopped the wagon between the house and barn.

Laila strode across the yard, jerking a white muslin duster cap off her head as she came.

Libby's breath caught at the sight of her swollen eyes. Thinking Joy might be the cause of her distress, she said quickly, "We saw Joy just now. She's with the Field girls."

"I know. I sent her. Things got a little intense around here." Features strained, Laila thrust the duster cap into her apron pocket. She swept an unsteady hand through her hair. "I was just on my way to tell her that Edina is gone and that Mrs. Seredy is waiting supper."

"Gone?" echoed Libby.

"In a great stormy hand-washing gust, ridding herself of her simpering fool of a daughter, to quote her loosely," said Laila in that flippant way of hers that hid deeper emotions. "With a tidy sum in her pocket, I might add."

"What's this all about?" asked Ike.

"Chester was here earlier. He paid Edina off."

Libby accepted Ike's help down from the wagon, saying, "But Chester told Ike that you'd dropped the suit."

"*I* did. Edina didn't. She was adamant that as Morgan's widow, she was entitled to something."

"And Chester gave in?" said Libby, surprised.

"He said fighting her was too much of a distraction, that it was taking time he wanted to spend with his wife. A sentimental soul might have been moved by that, but not Edina. She says he cracked under the pressure." Mouth crimping at the corners, Laila said, "It was a handsome sum they settled upon. I ate crow while Edina jeered at me for having lost my stomach for it. She said the deal was nearly sealed when I bowed out."

"You're not having regrets, surely!"

"Lib," murmured Ike, a staying hand on her arm. To Laila, he said, "Where was she headed?"

"Back East to my stepfather."

"That'd be Mr. Stapleton, her prominent attorney, I reckon," said Ike.

Laila's mouth quirked again. "Edina's boasting of him gets a little tiresome, but he *is* a shrewd attorney. He's been working behind the scenes on this lawsuit. The outcome bears his seal."

Quietly, Ike said, "The only seal worth havin' don't come from a law office, Laila, and it won't cost you yer integrity."

"I hope you're right, because I have a child depending on me to provide for her and nothing to work with but this piece of land and Hungarian helpers who, by the look of it, know scarcely more than I do about planting crops and raising cattle. God help me, I'm in a mess." Laila slipped up to the near horse, and laid her face against his neck.

Libby let her breath go, realizing it wasn't a firestorm. The fire had gone out of Laila before they arrived. This was ashes. Ashes and fear and second-guessing setting in. She moved closer, and slipped an arm around her. "You're not alone, Laila. Ike knows a little something about cattle. And so does Billy Young. He grew up on a ranch. He'd be glad to advise you."

But it was to Ike that Laila turned, her eyes dark and needy. A tear slid down her cheek. She caught it with the back of her hand, and said in a voice grown thin and reedy, "You told me once that I wasn't fatherless. How can I be sure, Ike? Will you tell me that?"

The evening that followed wasn't the one Libby had envisioned as the clock ran down on Ike's departure. With wisdom and understanding, Ike became the brother Laila needed him to be. They talked and prayed and showed to Laila the pathway leading to the Father who never abandoned His children. By the time they started home, Joy Stapleton was fed and tucked snugly in bed and Ike had a sister in the truest sense of the word.

A gentle night wind blew as Libby and Ike walked hand in hand with the moon and stars lighting their way through the woods and across the bridge and over the railroad tracks that would take him away at first light. Once home, they quibbled over who would tend the fire, then laughed and let it go out, and wrapped themselves in their wedding quilt. In the midst of their good-byes, Libby heard the twin oaks whispering in the yard.

At dawn, Ike boarded his train and waved from the window as the wheels crept forward and began to roll. The whistle piped down and smoke curled on an east-born wind, wafting along the siding, wrapping Libby in a swirling black mist. It lifted and floated on over the trees as she rose on tiptoe and followed a few strides, head back, red dawn in her hair, reaching her fingertips to the glass. Ike matched his palm to hers on his side of the window, throat growing thick as she beamed at him and mouthed the three little words he liked most to hear her say.

"I know," he said. "Me too."

25

The hardest part of good-bye was waiting for the next hello. Or so it seemed to Libby as she spent her first week without Ike, watching the mail for word from him. Mail was delivered to the grove on Wednesdays and Saturdays, so it was a long wait between deliveries. Libby's days were full, but the evenings were lonesome. Reading helped, as did writing.

Dear Ike,

When Mr. Elliot said a month, I took him at his word. Today is one day spent. Only thirty to wait. I weeded the garden this morning. The children stopped after school and "wallered" the chickens—Hascal's word, not mine. He stopped by to give me fish fresh from the creek and bend my ear a while. If Naomi's store was just a little bigger, I'm certain we'd soon have old-timers lounging on crates and cracker barrels arguing over crops, weather, and politics.

Dear Ike,

Laila was here today. We went to see Dorie and

who was there holding the baby but Chloe! Dorie
was overjoyed at their reconciliation and so proud
of little Earl. It makes me excited for what lies
ahead. Chloe was warm to me, but cool with Laila.
I wonder what Billy Young has on his heart? Any
thoughts on that? A train blew soot and cinders
all over my wash this afternoon. It was a for-
lorn-looking wash anyway, as there was nothing
of yours on the line.

Dear Ike,

I picked my first peas today. I wonder, is our baby
even that big? It brings to mind the verse about
being fearfully and wondrously made. Very Fine
painted a galloping horse on the side of the woodshed. Lafayette Field isn't the only painter in that
family! I'm enclosing some stamps and a few Gazette clippings I thought you'd enjoy. As you will
see, two were written by aspiring novelist, Libby
Galloway, and two by Mr. Gruben's new assistant,
William Young. A little while ago, I walked over
to the tracks and stood on a rail, thinking maybe
you had your foot on a rail, too, and it would
connect us. I know. They aren't the same rails. But
this whim operates on the same principle as Mr.
Brignadello's cookie tin.

Dear Ike,

I took the milk train to town today and went to see
Ida. She asked about you repeatedly, and yet, by
the time I hugged her good-bye, she was calling
me Catherine. Mr. and Mrs. Brignadello were
there. Mrs. Bee says that Chloe has her nose out
of joint with Billy, to which Kersey told her to—
well, you know what he told her, and of course
she just laughed like she always does and went
right on speculating. They gave me a ride back to

town. It was a good thing Kersey was along, or I
might have been tempted to tell Mrs. Bee about
the baby. I know, that's tantamount to putting it
in the paper. But it's such a delicious source of
conversation, I find myself having to work hard at
holding on to the secret. But I will. For a while,
anyway. I enjoyed supper at Verna's with Father,
Davie, and Teddy. Arthur is boarding at Baker's,
as well as Fritz and Joseph and Hans, so they ate
with us, too. Their English is improving, though
they seem to be dropping their g's. I wonder where
they picked that up?

Though Libby didn't tell him, it gave her heart a hard
twist to see Ike's men without him. They had all found
employment before he left. Naomi had hired Fritz to
help his brother Joseph part-time at Willie Blue's in
Edgewood. Fritz was also working part-time for Lester
Morefield. Likewise, Arthur was employed making
bricks and field-drainage tile at Lester Morefield's tile
factory, located midway between Old Kentucky and
Edgewood. Hans was working at the blacksmith shop.

Dear Ike,

I brought Davie home with me yesterday. He's
staying the weekend and going to church with
Laila and Joy and me tomorrow. Father insisted
I take Proctor and the buggy. He says it will save
him board at Woodmancy's Livery. Do you sup-
pose he's thinking I'll visit more often with a horse
and buggy at my disposal? Hascal dropped by
with three rabbits, skinned and ready for the pan.
'And don't ya be givin' 'em away to them little
chicken-cluckers,' he warned. That's what he calls
the Field boys. Chicken-cluckers. Lord love the or-
nery old rascal. I didn't pay any attention to him,
though. Dumplin and Purdy like rabbit too well to
deprive them.

Saturday afternoon was the first free time Ike had. He went to the post office in the nearest village and found several letters from Libby waiting for him in general delivery. He wasn't much at corresponding, but he could tell by the tone of Libby's letters that she was anxious to hear from him. He debated a moment, then bought six postcards, and wrote a few lines on each of them.

"Ma'am?" He sought the attention of the woolly-haired hawk-eyed matron behind the counter.

"Mrs. Esyster," she said, introducing herself. "May I help you?"

"Would ya send these one a day?"

Mrs. Esyster looked him up and down, faintly disapproving. He wasn't sure when he left whether she would do as he asked, or toss all six in today's outgoing mail.

Libby's second week was under way with still no word from Ike. *He listens to You, Lord. Could You tell him to write his wife?*

Not only was it futile to fret, it seemed a breach of faith. So, every time a worrisome thought popped into her mind, Libby picked up her Memorandum book and added a few paragraphs to a story she'd begun two years earlier and never finished. By the middle of the week, she was so engrossed, deliberating over words and phrases, that she neglected to cross the road to the mailbox until dusk. There were two postcards waiting for her from Ike.

Dear Lib,

Been a little dry here. Winter wheat looks good though. Work is going fine. If you see any of the boys, tell them hello for me.

Dear Lib,

The food's not bad, but I miss your maple sugar

cookies. How is Laila getting along with Saul and the Seredys?

Saturday rolled around again, and with it a paycheck. Ike cashed it at the store. Mrs. Esyster gave him six letters from Libby and a disparaging look as he bought more postcards.

"See here, young man. If I'm to be a party to this, I'm entitled to a question," she said, when Ike passed them back to her a while later with the same request as the previous week.

Ike shifted his feet and waited.

"Is this your wife you're writing?"

"Yes, ma'am.

"It's kind of the lazy man's way out, isn't it?"

Ike tugged at the red bandanna he wore to keep the cinders off his neck when he was working. "I'm not much of a letter writer, ma'am."

"I noticed," said Mrs. Esyster. "If I could make a suggestion . . ." Her dark gaze bored into his, daring him to deny her. "I've got a nice sale going on ladies' scarves."

Ashamed he hadn't thought of it himself, Ike had almost settled on a silky one the color of a dusty rose when he remembered what Libby'd written about standing on a rail at dusk. He walked back to the men's department, bought a railroader's bandanna, folded it up in an envelope, and sent it off with a note enclosed:

Dear Lib,

Something to hold me in mind. I'll be puttin' my foot down on the steel about seven and thinking of you doing the same.

Mrs. Esyster left little doubt as to what she thought of his purchase. But Ike stood his ground. "She'll like it."

"If she does, she must have quite a case," she replied dryly.

Dear Ike,

Laila and Joy came this afternoon. She said to tell you hello and that Billy is advising her in choosing heifers to fatten. His help seems to have bolstered her confidence in her cattle-raising plan. To hear her tell it, it's all very platonic between them; she's had only one great love in her life and intends to keep it that way. And here you thought she was toying with all your boys' hearts! Shame on you! Edina left the whole Field clan on Laila's hands. The Mar-key Day La-Fay-et (that's what Hascal calls him), has finished the mural and will probably be moving his family now. I'm concerned for the children. Please pray. Hans has quit his job with the smithy in Edgewood and gone to the C & A shops in Bloomington, where the opportunities are better. I miss you but am feeling well and thinking I might start a quilt for the baby.

Dear Ike,

I'm enjoying your postcards. According to Davie, so is everyone else in the post office, with the exception of Joseph, who as yet, can't read English. Father returns your greetings. And Captain Boyd, who has come out of retirement to take over Billy's mail route. The Marquis has found another painting job, though it's houses instead of murals. He told Laila he has enough work lined up to keep him busy all summer. She wants to ask him just when she might expect him to be moving his wagon off her property. I confess I'm of mixed feelings. I hate to see the children uprooted. I've

*grown fond of them, and it would hurt me to think
they might have a rough time of it elsewhere.*

Dear Ike,

*I've been to town again and had David here over
the weekend. Upon returning him home, I visited
both Ida and the Grubens and read my story to
them. It's about a schoolmarm losing her dashing
young beau to a banker's daughter who is as wild
as a March hare. The marm then falls madly in
love with a lumberjack, a man of the trees. (I
thought you'd like that.) Mrs. Gruben loved it. Mr.
Gruben was somewhat less enthusiastic. He recommended a few revisions. I intend to rewrite it
and send it off to the* Vermonter. *I hear they're
partial to trees and lumberjacks in Vermont! The
Field children continue to stop each day after
school and care for the chickens. They are growing so fast, you won't recognize them (the chicks,
not the children). Pretty Good and Very Fine are
equal to whatever Opal's lively imagination con-
jures. Often, Purdy and Dumplin infringe on their
play, violating the rules in their rambunctious
way. But even in their mischief, they tug at my
heartstrings, and it worries me what will become
of them, should they move away. I'm cutting tri-
angles for the baby quilt.*

Dear Ike,

*We're wearing away at the calendar, aren't we?
I'm feeling fine and am not suffering any of the
unpleasant symptoms of which Naomi forewarned.
The garden is flourishing as is Naomi's store. I
went to see Dorene and the baby today and noticed on the way home that the wild black rasp-*

*berries are doing well. They should be ripe by the
time you come home. If so, I promise you a pie.*

Dear Ike,

*After failing to get any definitive answer from Mr.
Field, Laila twisted my arm into going along with
her to call on Mrs. Field today. She answered the
door with a baby in her arms, and little Puddin
and Punkin hiding behind her skirts. The wagon
home was a wild disarray of soiled clothing, dirty
dishes, and so forth. You get the picture. Sadie
Field is passive and gentle and very loving to the
little ones, but she has no sway with the Marquis.
She said she hasn't seen him all week. Apparently
he's finding it more convenient to stay in Edgewood than to come home of an evening to his wife
and children.*

With over half of their separation spent, Libby had a
collection of eight postcards. She had shuffled through
them so much the corners were frayed and each word
was committed to memory:

Dear Lib,

*Some kids were playin on the railroad ties, jum-
pin' from stack to stack today. Three boys and a
little red-haired girl. Made me think of you.*

                                          Ike

Dear Lib,

*I should have thought about Proctor myself. He'll
keep the pasture clipped. Too bad school isn't out
yet. David could stay and keep you company.*

                                          Ike

Dear Lib,

Enjoyed the newspaper clippings. Billy's doing all right. Regarding the other, M.Y.O.B.M.B.

Ike

It didn't take Libby long to figure out his code: "Mind Your Own Business, Mrs. Bee." In other words, don't play Cupid. As if she would! While none of the cards was very newsy, each one carried the warmth of knowing he'd bothered, after a long day's work, to walk into town and send word he was doing well and thinking of her.

Separation, Libby had to admit, benefited her writing. The ambitions that had waned with marriage were fanned and she was dreaming once more of getting her start in magazines, and then trying a novel. Was it the thought of being a mother, or the children who filled her yard from the time school let out until they went home for supper that turned her thoughts to writing for children?

The story seed that rooted itself in her mind involved children similar in age and mischievous disposition to Purdy and Dumplin. Libby mused over it as she worked in the garden and at the sink and over the laundry tub. Maybe their father could be a fiddlemaker. No, not a fiddlemaker. How about a potter? Yes, a potter. And he could sell his pottery door to door as the family traveled about the country in . . . well, it couldn't be a gypsy wagon. That was a little too close to home.

Libby's back ached when she went to bed, but she supposed it was the weeding and laundering. She found a comfortable position, prayed for Ike's safekeeping, then fell asleep wondering how her story family would travel. By the next morning, she had the answer. They traveled by rail! The father was a world-famous potter. Scratch the selling door to door. He had exhibitions in large cities! He was so involved in his clay creations that his children, feeling unwanted, jumped the elegant private railway car in which the family traveled and landed in some farmer's yard and raided his wife's chicken coop. Yes! Now she was getting somewhere! Libby stretched a bit, trying to ease the pain in her lower back.

She returned to the story and scribbled away most of the afternoon. But her back pain worsened and by evening, much to her distress, her flow came in a rush. Could she be almost a month late? Or was it a miscarriage? Such a weight of disappointment settled over her that she couldn't even speak of it to Naomi. When the children came the following day, so bright and cheerful and full of energy, feeding the chickens and swinging on the rope and gorging themselves on cookies, Libby broke down and cried.

Alarmed, Opal got her mother. Naomi urged Libby to go see Dr. Harding. She put it off until the following day. Dr. Harding felt certain that what Libby described was a miscarriage. He gave her castor oil and recommended several days of rest. But the question that nagged, he couldn't answer. "Sometimes it's nature's way," he said.

Way of what? And who was this "nature," but God? Surely Dr. Harding didn't mean that this was God's way. God would not snatch this child from her womb. Heartsore, and too close to tears to confide in her family the purpose of her visit, Libby spent the night in town.

When she arrived home the next day, there was a postcard as well as a gift from Ike waiting in the mailbox. The blue bandanna brought more tears. Libby donned it and walked out to the rail at seven.

A train came along. She retreated to the yard, and watched the black smoke curl over the cab and slowly drift, disperse, and melt away. Like her dream of a grayeyed child trailing at Ike's heels, legs stretched out, trying to walk in his footsteps. *My gift to him is gone.*

Libby tried with trembling fingers to staunch the flow of tears. But the sobs pushed out of her lungs and couldn't be forced down. *I don't understand. God, what did I do wrong?*

Libby let two days pass without writing to Ike. The berries ripened. Naomi left Frankie in charge of the store and went berry picking with her one evening. She awoke the next morning in an agony of itching.

"Chiggers," said Naomi, when she came a while later. Chiggers were mites that tunneled beneath the skin and caused red itching welts. Naomi had them, too. She dug at her waist through the folds of her Mother Hubbard dress and confided, "I don't know about you, but I could bawl."

Libby could, and did. The misery went on for several days. Between scratching and soaking in a tub to relieve the awful itching, Libby managed to write Ike a few brief lines:

> *Dear Ike,*
>
> *Saul hurt his hand oiling Laila's windmill. I don't think it's serious, but it did require stitches. Naomi and I got into chiggers while we were picking black raspberries. She's miserable, and so am I. Maybe it's my punishment for not visiting Ida the last time I went to Edgewood. I should have, I guess, but it's depressing to see her this way.*

Ike frowned as he read the letter. The tone was different. And not a word about babies. Or the children. Or writing. It lacked . . . sparkle.

He looked toward the general-delivery case, thinking surely there were more letters. Mrs. Esyster met his gaze.

"That it?" he asked. She nodded. At length, he said, "Think ya better wrap up that pink scarf for me, if ya still got it."

Mrs. Esyster replied with matronly smugness, "Didn't I tell you?"

Ike included a short note.

Dear Lib,

It looks like it'll be another week before I'll be home to help you scratch your chigger bites. You aren't letting those chickens wear ya down, are ya? How's your quilt coming? What's Laila done about the Fields? Are they still around? How's Frankie and Opal? Are you doing all right, Lib? You aren't sick, are you?

Libby hadn't told him, and still she'd made him anxious. *Lord, I didn't mean to worry him.* Or had she? Maybe. Subconsciously. Always there had been someone to turn to. Her father. Her brothers. And lately, Ike. Now, when she needed him, he was away, and she was left to bear her bruising disappointment alone.

Alone?

The heart echo was too strong to dismiss. Her ears, for days, had been closed to Him. Libby bowed her head in quiet contrition and went inside to pray. When her soul had grown calmer, she leafed through His word, seeking underscored Scriptures through which He had spoken to her in the past. *Fear not. We walk by faith, not by sight. Let not your heart be troubled. My rest, my fortress, my God in whom I trust.*

She wasn't alone. God was here in the middle of her hurt. She was His chick, gathered beneath His wing.

The tears came and went and came again. A slow leaking of self-will until once more, Libby was His emptied vessel, willing and ready to be filled and poured out again in works God was even yet preparing her to do.

26

🐍 Libby's letter saying she had miscarried was waiting for Ike when he stopped by the store on Saturday. He sent word by one of the other men that he would be back by starting time on Monday, then boarded the next train for home.

It was evening when Ike arrived at the grove. Libby had no way of knowing he was coming, but as the train rolled to a stop, he saw her standing at the edge of their yard in the shadow of the water tower. It was hot for the end of June. Her sleeves were rolled up to her elbows, and her hands thrust into her apron pockets.

The pink scarf in her cascading curls was a delicate contrast to the blue bandanna tied at her throat. But it reflected her nature. Both sinewy and sensuous. Tenacious and tender. Enduring, endearing. She glanced with dilatory interest toward the crossing, then did a double take. Ike's heart kicked as her face lit up and his name broke from her throat.

She met him with a misty-eyed, tremulous smile. Until her arms were around him, he had feared that she would hold back, feeling stung that he hadn't been there when she needed him. He should have known better. A

261

rush of heat strummed through him as she clung to him without saying a word.

"You all right?" he asked finally.

"Yes." Libby placed one hand in his and wiped away tears with the back of the other. "You surprised me, is all. Happy tears," she added, and pressed her fingers to her mouth as if to steady the involuntary muscles making her chin quiver.

"You sure?"

Libby nodded, salt in her throat. "Where's your bag?"

"I didn't get your letter till I walked into town today. Wasn't time to go back for it."

"Then the job isn't finished?"

"No. Not yet. Got another week, anyway."

She mastered her disappointment. "You didn't have to come. I'm doing all right."

"Just all right?"

"It was hard at first. Not physically. I was just so . . ." Her eyes glimmered, but she fought back the tears and finished, "Looking forward to it."

" 'Course ya were."

Libby leaned into him and kissed his mouth. "I missed you."

"Me too," he said. The love in her eyes stirred over him, easing the constriction in his chest. He cupped her face and kissed her back, then slid his hands along her shoulders and down her arms and turned with her toward the house.

Arm in arm, they strode past flowers that had bloomed in his absence and entered the house by the back door. It was warm. Tranquil, with the familiarity of textures and colors that bespoke her caring attention to the details of their home.

Libby turned into his arms again. The fragrance of the sweet peas twining along the chicken fence wafted through the open window and melded with the dewy freshness of her mouth and the scent of her hair and the intoxicating taste of her skin. Her nose and cheeks were pearled in light freckles. Her fingers, stained from berry picking, were cool to the touch as they traced the line of his jaw, trailed over his ear, and splayed across his back.

"I'm sorry I wasn't here," Ike said.

"You couldn't help it," she murmured. "Anyway, it wouldn't have changed anything."

"I know. But you shouldn't have had to face it alone." His eyes followed her as she pulled away and set about fixing him a late supper.

"I thought that at first." Libby struggled to be honest. *Lord, it is good to have him home. With his hair curling over his collar and his boots, those dear scarred-up boots on my floor again.* By an effort, she stayed the course and shared the self-knowledge that had come to her over the past week of seeking and searching. "But when you *are* here, Ike, it's so easy to put my confidence in you. To let you be my strength when I'm hurt and helpless and at a loss."

"I want to be," he said, and sat down at the table.

"I know that, and I love you for it," said Libby. "But there's a danger to leaning too hard."

He turned his chair and watched her make pancakes and eggs and set a pitcher of their own sirup before him, waiting all the while for her to explain what possible danger there could be in a man taking care of his wife.

The small fire she'd built to cook his late supper made it uncomfortably warm in the cabin. His skin was shiny with the heat and musk-scented as Libby set his plate before him, then paused behind his chair to encircle him with her arms and drop a kiss on his temple.

"I want to be here," he said again, for the subject seemed unfinished. "But I have to provide."

"I know. And it's all right. You aren't meant to bear my burdens, Ike. Just to share them. Like you're doing now."

"Kind of late."

"No. Not really. You were doing what you had to do. To expect any more than that is to shift God from the center of my heart and to put you there instead. I've been doing that for too long."

Startled, he turned, trying to read her face. Her loose hair brushed his ear. "Lib, that isn't so."

"Isn't it?" Gently, with the glitter of tears, she asked, "Then why have I for all of these months thought of a child as a gift I could give you instead of a gift that God gives us? Why have I thought more of pleasing you and less of pleasing God?"

"Pleasing me?"

"It's true, Ike." Though Libby had eaten earlier, and wasn't hungry, she pulled out a chair and sat down across the table from him. "I've thought a lot since our marriage of giving gifts to you, and not nearly enough of how I might use for God the gifts He's given me."

Ike was struck by the sudden thought that she was assuming blame where she had no reason to. "You don't think God is punishing you, surely?"

"No," said Libby, though she had been tempted to wonder in the first heat of hurt and despair. "That's just another way of asking for a reason."

Libby thought how she might share the hard-won knowledge that she could endure being apart from Ike if she had to, but that she wasn't made to weather separation from God. The hurt had gone deeper because she had unwittingly clung to Ike instead of God. It was difficult to know how to phrase it so that Ike didn't think she was diminishing his place in her life. Far from it! She was trying to free him from thinking he had to be her whole world, as Mr. Gruben was Florence's.

Libby opened her mouth to the bite of pancake he offered, chewed it, and savored the sweetness of the sirup. "You make a good husband, Ike. You sweeten my life. But you're not my soul-keeper. And I'm not solely yours. I'm God's first, and He knows how to take care of me, though I may forget it sometimes."

"So what're you sayin'? No more pleasin' me?" Ike asked, smiling a little as he offered her another bite from his plate.

She declined it with an answering tilt of her lips. "No. I'm saying we'll both be better pleased if I give Him His place and you yours. Yours for a while, at least, seems to be with the railroad. I admit, I wasn't wild about you taking this job. But now that you have, I don't want you feeling pulled in two directions. Or guilty if you're not here when I want you to be."

He'd been wondering what this had to do with her loss and his absence. Suddenly, he saw that she hadn't strayed so far off course. She was offering him the peace of mind to do his part in taking care of her, even when it took him from her side.

"I'll have to leave by noon tomorrow," he said, for it seemed a fitting time to tell her.

Libby nodded. The brevity of time was why they had agreed, before he left, that there was little point in his coming home until the job was done.

"Maybe you can come along on the next job, since yer not . . ."

Seeing his gaze shift, as if he thought he had to tiptoe around it, Libby finished for him, saying, "With child? Oh, but I am, Ike. I'm with six of them every afternoon and some imaginary ones all evening. Story children. They talk to me, you know. And I talk back. On paper, anyway."

He was relieved to see the spark in her eye and the energy that flowed through her voice when she talked about her writing dreams. "I always did say you were never at a loss for words."

"Yes, well, wait till you see what I've made and we'll see who is at a loss for words." Libby pushed away from the table. "Don't go away, I'll be right back."

Libby went behind the screen and changed into the old bloomers and chemise she had altered into a swimming costume. She had embellished them with hearts cut from a blue railroader's kerchief just like the one Ike had sent her.

"It's what the fashionable railroaders' wives are wearing this season. To the swimming hole, anyway." She modeled her costume with a fine-turned ankle and a bit of clownish preening.

He laughed, a short-lived laugh that turned to a protest as she unlaced his boots, pulled them off and urged him toward the door, and a swim in the C & A's roofless water tower.

"Lib, it's pert near dark. I ain't climbin' that tower."

"Suit yourself," she said, and padded barefoot out the door.

Shoot. He couldn't let her go by herself. She'd break her neck, climbing the ladder. Or drown. Ike put out the lamp, shoved his feet into his boots again and caught up with her, still trying to dissuade her. "How about the creek, if yer bent on swimmin'?"

"There are snakes in the creek."

"Probably snakes in the tank, too."

"Long-legged, ladder-climbing snakes? There's one for the books."

"Skeeters'll eat you up," he warned, and slapped one off his neck.

"No, they won't. They can't fly that high."

Suspicious all at once, he said, "Lib, you been up there b'fore, haven't you!"

"Only once," she said quickly. "And that was to keep an eye on Dumplin. He doesn't swim so well with his lame arm, but he couldn't let Frankie and Purdy have all the fun." She wheeled around and asked, "What about you? Are you coming? Or do I get to have all the fun?"

The water was bracing to say the least. And she was wrong about the mosquitoes. But she was right about the fun. They splashed and laughed and played like children. By the time they climbed down again, Ike was relaxed and refreshed and more content than he'd been in a while. They shivered their way over the dew-drenched grass and back to the cabin. The warmth left from her cooking fire was welcome now.

Libby changed into her night shift and stood by the stove, combing her hair dry and talking about the children and her writing and the Grubens, about Billy's job at the paper, about Laila and her cattle and her Hungarian helpers. About his men, and her family, about Dorie and Earl and Chloe and all that had happened in the past month.

Ike watched her from the bed, thinking that, like the lamp, she gave off her own cheery glow. At length, she quieted, put her comb aside, and came to him. He had thought it might take some time before she would make herself vulnerable to the same disappointment again. But it wasn't so.

She was softness after weeks of uncompromising steel and iron and steam. The daily cacophony of machinery and men, of barked orders and banged knuckles, of hot sun and short tempers seemed a distant memory. *Drink waters out of thine own cistern.* She was water to him, cool and clear, deep and refreshing.

The pain of impending separation, the disappointment of loss gave way to whispered words and rustling corn-husks and love's healing touch.

27

❧ Having conceived once, Libby had no reason to think it wouldn't happen again. But the months passed, and her flow came and went and came and went, just as Ike came and went on his railroad jobs. Libby began to wonder if she had been mistaken on her wedding night, feeling born to mothering.

"We'll keep tryin', Lib," Ike would say. "You've got your little chicken-cluckers to look after and your writin', and I've got my work. We're young. There's plenty of time for a family."

Libby would fall asleep in his arms, knowing it wasn't a question of time. It was a question of purpose. God's purpose for them. But grasping that and yielding herself so that He could hand-tool her to His intended course was a slow uphill crawl.

Sometimes small private hurts crept in when she was a day or two late, and hope would rise only to give way to disappointment. Or when her friends chatted of childbirth and children, be it first words or first steps, the trials of runny noses or handprints on walls or muddy feet on fresh-scrubbed floors. It was natural they should speak of such things, for it was the fabric of their days, just as writing and waiting for Ike to come home was hers.

Libby knew that, and thanked God for the hands that rocked the cradles and for her little band of neighbor children. She thanked Him for Abigail's generous sharing of her growing family, and for Davie, too, whom she had had a hand in raising from infancy to the time of her marriage.

These precious ones gave her shared interests with her friends even as they enriched her life and increased her wisdom, for in all modesty, she could sometimes see with a clearer eye the strengths and weaknesses, even the needs they themselves could not or would not see in their children. Rarely was her advice sought, yet she prayerfully acted upon her insights and in so doing enlarged the circle of children who knew they could always count on time, tenderness, and a cookie from her.

By Libby's twenty-first birthday, it seemed to her that it had been a long time ago that she had caught her first glimpse of Edgewood at the tender age of seventeen. She remembered thinking, as she saw the lovely trees, how nice it would be to live among them with her pencils and tablets and spend her time weaving stories. That wish had nearly come true here at the grove.

She loved the lush shimmering green of summer and the red-golds of autumn. But winter and early spring came to hold a favored place in her heart. That was the only season Ike was home for any extended period of time, for Mr. Elliot, true to his original agreement, laid him off every sirup season. As for the rest of the year, Mr. Elliot saw a lot more of Ike than Libby did. Perceiving his varied interests and abilities, he gradually shifted Ike's chores from hammer, wrench, and steam to supervising duties and even surveying in preparation for new roadbeds.

Occasionally, on short projects when there were suitable accommodations close to where Ike was working, Libby traveled with him. The broadening of horizons was helpful in her writing, until one glad day, she made her first sale to a magazine. Payment was made in copies rather than cash, but it was a thrill to see her name in print, and one she couldn't share with Ike when the letter of acceptance came, for he was away. They celebrated when he came home, and in time, Libby began to be compensated for her stories in modest checks instead of copies.

As for her travels, Libby's longest stay away from home was three months, which she spent getting acquainted with Ike's mother and sister. They lived within a few miles of a new railroad bed Mr. Elliot's firm was preparing to build. Libby adored Nona Kay from the moment they met, for she possessed many of the attributes Libby had known in her own mother. Cicely, Ike's sister, was married to a rancher, and was about as uncompromising as the rugged acres their cattle ran. In time, they became friends. Before returning home, Libby had a family picture made by a traveling photographer, so that she could show Laila how strikingly similar she and Cicely were in physical features. Though Libby wouldn't have told Ike for the world, Laila was by far her favored sister, for she had become softer in a way that had nothing to do with social refinement.

Libby was glad Ike enjoyed his work, but as time passed, she grew increasingly concerned that the lure of the rails would crowd out his original dream of buying some land close to their timber and farming again. The lumber he had had sawn from his own trees had long since been stored out of the weather in Decatur's barn. Would he ever have time to build a barn of his own? Or had his dream changed so that he no longer thought of a barn as a necessity?

Separation wrought other changes, most notably a spirit of independence in Libby, and her own way of doing things. Likewise, for Ike. So while they anticipated for weeks, even months sometimes, the honeymoon feelings that came of reunion, there was also the reality of dusting off the art of compromise.

"This isn't one of yer little chicken-cluckers yer talkin' to," Ike would say when they butted heads over some perceived usurping of his authority.

"No, and I'm not some broken-down steam engine you're wrenching on, either," Libby would reply in response to what she perceived as an infraction upon her liberty.

After a day or two, they would sort out their roles and for the most part, limit their quibbling to good-natured exchanges over the woodstove, that source of contention so long-contested it had grown as warm and familiar as the glow of the stove itself.

As the seasons turned, Ike's men left the community one by one for Bloomington's Hungarian neighborhood and jobs in the railroad shops. Arthur Reiner was the only exception. He courted and married Chloe Berry in a whirlwind romance that kept Mrs. Bee chattering for weeks.

Chester Gentry clung vainly to hope where Ida was concerned, and made countless trips, taking her to renowned specialists to no avail.

Sadie Field and her children stayed at the grove, while Lafayette traveled the country, trying to scratch out a living from his art.

Laila ceased denying that her affections for Billy Young were platonic, and finally married him and bore him a son. Libby's friends, Catherine and Maddie, gave birth within hours of one another on New Year's Day, 1909.

Libby sent gifts and received thank-you notes. Catherine mentioned in hers that long-ago bet made in the cornfield amidst the noise of ears hitting the bang-board. It freshened the memory of predictions as to who among them would do the most mothering in future years: Catherine, Maddie, Libby, or the Berry girls. Catherine wrote:

*I'm having the seams let out on all of my gowns,
but I'm staying neck and neck with Maddie in this
race. She declares we're both losing badly. Dear
feisty Maddie, still marching to the beat of her
own drummer, trying to overthrow the natural order of things. She never changes! You haven't forgotten our ten-year cornfield reunion, have you,
Libby? We're almost halfway there. You had better get busy.*

Though it wasn't a deliberate unkindness, Libby's
nose prickled and her eyes dampened as she read the
note and questioned in a weak moment why her womb,
like the lilac bush in the yard, failed to bloom. She and
Ike had ceased to say "when we have children." It was
now "if we have children."

When Ike came home for sirup season, Libby mentioned adoption. Ike was silent on the subject, expressing
neither approval nor disapproval. That was his way. He
needed time to mull things over. Libby knew that, and
was in no hurry herself, for if it was God's plan, He
would bring it about.

*Is there a little child somewhere in need of our loving
home? Are You preparing us to meet the needs of some
very special little person? Help me to know, Lord, if it
is so. Give me the wisdom to see and to recognize such
a child.*

28

February 1909

Ike had been home for a month when Libby received word from Adam, saying Abigail was ready to deliver their third child any day and would Libby come stay for a while.

"Adam Watson, it's sirup season," Libby muttered to herself as she read the letter.

Yet, even as she mounted a heatless protest, Libby knew that she would go. Abigail needed the help, and Libby liked spending time with the children, even if it meant sacrificing a few days of Ike's precious time at home. She tucked the letter into her pocket, carried supper over to the sap house, and tended the evaporator while Ike ate. When he had finished his meal, Libby read Abigail's letter aloud.

Ike squinted in the lantern light, checking the thermometer. "What're you goin' to do about yer crew?" he asked.

Libby winced. Ike had dragged his feet a bit when she'd suggested hiring the Field children to help with some of the sirup work. With Billy, Decatur, and Frankie on the payroll, he'd thought he had all the workers he needed.

"But the children need the money and the experience," she remembered saying when urging him to reconsider, and more for her than the children, she suspected, he had finally agreed on the stipulation that Libby oversee in person whatever task she put them to.

The boys were eleven and twelve now, the girls fourteen and fifteen. They had helped wash buckets, drive the manufactured spouts that had replaced Ike's homemade ones, and hang the new galvanized buckets. Most recently the children had been coming after school on the days the trees ran to help gather sap.

Libby took the lantern and held it closer as he tested for sirup with the saccharometer. "You're satisfied with their work so far, aren't you?" she asked.

"Not bad fer chicken-cluckers."

Libby smiled at his teasing, and pointed out, "It's heavy work for the girls and Dumplin's lame arm limits him some. But he doesn't complain any more than average. And Purdy, I'm happy to say, is first-rate help."

"What're ya gettin' at, Lib?" The oxygen-deprived flame flickered low in the maple mists, making Ike's face difficult to read, but there was no mistaking his guarded tone.

"I'm not going to ask you to oversee them," she replied, "if that's what you're thinking. But Frankie could handle the responsibility until I return."

"Mixin' boys and girls out in the timber without any supervision?"

"It's just a couple of hours after school. You know as well as I do that Frankie could handle it."

"What do you suppose old Hack'd have to say about that?"

"What's that got to do with anything?"

"Lib, you know by now it doesn't matter how innocent a thing is, Hack can make it out to be lower'n a worm's belly in a wagon rut."

Libby backed out of his way as he reached for a bucket to draw off sirup. "Then let Hascal tramp out in the woods and keep an eye on them!"

"I reckon he will. From behind a tree somewhere."

"The old busybody. You'd think his own grandson would at least be safe from his clattering tongue." But she sighed, conceding his point. "What about Decatur?"

"He might welcome Purdy, but I wouldn't count on him molly-coddlin' Dumplin, and I know he won't go for the girls trekking along on the crew."

"Not even if Opal went, too?"

"Not a chance. But you can ask him about the boys if you want to."

Libby promptly did so. Decatur thought that he and Frankie could use Purdy's help. He wasn't sure how much help Dumplin would be, but when pressed, agreed to give him a chance.

The girls were disappointed at being "laid off," so to speak. They continued to be a part of Libby's "chicken project," but gave their share of the egg money to their mother to help with household expenses. Libby knew they had been counting on a few earnings that would be solely theirs. Very Fine had exhausted her father's supply of old paints, and was yearning for her own set of oils. Pretty Good's taste ran more toward fabric, as Libby was teaching her to sew. Libby had them both in mind as she packed her suitcase on Monday morning.

"Maybe when I get back, the girls and I will try making some maple candy and see how that sells," she said to Ike as he was eating his breakfast.

Libby put cookies out on the store counter for Naomi's two-year-old, little Floy. She wrote a note to Pretty Good, concerning chicken-feed sacks at her disposal for garment sewing, and another note to Dumplin, telling him to pick two hens out of those that had quit laying and take them home to his mother for supper. Purdy. She needed something for Purdy, so he wouldn't feel left out. Libby remembered a magazine containing one of her stories, sent to her from the publisher. Wasn't there a picture of an automobile in that magazine? She jumped up, grabbed it from her bedside table, and returned to the table, with both magazine and scissors.

"Reckon if we ever do have any little ones, it'll be hard for a man to get any attention around here," observed Ike. He drained his coffee cup as she flipped through the magazine.

"Aha!" said Libby, spotting the advertisement on the back of the magazine. "A Cadillac Model K Runabout."

"Shoppin', are you?"

"Hardly! Purdy has a collection of horseless carriage pictures."

Ike bumped the table, coming to his feet, then risked the sharp points of her scissors, hauling her into his arms. "This is good-bye, Lib, on account I have sap to boil and you're neglectin' me every which way."

"Neglecting you? And here I was just about ready to let you sit on my suitcase."

"Can't get it latched?"

"No, and I can't get it to the station by myself, either." Libby wrapped her arms around him and tipped her face in silent entreaty.

A grin worked at Ike's lips. "You wantin' to do our kissin' here? Or are you butterin' me up for the porter job?"

"Both," she said.

Ike laughed and kissed her and closed her suitcase. Before leaving the house, they prayed together just as they always did when he was leaving on a job. It seemed strange to Libby, though, to be the one who was going instead of the one waving good-bye.

With the trees devoid of leaves, Libby had a good view of the McClures' home from the train. It had grown two back bedrooms since little Floy's birth. A big-eyed mop-haired ball of joy, Floy accompanied Naomi to the store every day. He was tall enough to turn the door handle now, and toddled into Libby's cabin a couple of times a day to curl up in her lap with a book, or to "hep" with whatever little chore engaged his fancy.

The train picked up speed, then broke from the woods and onto open prairie. Laila and Billy Young's home lay to the east, beyond the creek. Billy had given up his job at the paper, and seemed to have finally found his niche in cattle-raising. He was helping Ike with sirup this season, and on the rare occasions Ike was home, he helped Billy with seasonal chores. Likewise, Libby and Laila shared heavy-duty household chores, socialized back and forth, and, when Ike was home, planned family outings.

The Fields lived on the west side of the tracks in an eyesore of a place just north of the McClures. Lafayette Field had traded the acre of untillable land with its smokehouse and a toolshed with a fellow who'd commissioned a mural and then couldn't pay for it. Lafayette pushed the two outbuildings together, called it a home for Sadie and the children, then resumed his meandering about the country in his gypsy wagon, painting everything from religious murals in sanctuaries to impressionist prints to painted ladies on the walls of saloons, hoping all the while to be discovered by the art world.

He'd become the butt of a lot of jokes locally. But Libby, seeing his family struggle, didn't see anything amusing about a man's family suffering for *his* art. She'd once remarked she wasn't certain how they kept the wolf from the door. Overhearing her, Hascal replied, "Reckon the wolf don't want ta be lunch for the Markey Day La-Fay-et clan, that's how."

For all his bluster, there were sparks of light in Hascal, evidenced in the fish and wild game he anonymously deposited on the Fields' doorstep. He was careful not to let the left hand know what the right hand was doing, and would no doubt deny it if asked. But Naomi, who lived near the Fields, had seen her father pass on his errands of mercy, and shared her sightings with Libby.

Why was making babies so easy to Sadie, when caring

for a large family came so hard and seven children suffered for it? The answer Libby received was similar to Ike's M. Y. O. B. M. B., with the heart-print, *Feed my lambs.* Libby continued to do so, not just from her garden and chicken pen, but from God's word, be it in the children's class she taught at Timber Creek Church every Sunday, the children's choir, or in her own backyard.

The Chicago and Alton Shops were on a sprawling west-side Bloomington acreage surrounded by neighborhoods of ethnic diversity. Between the shops, the roundhouse, the railroad yards, the offices, the station, the train crews, and the businesses that catered to the railroad families, railroading was the city's biggest employer. This spawned pride and a fraternal spirit among the workers. Though the pay was better than average, it was demanding and often dangerous work. Besides frequent layoffs, the men labored on long shifts. Maimings and sometimes death resulted from work-related accidents. But the hardships fostered a spirit of brother-keeping among railroad families that frequently lent itself even to the trackside hobo camps.

Adam was no exception. He and Abigail lived a block from the tracks. Hoboes came for handouts regularly enough that Abigail kept a sack of potatoes just inside the back door of the little white clapboard house. It was her contribution toward their simmering pots of mulligan stew, the mainstay of the hobo's diet. When Libby knocked on the door, Adam answered with two potatoes in hand.

"*Depart in peace, be ye warmed and filled,*" he quipped and dropped the potatoes into the basket hooked over her arm.

"Aren't you the clever one!" Assuming by the broad smile on his square-jawed face that she'd missed the birthing, Libby hugged him and cried, "Well? Don't keep me in suspense. Is it a boy or girl?"

"It's a boy. Another boy!" cried three-year-old Annie. She came running, blue eyes aglow and strawberry curls framing her cherry-cheeked face. "I woked up and there he was lyin' on the bed next to Mama!"

"Pipe down, now, or you'll wake Andrew, and Lib will have to fill the tank." Adam prodded Annie's round tummy with a forefinger.

Annie giggled and pressed her hands to her stomach. "My tank's empty, too."

"Then I'm just in time." Libby put her basket down to kiss her niece.

"Did you bring me a story, Aunt Lib?" chimed Annie, hunkering down on the floor, peeking into Libby's basket.

"Yes, I did, and some cookies and fresh eggs from my hen house and all sorts of little surprises, which we'll soon explore. But you'll have to wait for the stories. My books are in my suitcase at the station."

"I'll get it in a bit," said Adam as he moved her basket out of reach of Annie's curious fingers. "I planned to walk over and meet your train, but we've been kind of busy here. The doctor just left."

"Have you picked a name yet?"

"Abigail's deliberating. I think she's still awake if you want to go in and see the baby."

"All right. If you and Annie can wait for breakfast, I'll take a peek. Why, look who's up!" exclaimed Libby, turning as two-year-old Andrew toddled into the kitchen, a thumb in his mouth and dark curls tumbling toward his brown eyes. Seeing his bottom lip pucker, Libby extended a hand. "Maybe Andrew would like to wish his mama and his new baby brother a good-morning, too."

Abigail's eyes fluttered open at the sound of the whining door. She yawned and beamed as her little family gathered around, ogling the red-faced infant nestled beside her. Andrew climbed up on the bed and gave Libby an anxious moment as he tried to worm in between his mother and the new baby.

"Mama sick?" he asked.

"No, darling, Mama's not sick. Just tired. But Auntie Lib's here to take care of you for a few days." Abigail kissed Andrew's pudgy hand, then turned her gaze on Libby, who had rescued her new nephew from Andrew's careless wriggles. "Thanks for coming, Libby. You're going to have to get started on a family of your own if I'm ever going to repay you."

Libby covered a heart twinge with a smile. "Adam's already paid me in potatoes. Mulligan stew for breakfast, anyone?"

"No! Pancakes!" cried Annie.

Andrew clapped his hands and climbed off the bed to follow his sister from the room. Libby lingered a moment longer, stroking the baby's hands and studying his fragile ears, his puckered brow, his tiny fingernails. *Fearfully and wonderfully made.* She pressed her lips to one dimpled hand, then returned the baby to Abigail's side.

Abigail named the baby Abraham. He was a good eater and a good sleeper, which enabled her to rest and regain her strength while Libby took charge. Adam worked nights in the machine shop and slept during the day. In addition to the household chores, Libby tried to keep the children quiet. When they tired of stories and games, she bundled them up and took them for a walk.

The neighborhood was Hungarian, with small, well-kept homes in tidy rows. A whistle called the shifts to work, and twice in the night, Libby heard a boy knocking at the neighbor's window, calling, "Thornton! Mr. Thorton! Number 50, South. Three o'clock."

"Mr. Thornton's a fireman," Adam explained. "They send a caller out to rouse him for duty. The engine shifts depend on how regular the trains are running, so it's the only way to call them in."

Libby remembered that Abigail had complained when

they first moved there that their neighbors were stand-offish. But the people she met in the butcher shop and grocery store were friendly, and knew the children by name. There was a library, too, and a general store that carried caps and scarves and gloves and dungarees and sundry things for railroad workers. The children loved to go there, and so did Libby. It was cozy warm, and the aroma of the varied blends of tobacco wafted in the air. She made several purchases for Ike, articles she couldn't have found in Edgewood.

One afternoon, upon returning from such a jaunt, Libby commented on how she and the children were treated like old friends. Adam turned from the sink, his face lathered and a razor in his hand.

"You can thank Hans for that. He worked with me in the shop for two years before he learned I was your brother. He introduced me to a couple of other fellows who worked for Ike, too. Word spread, and the neighbors got friendly. It's been that way ever since."

Because of Ike's concern for his men. It pleased Libby, seeing a stone cast in kindness making ever-widening ripples.

By the end of the week, Abigail was coping well. Had it not been sirup season with Ike at home, having to carry the full burden himself, Libby would have stayed another week. Anxious for home, she asked Abigail on Friday if she was well enough to get along without her.

Abigail assured her she was, and thanked her again for coming. "Adam can walk you to the station when he gets off in the morning."

The children, learning Libby was leaving the following morning, begged for a walk before lunch. Libby obliged them. It was a cold day, cold enough that Annie, normally eager to show what a big girl she was, allowed Libby to tuck her into the perambulator with Andrew as they started home from the library. Upon their return, a closed hack was pulling away from the house.

Libby lifted Annie out of the wicker buggy, and had

her arms around Andrew when Abigail cracked the door just wide enough to sandwich her face in the opening.

"Take the children next door to Thorton's and come right back."

Startled by her terse tone, Libby shot her a seeking glance. Her heart leapt, for Abigail's face was as white as a Monday wash, her mouth a strained gash and her eyes full of tears.

"What's the matter?" cried Libby, forgetting the children.

"Hurry back," she said, and closed the door.

Dear God, the baby! Something must be wrong with the baby! Catching Libby's alarm, Andrew began to cry. Annie's chin was wobbling too by the time they reached the neighbor's door. The woman took the children without hesitation. Praying without knowing the exact need, Libby raced back across the muddy yard. Abigail met her at the door.

Slow to heed the warning finger on her lip, Libby cried, "What is it, Abby? Is it the baby?"

"The baby's fine. Shh!" she warned. "I don't want to wake Adam."

"Abigail, you scared me to death! What is *wrong* with you?"

Abigail swung the door wider, and there on a kitchen chair sat a little girl, not much bigger than Annie. Her golden ringlets were pulled back in a big glossy bow that matched the red satin dress beneath her lacy pinafore. She wore shiny black shoes. A purple cape trimmed in white fur was flung over the back of the chair.

Cold hammers pinged in Libby's head. There was something about the showy colors, the girl's tiny shell-like ears and rosebud mouth. But it was a muffled alarm. She couldn't peel away the veil from her throbbing subconscious. The child was a stranger, surely. She would remember a child so lovely. It was the eyes, the sad haunted eyes that cut Libby to the quick. All of this, an instant impression, made in less time than it took the sympathetic whooshing of air from her lungs to hang in the air as a single, heart-wrenched, "Oh-h-h!"

"It's Rose!" cried Abigail in a hoarse whisper.

"Rose?" The name rang like an explosion. "*Your* Rose!" Libby's hand flew to her throat, for it was so! This was the child Abigail had given up. The baby who'd gone to the Bigelows, owners of the circus that had played in Edgewood just after Rose was born. "How did she get here? Why is she . . ."

"Shh!" Abigail warned again. She flung a frantic glance toward the bedchamber where Adam lay sleeping. "The Bigelows were killed in a circus train wreck about a month ago. Their attorney brought her here."

"But why?"

"Because there's no one else to care for her. Look at her! How can I turn her away? But Adam . . . I don't know about Adam. I thought this was all behind me. What am I going to do?" White-lipped, she pleaded, "What am I going to do?"

"Go in there right now and talk to him, Abigail!"

"With her sitting right there? Her heart is already broken. If he uttered one short word, why it would . . . I don't know. I just don't know! My heart's pounding so hard, I can't even think!" cried Abigail, dashing at her flood of tears. "All the times I've wished . . . but we've never talked about it. I've been afraid to, afraid to remind him . . . as if he could forget. Oh God, how could I have ever been such a fool!"

Rose was watching them. *Did she know this distraught woman was her mother?* If not, she certainly knew their whispers were of her. The eyes of Abigail's heart saw true even in the midst of her frenzied panic. Rejection on top of bereavement was more wounding than this child could bear. *Dear God, it should not be!*

Impulsively, Libby said, "Do you want me to take her home with me while you talk it over with Adam?"

Abigail looked with a tortured gaze from Rose to

Libby and back again. Emotions and counteremotions swept across her face until Libby could almost hear her heart tear. Wanting Rose, yet fearing her as a threat to her family. *Was she right? Would the sight of Rose dredge up the past, shadow the harmony of her home, perhaps even doom her marriage?*

The answer rested solely in Adam, and Libby dared not offer reassurances. She would have pledged her life on Adam's character. But she didn't know his heart, the scars it bore, or the extent of his forgiveness.

But the child! Rose was spilling silent tears faster than she could catch them in her mittened hand. In her panic, Abigail had neglected to remove the girl's mittens.

Heart-wrenched, Libby crossed the kitchen, dried Rose's tears, and gathered her in her arms. Tears burned in her own throat as the little arms tightened around her neck and a smothered sob shook Rose's small frame. Libby wiped away her tears, and said softly, "I'm your Aunt Libby. I'm here to help Abigail with her tiny baby. He was born just a few days ago, Rose, and he needs a lot of attention right now. I was thinking maybe you could come home with me for a while. How does that sound? Would you like that?" she asked.

Rose's shining head bobbed against Libby's shoulder without hesitation.

"All right, then. Let's go to the station, shall we, and we'll catch the next train. It isn't far."

Libby helped the girl on with her coat, giving instructions to have Adam send her suitcase. She picked up the handsome tapestry valise, took Rose's hand, and started for the door, half-expecting Abigail to stop her, to come up with a plan of her own. But Abigail trailed them in mute misery all the way to the street.

Wanting no misunderstanding between them, Libby said, "Is this going to be all right with you, Abigail?"

Abigail stretched a hand, then let it fall just short of brushing Rose's cheek. Eyes filling afresh, she said, "I'll send word," then turned with a muffled sob, and retraced her steps to the house.

29

It was the first time Libby had been away when Ike was home and by Friday, Ike was missing her sorely. There could have been no worse time than sirup season. He and Billy and Decatur might be the muscle and steam that powered the camp. But Lib, with her willing hands and cheery industry, was the oil that kept things from clanking and grinding.

Even Hack Caton missed her maple-sugar cookies and her lively banter. On Friday morning, he asked when she was coming home.

"Next week, I reckon," said Ike.

"Wimmin got no business gallivantin'." Glowering at Ike's grin, he stumped off and banged the moisture-swelled door on his way out.

Billy came along at dusk to run the evaporator long enough for Ike to go home and fix himself some supper. Ike made his way over the bridge and was crossing the railroad tracks when his nose picked up the scent of Libby's home fires. The lamplight, spilling buttery light from the cabin windows, had never looked more welcoming. Ike quickened his step in anticipation and let himself in. The smell of frying sausage met him at the door.

"Lib?" Ike heard her moving behind the screen. He walked toward her with some notion of teasing her with the brush of cold fingers on her neck, but he was the one who got the surprise, for there was a golden-haired child asleep in their bed.

"Who've we got here?"

"Rose," whispered Libby. She caught his hand and drew him away from the sleeping child.

Her tone implied volumes more than the name. Nor could Ike fathom the strange light in her eyes as she kissed him in greeting, then drew him away from the sleeping child into the heart of their home.

Ike waited for an explanation. When it was slow to come, he scratched his head and offered, "I got yer card, sayin' you were bringin' me something. Somehow, I was expectin' overalls and maybe a cap."

Her mouth contorted, part smile, part quivering chin. Wary all at once, he asked, "Who does she belong to?"

"Let's go where we can talk."

Ike followed her into Naomi's dark store. His misgivings deepened as Libby freshened his memory on Abigail's past. The cold of the drafty porch crept into his bones. He knew instinctively what Libby was thinking, what she was trying to find a way to say. *She wanted this child.* He knew, too, that the wanting was going to snap back and hurt her. Trying to keep that from happening, he said, "She's a pretty little thing, but she's Abigail's."

"I only brought her home to give Abby time to talk it over with Adam," Libby explained.

"Her place is with Abigail and Adam, Lib. They'll both see that, and they'll come get her."

"I just said . . ."

"I heard what you said."

"You're angry," she said, surprised.

"No," he said, though he was. Not at her. At Abigail, for being blind about it and putting herself before Lib. He wanted to reach for her, but didn't, fearing if he showed any softness, she'd go on deceiving herself. "Rose has got a sister and two brothers and a mother and a father. That's a full family, Lib. She doesn't need us."

"I'm sure she needs any love she can get," Libby reasoned. "She's lost her parents and everything that's familiar."

"You're not thinkin' this through. That little girl isn't goin' to be yours."

"Ike . . ."

"No, Lib." He shook his head for emphasis. "It isn't goin' to happen that way. You're jest setting yourself up to get let down."

She was so quiet, he heard a stick fall from one of the oaks in the yard scraping the roof in the blowing wind. It was too dark to see her face, but he heard that tilt of a chin in her voice as she said, "Disappointment isn't fatal."

Failing at getting her to see she was opening herself up to needless hurt, Ike tried a new tack, and said with deliberate intention, "No, but sometimes it feels that way."

Libby heard the implication that he, too, was vulnerable. It hadn't occurred to her that he might feel that way. In fact, she'd been so caught up in the quiet whisper that Rose could be God's answer to her prayers regarding children, she'd given his feelings very little thought. Ashamed, she moved closer, twining her arms around him.

As Libby laid her cheek against his chest with that comforting, nurturing touch that had once made Ike so uncomfortable, his conscience twinged at having misled her. But how could he stand by and let her get her hopes up needlessly when he remembered so plainly her reaction to the baby they'd lost? A child God had only begun knitting. That child, a treasure laid up in heaven, was soul and spirit. This child was pink skin and sooty lashes and curls that Libby could see and touch and hold in her arms.

His protective feelings meshed with the emotions that had stirred at the sight of their lighted windows. He cradled her face in his hands and kissed her. Waiting for her to come home had been even harder than being away himself. It seemed as if she'd been gone much longer than five days. Her laced fingers tightened at the small of his back. She was supple lines, sweet scents, and warm curves, responding to his romancing in all the familiar ways. He stroked the silky underside of her chin with a rough thumb, then traced the slim column of her throat and felt her strongly beating pulse. He had nearly forgotten the little yellow-haired child when she mentioned her again.

"You're right, you know. I *was* thinking that if Rose needed a home, it might be ours."

" 'Course you were. You've got a motherin' instinct."

"And we *have* talked about adoption," she reminded him, breathless with the ray of hope daring to awaken within her, daring to be put into words.

"*You* talked about it, Lib," Ike said guardedly. "And I listened. But that isn't reason enough to bring home a stray child."

Stray? Jarred by the word, Libby loosened her hands, and drew back trying to see his face. Something wasn't right here. He didn't sound like a man who was afraid of getting his hopes up, only to have them crushed. Nor, she realized, was he generally so open to admitting vulnerabilities. But if he wasn't vulnerable to disappointment over Rose, then why would he say that he was? She asked, "Can't we at least talk about it?"

"Sometimes it's best not to let your heart get attached. That's about all I've got to say."

The truth struck with a wounding blow. His heart wasn't in danger of becoming attached! Why, he'd barely looked at Rose. And what a sneaky way of trying to sway her to his own way of thinking! Emotionally manipulative, that's what it was! Anger came in a rush. She sidestepped the hand poised to brush her cheek. "I left sausage on the stove."

The shift in her tone was like a cold wind over his rising blood. Knowing she'd seen through him, Ike let his hand fall. "I just don't want to see you get hurt, that's all."

"Then why didn't you say that?"

"I tried. You didn't want to hear."

What she heard was his reluctance to talk about the possibility of Rose needing a home. It was hard for her to say that Adam might not take her in. Even harder to say *I don't believe you, Ike. You just don't want her.* She stood in bruised silence.

"What did Abigail say?" he asked.

"There wasn't an opportunity to say much with Rose right there in the room. She said she'd send word. We left it at that."

"You're gettin' worked up needlessly, Lib. They'll come get her. Don't you see that?"

"I see that, Ike! I'm not arguing that point at all. But in the event that they don't, I think we should talk about keeping her ourselves."

Ike shifted his weight, for she *was* arguing. She was arguing against the inevitable, if not aloud, then in her own heart. He wished Abigail's troubles hadn't spilled over onto them. Here they were, coming to words over it, when all he was trying to do was keep Libby from another disappointment.

"That's what I thought," she said, finding her own answer in his silence. "You don't want her. Though I don't know how much of an inconvience it would be to you, since you're hardly ever home."

"That's unfair, Lib, and you know it."

"What about you playing on my emotions?" she flashed back. "Is that fair?"

Her strident tones made the reunion he had anticipated

impossible. He shouldn't have tried to mislead her, reasoning the ends justified the means. But even then, her resentment seemed out of proportion to his poorly thought-out attempt to protect her. "If you'd simmer down and listen to me for a minute, we could sort this out."

"Could we? I'm not so sure."

The glare of her swift anger illuminated an unhappiness that Ike hadn't guessed she felt over something that seemed to have little to do with the child in the other room. But by the time he neared the sap house, Ike could see that it had plenty to do with it. The issue wasn't just Rose. It was the same issue it had always been, and that was her desire for children.

He had once feared that should his bouts with malaria prevent them from having a family, Libby would feel he'd cheated her by not telling her of that possibility before they were married. And that she would blame him. Instead, she blamed him because he was away. She thought if he were in her bed every night, she'd have a baby by now.

So she brought home a child and tossed her down like a gauntlet? Was that it? What does she want from me? I've got to work. What kind of man would I be if I didn't provide for her? Does she think I like being away?

The swirling fog in the sap house, the flames licking in the firebox seemed in keeping with Ike's mood. He gave the door a push. Swollen from the moisture, it swung open again.

He swore and gave it a hard shove.

Billy swung around and looked at him in surprise. "That didn't take long."

"How long does it take?" countered Ike. *For a woman to tell you what's on* her *mind.*

Since you're hardly ever home. Libby was sorry for the words even before the eggs were done. She shouldn't have said them, and certainly not in that tone or context.

She'd been hurt because he had deliberately played on her feelings for him in hopes of deterring her from considering something he was apparently not ready to consider.

Wondering what was keeping him, she walked back out to the darkened store to tell him supper was ready. But he wasn't there. Gone back to the sap house, no doubt.

Tired over the tumult of the day, heart hurting for Rose, for Abigail, for Adam and yes, for herself, Libby sat down on a crate. Floy had left his tattered blanket on the floor. She picked it up, folded it, and cradled it as if it were little Floy himself.

It wasn't the homecoming she'd anticipated. Nor was Ike's reaction to Rose what she had thought it would be. Why had he reacted so negatively? The words weren't even out of her mouth, and he was on the other side of the fence.

I didn't help Rose's cause any, though, did I? She needs love, not contention. Abigail loves her. But she has given her up once. And she has Adam and three children to think of. Is she right? Will Adam resist? And if he accepts Rose, will he love her the same as the others? Guide their choice well, Lord. And should they choose to let her go, prepare Ike's heart to receive her.

Hearing stirrings in the next room, Libby got up from the crate and went to fix Rose a plate. They sat down at the table together. A quiet echo to her "Amen" at the end of the blessing rang sweetly in Libby's ears. She looked up to find Rose lifting her bowed head. Her small hands were clasped, her wrists braced against the edge of the table. Her soul easing a bit, Libby asked, "Are you hungry?"

Rose nodded, then as if remembering her manners, said, "Yes, ma'am."

A smile crept to Libby's mouth. "Why don't you call me Aunt Libby? What about you? I've been calling you Rose. Is that what you're used to?"

Rose's shining ringlets danced as she bobbed her head. She made Libby think of a little princess, with her back perfectly straight and her fingers laced and her eyes such a deep royal blue. Libby filled Rose's plate for her, and wondered why she made no move to pick up her fork.

Thinking perhaps the food wasn't to her liking, Libby asked, "Do you like gravy on your sausage and biscuits? I can make some if you like."

"Aren't we waiting for him?" Rose asked.

Puzzled, Libby said, "Who? Oh! You mean Ike! I thought you were asleep. I didn't realize you'd seen him. No, he won't expect us to wait."

Rose picked up her fork and was halfway through the meal before she met Libby's gaze again. A slight frown made puckers form over her delicate eyebrows. "Is he mad at me?"

"You mean Ike?" Startled, Libby said, "Why no! Whatever made you think that?"

"He isn't eating."

Not only was she pretty, she was perceptive. Though it wasn't Rose who was keeping him from the table. Libby hastened to reassure her, saying, "Ike had work to do. He'll be back later. I've put a plate in the warmer for him." Seeing the doubt in Rose's face, she tried to distract her by asking, "Do you like stories?"

Rose nodded. She lifted her deep blue gaze, and asked, "Shall I tell you one?"

The question surprised a smile from Libby. "Why yes! I'd like that."

Rose dribbled honey on a biscuit. She licked each finger, as dainty as a kitten, then spun a tale of a kidnapped princess and a pirate who tamed a sea dragon.

Pretty, perceptive, and delightfully inventive. Libby lost her heart before her coffee had cooled. And her perspective with it.

* * *

It was close to midnight when Ike returned to the house. There was a lamp burning low on the table. Rose was asleep on the feather mat that Libby kept for David, who often stayed overnight during the summer months. Ike thought Libby was asleep, too, but she called to him from the bed to tell him that his supper was in the warmer.

Ike hoped she wouldn't get up. Wasn't any point to it. They couldn't talk with Rose just yards away. He ate and banked the stove, put out the light, and knew, even as he undressed in the darkness, that Libby hadn't drifted back to sleep. But she didn't say anything when he crawled beneath the covers, or roll toward him as she was prone to do.

He had started out noble enough, trying to protect her from hurting herself, and it had escalated into silence, each hugging their own side of the bed as if danger lay in the middle. And maybe it did. Maybe it always had.

30

🌹 Libby awakened the next morning to find Rose handing kindling to Ike as he coaxed the fire to life. Ike, unaware she was listening, was conspiring with Rose in that gently teasing way of his.

"Catch that wisp of smoke there, would ya, b'fore it gets us in trouble?" he whispered. "Lib doesn't allow anyone smokin' up the place unless it's her."

Rose rose on tiptoes and put her hands together, and giggled as the smoke disappeared between her fingers. "Uh-oh! I missed."

It was a lovely sight to wake up to, Ike smiling at Rose, and Rose smiling back. Libby dressed and fixed breakfast, and they sat down together, saying grace and tucking a napkin under one dimpled chin and cautioning care with a full glass of milk, like families everywhere, with children at the table.

Ike soon donned his cap and coat and left for the sap house. He hadn't been gone long when Pretty Good and Very Fine stopped on their way to school to feed the chickens and gather the eggs. Libby introduced Rose and talked to them about trying to earn a little money making maple candy.

"If you'd like to try it, stop by after school," she told them.

The girls were eager to do so.

"Can we make candy now?" asked Rose, when the girls had gone on their way.

Thinking of an easy candy, made by pouring sirup over snow, Libby said. "Just as soon as the dishes are done and the beds are made and I've finished my pieces for the *Gazette*."

Floy arrived with Naomi about that time. Rose was captivated with him. She treated him as a life-size doll, wanting to hold him and rock him, while Floy, so full of energy, wanted only to race and play. Still, he enjoyed Rose's attention and cried when Naomi took him back into the store with her.

By midmorning, Libby had finished her chores. With Rose at her elbow, she cooked sirup to the soft-ball stage. They bundled up and walked over to the sap house with their pan of boiled sirup. Rose was awed by the mists.

"Did elves make these clouds?" she asked.

Libby and Ike chuckled, their gazes meeting briefly before swiftly falling away.

Hack Caton was there, looking on as Ike cooked. He brightened at the mention of snow candy. "Let's git to it," he said, then hitched his trousers and offered Rose his hand. "I'll take ya, young'un. Make shore ya don't git none of that yeller snow."

"Mr. Caton!" objected Libby.

He scratched his whiskery chin and cocked an eye her way. "By cracky if it ain't Miss Lib! Quit yer gallivantin' and come home to hep a spell, did ya?"

Hesitant about entrusting Rose to Hascal, Libby said to Ike, "I brought clean sirup filters. Did you want anything else?"

"Nothin' at the moment. Go on with Hack. Wouldn't want him settin' a bad example."

His words reminded Libby of the day after their wedding when they'd met Hascal and Frankie in the woods, and Hascal had been so ornery, she'd remarked to Ike that she wouldn't let any child of hers anywhere near the old scamp. And he had replied, *I wouldn't worry about that just yet.*

Libby flushed in looking back to think of how naive she had been. It had seemed so simple. You fell in love, you got married, you had babies. Here it was five years later. Five years! She was far beyond being ready. But by all appearances, Ike was as unhurried about it as he'd ever been.

She followed Hascal and Rose outside and soon returned with a platter of snow. Libby took the spoon from the pan, and poured the hot sirup over the snow. Hascal smacked his lips.

''Go ahead, Rose,'' said Libby.

Hascal caught Rose's elbow, restraining her reaching hand and mischievously attempting to get the first bite.

Libby whacked the back of his hand with the wooden spoon. ''Children first, Mr. Caton.''

''Gory be, Miss Lib!'' he yelped. ''That spoon's hot!''

Rose giggled as Hascal licked the sirup off the back of his hand. She pulled at the taffylike substance with both hands, pinching off some for herself, and some for Hascal.

Hascal chewed with lip-smacking pleasure, and remarked, ''Sticks to yer choppers, don't it?''

Rose laughed and fed him some more.

She had to be coaxed away, later, when it was approaching time for the Field girls to come home from school. Libby tied a dish towel on Rose as an apron, and let her help stir the sirup that had to be boiled to make maple-sugar candy. When it had cooled, Libby, Very Fine, and Pretty Good took turns stirring it until it turned from a transparent amber color to a thick creamy ivory. Rose licked the spoon while Libby and the girls smoothed the candy into molds Libby had purchased the previous year.

As the candy was setting up in the molds, Floy returned for another dose of attention from Rose. Opal, who was dusting shelves in the store, popped in for a while, too. In that unaffected way of children, Opal inquired about Rose's life with the circus, asking questions Libby had dared not ask for fear of rousing painful memories. While Rose didn't mention the Bigelows, she did speak of the animals and some of the circus people.

When Frankie, Purdy, and Dumplin had finished gathering sap, they tramped into the cabin to meet Rose and stayed to pull maple taffy. Their voices running over one another reminded Libby of birds in a summer rain puddle, chirping as they splashed and played. If only it could always be this way! A house full of children, spreading sunshine and laughter and brightening the long weeks while Ike was far away.

But bedtime came, and the silence and distance seemed all the more pronounced after the cheeriness of the children. Libby prayed and wrestled with her pride a while before whispering to Ike, "Thank you for being so sweet to Rose today."

"She'll make Annie a good sister," he said, and turned away.

Annie's sister. His way of telling her that he hadn't changed his mind, not to get her hopes up, that nothing permanent could come of this.

He lay with his back to her as if it were she who had injured him.

The following day, Laila, Billy, Joy, and the baby came for Sunday dinner. Joy and Rose played so sweetly together, one as dark-haired as the other was fair. Rose was even more fascinated with Billy and Laila's eight-month-old son than she had been with Floy the previous day. Here was a baby too small to slide off her lap and toddle away!

"Any word from her mother?" whispered Laila.

Libby shook her head. Unsure how much Ike had passed along to Billy, she didn't elaborate, for the whisper of hope was becoming more insistent. *Abigail gave her up once. She would do it again, if it came to a choice between Adam and Rose.*

Monday passed, and then Tuesday with no word from Abigail. Ike had a gentle teasing way with Rose, pretending his spoon was stuck in the sugar bowl, finding a magic penny behind her ear, tickling her cheek with a feather. His patience seemed unlimited, even when Rose got underfoot in the sap house, looking for the elves. But was he changing his mind? It seemed unlikely, for when night came, they lay like strangers, their backs to one another. *How could he be so sweet to Rose, and yet so distant with her, refusing even to talk about the possibility of making a home for Rose on a permanent basis?*

Her anger long since spent, Libby's isolation became painful to her in an elemental way, as hunger or thirst or intense cold was to her body. She prayed. But the words echoed hollowly as if she had lost her bearings in a confusing desert place where the shimmering daylight oasis of Rose's presence could not be stored to warm the cold and lonely nights.

Wednesday came and Libby awoke, remembering it was mail day. She butchered a chicken, made noodles, washed sirup filters and attended to other chores before there was time to play. Rose had admired Joy's braids on Sunday, and wanted Libby to braid her hair.

"Let's pretend we're Indian maidens," said Rose.

Libby chuckled. "How about just one braid for me?"

"Let me! I want to do it!" pleaded Rose, so Libby let her braid her hair.

After lunch they baked cookies and started for the sap house where the boys would come after school before going to the woods to gather sap. Libby saw Hascal Caton meddling with the mailboxes and thought again of Abigail. She was reluctant even to look in the box.

Hearing them in the road, Hascal wheeled around with a guilty start.

"Jest puttin' a penny in for a stamp for Naomi," he said, though Libby hadn't asked.

"Captain Boyd hasn't been by with the mail?"

"Ain't seen him. Did see Doc, though. He was headin' up toward the Fields'. Reckon there'll be another one in the cradle by nightfall," added Hascal. "Pay better if the Mar-key Day La-Fay-et'd paint a little more and pitch the woo a little less."

Libby blushed at his innuendo, and pivoted, her hand tightening on Rose's. Rose shot her a measuring glance, then set her own chin at the same angle as Libby's.

When they reached the sap house, Rose sought Ike in the steam. She folded her arms across her chest, and said, "Grandpa Caton was in *our* mailbox, and we don't like it."

Ike whistled off-key and tugged at one of Rose's braids. "Don't pay old Hack any mind. It's picture postcards he's pokin' around lookin' for."

"He needs to be poked. Poked with a big stick," said Libby.

The friction in her voice seemed out of proportion to Hascal's crime. Wary all at once, Ike asked, "Any mail?"

"The Captain hasn't been by yet."

So it wasn't a letter from Abigail accounting for the strain showing in her eyes and the blush upon her cheeks. Ike's gaze lingered for a moment on the wisps of hair that escaped her unruly braid. They twined like copper shavings against her white neck.

Libby caught Ike's sidelong glance, and was vain enough to regret having left her hair in the untidy braid. She strode through the mists, trying to tidy it and looked out the sap-house window just as Ike's team came out of the woods.

Decatur jumped off the back of the sap sled. He turned the horses in a wide loop, guiding them toward the snow-packed ramp. Libby heard sap running into the storage tank on the north side of the building.

A moment later, Frankie, Purdy, and Dumplin tramped in from school, dressed to help Decatur gather. At fifteen, Frankie was nearly as tall as Decatur. His crop of red hair made a fringe around his cap and spilled over the collar of his worn coat. "Hey, Lib. What happened to yer hair?"

Rose said, "We're Indians."

Dumplin spied the plate of cookies and grinned at Libby. "I like your hair, looks nice that way," he said, and patted his pudgy stomach.

Purdy, as compact and straight up and down as a barber pole, was always hungry. He nearly walked over Rose's feet, getting to the plate of cookies.

Libby heard a train whistle blow. Wondering about Pretty Good and Very Fine, she asked, "Where are the girls? I thought they were going to stop after school and make candy again."

"Very Fine wasn't feeling good this morning, and Pretty Good just went home with the chills." Dumplin showered cookie crumbs as he talked with his mouth full. "The small fry have been puny all week."

Libby wondered if Hascal had misunderstood the purpose of Dr. Harding's trip up to the Fields' house. "What's wrong with them?" she asked.

"Dunno. Just sick," said Purdy, reaching for another cookie.

Libby was about to question them further when Decatur limped in, face ruddy from the cold.

Ike angled him a measuring glance. "Favorin' one foot, aren't ya?"

"Wrenched an ankle out in the woods. Durn fool trick." Decatur turned his gruff voice on the boys. "You fellers go keep an eye on the gathering tank while it's emptyin'. No need in ya burnin' daylight in here."

The boys stormed the cookie plate one last time and trooped out.

Decatur pulled up a crate and sat down. "If Billy's goin' to be around, I may git off this foot a spell and let him take the boys to the woods."

"Billy had something planned today. The boys'll just have to go by themselves," said Ike.

Decatur snorted. "Ya take one to the woods and ya got one boy. Ya take two, and ya got half a boy. Ya take three and ya got no boy at all. Unless'n ya stay after 'em, it's nothin' but highjinks. Duncan, in particular. Frankie kin empty three buckets for his every one."

"One to three isn't bad for a boy usin' jest one arm," reasoned Ike.

Decatur lowered himself to a crate, massaged his ankle through his thick muddy boot, and drawled, "It ain't Duncan's arm that's holdin' him back, it's his finaglin' work-duckin' attitude."

"That's *Dumplin*," said Libby.

"Duncan," countered Decatur with a stubborn set to his chin. "Dumplin ain't no fittin' name for a boy. I ain't too partial to Purdy either."

"How about Purdue?" piped up Rose.

Decatur shot her a sharp glance. Between his size and his shaggy hair hanging down on his shoulders and his rough-hewn features, he was more accustomed to children ducking away from him than speaking up. "Purdue? What kinda name is that?"

Doubtful Rose would recognize the twinkle in Decatur's eye, Libby patted Rose's arm. "Thank you, Rose. You too, Mr. McClure. New names—a most sensible idea."

Rose wasn't put off by Decatur's growly voice. She eyed him a long moment, then tugged at his coat and indicated Libby. "We're Indians."

"That so?" he countered.

Rose nodded and took Libby's hand and hummed to herself, winding halfway around Libby with their hands still linked.

Ike saw Libby's hands stroke Rose's back, pat her

braids, straighten her ribbons. It struck him how contented they looked together. Almost as if they belonged. Hearing the sap house door creak open, he turned in that direction. It was Adam Watson, appearing in the mists as if in rebuttal of that one double-minded thought.

The dread that had settled on Ike five days earlier slammed home as Libby turned to see her brother. Her eyes lit in spontaneous greeting, then darkened as realization set in. Color mounted her cheeks. Her mouth opened, then closed and suddenly, she was seeking Ike in wordless entreaty. The need to shield her whipped like a snarled rope in the pit of his stomach. But how was he to help her now?

Seeking Decatur's eye, Ike said, ''Why don't you take Rose out and show her the horses?''

Libby's chest was a tangle of emotion, loss on the one hand, respect on the other, for once again, Adam was proving himself. Abigail's fears were unfounded. Libby was proud of him, and at the same time felt as if she were falling from some great height, awaiting the pain of impact as she struggled with the knowledge that Rose was not to be hers. As if sensing her distress, Rose stopped humming and looked at Libby, then at Adam. Taking Rose's hands, Libby bent her knees to meet her inquiring glance. She was about to introduce Adam when Ike's hand gripped her shoulder.

Decatur hobbled off his crate, beckoned to Rose, and said gruffly, ''Come on, little Injun, and I'll set ya up on one of them horses.''

Having no idea that she was the reason Adam had come, Rose let go of Libby's hand and trotted after Decatur.

Adam stepped aside, his gaze following Rose until Decatur pulled the door closed behind them. He tramped the snow off his shoes, then shook Ike's hand in greeting before turning to Libby.

''I'm sorry about the wait, Lib. Meant to come Saturday and get her, but the neighborhood is full of influenza. Annie came down with it, then Andrew caught it, and there wasn't any way I could leave, not with Abigail just barely on her feet. Did you get her letter?''

"No,'' said Libby. She swallowed hard. "But that's all right, Adam. Ike said you'd come. Are the children better?''

"Andrew's still whooping a little, but Annie's fine. She's more excited about having a sister than she is about little Abraham.''

Struggling with herself, Libby asked, "Then everything is all right? With you and Abigail, I mean?''

He looked pained that she would ask. Putting a crimp in his hat as he turned it, he said, "I don't know why she got so upset. She should have known I'd want Rose if that was what she wanted.''

"How, Adam? How would she know if you never talked about it?''

"Lib,'' warned Ike.

His gray eyes flashed that M.Y.O.B. message. But Libby stood her ground, for five days of keeping Rose and this pressing hot knife in her heart made it her business. "It isn't just Rose,'' she reminded him. "There are six people's lives involved. You have to be sure.''

"I wouldn't be here if I wasn't,'' said Adam.

Seeing him prickle defensively, Libby embraced him just to remind herself that he was her brother, and not the enemy. Manlike, he didn't understand. He clapped her shoulder and said, "I suppose you're wanting to say good-bye.''

It was a difficult good-bye, for the attachment ran both ways. But when Rose grasped that it wasn't final, that this was family, that there would be visits, and that she had a little sister and a brother waiting to meet her and a baby to hold, she accepted Adam's outstretched hand.

Fighting the crushing sense of loss, Libby said, "She's got a few things at the cabin.''

Adam checked his pocket watch. "We're running out

of time if we're going to catch the Prairie Express back to Bloomington. I've got to be at work in a few hours.''

"I'll send them," said Libby, and kissed her niece, once lost and now found. She watched her walk away, hand in hand with Adam, and already missed the sweet fragrance of Rose.

31

Ike couldn't leave the evaporator. He thought Rose might come in to say good-bye, but she didn't. He watched from the sap house window as Adam took her away.

Libby had her back to him. He saw her elbow bend, saw the furtive flutter of fingers and knew she was wiping away tears. In the next instant, her hand was in the air, waving to Rose, who had looked back.

"We love you, Rose. Come see us again!" he heard her call. If he hadn't known her so well, he wouldn't have guessed what it cost her to see Rose go.

He turned back toward the pans, unable to watch any longer.

In a moment, Libby slipped into the sap house.

"You all right?" he asked, when the silence grew heavy.

Libby looked down at her laced fingers, then up again to see Decatur stumping past the far window. He'd be to the door as fast as his limping ankle allowed. Knowing she had only a moment, Libby swallowed the hard knot in her throat and said, "You can say it. You tried to tell me."

"Decatur's comin'," Ike warned.

Libby stopped where she was, just short of seeking his arms, his strength. *Had she assumed too much? Read too much into his concern?*

"Billy's comin' to cook for me for a couple of hours this evening," he added. "Maybe we can talk then."

"About Rose?"

"And some other things. My bein' gone, for one." Ike ran the ladle through the finishing pans. "And you, bein' unhappy."

"Unhappy?" Libby felt scalded by his words, as if the thick amber sirup sheeting off the ladle had flown all over her. "I didn't say I was unhappy."

He busied himself reading the thermometer and didn't answer.

Those words of five days ago rang loudly in Libby's ears. *Since you're hardly ever home.* She wished a hundred times, a thousand times over she hadn't said them.

Decatur let himself in, seeming unaware of tension thicker than the swirling curtains of steam. "Temperature's fallin'. Hope them boys don't dally."

"They'll be all right," said Ike.

Libby was looking through her tears, knowing she'd disgrace herself if she stayed any longer. She patted down her coat pockets, checking for her scarf and gloves. "I'll go with them."

"You sure?" asked Ike.

Libby nodded, already moving toward the door, where she'd left her timber boots. She needed the wind to sweep over Ike's words and soften the edges. If it could.

"They've struck for the south piece, and they need to git 'em all gathered," Decatur called after her. "Ya gotta watch Duncan. He'll miss one now and then."

The manufactured buckets had lids to keep out the weather and the debris, and were light enough in weight to hang on the tree at a comfortable height. But they weren't as forgiving as wooden buckets, and would burst if a freeze caught them holding sap.

A north wind, fading daylight, falling temperatures and hidden branches buried in the snow made cold hard work of the gathering. Yet, it was no harsher than the three-syllable word still echoing in Libby's head. *Unhappy*. Ike thought she was unhappy. And he hadn't been talking about Rose.

The ring of the boys' voices in the clear air couldn't deafen the word. Nor could the crunch of horses' hooves breaking through the crusty snow, the creaking of leather traces or the slosh of the sap splashing from bucket to gathering tank.

Feeling in danger of bursting herself, Libby lifted her eyes to the winter-bare trees, their broken limbs and knotholes and sap-dampened wounds reminding her of her own hard, hasty words. Of sunsets falling on anger. Five suns. Denying fault, hugging hurt, and accusing Ike of turning his back when she was turning away, too. What about him? Was *he* unhappy? Was that what had prompted the comment? She shuffled along through the snow, repeating the question to God and listening for answers that came from someplace besides her own blind heart.

Frankie was strong and tireless, but Purdy's and Dumplin's strength was waning as dusk approached and only a short stretch of timber remained to be gathered. Libby hurried along, knowing they were anxious to go home. She thought fleetingly of the doctor going to the Fields' home, and was concerned with what awaited the boys there.

The wind stung Libby's eyes as she tramped to the next maple tree, then on to the tank where Dumplin used his lame arm to steady the bottom of the gathering pail as he emptied it into the tank.

"How much daylight's left?" he asked.

"About twenty minutes," Frankie answered. "Looks like some weather movin' in, too."

"Air's cold," said Purdy, shivering a little.

"Yup," said Frankie, sounding just like Decatur. He wiped his dripping nose on his coat sleeve, then poked a stick down in the belly of the gathering tank, measuring how close it was to being full.

Libby had been going to check it to see if there was room in the tank to collect the buckets of sap that remained. "What do you think?" she asked, as Frankie tossed the stick aside.

"Goin' ta be close." Frankie motioned to Dumplin. "Pull her ahead, Dumplin. You and Lib get the close ones. Purdy and me'll do the walkin'."

His boyish gallantry touched Libby's bruised heart. She hurried on to the next tree and sang a terse little song as they raced the setting sun.

They'd nearly finished when the hitching pin on the sap sled broke. There was no way to get the sap sled back to the sap house without a pin. They didn't have a spare there in the woods and it would be dark in the time it took one of the boys to run back to the sap house, then return with a spare.

"Can we leave it until tomorrow?" asked Dumplin, hunching his shoulders against the cold.

"Let it freeze and bust Ike's new gatherin' tank? I don't reckon he'd thank us for that," said Frankie.

"Purdy, you and Dumplin empty the rest of the buckets. Just dump them on the ground," said Libby.

"On the ground?" echoed Purdy, seemingly troubled by the waste.

"It can't be helped. We'd better come up with a way to get this hauled in, or we'll have to dump the tank, too," said Libby. It was turning cold fast and she didn't want to risk the tank over a single load of sap.

"I'll whittle an oak plug. Maybe that'll work in place of a pin," said Frankie, reaching for his pocketknife. "Jest in case it don't, you better run on back to the sap house and git another pin."

Unwilling to leave the boys in the cold, Libby sent Dumplin instead. As he loped off through the trees, she helped Purdy finish emptying the remaining buckets.

By the time they'd finished, Frankie had an oak pin in place. How he did it, Libby wasn't sure, for the sun had set. It made her uneasy to hear ice sloshing around inside the tank. Uncertain how long they dared wait, she said, "Maybe we should dump it while we still can."

"It's still plenty loose. We got some time yet." Frankie made a wide turn with the team and took them along a path leading toward the road that ran from Edgewood past the sirup camp and north. "Be easier to see and maneuver on the road."

"How is Dumplin going to find us?"

"Reckon ya better sing a little louder," said Frankie, a grin in his voice. "Or Purdy could yodel."

Purdy was giving it a good effort when the oak pin broke.

"There she goes," said Frankie, planting his feet hard and pulling back on the lines to keep the horses from heading home without them. "Purdy, get me a good stout oak stick and we'll try 'er again."

"How am I supposed to tell in the dark what's oak and what isn't?"

"Never mind," said Libby. She took the lines from Frankie before the boys got into a fuss. "You two have done enough. Go on back to the sap house. If Dumplin isn't already on his way with a pin, send Ike. Then go home where it's warm."

"What're you goin' to do?"

"I'll wait here with the team."

Frankie started to protest, but Libby was firm. They went on their way, yodeling and hollering and making enough racket, should Dumplin or Ike be in the woods looking for them, they'd be sure to hear.

The team was hard to restrain without the weight of the sap tank to hold them back. Libby knotted the lines through the hole where the broken pin belonged, and found it to be sufficient to hold them. She climbed up on the sled to keep her cold feet out of the snow, and was relieved to see a light coming her way. But it wasn't Ike to her rescue, rather Dr. Harding heading home to Edgewood.

He stopped his team and climbed down. "Libby! I just left word for you."

"For me?" echoed Libby.

"Mrs. Field and several of the children are ill with influenza. Mrs. Field being in the family way adds to the danger."

"Hascal saw you pass. He assumed she was about to deliver."

"No. I hope not anyway, not for a month or so," said the doctor. "However, in her condition, influenza presents additional concerns. Can you lend her a hand?"

"Yes, of course," said Libby without hesitation.

"I'd be happy to drive you."

Libby accepted, adding, "But I'll have to wait until Ike gets here. I can't leave this tank." She was explaining her predicament when a man strode out of the trees. *Chester Gentry?* Surprise stirred through her, a surprise shared by Dr. Harding.

"Chester!" he exclaimed. "What brings you out this way?"

"My tenant and I were checking on the cattle just beyond the trees there when I heard someone caterwauling. Thought I'd better check and make sure it wasn't a call for help."

Realizing it was the boys' noise-making he'd heard, Libby repeated what she had just told Dr. Harding concerning the broken pin and the tank full of sap.

"Melville's checked his toolbox for a pin and come up wanting, I assume," said Chester, more in tune to Libby's problem than the distracted doctor.

"Not yet, I haven't," admitted Dr. Harding.

The doctor checked and found one. In short order he and Chester had Libby's team hitched to the sap sled.

"You look cold, Mrs. Galloway," said Chester. "Why don't you get in the buggy and I'll drive the team back to camp for you? Or is that Ike coming?"

It was. Relieved, Libby walked to meet him. She repeated the doctor's request, only to learn that Dr. Harding had already stopped by the sap house, looking for her. Ike expressed neither approval nor disapproval of her going, seeming to know that when it came to the Field children, she had no choice but to go.

"Let's get this sap in from the woods, then I'll take you," he said.

"I was just saying I'd drive her, if that's all right with you, Ike," offered Dr. Harding.

"Be quicker, I guess, if it doesn't put you out."

"Where's Mr. Field?" asked Chester.

"Mrs. Field says he's in Bloomington on a painting job for some west-side lodge." The doctor paused within yards of the buggy to pack his pipe.

"It makes my blood boil to see a man take so little thought for his wife and children," said Chester.

Libby missed the doctor's reply as Ike helped her into the buggy.

"Better have Doc stop by the cabin and get you a change of clothes. Some blankets, too. That place of theirs is likely to be drafty, and there's no need in you gettin' sick," said Ike.

"There's soup on the stove at the cabin," Libby told him. "I'll leave some for you and take the rest with me for the children."

Ike nodded agreement. "I'll be up in the mornin', see if you need anything."

"I wish you wouldn't," said Libby, his past illnesses in mind. He burned his candle at both ends during sirup season. She couldn't help thinking it made him susceptible to sicknesses that came around. "I'll come home when they're well enough to get along without me."

He let it go, and said, "I got to get back. Frankie's cookin' for me."

"Ike?"

He turned, but it was too dark to make out his features

clearly. There was so much she wanted to say. About Rose. And their quarrel. And her hasty words. And that she wasn't unhappy. Not in the ongoing way his word seemed to imply. But they weren't the sorts of things you said in front of others. "I'll be home as soon as I can," she said, and he nodded.

Ike stood with the lines of the team in hand as the doctor turned the buggy around and started back the way he'd come, Libby on the seat beside him.

Chester lingered there on the snowy road. He shoved his hands in his pockets. "I hear the C & A's renewing some of the work they canceled three years ago."

"Cutting through the Shirley hill," said Ike, nodding.

"You'll be working on that, I suppose."

"I don't know yet. Mr. Elliot hasn't said. Be nice, though, to have work close to home."

"It would be a relief to your wife, I'm sure."

Ike nodded, though he hadn't told Libby yet. He was waiting until he was sure it wouldn't fall through.

Chester dropped his head back and looked up at the trees. "How many buckets did you hang this year?"

"Seven hundred, somewhere thereabouts."

"Expanding a little every year. That's a good plan. Though I'd say you've tapped about to your maximum, between your trees and Mr. McClure's."

"Just about," said Ike.

"Maybe we could come to terms next year, if you're wanting to keep growing."

"Tap your woods, you mean?" asked Ike, surprised.

"It should serve us both well."

Old habits die hard. It was on the tip of Ike's tongue to shut him off right there. But he thought better of it, and stepped up on the sled. "I've got to get this sled back to the camp before it turns to ice. You can come along if you've got nowhere you have to be."

"I've got a team of my own wanting their stalls. But maybe I'll come watch you make sirup sometime."

"All right," said Ike. "Be glad to show you around."

Chester lingered. He cleared his throat, and shuffled his feet in the snow. "You know, Ike, I'm having some tenant problems."

Again, Ike fought remnants of old feelings that made him want to drop a brick on the conversation. But there was no heat to those feelings anymore. The resentment of all those years ago had died on the steps of the New Hope Church, then turned to pity when Ida came calling and took Lib's cookie jar away with her. This was the first he'd talked with Chester since that day. It wasn't that he'd avoided him. Chester spent most of his time with Ida these days, and he was gone so much, their paths simply hadn't crossed.

"Serious problems," said Chester. "Like missing cattle."

"Broken fences, you mean?"

"I'm still checking into that."

They both fell quiet, each waiting for the other. Ike could hear the wind in the trees. The twin oaks would sing tonight, but Lib wouldn't be there to hear. Sometimes it sounded like music. Sometimes a bit threatening, for the cabin was in direct line of its lean.

"Just thought you might like to know I could be looking for a tenant soon," said Chester.

Ike's thoughts shifted. "Don't suppose you'd consider selling off a piece of ground."

"I don't think so, Ike. I've got grandchildren coming up."

Like Miss Maudie, keep it in the family. Seemed to be the way of folks who had a little something. Had to hit on hard times b'fore they'd sell off a piece.

Chester started for the trees. At the last moment, he turned back, and said, "I was planning on taking the train into Bloomington tomorrow. Maybe I'll make it my business to look up Mr. Field and send him home to see after his family."

And get your wife home where she belongs. He didn't

say it, but somehow Ike knew what he was thinking. He was questioning his good sense in letting Libby go. Ike questioned it himself. Except that with Lib he wasn't sure he hadn't already lost a part of her. A part that was her mothering heart, wandering after her chicks.

He squared his shoulders, and said, ''I'd take it as a favor if you would, Chester.''

''Consider it done.''

Ike got back to the sap house, and found the Field boys still there with Frankie and Decatur. He hadn't thought to tell the doctor to stop and pick them up. Maybe it was just as well. With everybody in the house sick, it seemed pointless to send Dumplin and Purdy home. Just be extra work for Lib, looking out for them.

''You boys want to stay overnight at the cabin?'' Ike asked.

They lost no time in accepting. Ike sent them out to empty the sap tank. Frankie went, too, then he and Decatur rode the team home, promising to take word to Libby not to be expecting the boys. The Fields lived just beyond the trees to the north of McClure's and it wouldn't be far for him to go.

Remembering the boys had school the next day, Ike shut down earlier than he'd originally intended. He shared the soup Libby had left on the stove and gave them the choice of sleeping in the bed, which involved taking a bath first—Lib would have everybody's hide if they got her wedding quilt dirty—or sleeping on the floor on the mat Rose had been using.

It was an easy choice for the boys. They curled up on the mat like a couple of pups. Long after they were asleep, Ike sat in his chair by the stove, his feet propped up on the kindling box, his thoughts reaching over the past few days and beyond. Wasn't much point in regrets. Yet he couldn't help wishing he'd handled the whole matter of Rose differently. Initially, it was simple protection he was trying to offer Lib. But in retrospect, he could see that nothing he could have said would have kept her from hugging that secret wish to make Rose hers.

Libby had once told him it wasn't his place to bear her burdens, just to share them. He wasn't sure he'd succeeded even at that. What was it that had distracted him? Getting his back up, thinking she was blaming him because there had been no babies? Blaming him for being gone? Bringing a child home and saying, in effect, *There's more than one way to skin a cat.*

Was she saying that? He wasn't sure yet. He'd made her unhappy, though, and he was sorry. Was he sorry enough to seriously consider Chester's words to him? Looked like there'd be a job for him if he wanted to ask. It wasn't his dream of owning his own land. And it wouldn't be anywhere near the money he'd been earning.

But it was close to his sirup camp. He wouldn't ever have to leave Lib again. And if babies didn't come, well, they'd know then it wasn't adverse circumstances, or for lack of trying.

He walked out for a couple of pieces of firewood, lifted his face to the starry night, and said aloud, "What about it, God? Should I talk to him? Or am I just asking for trouble, thinking there could be a future on Gentry land?"

Gentry land?

It fell over his spirit like a deep, good-humored chuckle from the One who'd made the earth, reminding him that while the land might bear a man's footprints, it was only on loan from the Creator.

32

✿ The stench of sickness permeated the Fields'
home, a drafty dismal affair with too many people living
too close in primitive quarters. Newspapers were tacked
to the board walls in layers and rags stuffed in open
knotholes, both in the walls and the plank floor, in an
effort to hold in the heat and shut out the cold.

There was a loft built over the ceiling joists and a
ladder leading up to where Puddin and Punkin, five and
six, lay resting. Pretty Good, Very Fine, and Sweet
Thing shared a room and a bed at the east end of the
house. Sadie Field had a space scarcely large enough to
accommodate a bed in the west corner.

A single candle burned on the nightstand, dimly il-
luminating Sadie's flushed face and dull eyes. Her gown
was faded and wrinkled and worn thin over the generous
mound of unborn child. She smoothed it with fretful
hands and struggled up on one elbow to thank Libby for
coming.

"I'm ashamed, you catching me in bed like this. But
I've been nursing the children for days, and I just
couldn't keep my feet under me any longer."

"You've done your best, Mrs. Field. Lie back now,
and rest," soothed Libby.

Tears glimmered in Sadie's eyes as she urged Libby to call her by her given name.

Libby did so as she slipped out of her coat, asking, "What can I get you, Sadie?"

"If you'll just look after the children . . ." Sadie fell back on the pillow in mute misery. A tear trickled over her temple and into hair that was dull and damp from sweats and fever.

"I brought chicken soup from home. Could you eat a bite?"

"I don't want to be any trouble."

Libby pulled the covers more snugly around the woman's trembling shoulders and assured her it was no bother.

But that soon proved to be optimistic on her part. The dishes were all dirty. There was no water reservoir on the stove, no pump at the sink, and very little wood in the wood box. Nor could Libby find any oil for the lamp.

One building had been linked to another to form the home. The floor didn't meet at the same height where the two came together, so the stove, which was in the cental part of the house, was a step higher than the sink, the cupboard, and table and chairs. It was a step easily missed while trying to work by candlelight.

Libby donned her coat again and hauled water from the well out back and put it on the stove to heat. By the time she'd washed the dishes and reheated the soup, Sadie was sleeping the hard sleep of exhaustion. Punkin ate only a few bites, but Puddin ate as if he were starving, then promptly vomited into the slop jar.

Judging by the odor in the house, the slop jar along with the chamber pots had been in popular demand the last few days. Even now, Puddin and Punkin, whose fevers had broken, were too weak to make it down the ladder and along the path to the privy.

Having seen her father and brothers and more recently, Ike, through some serious illnesses, Libby had acquired a fair degree of skill in nursing. But she'd never tried to care for six people at once.

When Frankie knocked on the door to tell her that the boys wouldn't be coming home, Libby was so relieved, she didn't think to ask where they would be staying. Anyplace would be healthier than this! She had Frankie bring an armload of firewood from the woodpile out back and leave it at the front door. But the wood was damp from the recent snows. It made a finicky fire that required more attention than Libby had time to give it.

Very Fine and Pretty Good, in the early stages of the sickness, complained of raw throats and refused food. It was all Libby could do to get a few sips of water past their cracked lips. She returned to their bedside intermittently to change the rags on their fevered brows for cool ones.

Sweet Thing, only three, whined pitifully for her mother. When the rest of the family finally dozed in fitful sleep, Libby wrapped the little girl in a blanket, blew out the candle, and sang her to sleep before drifting off herself. She awoke some time later with a painful crick in her neck and a chill in the room that came of a dead fire and thin walls.

Libby returned Sweet Thing to her bed, then laid a fire with the damp wood, but couldn't get it to burn. Frustrated, she donned her coat and trekked outside to empty the chamber pots, and in so doing found a bucket of corncobs in the privy. She took it inside and relaid her fire, beginning with newspapers torn from the walls, then added the cobs and finally the damp wood.

Dear God, how do these people survive?

The crudeness of the place gave Libby a fresh appreciation for the improvements Ike was constantly making on their home to make it comfortable and convenient to her needs.

Libby's thoughts, pain-laced, skipped from him to Rose and back again as she nursed the fire to life. She wrapped up in the blankets she had brought from home

and returned to the rocking chair, remembering the word
that, on the heels of losing Rose, had sent her fleeing
out the door and into the woods with the boys.

Unhappy. Was it five nights of lying, backs turned,
not talking, not touching that had given Ike that impression? Surely he knew that that nightly distance had
seemed as great to her as if he'd been on a job halfway
across the country. Or did he? That very afternoon she
had faulted Adam for his long-standing silence with Abigail in regard to Rose.

Why hadn't she bridged the distance with a touch or
a word? Pride? Fear of being rebuffed? Reluctance toward having the gesture misunderstood as surrender? A
little of all three. But it should not take the sickness and
deprivations of poor Sadie and her family to see the
wrong in hurting one another that way. *Up-and-down
faith.* That spirit impression touched her again.

*You never intended me to have Rose, did You? I put
myself in the middle by bringing her home with me and
then felt hurt when Ike questioned the wisdom of it. And
hurt again when Adam took her away.*

She had done it to herself. It wasn't honest to feel
bruised by Ike, Adam, Abigail. It felt better to say it, to
have it out in the open between herself and God.

Sweet Thing awoke with a cry. Libby took her a cup
of cold water and a rag to cool her brow. When she had
soothed the little girl back to sleep again, Libby returned
to her chair in the next room and closed her eyes. It
seemed only moments had passed when dawn's gray
light crept through the near window.

The day that dawned was a repeat of the previous
evening, except that in the stream of sunlight coming
through the windows, Libby saw that the little home had
a few familiar touches. There was a bowl of pine cones
in the middle of the table. The rickety lamp table in the
girls' room was covered in a doily, made off a pattern
of Libby's own invention, one that Very Fine, with her
artistic flare, had improved upon. There were sketches,

too, from Very Fine's hand, and a dresser scarf that Libby had helped Pretty Good stitch as her very first sewing project.

Purdy's automobile pictures were pinned to the eaves in the loft. Stacked in an upturned orange crate were books that had belonged first to Libby's older brothers, then to Libby and now to Dumplin. They had seen considerable wear since leaving her house, an indication of the enjoyment they were bringing.

Somehow, it cheered Libby to see that her presence in the children's lives, however small, had been felt. Encouraged, she found fresh strength in her nursing.

Naomi came to the door early with soup, then went on her way to open the store. A while later, Ike came with dry wood. He had learned of her need from Naomi, just as she had learned from Naomi that Purdy and Dumplin were staying with Ike.

Libby stepped outside so that he wouldn't come in. "Stay back," she warned, as he drew near. "You don't want to catch this."

Eyes dark with concern, he said, "Maybe you should come home, Lib."

"I can't. Not yet." The word *unhappy* rang in her head, for his demeanor reflected it. *Had she done this to him?*

Unhappy, thought Ike. In his fear and pride, had he done this to her? Why couldn't he just ask? Or say he was sorry he'd failed her? What was he scared of, anyway? What was the worst that could happen? She'd already figured out he wasn't as strong as he would like to be. Or as noble. Or selfless. Or wise. That he couldn't always protect her and give her what she wanted.

It was a complicated business, sharing lives. He stood with his elbows bent, fingertips hooked in his pockets, the morning breeze stirring his hair, and studied her face as she studied him. At length, he asked, "How are they doin'?"

"The boys are improving. The girls are holding their

own. But Sadie can't even lift her head off the pillow this morning."

"You pinin' for Rose?"

She shook her head, realizing it was the truth. Throat filling, she murmured, "Just for you."

"Me too."

Libby saw the somber line of his mouth ease. The sun, coming through the trees, flitted over his face, lighting the shadows, softening the planes as he moved toward her. This time, Libby hadn't the will to stop him.

Her eyes filled as he folded her in his arms. Like salve to a wound, those hard-muscled arms. He hadn't shaved that morning, but even the roughness of his beard grazing her cheek was a comfort. Snug against him, holding, being held by family. For he was her family, whole and complete. He had tried to tell her that once.

But instead of counting her blessings, she had counted what she thought was missing from their lives. With her hands outstretched for more, she hadn't realized the worth of the original blessing. Instead, she waited for the gift she had vowed on their honeymoon night to give.

But it isn't mine to give.

Her gift to Ike was and had always been herself.

Libby supposed it was Sadie's condition that made her so slow to rally. Three days passed, and then four. The younger children were well, and the older girls much improved. Yet Sadie's fever persisted, and Libby was reluctant to leave her for fear she'd lose the baby if she tried to resume the care of her children.

Naomi and Laila took turns bringing food, and Ike came each morning to check on her. On the fourth day, Hascal Caton brought fresh game from the woods. Libby saw him pause at the edge of the yard, seeming at a loss. It was, she knew, his fear of disease of any kind that prevented him from leaving the meat in front of the door and slipping away. Yet he was reluctant to hail her and draw attention to his good deed.

Libby swung the door open and solved his dilemma. "Good morning, Mr. Caton. What've you got there?"

"Fresh rabbit."

"That was kind of you."

He ran a hand over his grizzled chin. "Well, I figur't I jest as well cut out the middle man."

Libby puzzled over that for a moment, then realized he meant her. In the past, when he'd given her game, she'd nearly always passed it along to the Field family. She thanked him again, saying, "The younger ones are getting their appetites back. Though Sadie and the girls are a little slower on the mend. How about you, Mr. Caton? Are you staying well?"

"I'm feelin' spry, but influenza's takin' a toll on the young'uns and the weak. Family in Edgewood lost a young'un to it. Miz Morefield succumbed to it and passed on the day b'fore yesterday."

Libby caught her breath. She hadn't known. "I'm sorry to hear that."

"Miz Gentry, too," said Hascal, slapping his hat against his thigh. "Though from what I hear, that was a blessin'. Stout, weren't she, ta hang on all this time? Hear tell, though, she hadn't knowed nobody in a while."

Libby had last been to see Ida at Christmastime. Chester, always gracious about her visits, had thanked her for coming. But she had sensed that it was painful for him to have her see Ida in the final stages of her illness, so emaciated and unknowing, and that he now wished to spare Ida being remembered as anything less than the vital, vivacious beauty she had always been in his eyes.

Perhaps losing her by degrees was the only way he would ever be willing to let her go. Libby looked through the trees toward heaven and thought of Ida enveloped in yellow, healed of every weakness and trilling once again in that light, cheery voice that made Libby think of canaries.

Libby was still caring for the Field family and couldn't attend Ida Gentry's funeral, which was held at the New Hope Church in Edgewood. Burial was at the grove, where Ida had lived as a girl. Ike went on Libby's behalf and stood amidst the landscape of bleached tombstones as Pastor Shaw spoke a few final words.

Ida's children, Catherine and Angus, along with Angus's wife Maddie, caught up with Ike before he left the cemetery. Angus shook his hand and thanked him for coming. Maddie asked about Libby. Upon learning she was trying to nurse Sadie Field back to health, Catherine said, "Come to Chester's with us, Ike, and have a bite to eat."

"Yes, do," urged Maddie.

"Thanks, but I can't," said Ike. "I've got sirup to cook." Noting that Chester wasn't at the cemetery, he asked belatedly, "How's Chester doin'?"

Angus said, "He's pretty broken up."

"I don't believe he could bear to watch them put her in the ground," murmured Catherine, dabbing at eyes the same violet hue as her mother's had been.

"He's a survivor," said Maddie. "He'll pull himself together."

Ike supposed she was right. Though it seemed a bleak survival, learning to live without the one you loved.

It was a full week before Sadie began to show some improvement. After the three school-aged children left for school on Wednesday, Libby left Puddin and Sweet Thing building houses with sticks from the box of kindling Ike had brought, and sat with Sadie a while. Finding her fever had passed, she helped her bathe, put on a clean gown, and brush her hair.

"It's time you went home," Sadie said. "The girls

are fine now. They can stay home from school tomorrow and look after the younger ones.''

''I know. They're good girls. They have your mothering touch.''

Sadie flushed. Her chin quivered. Was it that she was weak and sick? Or hadn't she heard a tender word in a while? Libby took her hand and stroked it gently. She asked, ''When is your baby due, Sadie?''

''Late in May or early June. When the lilacs bloom.''

Libby thought of her own barren bush. She let her gaze wander over Sadie's face. She must have been quite pretty once. Her skin was clear, her features pleasing. But her deep-set eyes were prematurely lined with the cares of too many babies too soon and limited resources with which to care for them.

''Have you thought of a name?'' asked Libby.

''If it's a girl, yes, I've settled on one.'' Sadie smiled, but declined to say what it was.

Libby worked all day, cooking, cleaning, washing bedclothes, preparing to leave Sadie's household in the girls' hands. That evening, as she was calling the children to supper, Mr. Field came through the door.

''I understand we're in you're debt, Mrs. Galloway,'' said Lafayette Field with a courteous lift of his hat.

He was a dapper little villain with his slim moustache and neat white shirt and polished shoes, for what else were you to call a man who took so little care of his family, but villain? Yet the children were so glad to see him, Libby couldn't injure them by snubbing him the way she felt like doing. He wasn't her problem, she reminded herself. And thanked God it was so.

Ike was waiting for her at the edge of the Fields' muddy yard.

''So? Have you got that stove glowing nice and hot?'' she asked.

He smiled and took her arm. ''You'll thank me when you climb into that warm tub.''

''A bath! That sounds like heaven.''

"Walk a little faster then, because I've got water heating."

She looked at him in surprise. "Ike! Do you really? How'd you know I was coming home?"

"A little bird told me."

"Named Hascal Caton?" she said. He laughed, and she knew it was so. "Where are the boys?"

"In the sap house with Decatur. He's got it in his head Dumplin's goin' to quit using the arm for an excuse and make somethin' of himself."

Libby frowned. "He's a little hard on Dumplin, isn't he?"

"And yer a little easy," Ike replied.

Distracted by his shoulder brushing hers, the familar light in those smoke-colored eyes and the gentle baiting tip of his mouth, Libby slipped her arms through his and declined to argue the case.

33

❧ The weather warmed at mid-March. Sirup season was nearing an end when Ike received word from Mr. Elliot that he was expecting him in Grand Rapids as soon as the weather broke.

He lifted his head from the letter to find Libby at the table, scribbling across the page, intent on the children's book she'd been writing and rewriting ever since he went to work for Mr. Elliot. To the best of his understanding, it featured the thinly disguised capers of Dumplin and Purdy. He didn't hardly see how there'd be much interest in that.

"Grand Rapids." Ike joined her at the table, stretched a hand toward the lamp and adjusted the wick before reaching for the *Gazette*. "Don't think I've ever been there."

"Mmm," said Libby.

But she was as far away in thought as those steel rails ever took him. One dreamer per family seemed a good ratio. He settled then and there on talking to Chester.

Ike got his chance a few days later when he saw Chester step off a northbound express at the grove. He'd been heading for the sap house, but he changed course. The boarding whistle blew, beguiling his ears and drawing his eye to the silver-lined mane of trailing smoke and steam. There was something intoxicating about the sight, like the rippling muscles of a workhorse or a hawk riding the wind. A siren call, that whistle. He had answered it time and again. But this time, it blew for someone else.

Ike walked to meet Chester and offered his condolences concerning Ida.

The loss was too fresh to linger over. A muscle flexed along Chester's jaw. He set his package down to rub his spectacles dry, and asked in a throaty voice, "How's the sirup coming along?"

"Been a good season," Ike told him.

"I saw a robin in the yard today."

Ike nodded. He had been seeing them for a week. Geese flying north, too. Spring couldn't be far behind. "You headed over to the farm?"

Chester nodded and picked up the parcel, wrapped in brown paper and string. "The shape the roads are in, it seemed easier to take the train and walk the rest of the way than to get a buggy mired in the mud."

"Have you got time to step in and watch some sirup-making?" Ike asked.

Chester considered the offer as they picked their way along the soupy road toward the bridge. He shifted his package. "Perhaps I will. Then, if you're of a notion, we could go over to the farm together."

"What's your tenant goin' to make of that?"

"He's gone," said Chester.

"So the job's open?"

"Yes, it is."

"Wouldn't be stepping on any toes to have a look, then, I guess."

They passed the distance to the bridge in silence. Chester broke it to say, "The girls helped me go through some of Ida's things last week. I found something that belongs to you."

"To me?" Surprised, Ike regarded the package as Chester held it out to him. "Don't know how that could be."

"You will when you see it." Chester motioned with a gloved hand for him to open it.

Ike pulled away the brown paper and found the rose cookie jar Ida had collected from Lib's table three years ago.

Watching him, Chester said, "It belonged to your Grandmother Rachel."

"That's what I hear." As he folded the paper back around it, Ike knew that Chester would have stopped by even if he hadn't met him halfway. Somehow, he was glad that he had. He cradled the jar carefully in the crook of his arm. "Thanks, Chester. Libby'll be pleased."

"I hope so. There wasn't anyone any better about coming to visit Ida than that little wife of yours." Struggling once more with rising emotions, Chester tucked his chin and opened his coat to pull a paper from his pocket. "The last time I asked you to farm for me, you turned me down."

"Chester . . ."

He held up a hand. "Let me finish. Some time has passed, and I was hoping you might be willing to reconsider. With that in mind, I took the liberty of having Angus draw up a lease agreement while he was down last week. I hope the terms are agreeable. Go on, look it over," he said, waggling his fingers.

Ike unfolded the paper. It was a lifetime lease on the forty acres at a dollar a year. *Just short of giving it to him.* The water rushing beneath the bridge was no muddier than his thoughts. *Why would he do that?* "Mighty generous terms," he said.

"The risk is all yours, you know. None of this fifty-fifty. You sink or swim on your own capital."

"Too generous. I'll buy the ground, Chester. Or share-crop. Or pay rent. But this . . . it's like . . . charity."

"Nonsense! Do it for your wife."

Ike was silent a long moment. Why wouldn't he just let him buy it? Why did he have to do it this way, and make it stick in his craw? At length, he said, "I don't think I can."

"Yes, you can," said Chester, an inflexible edge creeping into his voice. "I've been watching you for some time now, thinking that you just might be a better man than your father. But when Angus mentioned your being at the cemetery, I began to see you are a better man than either one of Rachel Galloway Cearlock's sons." Throat working, he got a tightness in his jaw again. "If you can't do it for yourself or Libby, then do it in Ida's memory. She always did say I was wrong about you," he finished, his words trailing to a thin conclusion.

Ike gave his words full attention, struggled to put away all that hindered him, and, at length, met Chester's outstretched hand.

It was unseasonably warm for March. Libby's wash was flapping in the breeze. Another day or two of this, and Ike would be taking down buckets. Libby dreaded seeing the season end, knowing when the last spout was pulled, the sap house cleaned, and the pans taken off the arch, Ike would go. She had found the letter from Mr. Elliot mixed in with the *Gazette*, as she was looking for some paper in which to wrap her children's book before sending it off to a New York publisher who had agreed to read it.

Libby donned a coat and went outdoors to enjoy the late-afternoon sunshine. She was raking a damp covering of leaves off the west lawn beneath the twin oaks when a squirrel's nest high in the branches of one of the trees caught her eye. It was built of sticks and leaves and didn't look all that sturdy. Yet it held together, withstanding the winds that thrashed the tree over the winter.

I'm a nest-builder, too. You made me that way, Lord.

What would You have me put in my nest? Getting no answers, she smiled and quipped: "Acorns?"

"Huh?" answered Dumplin.

Libby swung around. "Dumplin! Where'd you come from?"

"It's Duncan," he said, for he'd taken a shine to Decatur's renaming him. "Mom sent me to tell you we've got a new baby."

"Baby!" cried Libby. "What do you know about that! So do you have a brother or sister?"

"Another sister." Dumplin wrinkled his freckled nose, attesting to what his choice would have been. Then he tilted his head, a light coming into his eyes. "Guess what she named her?"

"Sugar Plum?"

Dumplin snickered.

"Poppet?"

He tunneled a hand beneath his knit cap and scratched his head, as if he'd never heard that one. "You're about out of guesses."

"Lovey?"

"That's close. Livvy. Actually, Elizabeth. For you. But we're going to call her Livvy."

"Really?" Touched, Libby said, "I'm flattered. And they're doing all right? Your mother and the . . . Livvy?"

"I guess so. Doc's still there, checking Dad over."

"Your father's home?"

He nodded.

"Is he ill?"

"No. He fell off a scaffold. He said it wasn't the fall that hurt so much as the landing."

"Dear me!" Libby tried to be sympathetic.

"Hit a sawhorse."

"That sounds terrible."

Dumplin nodded and laid a hand over his growling stomach. "I was thinking maybe some fried chicken would make him feel better."

"Perhaps it would, Dumplin. *Duncan*," Libby corrected herself, though the boy by either name was just as much a chicken connoisseur. Holding back a smile, she said, "Take a couple of those hens that've quit laying. And tell your mother I'll be up to see the baby as soon as she feels like some company."

"I will. Thanks, Libby."

Libby watched him make his way toward the hen house. Her mouth tipped, for on his head was a round woolen cap that looked just like the cap of an acorn. Purdy had one like it, made by Sadie's hand. They were acorns, both of them, with the potential to be oaks. As were all children. Even grown-up ones like her and Ike, making nests of their own.

Libby worked her way toward the front of the house and was raking around the base of the lilac bush as Ike came whistling down the road. He was carrying something. It was the brown paper wrapping that caught her eye. It looked just like what she needed to wrap her manuscript.

She smiled as the distance fell away. "I looked the house over for brown paper and here you come, bringing just what I need."

"You might like to have what's in it, too." Ike pulled off the wrapping.

"A cookie jar just like Ida's!"

Ike grinned at the lilting delight in her voice, and watched surprise round her mouth as she found the knick in the lid "Why, it *is* Ida's jar. Ike! Where'd you get this?"

"Chester sent it to you."

"Well, wasn't that sweet of him! Where'd you see him?"

"We did some business together." He reached a hand toward the lilac bush, bent a twig his way, and said, "Looky here, you're going to have some blooms this year."

"You mean those aren't just leaf buds?" Libby

shifted the cookie jar in her arm and gave the bush a closer look. It was as tall as her shoulder now, the branches purple-tinted with new growth and buds where the leaves would crop out, and yes! Tiny nubs that just might be blooms. "I think you're right! And just when I was thinking I might just as well have you chop this thing down!"

"Anyway, about Chester, he's lost his tenant," said Ike, watching her beam over a simple cookie jar and a few tight lilac buds.

"Poor Chester. He's having a terrible time." Libby tugged at the lilac branch, trying to get a closer look at the buds. All at once her mouth turned down. "Our first lilacs, and you'll be off in Grand Rapids."

So she *had* been listening the other night. Ike smiled. Anticipation crowded his chest and put a tickling in his throat. "I'm not goin' to Grand Rapids, Lib. Or anywhere else. Don't get me wrong, I'm grateful for all Mr. Elliot's taught me. But here lately, the price of goin' has gotten too costly."

Libby whirled around so fast, the lilac branch broke off in her hand. Clutching it tightly, she gave him her full attention. "What do you mean you're not going? What will you do?"

"Oh, I don't know. Maybe your book about the Dumplin-Purdy gang'll sell."

"Ike, it isn't . . ."

"Or I could take to checkin' mailboxes for postcards. And huntin' and fishin' and runnin' a trap line with Hack."

"It's fiction. Purely fiction."

"Or we could try livin' on love, Mar-key Day La-Fay-ette style."

"Now that *is* fiction." Libby smothered a laugh. "What's got into you, anyway?"

"Like I said, Chester and I have been doing business. Take a look at this." Ike pulled the lease agreement from his pocket.

The lilac branch was tangled in the brown paper. Libby shifted both under her arm, braced the cookie jar in the crook of it, and took from Ike what seemed to be a legal document. She skimmed it first. Then read it more slowly. Her heart gave such a lurch, she nearly dropped the cookie jar. "Ike! Does this mean right away? This year?"

A smile broke over her face like gleaming pearls. Eyes glistening, chin wobbling, she seemed caught between laughter and tears. Ike reached for the jar, saying, "Give me that before you drop it."

He got the jar, the brown paper, the lilac switch and Libby, all in one armful. But then, hadn't he known when he married her that he'd gotten more than he'd bargained for?

Much later, Libby was lying next to Ike in bed when a lumbering dish-shaking train rumbled through the grove, whistle keening. When the sound of its passing faded away, and Libby could hear the twin oaks in the breeze, she rolled closer to Ike, thinking of those lover trees. Nurtured by sunshine and showers, withstanding storms. Leaning into each other, even as they drew from unseen resources deep in the soil. In those trees she had come to treasure were lessons she was still learning. Lessons of endurance. Perseverance. Partnership.

Once, Ike had showed her while they were cutting firewood how to count the years of a tree by the growth rings. The rings were irregular, the wide ones grown in the favorable years, the narrow ones representing years of low moisture and struggle.

Some would say it worked just the opposite in people. That the real growth came in adversity. Libby wasn't sure. Perhaps, like a tree, you had to reach the sum of your years for that knowledge to be revealed at heaven's gates. For it was when the tree had fallen that you counted its rings.

Eyes growing heavy, she nestled closer. Ike's heart

beat against the palm of her hand as he breathed the deep, even rhythm of sleep. A log shifted in the stove with a soft drawn-out sizzle. Family. Home fires. And on the sheets, the scent of lilacs.

Epilogue

1915

❧ October. The earth was golden with harvest. Libby left her white clapboard house built of lumber once meant for Ike's barn, and ambled past the sap house and into the woods to keep a commitment made in a lighthearted moment ten years earlier. Catherine was coming from St. Louis, Maddie from Springfield, where Angus was now serving his second term in the state legislature.

Libby had spoken to both Dorene and Chloe in the past week and been assured they wouldn't miss it for the world. Of course Chloe wouldn't. She and Arthur had four children and a fifth one on the way. That made her the undisputed winner of that long-ago bet.

Hearing her name, Libby stopped and turned to see Pretty Good hurrying toward her. She had married a local boy two years earlier, and carried an infant in her arms. Joy Stapleton, teetering between adolescence and womanhood, trailed a step behind. She had her hands full with Precious, Pretty Good's eighteen-month-old daughter.

"What a nice surprise," said Libby. She put her baskets down, embraced both young ladies, and swept Precious into her arms for a hug and a kiss. "You're not walking to town with the children surely?" she said, as she passed the child back to Joy.

Joy laughed. "Of course not, Aunt Lib. We're coming with you."

Pretty Good had a twinkle in her eye as she patted her fussing infant. "I suppose you thought once we grew up, we'd quit trailing you like chicks."

"Don't be silly! The girls won't mind," said Libby. "You're more than welcome."

"The girls?" echoed Joy, with a sassy quirk at the corner of her mouth that reminded Libby of Laila.

"All right, so we're not exactly girls anymore," conceded Libby cheerily. "But we're not ready for rocking chairs, either!"

"That's all right, Joy," said Pretty Good. "I used to think twenty-eight was over the hill, too."

"*Twenty-eight!* Aunt Lib, are you twenty-eight? Precious, you'd better walk and let me give Aunt Lib a hand," said Joy.

Libby laughed and assured her she was managing nicely.

Joy reached into one basket, lifted the corner of the patchwork cloth and peeked inside. "Is this the one we've been waiting to get our hands on?"

Libby laughed again. "All right, so you caught me. I'm shamelessly promoting."

"Is this one about Purdy and Dumplin, too?" asked Pretty Good, admiring the hardback book Joy held up for her to see.

"Now there you go again!" Libby complained. "Why is it that Duncan and Purdue are the only ones who believe me when I say the books aren't about them?"

"Probably because you've disguised their devilment so well, they don't recognize themselves," said Pretty Good. She hugged baby Joey to her heart, and said,

"Would you write one about Precious and Joey?"

"Very Fine could do the artwork," said Joy.

"Not for a while, she can't. She's leaving for New York tomorrow. Mom's so proud she doesn't know what to do. At the same time, she complains that the house is empty, with Dad gone so much and Livvy in school."

Libby supposed it *was* quiet for Sadie after all those years of having little ones underfoot. There'd been no more children since the Mar-key Day La-Fay-et's fall from the scaffolding six years earlier. His art, however, had gained recognition at long last and was much in demand. He had bought Sadie a Sears and Roebuck bungalow from his earnings and was now sending Very Fine off to art school. Libby wished Hascal Caton could have lived to see it. It would have baffled him to no end!

Joy and Very Good quizzed Libby about her latest book the rest of the way to the field where Libby was to meet her friends and their children for a picnic. The table Ike had erected the previous evening was strewn with covered dishes and waiting plates and tableware when they arrived.

The bang-board cadence of flying corn rang from Ike's field, with a faded back beat of an answering ring from nearby farms. It was a fitting harmony for a harvest reunion of familiar faces and embraces while children raced and laughed and played.

Abruptly, the bang-boards were silenced. Frankie, Purdue, Duncan, and Puddin and Punkin, who had renamed themselves Paul and Rankin, came in from the field where they'd been helping Ike harvest corn. Six-year-old Elizabeth and Very Fine were with them.

Libby opened her arms to Livvy, and wrote words of pride and love on the inside cover of the book she presented to Very Fine, a parting gift before she left for school.

As they were chatting, Libby's gaze wandered over the food table. Was there enough to feed all these unexpected guests? Each was too dear to risk hurting by pointing out that this was to have been a simple matter of five old friends and their children getting together.

Why, even David had come from town. And with him, a young woman Libby recognized with a start as Maddie's niece, Francis Kay! She had once been a lonely possum-faced little rich girl stirring Frankie's ire with her autocratic ramrodding of backyard play. But she had blossomed into a lovely young woman and was, by the look of it, stirring different emotions in Frankie today. He shouldered Davie to one side, took off his hat, and bowed over Francis Kay's hand.

Francis Kay responded with a coquettish twitch of her lips and a widening of her eyes. "My goodness! It's Red."

"Yes, it is," said Frankie, surprising a laugh out of Libby, for reference to his red hair had once been fighting words.

"He's grown up fine and straight, hasn't he?"

Libby turned to find Ike had slipped in from the field, too. His face, weathered by the elements, was dusty and damp with harvest-toil. His gray eyes met her ruffled glance and crinkled between sooty lashes. "Don't worry about feeding all these folks; Opal's got everything under control," he said as if reading her mind.

"Opal? Who's keeping the store?"

"The old-timers. They got nothin' better to do than hold down the cracker barrels, anyway," Ike said. He tipped up her face and kissed her right in front of everyone.

Not that anyone noticed. The children clamored to eat. Chloe and Dorene bickered good-naturedly, as they were prone to do. Catherine, with a baby on one hip, waved a small branch over the dishes to shoo the flies away. Maddie beat on a pan, and used her foot at the same time, trying to prevent her youngest daughter from wrestling a cousin to the ground.

"I'm afraid it's out of hand," murmured Libby, leaning her shoulder against Ike's.

"It only looks that way." He grinned at her bewilderment, and forestalled her puzzled glance, saying, "Shh! Maddie's going to start rappin' heads with that pan if folks don't simmer down and give her an ear."

"Everyone who wants to eat raise your hand!" bellowed Maddie. "All right, then. Line up! No, no! Not like that. In families. We have to count heads."

Libby gave a short laugh, inadvertently garnering Maddie's attention.

"Is that Ike, or is something else tickling you, Mrs. Galloway?" she demanded, as despotic as her mother ever thought of being.

Libby flushed hot. "Well . . . er . . . it just seems silly to let the food get cold when it's obvious that Chloe has the most children."

Maddie heaved a sigh. "Oh, what do you know, Libby? You're a writer, not a counter. Line up, now. Line up! Saints have mercy, you people would never make the muster in a suffragette march! Don't you know how to make a line?"

Catherine, in a yellow gown, made Libby think of Ida as she giggled and bounced her baby and tried to get her remaining three children in a straight line behind her. Dorene's three made a stair-step line. Chloe's children trooped behind her and stood straight as soldiers while Maddie's little group of nonconformists made more of a cresting wave toward the table than a line.

Looking at the uninvited guests clustering behind her, Libby nudged Ike. "I didn't bring enough plates."

Opal, standing just behind her, overheard. "I did, Lib," she said, then whispered something to Francis Kay, who had trailed along with her and Frankie.

"Chase, dear, would you like to count for Mother?" asked Maddie.

Everyone groaned.

But Chase, a good-natured boy like his father, did so silently.

"And the winner?" chimed his twin sister Lacey.

Chase looked at Chloe's troop and stretched out an arm, then swiveled with a slow drama that made his twin giggle, and pointed to Libby.

It was clearly staged. Libby would have laughed it off as some prearranged joke by her friends, but their smiles were so tender, so all-inclusive. She swung around and looked behind her, and, slowly, like sand sifting through an hourglass, it settled in. They had become hers in part: Her own dear brother David, Frankie and Opal, Pretty Good and her little ones, Very Fine, Purdue and Duncan, Puddin and Punkin, Livvy, and Joy.

"No fair!" Chloe sang out. "Francis Kay belongs in Maddie's line and Precious and Joey don't count, they are . . . well, they're grandchildren."

"Yes, they *are* grand," replied Libby, and covered brimming tears with bright laughter.

"Hush, both of you, I'm running this show," said Maddie. She grinned at Libby. "The common consensus, aside from one obviously biased dissenter, is that you, Libby Galloway, have outmothered us all. And that, after all, was the bet."

A cheer went up from the flock behind Libby and Ike. They closed in around them. Brusque shoulder pats from the boys and kisses and embraces from the girls thickened the rising lump in Libby's throat.

Just as she feared the dam would burst, Maddie gave the dinner shout and Libby's tribe quickly deserted, leaving her alone with Ike and the fragrant spirit reminder of that ancient promise. *Exceeding, abundantly above all she could ask or think.*

And it was so.